THE HAUNT ON THE ISLAND OF ESMER

Justin A.W. Blair

Prologue

Travelogue of Vohn Cearhardt, known as Scrolls of the Relic Hunters of the 9th: Awarded-Scholar of the University of Mhars

I leave these pages in the travelogue of the Relic Hunters of the 9th so that a record exists for posterity of our travels, our travails, our victories, and defeats. May the God of Scripts and Learning bless these words and may the God of Ink and Letters safeguard them against time, weather, war and lies.

Our troubles and treasures past, one can read recorded in

prior pages...

 Our latest voyage has brought the Relic Hunters of the 9th to this southernly city—the free-city of Port Shamhalhan, or Sem-hel-hen, in the tongue of the Old Kings who by measuring, founded it.

 It is a city of tens of thousands of men blessed by strong trade winds and a warm climate, which stifles those of us with northerly blood. Spice traders, flesh traders and exotic beasts fill the common markets. Beer-blooded sailors sleep at night beneath the stars atop the city's seawall of yellow sandstone. The wall embracing the day's sun, captures and preserves it for the vagabonds who sleep on it at night. All sorts crowd and crawl the alleys and wander the portside of the city.

 As any well-educated traveler will know Shamhalhan lays outside Throne control, though traders and armed ships flying their banners ply the shores and find free harbor here.

 Scrolls paused from his work and mopped sweat from his brow with his crumpled silken handkerchief laying atop the hardwood writing table. Soon, he would board the Black Boat to Esmer, Cole had told him. He wanted to put down a few words before embarkation. Once they set out to find the Haunt, he didn't know when next he could take the time to recall recent days, or *if* he would have the time, again.

 He resumed writing, irritated at the drop of perspiration which dripped from his brow and blurred the ink he had committed to parchment. He sniffed. Waving away the gnats swarming about the candlelight, he dabbed at the parchment and sighing, returned to his labor.

 We have stayed in the city for some time, recovering from past exertions, waiting for contact from allies, waiting for those who remember the 9th, purchasing the material we will need that we cannot ourselves devise through magecraft, alchemy or otherwise; above all, waiting on the Black Boat and its cargo to appear in port.

 Few of these tasks involve me, except for the study of maps in relation to the selection of our next expedition. When I do not write, I consult with our mage, (may his true name never a parchment hold) or if he is indisposed, I speak with master physician, Aodlen, on peculiar matters best left the subject of other ink.

I take my leave of this richly appointed room, an old, rundown palace we procured some time ago and I walk the sandstone-colored cobbles of Shamhalhan when the heat of the afternoon sun subsides. I have spent many hours strolling the narrow alleys of the city, seeking scrollsellers. I have found a few curious folios to add to my personal collection, though I fear I will have to leave the majority here in Shamhalhan and retrieve them at a later date.

A later date.

This phrase assumes much. Will I ever see a return of these books and artifacts to Cearhardt lands? Or should all my possessions stay scattered across the broad world? A dozen domiciles both leased and purchased hold my trunks; they gather dust, silent, books inside them, silent, landlords paid to ask no questions—mansion or hovel, my books wait. My work inhabits both cellars where damp straw mats are mute and the finest lodgings; villas and safehouses in the heart of the Throne City itself. Chests with books, chests with maps, chests brimming with artifacts unsold. Gold. Coins minted in forgotten kingdoms and kingdoms which flourish and will fall. Dust. Dust over everything. Waiting.

It pained him, but Scrolls crossed through the last lines above. A travelogue, even a personal account, had no room for such sentiment, so the teachers of rhetoric in Mhars had instructed him. Another bead of sweat rolled from the tip of his aquiline nose onto the ink. The Gods signaling their lack of appreciation for his prose, editing for him with his own sweat. Insult and eraser.

It takes time to find the types of markets which relic hunters can both buy and sell at, though in a city such as Shamhalhan, the most important figures are known to us already.

These mapmaker markets, scroll bazaars and arcane book

mongers, even in a free-city such as Shamhalhan, are simultaneously hidden from authority and protected by those same authorities who are paid percentages to pretend they do not exist. These places, we know in dozens of cities across this broad land. Shamhalhan is no different.

Days of languor, days of boredom. I found introduction to a previously unrealized greymarket scrollseller through students I befriended at the taverns near the university—an unremarkable place filled with unremarkable minds.

But the scrollseller's collections were useless in guiding us to a new destination.

In short, nothing of worth could I find in Shamhalhan. So, readers will ask how we came to set sail for Esmer. Cole found the map. That is what he related to me, so, I will assume it is fact.

Scrolls was comfortable with his own lies and writing them. He was a scholar and a scribe after all. But there had been something odd about Cole's story. He pressed the end of his stylus against his cheek, felt the cold metal there. The taper flickered. He spun the inkpot and laughed to himself.

Some night's past, Cole visited my private quarters and set down on this very writing desk where I labor now, a large, ragged piece of old vellum. While studying the material beneath a long glass, I asked him where he found it.

He and Allred had met a man who lived in one of the temples of the city which houses the divinely mad—men who never recover from Downside Fever abide there, they who have left their souls in the Haunts. They harbor many species of madness these temples. The white robed women sing quiet songs to ease the feverish, you have heard them sing, have you not? From open doors, down alleys you have no business travelling, you have heard their sweet lyrics mixed with the cries of the damne—

He felt a sudden clenching in his guts. A bit of Upside Fever wracked him on recollecting those temples. The room felt fragile and everything—his flesh, his thoughts the walls and the air appeared as if it were made of glass on some shrill edge of shattering.

"No."

Scrolls shook it off, assuring himself that a trained mind such as his would never end up in one of those terrible temples, cowering, relying on the priestesses to shelter him from the Optri and his own tormented thoughts among the unclean.

The old man sat hunched against the ochre wall of the temple—eyes closed, palm out, collecting alms, drowsing in the morning sun. On approaching, the man looked up at Cole and Allred and said the word "brothers" in the Thronelands tongue. Then he stood and retreated through a low door to the temple, gesturing for them to remain standing on the street.

Cole told me they stood and waited, both agreeing the man's mind was emptied by Downside Fever, or his spirit entangled in Upside Fever, or both. He had the look of an old relic hunter about him. He limped like a fighter and his eyes had known the under places.

Soon enough the man shambled back outside, grasping something in the folds of his old cloak. Allred would have thought it a knife and probably laid a hand on his own dagger. But the old man withdrew the map, looking about him furtively and shoved it into Cole's hands, speaking a few words in a language they did not share. Then without another word, he turned and resumed his exact pose in front of the temple, hand outstretched as if he were a piece of the temple stonework instead of a man of blood and flesh. He remained like that, the sun playing on his thin smile, immune to their presence and deaf to Cole's quiet questions.

Allred put two solid gold coins in his trembling hand.

In the evening darkness, candles brightening the room, the spring moths bouncing against the fine glass panes staring onto the courtyard below—Cole stood above me telling me this tale of the provenance of the map I studied. I nodded and believed him just enough to say nothing.

It was one large piece, faded and fashioned of strange leather. To the touch, it felt smoothed by centuries, as if beneath the crust of the page fats congealed beneath. On this odd surface, fading lines indicated Port Shamhalhan at the top. Below it, the outlines of the hundreds of small islands which populate the waters south of here. On one of those islands, seemingly enlarged in scale to attract the reader's eye was marked in faded ink, the old Sem-hel-hen word for what we call a Haunt.

Their word for it translates differently, Haunt *being a neologism of the last few centuries, likely originating around the city of ...*

Scrolls stopped writing. His pale blue eyes pursued the last lines again. He must not launch into a history of etymologies of words here. He glanced over his shoulder at a trunk, iron locks dangling from chains beside magemade locks where the top of the chest met the body in a mouth. There he could write his etymologies and store them.

Would he have time to summon the porters before they left? He turned back to his writing.

An arrow indicated an island, near the word, whose position it was clear was the purpose and subject of the map itself. Above the illustration of this small island the scribe had written the name of it in a clever fit of fancy. A volcano on the island had been drawn spouting plumes of smoke and these plumes of volcanic ash animated so skillfully formed the letters which spelled the name of the island: Esmer.

And the map read: The Haunt on the Island of Esmer.

Cole stood there, quietly, while I read, shoulders-back, the fire-scarred side of his head pitched down, away from the candlelight, listening to his own thoughts and awaiting my answer.

I peered up from the map at my commander. His green eyes spoke of the hawk's calculation, and he smiled at me, and it wasn't cruel or kind. The room appeared distorted, twisted and out of shape. He stood straight, unmoving as if behind a fog.

I assumed a bout of Upside Fever had seized upon me. Then I noticed that I had been so enthralled by the map, I had forgotten to take out the looking glass from my eye. The lens meant for reading close detail had deformed the room and distorted his face.

I popped the glass out from my eye with great relief. I wiped the vapor from the glass the humidity caused, cleared my throat, and said, "The map appears authentic."

Cole nodded and turned from me and lit his pipe. He went to the large window and stared out onto the courtyard below, and replied "Good. Then that's where we're bound," he said.

I asked Cole to give me an evening, to study the map more and match it with documents I already possessed—perhaps to consult with the scholars near the small university. They did not know my true name, instead, I had told them I was a traveler, a writer, the son of a wealthy house, which I left unnamed, far to the north. A mix of truth makes lies easier to tell for a scholar such as myself.

Cole agreed and said he would make his own inquiries and left, slipping out of my room, without another word. We have all learned to walk quietly in the last few years, though he seemed born to it.

I found one reference to a Haunt on an island named ElSamar, in the Old Semhelhen language in my own folios that night. As I sat on the floor rummaging through my papers, batting away the gnats which swarm to lamplit places on this southern isle, I became sure we would find the Haunt where the map indicated.

The next day when I asked the scholars about such an island, no one had heard of it. There are a thousand islands to the south and few of interest, they told me. I did not mention my design, to learn if Esmer might possess a true Haunt. Such subjects aren't the topic of idle conversation, even in a free-city like Port Shamhalhan.

Upon further inquiry and coaxing, I was told the islands south are inhabited by a mild and inconsequential people. Small traders, farmers and fishermen, distant relatives to the people who live in Port Shamhalhan, but of a more primitive mind who kept the old ways of the Bead.

But the specific island of Esmer? The name brought only shrugs and headshaking.

I did learn a few ships brought Throneland veterans to settle there amongst those islands a long while ago. The land was had cheap, though not ruled directly by the Throne. There were useable navigation maps they assured me and a steady stream of small boats hauling goods between the most northernly of the islands. But why bother with such places, they asked? Port Shamhalhan held mystery enough for an enterprising northerner.

I let them believe myself ignorant. I stared open-mouthed at their words, pretending amazement at their worldly ways; me the simple northerner. I let the subject go. I grew tired of their pleasant scorn for me and for a moment the idea possessed me to tell them who I truly was and the name of my outfit.

I am told I do not hide my indignation well. I remembered myself and put on a hollow smile and left their company in haste.

Cole returned that evening with a bundle of documents and said, he had spent the day near the harbor, elbow to elbow in crowded inns with Allred by his side.

He let the name Esmer float around the taverns, above the crash of slamming wooden cups emptied of pale ales. He trialed the name Esmer before the faces of sunburnt sailors, their eyes heavy-wild, fixed on the sloshing dregs of rotgut wine. The sailors sang and swayed on legs that had forgotten how to stand on solid land, and laughing, they said, no, they had heard of no such island.

A lot of nothing south. A long way before reaching anything important. That was the consensus.

One publican, a former ship's captain, told Cole that down the wide boulevard which hugged the shore, he could buy access to maps at the Navigator's Guild.

There he might find the names of smaller islands. There were hundreds, maybe thousands if you counted every spit of land. It was a place so unimportant, even the Throne hadn't made a play for it. Rich in nothing to concern the outside world.

Cole thanked the man. Allred stood unblinking, his hand resting lightly on a hidden dagger and watched with a bored look on his face as a fight broke out.

The barman cupped the coin for the drinks Cole had ordered, then over the racket and crash of cups and plate, he said: "Sounds like a paradise—Esmer, a place where nothing happens. Then he shook his head and pulled from beneath his crude bar a club with a handle worn smooth from keeping sailors at peace. He hopped over the bar top with a cheery, "Fortune!" to restore order.

Cole and Allred had gone to the Guild and paid handsomely for copies of navigation maps. He placed them on my desk, and we compared them with the ancient map. It took some time, but we found the island of Esmer, still unmarked and unnamed, too small to matter on the charts but matching the older map.

"It's enough," Cole said.

The Black Boat had arrived in harbor that very night. He had decided where it would take us. I knew, we all knew it would take us into another kind of hell. It had just been uncertain where the entrance was located.

Stoneburner, our quartermaster already worked the night markets near the port to supply the ship. He hefted his bulky body from stall to stall, good-naturedly complaining how his feet hurt, flattering market women. He does much our dealing and less the fighting. Grinning beneath his bristling moustache, most don't notice his shrewdness beneath the friendly patter. He's all the more convincing because he is a kind man, our wise provisioner.

Cole said porters were on their way to help me prepare to board. And then, he turned and left.

And so, we set off tonight in our Black Boat. Glume at the helm, crewed by the quiet sailors from his clan, full of what Cole calls the Black Boat men.

These Black Boat men, Cole says, will play a role. That role I am not yet certain I understand. Cole commands. I follow. That is enough for those who remember the 9th.

On the staircase below already, I hear the plodding feet of the porters come to haul my baggage down the spiral staircase and into the muggy night air where mule and cart awaits to take it to the port.

Scrolls put his ink away and shuffled his papers, casting a mournful glance around the room. It looked enticingly more comfortable now that he knew he would leave it for the confines of the ship and this island called Esmer.

1

Allred

Half a day up the trail, he ran into heavy action walking point. Dhlams came raging down the mountain and it was good fortune the path ran straight there. The old map from the madman in Shamhalhan looked to pay off.

Means we found it.

Allred raised his hand in a fist. The men behind him clattered to a halt and the battlemage raised a feint. He felt the press of the spell weigh down on him, as the mage bewitched the air with a scurrying set of consonants from behind his bronze mask. With a twist of his deformed hands, he hid them under an envelope of magic.

Under the tropical sun, he was sweating, and the linen-wrapped hilt of his sword was damp. His light boiled leather armor felt heavier under the press of the feint. A fight was welcome enough.

The Dhlams stopped on the trail, confused by the feint. The buzz of insects mixed with their sibilant hissing. They searched for their prey, now disappeared. Claws erupted from scaly hands, retracting and protruding, hungry. Three of them stood ten paces away in the middle of the game trail.

"They still smell our mage," Hartha said and laughed.

The blond giant's voice boomed out against the unseen walls of the feint.

"The Haunt answers," Hortha his brother replied.

"Close in on the mage," Allred said.

The twins, blond-bearded, horn-handled axe-wielders, torc-rich, shield-bearers, stepped closer to each other. Both men hoisted their Green-Island shields higher, sheltering Mage between them.

From the back of the group, Scrolls called up to him.

"How many?"

"Three in front. More ahead," Allred answered, chewing the end of his redleaf stick. It was unlit. "Can't run."

"Never," Hartha said.

"Can't hide," Hortha chimed in.

"Never," Allred whispered to himself.

The longer Mage held the feint, the less craft he could manage later. Time to decide. Time to war. Besides, once the battle ended, he could finally light the redleaf in his mouth.

"Fine," he said, quietly. Then louder, "Ready."

No danger of the Dhlams hearing them. The feint captured the sounds of their voices within its aura. He never got used to it though. He always kept his voice low inside the confines of the spell as if testing it with a loud voice somehow made the magic lesser.

Some men never get used to hiding in plain sight, he thought. If anyone should have mastered the skill by now it was Allred and the Relic Hunters of the 9th.

"Drop feint on my signal. Hartha and Hortha stay on the mage. Scrolls watch my back. I'll move up. Once the three fall, the rest will come. They look fast. Don't waste yourself, mage. Not unless they come in number."

"Heard," the twin giants called out in unison. Mage said nothing.

The sound of a bowstring drawing tight. Behind him, Scrolls

nocked an arrow, "Heard," he echoed.

They still leaned on the old command language learned in the Throneland's Army. The short, simple words felt bitter but familiar in his mouth.

Just outlaws now, he thought.

The three Dhlams were slashing at the low ferns around them, unhappy their prey had vanished. They ducked in and out of the foliage. Fast, wicked-looking things. If he hadn't been used to seeing demons, the sight would have turned his blood cold.

Dhlams, Undersiders, Demons—there was a thousand different names for the things that surrounded Haunts on the Upside or lived within the Haunts themselves and they took a thousand different forms.

They all died the same way, the only important way—before he did.

These stood, hunched, nearly the height of a man. Tough olive scales for skin, short arms, short legs, and a broad naked torso thick. They stood on two feet but with the sweeping arch of back which told him, they could and would fall to fours and run like a beast.

Their faces were a mix of something old—angles and bones prior to mankind but he couldn't help seeing something human in their eyes. Creatures warped by a birth in the Haunts.

Or so the legends told.

These wore no armor but their own thick hide and there was intelligence in their eyes, but it was dimmed by a raw physical speed, some lower order of thought which screamed—kill. He had heard the same word on the tips of forked tongues. He had heard the same word on the tongues of ordinary men in a hundred dialects—kill. He knew how to speak it, too.

Allred held his hand clenched high in sight of the warriors.

Then dropped it.

The feint went down with a low whoosh like a sudden gust of wind. Palm fronds and leaves shuddered along the trail. Behind him, the first arrow from Scrolls hit the closest Dhlam square in the body. It screamed and bolted forward. Another arrow embedded in its long snout. It crashed to the jungle floor, scrabbling off the trail through the ferns.

He went to one knee, aimed his crossbow. Waiting, patient.

The other two Dhlams barreled straight towards him. He pulled the trigger. The second Dhlam ate the bolt, spun and began to circle, thrashing in the loose dirt of the trail and perished.

The third didn't stop. It dropped to all fours like he figured it would, low to the ground. Just before it leaped on him, fire erupted over its body. The jungle filled with the smell of burning demon flesh and singed, wet vegetal matter.

The mage's work spoke of fire today.

"Three down," Allred said, calmly. He rose and pulled his sword from scabbard. "More coming."

As soon as the words were out of his mouth, the rest of the Dhlams burst from the underbrush, heading straight for the mage.

Two more Dhlams fell in the mage's flames, erupting from the words he sang behind his bronzemask. The fire smelled like the tar sailors used to cure a ship's hull mixed with incense.

Allred swung his blade. Edge met armored skin. Through it. Past demon flesh.

He took a nimble step backwards. The demon rushing him swung clawed hands. A half step to his side and a tight circle of the blade, metal gleaming in southernly sun—the wet sound of steel rushing, chopping through the Dhlam's head.

The demon's squat legs kept turning for a moment, as if trying to run, but now the creature's feet met only air.

Two more burst out of the brush near Hartha and Hortha. One of them leapt into the air and met the great upheld shield of Hortha as if trying to scale a wall. The giant man heaved the demon back into the jungle. The other went low and grabbed Hartha's boots, biting and slavering. Hortha lopped off its arm with his axe freeing his brother's foot.

Allred felt the cold cut of a claw on his shoulder piercing his armor. He spun low and the blade cut through both Dhlam's legs. Its trunk fell sideways over its twitching legs.

Covered in strange hissing, the smell of burning demons, a bit of blood in his eye, Allred did what he did best—fighting.

To his left, Mage worked his spells and brought down two

more demons. The black-cloaked, bronzeface worked his terrible magic, shifting his disjointed, elongated fingers in impossible patterns--the sound of bones shifting, flesh oozing like burned candle wax above the joints troubled the air.

The smell after a lightning strike perfumed the narrow trail, the dealer of magic crouched beneath the double shadows of the two high shields. Hartha and Hortha smeared in blood, four eyes bulging in paroxysms of war-laughter, hacked with their axes, sheltering the mage with shield-bound arms.

Demons and men at war. In the melee, lost in his movement, lost in the perfect dance of steel, Allred forgot the differences between man and demon. Lost himself in the simplicity of bloodshed. Disappeared.

Then it was quiet.

"Circle up," he said.

He watched the path behind them. No movement, only the twitching of one of the Dhlams nearby. A mountain breeze rustled the tops of the lush tropical trees.

The blood-smeared Emerald Isle giants chuckled. The fight over, they beat their silver torc-laden arms against chain-heavy chests in triumph, counting their kills with each strike, arguing amongst themselves which demon corpse was their own and which belonged to the other. "Mage needs rest," Hartha and Hortha said in unison.

"Then rest," he answered.

He sheathed his sword and checked the light wound on his shoulder. Nothing much.

Mage moved low and quiet to the ground beneath his flowing black cloak. Still whispering the tattered ends of spells, the battle over, he transmuted curses to prayers.

You couldn't listen too long to a mage that powerful, or your mind would start to undo itself. The Relic Hunters of the 9th had grown accustomed to it, could tolerate it more than common men. They had spent years fighting and dying with him.

Still, the chaos of the magic made his head swim, and his hands shake. Allred lit his redleaf smoke from the small coal-carrier he kept in one of the pockets of his leather vest and took a long drag.

Hartha set down his axe and pulled a light grey cloth he kept folded and bunched between his belt and belly and draped it over the mage. Hortha dug a shallow trench in the dirt to fit the curve of the giant shield's bottom. The brothers positioned their shields to stand upright in the ground, tilted to lean on one another, creating a makeshift shelter where their battlemage lay talking to himself in its shade.

After spell casting he would rest away from the light of the sun which broke through the jungle canopy onto the trail itself. It was a small bit of battle magic the man had used, but he had been fighting for many years and the weight of the Haunt on the island disrupted the man's mind.

"Hartha and Hortha, good?" he asked.

"Aye. No wounds."

"Mage?"

He learned years ago it was best not to utter any of the mage's specific names, especially while at war. The man had too many names, some real, some not—Bronzface (an affectionate nickname he sometimes used himself), Les Aments, L'Eintzamets, Mehry-meh-rhin, Elaohir, Shadowspate. A true-trained battle-mage was blown apart by the entities he contacted, channeled and consumed. A battlemage at best was always a bit mind-fractured, at worst shattered. Allred understood what war could do to the spirit but the depths a trained battlemage descended, even he couldn't fathom.

So, except in the most private of moments, the relic hunters just called him, Mage.

A different language echoed from within the makeshift tent where he crouched. He looked like some disguised, dangerous animal under it. More words poured forth, steely sounding around the bronze mask. Allred took it as an affirmative that he was uninjured.

"Scrolls?"

"Whole and hail," the scholar answered and slung his small bow over his shoulder.

The fight over, Scrolls joined him at the front of the group.

The man could fight well enough, the result of years of practice in the courtyards of a lord's house. Still, he was foremost a scholar and Allred tried to keep him farthest from the battle.

That was it. No more names to call. He considered other names he had called in the past. A roll call of the dead now.

Best not to utter the names of the dead in strange places.

"I have commerce with the dead," Scrolls said.

"I'll go with you," he answered, "Make sure nothing else is coming."

They had survived another day.

The day was still long.

Allred winced. He turned his head, blew some smoke on the scratch on his shoulder, sighed. He should take the time to clean it properly.

In his vest, he plucked a bit of cloth, pre-soaked in one of Doctor Aodlen's remedies, prepared for their scouting mission the night before. He poured it past the cut in the leather armor, smelled it cauterizing the wound.

He smoked while the flesh bubbled, staring hollow-eyed at the gore-filled trail. The wound fell quiet. He lit another redleaf smoke from the end of the one he'd just finished, listening to the jungle and considering the next move.

They were less than a half day's hike up the trail from the smaller camp where Cole and the others waited below. From there, it was further down the mountain to the beach where Captain Glume guarded the beach with the Black Boat men and the bulk of their supplies.

In the morning, Cole had said to him, "Go up until you find trouble. Then come back."

Well, that's what they had done.

He checked his crossbow, locked it back into place on his belt loop. He unsheathed his sword again, examined it, wiped the blood from it on his trousers then sheathed it again.

"You want a closer look at the Dhlams?"

"I await your signal," the pale scholar said, impatiently.

"Get on with your butchery, then."

"My work is within the purview of the arts and sciences,"

the scholar scoffed and withdrew a short knife from his belt.

Scrolls maintained his aristocratic manners even halfway up the side of a mountain on a nowhere island, covered in blood and jungle sweat. Years before, when he first met him, it bothered him, but after all this time, he was glad Scrolls had stayed the same. He would never tell him that though.

"Go," he said.

The two men surveyed the trail as they walked. The Dhlams lay where they died. Scrolls pointed to one felled by a crossbow bolt, unmarred by magic or steel.

"This one suffices. A relatively untouched specimen."

To Scrolls these things were not just enemies but clues to a greater mystery.

"Then do it well," Allred said, "Salvage my bolt, too, while you work."

Scrolls took a knee beside the Dhlam, delicately lowering himself to the ground and began to saw the hands from the demon. Then the feet.

Allred turned away. Something about it he didn't like. Old prohibitions from his homeland about defiling the dead. Even Dhlams, inhuman things, fought and died for whatever unholy orders they followed.

Scrolls pulled his crossbow bolt from the demon's flesh with a wet sucking sound and held it over his shoulder, not bothering to turn away from his toil. Allred muttered thanks and took it and put it back in one of the loops on his vest which carried more.

Behind him, Hartha and Hortha hummed a tune from their land, a song sung after battle—a recitation of the names of the ancestors inscribed on their shields. The melody was cold. A mournful tune of salt, rain, and steel, contending with the humid jungle surrounding them. The Songs of the Shields of Green Island. Names of the dead lending weight to the iron they carried. Allred didn't know the language, but he had heard it so many times, he could sing along, anyway.

Scroll's knife sawing into Dhlam-flesh kept rhythmic counterpoint to the giant's melody.

"How much longer?" he asked. The jungle was quiet, but he

was feeling nervous. Time to move.

Scrolls looked up, light blue eyes like ice in the southern sun, "The more I ascertain about this particular type of Dhlam and the Haunt they guard, the better I can suggest answers to the layout and provenance of the Haunt itself." He lifted some black-grey organ above him, sloppy with the wet edge of flesh in the sunlight. "Through study, I might recognize patterns which will aid us in our business and calibrate the bronzeface's magic all the better."

"You talk about him like he's a weapon, not a man."

"He is—" The scholar's blade worked bone and gristle. A hunk of flesh came loose in his hands. "Both."

Allred grunted agreement. A look of irritation crossed Scroll's face. A refined face, despite a scar here and there. It reminded him of the slightly disdainful and curious stares of ice foxes back home in Darkridge.

"Nothing is known for certain until we observe it ourselves—" The man looked lost in thought for a moment, "Aodlen will wish to scrutinize these on our return."

He is what he is, Allred thought. *Effete*.

There was a word he had heard someone use once, probably Scrolls himself. He was the most knowledgeable man Allred had ever known and brave enough, he could count on him— the son of a march lord.

It didn't mean he had to like the man's work or wit.

"My task has concluded," Scrolls said.

He deposited the last of the demon's body into what looked like a small, common, potato sack. He wrapped and folded it and then placed it inside his own larger bag.

Fussy. That's the word. Fussy but effective.

He turned from the gruesome work and looked at the map he built of Esmer inside his own head. His was a scout's mind, holding a scout's map—an unfilled-in thing, made of loose rocks, slick dirt, bends in the trail where it was difficult to see ahead; the sound of the ground you tread, notes of places where a man could fall back to defend, fall back and hide, fall back and attack. It was a living map, composed of sound, terrain, weather, angles. The odds of surviving encounters he hastily scrawled in the margins.

It was a useful map.

They walked back to join the others.

Mage still huddled by himself beneath the gossamer grey, magecrafted blanket. Hartha said, "He needs an idle."

"Time to move," he answered.

The twins nodded and lifting their shields helped the mage to his feet.

He lit another redleaf smoke and looked up the game trail ahead. The Haunt should stand somewhere up there, past the shadows of the jungle of this island called Esmer.

He gathered up the men, took the front of the line and set off back down the mountain to the camp to tell Cole what they had found.

The hike back down, they accomplished without incident and good speed. Sometimes it was faster going down a mountain. Most of the time it was not. In Allred's experience, there were unfortunate times when it was too fast, the going-down of mountains.

They neared Cole's position around dusk, and he whistled a mimic of a greydown hawk to signal their approaching. A similar whistle returned.

They rounded the last small turn of the mountain before the camp. The vegetation grew thicker here, the closer they were to beach and the sea. Up higher, the trees thinned out some, more palms, less broad-leafed ferns.

He glanced backwards. All accounted for. He whistled once more and walked forward, slowly. Cole stood in the little clearing watching them.

The man's face was familiar to him. He'd seen it on returning from uncountable missions, welcoming him back. A mix of black hair streaked with auburn and grey fell around his shoulders and hid most of the flat scars of fire that ran down one side of his face and neck. His eyes were green. War and thought had hooded them. He was a man of average height, wearing the same expensive light armor, magewoven, many of them wore. His armor covered broad-shoulders above simple looking trousers, sturdy but worn with mud and bits of green jungle clinging to it.

He nodded to them as they came into camp and Allred felt relief seeing him. He was no longer in command, Cole was, though he wore no badges or insignia of rank now to show it. Once this simple-looking warrior had boasted high command in the Throneland's armies.

He stood watching and waiting, statue-still, a pipe in his face, unlit, Cole chewed. He showed no sign of relief or fear, as he surveyed his men returning to camp.

They greeted each other quietly as they walked into the small camp. Stoneburner tended a fire near where the trail sloped down the mountain. A small iron pot above the flame simmered with a simple camp soup. Stoneburner's bushy moustache bobbed upwards on his thick face. The oldest among them, the least fit of their band, he offered a wide, warm grin and began to ladle out his stew.

"You found something," Cole stated.

"We did," Allred said.

Doctor Aodlen stood leaning over Stoneburner, talking in his frenetic, staccato way. He gave a short frantic wave with one tattooed hand then resumed pointing at the soup, harassing Stoneburner about the portion of this or that in the recipe. He was sweating as usual. Allred hoped he wasn't sweating over the soup.

"Is the mage sound?" Cole asked.

Mage didn't join them in the clearing but walked off to some trees near the cliff's edge and sat alone, pulling his cloak over himself.

"Enough so."

The hike back down had been uneventful. The last half, Hartha gave his shield to his brother and carried the mage down the mountain like a child. The thin man, his warped body strangled by his shimmering cloak was no difficult weight for the giant to carry. He likely weighed less than the giant's shield.

Mage's unpredictability grew every day. He had expended a fragment of his power fighting the Dhlams, casting simple magic and holding a feint. Allred had seen him do much more than that in other battles—much more. But these days, even simple magic wielding could throw the mage into odd moods, his whole being alight with chaos for hours after.

Less the fight itself, Allred thought, *than the fight with whatever hounds his spirit.*

The bronzeface wrestled with interior voices. They were manifold. He voiced them out loud sometimes and then replied to them in his own voice. Or sometimes he set to disputing in the shared language of the Ninth—the tongue of the Thronelands—and then changing to older languages mid-sentence. Mage talked to the Keys, to the Haunts, to the things inside the Haunts, to entities unseen, to animals, to himself.

It was getting harder and harder to speak to his friend.

They settled down around the small campfire. Stoneburner brought food, hard bread and soup. Handing him his bowl, he said, "No flesh in it."

Allred hadn't eaten meat since the day before he earned his name. During his time in service to the Throneland army a few men had asked questions about his diet. The questions stopped when the truth got around.

"Fortune."

Cole let them eat in peace, before launching into questions. As the sun grew low in the southern sky, night insects began to chirp. The brush beside them stirred with the first tentative motions of small predators beginning the night's hunt. A cool breeze came down from the clouds and found its way through the trees washing through the leaves.

Aodlen sat across from him, fidgeting and shuffling a deck of flesh-stained cards, investigating him with squinting eyes in the falling dark. Allred nodded a greeting and tried to ignore him but Aodlen must have smelled his cut, because with a flick of the wrist, he retired his cards to his belt pouch and came to crouch beside him, prodding and poking at the wound on Allred's shoulder.

"You should have told me. Ha!"

"Already shook some of your medicine on it. Burned like fire. It's fine," Allred said and waved him off.

It was hard to eat with the man flitting about him. He was

22

wiry and smelled of his own unguents, salves and saps. Allred didn't care for doctors, barbers and surgeons much. This one had saved his life, stopped his bleeding, and even restarted his heart with his cruel potions a few times, so he let him hover about.

"I'll check on it later." Aodlen said, mollified enough for now to let him eat. "I have a lot of vitality, you see, ha! We've been sitting here all day, waiting for you lot. So? What is it? Did you find anything? Another foray into the downdowndown into the darkness, is it? I must prepare. Ha!"

The doctor hopped up from his crouch, nearly knocking the soup bowl from Allred's hands and began pacing; then reaching back into his belt purse, his fingers jumbling vials and glasses full of distillations as if taking inventory, he recovered his dirt-caked cards and set again to amusing his nervous hands.

"Looks like you kept busy enough with sampling your own medicines while we marched, good doctor, Aodlen!" Hortha said in his cheery, guileless way.

Hartha laughed at his brother's soft mockery, sat his soup bowl down and took out his bone cup and dice, slapping his brother on the chest with the back of his hand, to bring his attention to the game.

"Play a round while we have time, brother," Hartha said.

Hortha smiled and the men set to rolling dice from the cup in the dirt and tallying, rule-calling in their Green Island dialect.

Aodlen looked for the answer to the giant's jest in his cards, "Yes, yes and again yes! If I don't sample the medicines, then they won't be perfect to keep you fools alive, ha!"

The doctor circled back around the little campfire, shuffling his cards, plucking one from the top of the deck, spinning it, tossing them from hand to hand in waves, hiding one, revealing it to himself, and chirping with frantic laughter. He stopped, his mood turning morose and sat near the fire with the rest of the men.

The Haunts and the years and the hiding had made Aodlen sleep-deprived. The men he couldn't save through the years grew large purple circles of flesh around his eyes. These doctor's eyes, both cold and warm, were set below a few wild grey hairs he missed with his surgeon's clippers on his otherwise close-shaved head.

Never judge a surgeon by his barber skills, was generally a bad piece of advice but in Aodlen's case it held true.

"Well, Allred, my mute man, our silent scout, will you say what's what? Will you tell us what we are in for? Ha! Ha! As if we don't know."

Allred laid down his empty bowl in front of him, plucked some loose sand and splashed it in the bottom of the bowl and rubbed it around, scouring out the bits of vegetables and Rhu grain clinging to the wood. Least he could do for Stoneburner. Keep things clean.

Cole had ignored all the camp talk and conversed quietly with Scrolls. The scholar sat beside Cole, delicate hands passing him sketches he had made from the day's research. Research is what Scrolls called nearly everything.

The campfire crackled. Stoneburner refilled two more bowls for Hartha and Hortha and they thanked the man, not breaking away their gaze from the dice game which was growing heated. Allred never fully understood the rules of their simple game, but it involved rolling the dice from the cup made of bone and then slapping each other in the face and laughing. It was a game only Green Island men could truly master.

Cole and Scrolls kept talking quietly and Aodlen sprung back up and stood, leaning over Cole's shoulder and looking at Scroll's sketches.

Mage hadn't joined them.

The bronzeface tended to climb trees, linger in the mouth of caves and caverns, or perch in high places alone. Not a particularly odd behavior for a mage with his powers. His mere presence and proximity could drive others around him to distraction, nervousness, or in time—madness. Some people's minds just closed off around him and didn't notice him at all, especially with the prompting of a simple spell.

The Relic Hunters of the 9th didn't react that way to him. They had all grown accustomed to the presence of magic and its chaos.

Too accustomed.

He's disputing with all the demons, Allred thought, *We are too but we don't have the words for it.*

The familiar black cloak, velvet-dark, like the sleep beneath a star-rich sky was waving in the gentle mountain breeze halfway up the low twisted branches of a tree the name of which, Allred could not lay claim.

Sometimes a man needed space. Even if you were barely holding on to the idea of being a man, like the mage. Allred nodded to the figure. Something friendly-sounding escaped from behind the bronze masked figure in reply.

This is what's left of the 9th. These are the survivors.

He pulled a small knife from his vest and began to pick and scrape at his fingernails.

Across the campfire, Cole motioned for Scrolls to leave off and turning his hard, careful eyes at him, puffed his pipe and asked, "What's the land look like?"

He put away the knife and stopped cleaning his fingernails at Cole's inquiry.

"Just the one fight. That was it. Heavy and fast. My gut tells me we have the right trail and what we're looking for will be at the top of this mountain. No villagers around, so that's one less thing," Allred reported.

"Good," Cole said.

Odd how some men appear separate, even when they are huddled around the same fire, shoulder to shoulder with men they've known for years.

That's how Cole's always looked, he thought, *apart from things, even before the fire.*

It wasn't the aloof ways of Scrolls, the aristocrat and scholar. That was different. It wasn't the sad tendrils of madness of Mage, a life shaped in pain. (Allred shivered at the thought of the man's hands and it took a lot to make him shiver these days.) Nor was it the physical difference between the two giant twins, Hartha and Hortha—they were Green Islander twins and not true giants after all, though they stood a good three heads taller than most average men.

It was the years of command that kept Cole apart. Every

death ultimately fell on Cole. He sent men to die, and they did. That's why when he looked at you, everything around him seemed to eclipse until he dismissed you.

And, yes, Allred knew, there was something else besides that, but he couldn't quite muster the strength to consider that too closely, not after all the miles they'd walked together and maybe it was best just never to figure it out besides.

Cole came from near the same country he did but out near Port Coldewater. A larger town where the hills sloped away toward the sea and the clans didn't fight but had been staid by the rulership of a house.

He knew a bit of the man's past, told in pieces over innumerable campfires in enemy country, after battles where the scent of the recently dead drifted in over the cookfires to tap the living on the shoulder and remind them they were alive, so might as well talk.

He was likely a few years older than Allred. He hailed not from a named house but said he was the son of a farrier and small trader of horses bred for Throneland service. Joined the Throneland army when he was old enough. A market town boy, he had never ridden with the clans on raids as a child like Allred or known war and death as early as Allred, but he knew command and came to master it and rose high in war until that fateful day that sent all the Ninth to running and marred Cole's face with fire.

Cole had earned command. It stuck to the man with every breath, every step, even the way he smoked his pipe—a calculated and cold balance. And every man around this campfire and many across the sea would die for him at a simple command.

That was one story, anyway. Allred knew there were others.

"Describe the fight to me in detail," Cole said.

So, Allred did. He told how the Dhlams fell, described their smell, their sound, went into detail on their claw-like hands. Estimated their speed.

"Good. Anyone else want to add anything?" Cole asked, looking around the fire.

"An excellent recollection of the melee from Allred. I can however bring to your attention the specimens I procured. I simply thought it best to wait until less-scholarly minds had finished eating," Scrolls said.

Scrolls opened the bag where he had stowed the body parts of the Dhlam. He handed a foot to Cole, who turned it over and examined it in the flickering campfire. Then the hand of one of the creatures with the long black claws. Eagerly, Aodlen took each body part from Cole as he passed them across the fire. The doctor issued his little burbles of laughter, inspecting the demon flesh.

Cole looked up to the trees.

"Mage, can you speak?"

"The Keys, the Haunts. These spirits keep waking me up," Mage called down from above them.

"He's fit?" Cole asked Hartha.

"Tired," Hartha said.

Hortha said nothing. Just agreed with his brother with a soft, "Aye." And rattled the dice against the bone cup.

The sorcerer spoke something indecipherable again from the treetops; then lightly he jumped down to the ground, cloak snapping, the material flashing and reflecting liquid designs in the firelight. He stood, looking back and forth, one pale finger pointed to the sky as if suspended in the middle of a secret debate with the stars. Then he pulled his black cloak further around him and took a seat around the fire.

For a moment, there was a constant outpouring of strange syllables and sentences from behind his bronze mask. He answered himself with a series of lilting sentences which sounded like admonishing questions—then a blunt pause followed by another voice as if answering the others and the conversation stopped all at once.

Mage's ivory white skin looked even paler in the firelight. He managed a thin-red-lipped smile and carefully as if remembering their shared language, opened his mouth revealing jewel-studded teeth, "I might eat."

Stoneburner offered him his bowl of soup, "Yes, best eat something."

The black eyes of the mage peered through the eyeholes of his elaborate bronze mask which stayed fitted to his face by invisible means. He took the bowl in his least twisted hand, his movements like a wary animal, tentative and stared through the fire straight into Allred's own eyes.

He didn't blink. He met the man's gaze and returned a sad smile.

Then a strange and wild kindness showed back, the eyes of a child—a blend of an ancient man and an animal stare and something alive which could not be categorized; all there in the brief glance, behind the bronze mask.

Allred felt his shoulders tighten, as if suffering the stare of some minor god or the wild-souled spirit of a wilderness sprite.

Then Mage broke off his gaze, shrunk back into his cloak a bit and cradled the bowl in his lap and said, "Thank you," in perfect, precise imperial-diction.

He pulled his hood further over his face, then, stifling a sound of pain, he prised away the bronzemask clinging to his skin. He laid it on his lap beside the bowl, face up, blank, eye holes staring at the stars. He spooned his soup into the cavernous shadows of his cloak.

Cole asked a few more questions. Mage answered, sometimes in Imperial, sometimes in forgotten languages which Scrolls helpfully translated where he could.

"Might get there tomorrow. Maybe the next day," Cole said.

Allred wanted to say, "Another Haunt might kill us."

He wanted to say, "We're on the edge of permanent madness. We should stop."

He wanted to say, "It's time to return home."

But he said nothing. Stretched his legs, figured on sleep soon.

The men traded some quiet jokes—the same jokes they had been making for years. A flagon of wine made a round. The crisp wine mixed with the smell of the vegetable soup blended with the smoke from the small fire and could convince a stranger who came upon the place that it might just be peaceful and pleasant enough life, if he didn't look closely.

It's either forward or backwards, Allred thought, *That's what it all comes down to.*

Stoneburner put the bowls away and brought out his small lute, took a swig of wine and strummed it. The instrument was the one thing Stoneburner never left behind no matter where they tread—Allred had heard it played even in the depths of the Haunts. A simple wooden instrument, easy enough to carry and it birthed songs and legends and brought quiet to the troubled men's minds.

Mage put back his mask. Cole folded his hands, shook some ash from his pipe and refilled it. Someone won the dice game between the giants but it wasn't clear. The men grew quiet in the music.

"The deeds of the 9th are known, to shake the throne," Stoneburner sang.

Allred watched the man strum and pick at the lute. The gentlest among them, rare to pick up a sword, Stoneburner did something more important—he packed bags properly, portioned food, found and stored water, ordered men, supervised digging of ditch and latrine, cared for pack animals, washed bowls or ordered the washing of them, made lists and checked lists, bought and sold goods both mundane and illegal. Flint and firepot, bowls and bandage, twine and taper, he stored them, packed them. Stoking the fire, knowing when to fetch another flagon of wine and when to put the wine away. Men like him shared little fame in the stories of heroes.

A thousand other tasks, Stoneburner understood, which kept an army, or a band like their own fed, safe, warm, dry, rested—prepared and capable to fight.

And he sang.

Over the years, those songs were heard, picked up and sung by other voices in rebel lands, inside inns, at festivals, around campfires and even at courts.

Stoneburner made myths of them.

The portly man stepped nimbly around the fire, avoiding the crossbows and swords and axes which the warriors kept close at hand. He put the lute down and began rolling out packs for the men for the night.

Cole said, "Tomorrow we head straight up to the top of this mountain before we call the criminals up."

Tired men muttered assent.

"Trail is clean. Easy so far. I'll run point," Allred said.

"Good. Rather deal with any villagers we come across without the Black Boat Men in tow. So, first light we make fast the ascent and push to the top of this trail." Cole said.

Scrolls lay out on his camp blanket. He had managed to make it look prim and square in the sand and grass, "If my measurements are correct, and they are, we can gain the ascent in around a day's march."

"Sleep while you can," Cole said, "It's going to be a long few days."

The men turned their faces to the stars gazing down on them through the thick, tropical air. Through the canopy, some offered private prayers or studied the symmetry of the night sky. Mage laid a ward over the area and scuttled back up his tree.

Not Allred. He couldn't sleep. He took a seat across from Cole and said nothing. Both men kept private their thoughts as the last of the campfire starved and the clearing grew darker.

The trail gave off the reverberations of old spells, and in the night ancient arguments floated down from the jungle canopy higher up the mountain. Hortha started snoring and his brother joined him and then that subsided. Allred lit a redleaf roll and Cole smoked, too and the fire dimmed to nothing and the two men sat quiet, listening.

Far off, he thought he could hear the surf below.

2

Lookout

The Attman had brought the horse all the way from Port Shamhalhan—that was the story. It was the only horse on Esmer, brown and tan and white. He had seen it for himself, so he knew what a horse looked like—bigger than a donkey—though he never observed it doing anything more than standing in a roughly-built shed, chomping grass that once. The Attman was too fat to ride.

He also knew what horses looked like from Boph's recitations of *Kings, Princes, Kingdoms and Empire*. There were many horses in those stories. Warhorses.

Tonight, Lookout stood at the summit of the watch tower of Esmer. It stood in a clearing, close to the top of one of the highest peaks on the island. The only higher point was the volcano. So, he had been told by the Attman. He had never been.

He surveyed the scene, the scope of his lonely remit, in the twilight below.

Nothing moved. Nothing happened. It almost never did up here. The ground, the air, the mountain in the distance looked soft to the point of bleariness in the night's sultry stillness. Waves of chirrups, the dialogues of insects, pulsed from the surrounding jungle brush.

He took another pull from the bottle of cownut liquor. The liquid warmed his guts. Last bottle from the last delivery. He steadied himself against the rickety railing which encompassed the one room shack at the top of the wooden platform.

The tower didn't stand tall. From below, if he jumped as high as he could, he could touch the platform with the tips of his fingers. He knew that because sometimes, he did that when he felt bored. He did it a lot.

So, this night, like many nights alate, deep in his cups, he imagined himself as a knight, armored, on horseback in the clearing below his tame, rotting tower. The more he drank, the better he could imagine it.

He spurred his imagination on. The horse neighed. The horse shifted. The horse was decidedly not present except within his liquor-driven dream.

There—taller, stronger, mounted on a great steed (steed was a word for a horse he had heard from the tales Boph told him) he sported a set of shining armor. Sometimes it was gold-plated, sometimes a dull silver but mostly the dark Throneland-crimson the likes the prince had worn riding into battle in the "Tale of the Crimson Knight."

The more he drank the more elaborate the armor became. It never felt heavy or burdensome because it wasn't real. And so, the armor grew very elaborate, because it could.

Shouldn't the steed change, too? The horse brown, no dun; dun was a word used in the legends—no black, no white, yes white, a white steed! Pawing at the sandy ground where the patchy grass grew yellow in the shadow of the tower, the steed stood waiting.

The armor he wore as a knight in his imagination differed a lot from what he wore when the sun rose, and the headaches set in.

A helmet too large for his head from his father's old infantry days, Lookout possessed. It was a kind of armor and his only real piece. His father had given it to him before he took this post. That felt a long time ago.

The helmet was stored inside the one room shack. He wore it for a few weeks when he first arrived, but it made his head sweat and the sweat dripped in his eyes. He stopped wearing it. Why armor yourself against nothing besides boredom?

It was one of the best days in his life, when his father had gifted the helmet to him. Before arranging the meeting with the Attman, his father had brought it to him, in front of their small wooden house which stared with hollow windows out onto a weedy yard and rows of cownut trees.

His father had fitted it on his head with his thick knuckled hands swollen from infantry service and worse—farmer's hands. When he had fitted it over his head, his father had stepped back a pace, and with the first smile he had seen on his face for many years, said:

"It'll take time, but you'll grow into it."

That's what his father had told him.

His father, well, his soldiering days were long past. He didn't have much to give his son. The farm had produced nought but a scattered cownut grove. They kept chickens for eggs and enough of a garden to ward away starving. That was the patrimony his father earned from a life of service in the Throneland's military.

That and the helmet.

Perhaps it was against regulations to not wear the helmet, he didn't know. The Attman hadn't given him much instruction concerning his post at the tower—just go sit up there night and day. Don't leave. A boy named Boph will come up every two weeks with supplies and half-a-hand of copper coins for your pay.

His official title was *Guard of the First Tower of Esmer*, the Attman had told him. From the way the Attman had said it, Lookout wasn't sure he hadn't just invented the title there and then in the action of bestowing it on him.

It came with no benefits of armor. There wasn't a Throneland armory on Esmer or Throneland troops. Just the Attman, a kind of forgotten diplomat, who shipped over with the few dozen colonists in his father's generation. The only other Thronelanders were a handful of ageing veterans like his father who had been doled out their land allotments here on Esmer. They weren't active soldiers. Most weren't even active farmers. Most were dead. The Attman oversaw the remnants.

He possessed another piece. He had one leather gauntlet somewhere. This the Attman gave to him in lieu of explaining to him what he was supposed to do up here.

"What am I to look out for up there?" he had asked, "They say there's geists and were-creatures far up."

"Island fables ... hmm, but stay near your tower. Go no higher up. Here. Take this." The Attman had pulled the old gauntlet from a heap of this-and-that crowding one corner of his quarters and handed him the gauntlet.

He had kept it near the helmet for some time. A few months ago, he realized he had misplaced it. To his embarrassment, first, he had accused Boph of stealing it, though the island boy denied it saying, "Why would I steal your trash glove?" or something to that effect in his Imperial pidgin.

That had provoked a row which ended in the two boys punching and kicking and no one particularly hurt. Still, was it not a serious thing for his servant to speak like that to him? When he told Boph this after the fight, the fight resumed. Boph had never accepted the idea that he was a servant, attendant or a retainer. Lookout had tried a lot of different words. None worked.

Where was Boph, anyway? This was the last bottle of cownut liquor. That he kept careful stock of.

Eventually a steady enough peace resumed, when Lookout admitted he might have misplaced the gauntlet while drinking. Boph shot back that it wasn't a gauntlet but just an old leather glove with holes. Lookout was too tired to fight. He let the comment pass.

Rounding out his uniform he owned a thin shirt which had

developed many holes, more so than the gauntlet. It had been clean once. Now it was the color of sweat. On his enrollment by the Attman—a hurried ceremony with little grace—the Attman *had* given him an allowance to purchase a new tunic in the village. And that he did.

Once Lookout made it to this lonely place, he decided it wiser to preserve the new tunic and not wear it. So, for most of the day he simply wore the old shirt or went shirtless. It was humid and hot on Esmer, the island of his birth, even this high up the mountain. He was of northern blood, after all, and sweat more profusely than natives of Esmer, like Boph.

He blinked. Watched himself sitting on the steed below. The horse on which his imaginary-self bestrode grew impatient and dug at the ground with a hoof.

"Silence war-steed. I command you," he muttered.

He wasn't sure how to ride a horse, or how to talk to one or if talking to a horse had any effect. He had grown accustomed to talking to himself up here though. He knew talking to an invisible horse was talking to oneself. Yes, he knew how to do that.

The first few times, it frightened him a little, his own voice unanswered at the top of the mountain. After a few months, he decided it was perfectly fine, especially if he was talking to a figment of his imagination.

The war-horse calmed down.

Lookout held a great lance astride the steed and a great sword, too. He wasn't sure the name of the sword or its provenance. The swords in the legends were often named-things. He wasn't so sure how men could carry so many different weapons in the legends. The tales glanced over the details.

His father had been proud when the Attman offered him the sinecure—that's what they called it, a sinecure. The Attman and his father had talked in the Attman's little humid room, so close to the beach and sea, behind what stood for an inn at the main village. It was also the Attman's domicile.

The two men who got along well, arriving together on Esmer as they had, spoke words like 'sinecure' and 'pittance' and others Lookout didn't understand. The Attman raised his fat arms above his head to emphasize some catastrophe Lookout didn't quite understand. He remembered turning away from the sight of the Attman's old arms, drooping heavy with fat.

At the end of their talk, after sharing stories of their service, and half a bottle of cownut liquor between them, the Attman by authority of the Throne had taken a small bag of coins and given half to his father and half to him. Then came the oath to the throne. That was that. The next day a village boy would guide him far up the mountain to the tower.

Boph was his name.

Boph shows up tomorrow, he thought and smiled.

Not the yesteryear tomorrow, the tomorrow, tomorrow. He looked forward to it. If he didn't arrive with his supplies, his cownut liquor ration and Orangeroot grain, Lookout would be displeased.

"I would be most displeased," Lookout said to himself, mimicking the cadence of the old Throneland tongue used in the tales.

Down below the image of the knight vanished.

A year ago, when the Attman had introduced him to Boph the insolent attitude began immediately.

Insolent—a word he didn't know at the time. Boph would later explain the word to him while reciting the story of *The Cave Apprentice and his Son*. Lookout found it doubly confusing and irritating to learn vocabulary from the very servant you needed to deploy it against.

A One-Bead boy, not even the son of a colonist, and certainly he had no official place in the Throneland's Guard like Lookout did—Boph, his friend. He had a way with words and he suspected the boy of dwelling in magic.

He didn't even come from Esmer but some smaller, even lesser, nameless atoll nearby. He wore one bead beneath the overgrown skin-scar on his arm marking him as free to move about. Low caste but clever.

"A clever servant," Lookout said.

Where was that horse?

Boph had a donkey, not a horse. His parents were sick and then they were dead, and the boy was quick-witted—even Lookout knew it was so upon first meeting him.

So, the Attman hired Boph out to haul supplies up to the tower, to carry messages and do other errands for him which the Attman had grown too lazy to accomplish himself.

The Attman wasn't a cruel man despite the island-torpor he had adopted upon taking up his sinecure in Esmer. In fact, Lookout liked him. All the villagers liked him well enough, too. And Boph told him later that it was the Attman who'd taught him to read Imperial script and let him spend hours reading and memorizing the few books he had brought with him to Esmer from the Thronelands.

The first day upon meeting Boph, early in the morning, Lookout was sore. He had slept out on small porch of the Attman's office on an itchy blanket. His father had left the night before, back to the farm, avoiding any parting words. He had given him a fast hug, a last look, a pat on the old helmet and then set back up the mountain.

In the morning, he awoke to an uncertain future, red bites from bugs in the blanket, a crick in his neck from sleeping on the porch and the tawny, bald-headed, sharp-tongued, false-servant, no-good, lazy, scheming, errand boy named Boph staring down at him beside a donkey.

"You're the new lookout?" His voice oozed with impertinence even at his first words.

"Yes," he had answered.

"Well, let's go," Boph had said.

"Is the Attman—"

"Still asleep."

He folded the rug up neatly and laid it by the door of the inn.

The two boys and the donkey climbed the mountain road from the main village. The road soon turned to a trail. It grew narrower and narrower with every step but could still fit a cart, even two, if one cart ran a wheel close to the edge of the precipice.

Somewhere along the way, Lookout had decided to refer to Boph as his attendant. He would need a proper way to refer to him, he figured, and no instruction had been provided by the Attman.

He told him so.

"I'm not your attendant or servant. You got this role because Attman knew your father and the other man up there ran away, or something. You're just a lookout, so that's what I'll call you," Boph replied.

On recollection, Lookout knew, he had said it quite insolently.

"I thought the Attman said you were a servant?" Lookout ventured. "Was certain, yesterday when he swore me my oath, that he called you a servant."

The Attman had said no such thing with regards to Boph's status in relation to his own, he hadn't even mentioned it, but he figured he would try it on for the truth.

"No," Boph said.

"Look at you, you're hauling my food and drink and other things on your donkey. That's what a servant does. I'm not just a lookout—or I am that, yes, but also a Throneland soldier, er a Guard at least—"

Boph had interrupted with a sharp sigh of exasperation.

He answered the sound with, "I took an oath."

Met with the same rude dismissal in the form of an exasperate sigh, he fell silent.

This set the tone for months to come. As they passed by other villagers laboring up and down the main mountain trail, they bickered. They would sometimes stop arguing and talk of other things for a while in a friendly way, as if the steep incline and the long walk made them forget their dispute. Sometimes they would break off from a spat and greet a passerby with friendly greetings. Then as sure as the ground beneath the trail itself, they would pick up their dispute out of boredom as much as belief.

"No shame in service," Lookout had tried, "Especially for a One-Bead."

"You aren't paying me. I'm not in your service. The Attman is the one who pays," Boph answered.

At a familiar crossroads, a full day's hike up the mountain— they weren't particularly setting a fast pace—they stopped to sleep and shared a meal of dried meat and orangeroot flat bread. It was there, on two thin blankets Boph provided, both gazing up at the stars, the harsh words put away, that Lookout explained his dream of becoming a knight.

That dream was only another impetus (a Boph word) to insolence (another Boph word).

He was considering Boph's status in light of that dream, couldn't he see? Besides this wasn't about status exactly, it was about establishing proper roles by which both could prosper! He as a renowned knight in service to the Throne and Boph as a loyal retainer, honored in his own right.

The tang of the orangeroot bread lingered in his mouth while he watched the sharpness of the stars whirl slow overhead.

Boph had scoffed, "What do you know about knights? Have you ever seen one? I know all the stories about them because the Attman taught me to read. Did you know that?"

Lookout had considered this for quite some time, staring up at the mighty constellation of Allweln above. He chewed on a horne-fruit twig he had snapped off the side of the trail. A servant who could read was a major boon to a future knight like himself who could not read letters.

"Maybe you could tell me some of the legends, so I could know them better?"

Had he spoke those words, or were they words breathed in sleep? Allweln circled above. Boph muttered, "Maybe, I could, yeah."

And that was good enough.

The next day the argument resumed as they passed the last few small trails which led to the poor weedy farms of the remaining colonists. Lookout paused at the one which led far away back to his farm but said nothing.

Instead of mentioning his home, Lookout first broached the idea of a trade—Boph could recite to him the stories he knew from reading the books and for that, he would pay him a small extra amount from his salary.

Boph took the offer but refused to allow it to be attached to a change of his status as a free islander.

When the main trail had dwindled to nothing more than a

muddy track for goat and deer and boar and they had passed the last points where side-trails led to the high pastures of the herders, they continued in their disputes—but soon the silences of the high places muted all rancor.

Coming to the tower itself, the fight over status waned entirely. A desolate place stood before the two boys and the donkey and they all three stopped to take it in.

Away from man, the heaviness of the quietness up here fell upon them both. Only the sound of the mountain winds shifting the wooden tower in creaks and timber groans greeted them. The whistling wind through the loose clapboards at the top of the tower made Lookout suppress a shiver. The top of the tower formed a square composing the one room abode of Lookout, the future knight.

All at once, he decided to become genial. Without the boy's faithful delivery and his donkey, this far up the mountain, even a Throneland auxillary could run into problems.

"What happened to the last man up here?"

Boph turned to face him, one hand laid protectively on his donkey's neck.

"If not for me, you'll die up here or get lost or go mad," Boph had answered.

"Yeah. But the other guard?"

The boy just shrugged, "Don't know. I came up here and he was gone and that's it."

"No one ever found him?"

"No."

This scared him. So, he changed the subject.

"That doesn't mean you aren't my servant, it just means you're a good and useful servant," Lookout had countered.

"What?"

"Well, me needing you to show up and all. It just means...well, it's good, that," he had said.

He couldn't help countering. When he wasn't drinking cownut liquor—and a year ago when he started this sinecure, he didn't touch the stuff much—he felt he could clearly argue his point.

These days a little less so.

"The Attman pays me to bring you up here and leave you. He pays me to return, to make sure you aren't dead yet and deliver food and things. That's that, get it?"

Lookout had tried on a cool air of not concerning himself with such trivialities upon arrival at his post. The effect was lost as he stumbled on an upturned rock at the end of the high trail. The weight of his own pack he carried, tipped his thin frame over and he fell to the ground.

Boph didn't laugh. The donkey nudged him with its head. The wind blew terrible and made the tower sway. He got back up. Boph pretended not to notice.

They left the matter there.

Allweln spun in the sky and many nights came and went beneath his sure gaze.

Months later, Boph found him in his tower sick with fever. Lookout hadn't noticed the boy and his donkey approach the tower. Through swollen eyes he watched as Boph carefully unpacked the supplies from the donkey's packs and lay them around the base of the tower, then carry them up the small ladder.

"You got a fever on you," Boph had said, standing in the darkened doorway.

"I'm cold, then hot."

Sometimes, he could feel the presence of the boy hovering over him and then, gone.

"Fever. They say the demons wear fever in the high places to keep warm."

The light coming through the gaps in the wooden walls and the hot and the cold and the blurry, far-away feeling dulled the fear of these words.

He mumbled something he couldn't recall. He wanted to ask Boph to stay near or find his father and bring him here, or better his mother. It wasn't the first fever he had suffered. The colonists and their families were particularly prone to these, more so than the native inhabitants.

Pride kept his mouth closed. Would a knight beg for his

mother? Beg for his own life?

Lookout had tried to convince Boph that he was a good attendant, but the words came out wrong.

The sound of branches snapping somewhere off in the jungle floated up to the tower. He heard a discussion between a spirit and a grey panther. Was the donkey adding to the argument of the fever-drenched night below? It was just day. Short, clear, braying sentences of logic, he heard.

Then there was no sound and Lookout grew afraid. He thought it possible he had even cried. Later, Boph said he *had* cried but Lookout denied it to this day.

Sometime later, Boph had brought him something foul to drink in a rude wooden bowl.

"Here, it'll help," Boph had said.

Lookout recalled sitting up, looking at the bald, tan boy with the large eyes holding a wooden bowl in the dark of his room, illuminated by one cheap taper. The liquid smelled like dirt and berries, fragrant and on the edge of rotting.

Boph made him drink it.

That night he laid back on his blanket and sweat. Boph stayed and the next day and into the next night and built a small fire below the foot of the tower. Lookout had not commanded it to be done but allowed it to be so. Good initiative for an attendant, he had thought. He also didn't recall Boph helping him down the ladder to warm-up beside the fire but that too had come to pass.

"Do I live?" Lookout had reportedly said through tears.

Later, he disputed asking this. Boph told the story differently—that Lookout in the grips of fever sobbed and blabbered. Certainly, not the case. Impudent (another Boph word!) recollections.

"Probably," Boph had said.

The next event was much in dispute. The way Boph told it, he had begged for him to tell a story to him, something of brave knights from the legend book of the Attman. Boph had read to him. It was good for a servant to learn to read, though warriors such as himself did not have the time, nor had his father in his long years of service in the Throne's army learned his letters.

42

Lookout recalled it differently. In battling his ague and already in the process of expelling the weakness he sat up and commanded Boph to recount stories of the empire's history.

Either way, Boph had told him many stories from the legend book around the small fire as Lookout's fever slackened. He saw the fever itself, drifting away from his body and wandering off through the jungle brush in the dawn. It did look like a demon's coat but also like fog.

The knight below him blurred for some reason.

He took another drink of cownut liquor. Why was the knight below him blurry? No enemies, there was nothing, not even a fever hiding in the brush, no grey panther watching, and Lookout learned to face the first real enemy of any soldier, boredom.

So, he drank and waited.

Nearly a full turn on top this mountain. His father back on the farm, eking out something, a few vegetables and a cownut orchard. Even with all the rain, the ground stayed hard and fruitless. So, he had no time to visit his son. Then gone. Gone. No goodbye. His mother, not long after his birth fell to one of the various fevers widespread on the island. He couldn't recall her face.

In some dark moments, Lookout thought the very same fever attacking him had carried his mother away so many turns ago. That maybe fevers never truly died, just rushed in and out of bodies and spent time hiding outside, waiting.

The idea could frighten any man to tears, let alone an orphan.

Reportedly.

And so, Boph and his donkey, came and went. The Attman sent tidings, encouragement and even once, an extra pittance, some copper coins which Lookout first hid and made elaborate plans over, then used to buy more cownut liquor from Boph.

The knight disappeared below him. He did not charge forward or dismount. Instead, he just vanished in a haze. First, he saw the knight swaying, dizzy and retching. That made no sense. The guard rail around the top of the tower creaked and gave way and then he was pitching forward through the night air and no brave steed to break his fall.

He hit the ground. He heard horse hooves. The clatter of armor. A knight bending over him to pick him up but no, what? Who? Brave Eadrick? No. Allweln before the gods cast him into the inky black of forever skies? No. Still, a hand did brush his shoulder and patted him, giving him strength.

He heard the knight slowly clatter away down the hill back towards the village, swigging from a bottle of cownut liquor beneath the constellation of Allweln; and Lookout bruising yet unbroken fell to slumber where he lay, in the summer shadow cast by the tower of Esmer amidst short, yellow, sun-lacked grass.

3

Allred

Plans became orders. Orders became actions. It was morning.

"You take point," Cole told him.

"Always."

He had slept some. Now, he stood, rolled his camp blanket up. He went through the same checks he had in the army. Weapons in good order. Armor fit. Boots smart. Crossbow darts counted and caressed. He could smell the oil on his sword's blade he had applied the night before. Each strap buckled, trapped and locked tight against his body.

Sword sharp.

That done, he stretched and felt all the broken places in his body like a tightness, then sat again and waited for Cole's orders.

Same type of dawn, he thought.

Stoneburner plucked up a few pieces of charcoal with small tongs, storing them in his firepot. He had already been to the little creek that ran down the mountain parallel with the trail refilling flagons.

Hartha and Hortha stood waiting, talking to each other in their native tongue. It was near enough to Allred's own, but the words were stretched and singsong sounding. The mage stood near them, muttering incantations, swirling the bottom of his cloak back and forth in half-circles like a child. His eyes almost looked human in the faint light of morning, he even said, "Good dawn," to him.

Cole drank strong Kler tea and scoured a map one last time with Scrolls. Stoneburner handed Allred his own cup of the acrid brew. He drank and felt the surge of energy down his throat, into his chest, massaging away the tightness in his body in the places where war had torn bone and flesh, where time and costly magic had knitted them back crudely.

Aodlen looked nearly sober this morning. None the better for it. He sat drinking his tea and prodding the ash of the campfire with a branch. The end snapped off and he jerked, cursed and tossed the rest away.

The sun warmed the top of the jungle as the morning sky turned to fire. Dew-dripping broad leaves waved in gentle wind beside the trail. A few birds landed in the grass near the cliff edge; slick and white-feathered, orange bills pecking viciously at the ground and then pausing. They walked delicately on orange scaly legs, high quiet steps through the grass; then freezing, listening to crawling things amongst the morning grass, and then plunging their beaks into damp shadows the ferns cast.

Their beaks matched the vivid color of their legs. They moved in slow, soft steps—then they plunged their beaks into the grass over and over, vicious sabers stabbing, their necks the movement of serpents, shaking their white-feathered heads.

He'd learned a lot about scouting from watching animals. He drank his tea and watched the birds and waited.

Quiet. Strike. Quiet. Strike. Strike. Strike.

"Move," Cole said.

The men shouldered their packs. The Green Islanders hoisted their ancestor-shields. Mage took his place between them.

Allred walked to the head of the trail. One last check of his crossbow.

Everything came together in the way it does for small units. No need for orders anymore. Cole didn't even say anything. The campfire which had been camouflaged by Stoneburner with some fallen palm fronds Cole stared at and then motioned to Allred. They started up the trail.

Gummy green leaves, waxy, reflected the morning sunlight back white and bright. Here the brush beside each trail tended to low palms in scrub, sandy soil which sloped off the mountain's side. Farther ahead the trail grew steadily steeper. The sun was behind them for now which favored them in a fight.

They covered the distance of yesterday's scouting mission fast, soon arriving at the sharp incline in the trail of raw rock. Not steep enough for climbing gear, it still rose to the height of five horses.

Scrolls signaled them to pause. He took out a small spade and dug down around the rock, turning up soil. He pointed at a broken fragment of stone, then consulted with Cole.

"What remains from an old Semhelhen road, one can see here," Scrolls explained, holding up the stone. "The jungle devoured it. Here some sort of upheaval, likely natural. We see the cliff rock mixed in with the remainder of the old road. We are on the right track. This discovery accords with the remnants of the old stone marker I observed at the beach below and with yesterday's encounter with the Dhlams."

Cole took this in, said nothing, then motioned for him to move on.

He remembered the old time-smoothed stone marker down on the beach near the estuary where the Black Boat anchored. Scrolls had found it when they arrived. The script if any there ever was etched on it had faded but the scholar had explained it was a common type used in the ancient Semhelhen roads. He had then gone on for nearly an hour about the different styles of road markers in the previous age and how they had evolved, eventually only Aodlen listening, interjecting with his chirping "ha!" while the rest secured the beach and looked for things to eat.

Scrolls saw clearly the past. Allred saw the present. He

feared Cole saw the future.

Today is today and today meant marching. The creek meandering downhill near them would make for a good water source for the animals of Esmer. He saw boar prints, deer prints, the prints of birds, a hole where snakes burrowed.

After a long time, he turned and signaled halt. He reckoned they stood close to yesterday's battle site. He walked back to Cole and told him so.

"Feint up," Cole said.

Mage obliged.

That familiar fading took over. The air ran thinner and dead across his face. The green jungle turned grey.

"I want a look at the Dhlam bodies if they remain," Cole said.

"Up there where the big palm stands on the left of the trail, the one with the red fruit popping out in the center like a flower. That's where the fight happened," he said.

Cole motioned him forward.

Allred looked up the mountain ahead of the rest. He laid his crossbow across his knees and waited.

Still felt quiet. He could hear Aodlen talking to Cole and Scrolls and Mage muttering his twisting syllables to hold the feint, on the edge of which, Allred waited. An orange and red bird screeched from the top of a tree. A monkey darted from branch to branch.

Cole came up the trail.

"Dhlam's still there. Something might have chewed on a couple of them over night."

"Big boars up here, maybe some panthers. I've seen the prints."

"I want to reach near to the top by nightfall. Doable?"

"We can trudge it, assuming the trail stays easy."

When they had arrived on the beach, Scrolls used his surveying instruments and a looking glass to gauge the elevation of the mountain they now ascended. Allred thought of distances in terms of how fast he could reach a place, or how fast a good horse could reach a place. Scrolls used other numbers.

By Scrolls estimates and his own scout-figuring, he knew they could probably get close to the top but not the peak itself today. Near the peak, the game trails might run out.

"No human tracks so far," Allred said.

"It's the Dragon Wash side. Most of these southern islands don't build on that side, Scrolls says. Prohibitions, old legends," Cole said.

The Dragon Wash was a wave and a current. You could see it up in Port Shamhalhan, the lines the priests marked on some of the seawalls. The wave didn't follow storm season. It came when it did. Astrologers in Shamhalhan and around many port cities built their forecasts and predictions around it. It varied in strength. It mattered for navigation and it figured in the beliefs of many of the people in the southern seas but Allred knew nothing of boats or sailing or the south and its seas and didn't much like the water.

"I'm going to let Mage drop feint as long as it stays quiet. Need to keep him fresh. He'll call it up on your signal."

"Heard."

He unlocked the safety on the crossbow and started marching.

Too easy, Allred thought.

It put him in a dark mood. Too easy for too long, something readies itself to go wrong. That's what his body told him.

Like most relic hunters, his lived in a state of apprehension from the Upside Fever, and he knew it, so he tried to account for it. Waking up in the middle of the night. Sweating. Doubt. Noise which once seemed mild, made him jump. He didn't talk about it. More noise, talking. What's the use?

Still alive. Whole lot of other people aren't. I'll trust my gut even if my soul is shot through.

The jungle thinned out the higher they marched. The trail widened, less damp, less fragrant from jungle flower. The dirt interspersed with clumps of tall weeds, stuck to his boots. He smelled smoke and called a halt behind him with an upraised fist and low whistle.

He felt the feint go back up and cover him. He walked back. Told Cole about it. No one argued with him. They could hear distant shouting up the trail.

"Sounds like two youths attempting to speak a pidgin-Imperial," Scrolls said.

Cole pointed and Allred knew it meant 'get eyes on the sound.'

He edged up the trail, careful since a feint could be broken by another mage or detected in a few other ways. Careful because that had been his practice and he was still breathing and a lot of other men weren't.

The trail ended in a large clearing. Stopping on the edge, he got down on his stomach and peered through the ferns and brush.

Nearby the remnants of an old barrier about the height of his waist at its highest point disappeared in the jungle to his right and left. It had fallen down completely here, and nothing more than an outline showed through grass. To most people it would have just looked like an old fence. It meant they were close.

In the center of the clearing stood a squat, wooden watchtower in disrepair. On top of it against what would be the outer wall of the room in the center, cut crudely into the wood itself, a Throneland insignia.

Unexpected.

Two young boys chased each other around the base of the tower. They were shouting what amounted to "you idiot, you dummy, you're a servant, no, I'm not" in ragged Imperial pidgin.

The smaller boy, browner than the other, had a shaved head and wore simple island garb. Allred watched quietly for long minutes. A donkey stood in the shade of the tower and watched the two boys.

The donkey looked at Allred. He looked back. Nothing much happened.

The boys yelled at each other. Both laughed. One of them threw something at the other and that one hurled it back and they started running around again.

Beyond that, the jungle reconquered the clearing and he could make out another trail leading further up the mountain peak.

That's where it'll be.

He sighted his crossbow on the taller, paler kid just in case. He considered the distance, noted the wind, got a sense of the shot, then lowered the crossbow and slithered backwards.

Cole asked.

He told.

"There's a watchtower. It's not real Throneland engineered, though. Peasants built it, looks like. Two boys. Unarmed. One taller and pale. Northern. Could be a colonist's kid. The other one is a One Bead boy. Both might be slow in the head. I think they're throwing dung at each other."

"Dung?" Stoneburner asked.

He had joined them from the back of the line and was resting his hands on his knees catching his breath.

"Yes."

"Their own dung?" Aodlen asked.

"No. There's a donkey there, too."

"Ha! Donkey dung, they're throwing?"

"Donkey dung," Stoneburner affirmed, head nodding, then bent back over to rest some more.

"That's unclear," Allred said.

Hortha and Hartha smiled, as if this all made perfect sense. They had likely engaged in the same practice. Scrolls cocked his head as if confused.

"They're going to run when they see us," he said, "Going to have to decide about that."

Cole thought for a moment, then spoke:

"It's getting dark. Everyone follows me around slow through the trees to cut them off. Mage, for now, stay hidden. Don't need the boys going into magefits. If they run, grab them. Can't let them run off and tell someone, so...Hold the feint on Allred until he reaches the tower, then bring it down on us while we go around," Cole said.

"If they run?" he asked.

"I want to talk to them. You didn't see any arms?"

"No, could be these are the kids of some guards—"

"Shouldn't even be a Thronelander this far south,"

Stoneburner grunted.

"Are you hail?" Aodlen asked.

"Yes, yes, just old and fat and out of breath."

"Up the tower. Whistle when it's clear. No blades. Mage, you hear me?" Cole asked.

"I agree with nature," Mage said.

That seemed like acknowledgment enough.

Allred skirted the tree line, keeping his eyes on the boys. They were still busy arguing about something. He walked up to the tower still under the feint, found the ladder, which was in bad repair and shimmied up.

At the top, stood one large room in the center. It held a sleeping pack, an old helmet, a makeshift table with an empty bottle atop, a dirty wooden bowl and wooden mug and a collection of small, whittled statues of humans and animals. Allred picked one up—a horse with a rider wearing armor and holding a lance. The horse reared back on back legs preparing to charge. Allred set it back down gently on the rough table. Fine work.

He went out to the blind side of the tower. There a piece of the railing had split and broken and lay in the yellowed grass below. He signaled all-clear with a low whistle, and felt the feint leave him.

From up here, he could drop both boys with the crossbow. He calculated the distance to the trees from where they stood.

They're still just boys, he thought.

Years of war taught him to see like this and he didn't like it but it only bothered him when he woke up screaming, so at least it didn't get in the way of the daylight.

To see like this—Immediately. Distance in terms of time, time in terms of ability-to-kill, ability-to-kill in terms of ability-to-survive, ability-to-survive in terms of time...repeat... outward spirals of gory reason.

He sighted his crossbow on the tallest boy, kept his finger off the trigger.

I'm not a monster.

When they saw Cole and the others moving towards them, they didn't run or scream. The taller boy stood there, mouth open, like he was going to say something but didn't. The younger kid turned and stepped into the twin bulk of Hartha and Hortha. Hartha laid one heavy hand on the boy's shoulder. Allred couldn't hear his words but saw the Green Islander smile.

The donkey watched all with a dignified calm.

He walked around the tower, surveying the entire perimeter again. No one. A desolate spot. Cole motioned for Allred to come down from the tower. He saw the surprised look on the tall boy's face before he turned and descended the ladder the few steps to the ground.

Cole had started questioning the boys.

The smaller boy was saying, "He's Lookout. My name is Boph. I carry supplies up here."

"And you're a guard?" Cole asked.

Cole squatted down in front of the taller boy, brushed back his hair revealing the fire-scarred side of his face and neck. The taller boy blanched a bit at the sight and fidgeted.

"This is the Watch Tower on the Island of Esmer and I'm a Throneland Guard, er at least Auxillary—

"Junior Guard, maybe," Boph said.

"—and I guard this place," Lookout finished, shooting the younger boy an exasperated look.

"Is there anyone else up here with you?"

"No, not anywhere. It's an isolated station," Lookout said, "Are you Throneland soldiers like me?"

Cole put a friendly look on his face, turned his head to hide the scars and took his pipe from his vest, gesturing expansively with it.

"Throne-sanctioned explorers, yes, of a kind. On a quiet expedition though. So, it's important our presence is secret," he said.

A skeptical look took quick passage across Boph's face. The taller one, Lookout, appeared to believe Cole's tale immediately. He had a desperate look, the kind of person that wanted to believe someone with a good story, like most people did.

He figured both were too young to enter Throneland service

by several turns. By the age of the older one, he had already rode out, raiding cattle and horses, clashing in the hills with other clans and drawn blood and earned his name in the Battle of the Bales.

The world differed, and the people in it, too.

"Do you have Throneland writs?" Lookout asked.

He stifled a snorting laugh that surprised him. The boy had some courage after all, then. The scrap of a uniform and the empire's insignia on the rotting watch tower must have given him some spirit.

Cole didn't laugh or stutter, "We do. Scrolls, would you show the guard?"

"The permanent writ, Cole? Or the less permanent?"

"Not the permanent, no, not necessary."

Scrolls blinked, took off his pack and while turning surreptitiously slipped a thin, mean knife back into its sheathe; he delicately removed a leather-covered folio from his pack, flipped through it, found a piece of paper and handed it to Stoneburner who looked over it and then formally presented it to Lookout.

The papers were fine forgeries. Scrolls carried many different documents, claiming many different things. Papers written in different scripts, signed by this or that authority and sealed as well. They had crests, warrants, writs, badges, notes, correspondence, requests for favors from this or that prince or merchant house or king, of this or that princedom or merchant conglomerate, company or kingdom. Scrolls could produce a paper to satisfy nearly any institution, any guard, any customs agent, any port police, anyone who carried a weapon and had orders to ask questions—the Relic Hunters of the 9th usually had an answer prepared.

The boy looked at the paper, barely touching the corners as if amazed by the document itself. From the way his eyes moved around it, untrained and loose, he could tell the boy couldn't read. He handled the paper gingerly, then looking at his own dirty hands, nearly dropped it, afraid he might sully the clean parchment.

Which told Allred this island was a poor place. Here was a Son of Empire, a colonist's son, and some sort of quasi-guard who looked quite astounded by the feel of a good piece of parchment.

"Is it alright if I have my attendant examine this?" the boy asked, sheepishly.

"Of course," Cole said. He pulled a metal plate from a chain around his neck from beneath his tunic under his light armor, "You've seen these before, I'm sure. The plates imperial soldiers carry. Have you misplaced your own?"

Lookout's face dropped to the ground.

"Oh, well, the Attman you see, he says that...I'm not sure exactly, maybe since I'm only now a junior guard, and this is a small island and it's not really exactly imperial land, Esmer, after all...not even really anything much." The boy spoke fast. "So, the Attman says some of these matters are complicated. Says I'm his official agent and...he has a plate like that—I've seen it. My father, I've seen his, too. He has one, but me, not yet, no."

"I see," Cole said and let just a hint of disdain and hardness slip into his voice. The boy firmly fell into place. "Well, while your... helper peruses the writ, perhaps you can tell us what is this outpost for?"

Lookout carefully handed the parchment to Boph, as if he were a priest transferring a holy writ. Allred studied Boph's face and saw that he could read.

Surprising.

"It's to do...it's, well, I was told to come up here and watch," Lookout said.

Cole nodded. He acted like he was taking the boy seriously but allowed disappointment and suspicion to lace his words now.

"Watch for anything in particular?"

"Just watch. There's nothing much up here, to tell you the truth."

"Would you like some wine from Port Shamhalhan? Good stuff," Stoneburner offered his flagon.

Lookout didn't hesitate. He took the wine and drank. Wiped his mouth with the back of his wrist.

"It's good," he said.

"Would you mind, if we made a small camp here?" Cole asked.

"Oh, of course. I would think, I should do anything I could to help anyone with your papers and such." The boy turned to Boph. "Right?"

The boy nodded his agreement and didn't meet anyone's eyes.

Cole motioned for the men to settle, drop their packs. Stoneburner started surveying the area.

"What do you drink up here, on this island?" Cole asked.

"Cownut liquor mostly. That's part of what my attendant does. He delivers my portions from down in the village. The Attman hires him out to carry stuff just like he said."

"I'm a hired courier," Boph offered, "By way of the Attman. He pays me because he doesn't want to make the trip up here."

Boph waved off the offer of the flagon.

"Well, as I said, the Throne itself sent us here," Cole's face darkened at his private jest, "Where is the rest of your company, your commander and the others?"

Cole often asked the same question slightly differently, just to make sure he got the truthful answer.

"Oh, that's funny. I'm the only one. There're no soldiers on the entire island. I don't think on any islands around here. Not that I've heard or seen. Just the Attman in the main village. He's kind of retired. He does tasks. He says it's called administration. Then there's some colonists around, veterans who retired and got their lot of land, like my father," Lookout said, "That's it."

"No soldiers here," Boph agreed.

The bald boy was eager to make that clear enough.

"How far is the village?"

"Down a couple days to the coast that way," Boph said, pointing at a trail visible on the opposite side of the clearing where the Relic Hunters had emerged.

Cole offered the wine to Lookout again who clutched it a bit too fast. Young kid, but Allred could see he had learned to drink. Recently. He wore bruises on his arm and his face was scraped. He thought back to the railing around the tower.

"So, the village is all Throneland colonists?" Cole asked.

"No, most of us are like Boph, Bead people. He's got his own names." He turned to Boph. "And it's not because we don't

56

know how to farm that the colonists died. But maybe because the weather isn't the same. The village is just small traders. A few old veterans spend time at the inn down there."

"What are you watching for here then? What's up this mountain, do you know?" Cole persisted.

"Never gone up there. Nothing, I guess," Lookout said.

Boph didn't say anything. Cole caught that and turned to the younger boy.

"You've gone up there?"

"My people know not to go to the high places," Boph said with lowered eyes.

"Why's that?"

The boy didn't answer for a bit, chewed his lip and looked at his donkey. A fly spun around his face and he waved it away.

"Old things ... Best to just stay away. Old buildings." The boy was going to stop, then his pride got the better of him. "I can read. The Attman taught me. There are stories about the high places where there used to be altars from the ancient kingdoms, when the Sem-hel-hen ruled. Anyway, it's hard to go up to the high places. The ground and air and trees trick you."

Boph's Imperial wasn't bad. The way he heard the two boys talking to each other changed when they talked to the Relic Hunters.

"As explorers we go investigate those places," Cole said.

"No one goes up this high, even here where the tower is. No one ever thinks to go up this high." Boph said, pointing to the last mountain peak. "Why go? Nothing good to find there. The last man disappeared from here. I bet he went up higher."

"Hey, you never told me that," Lookout said.

"Didn't want to scare you."

Cole listened to the boys. Scrolls too, his face unmoving but recording every detail of the exchange.

"You think up there," Cole pointed to the trail that led up to the last part of the mountain. "You figure one of the old places is up there?"

"Don't know. It's the kind of place where it *would be*. I've snuck some looks at the trail that leads up. Looks like an old, old path. I don't know," Boph said.

Cole nodded.

"I have decided to engage you both in our service for the immediate future," he said.

Lookout looked excited at this news. Boph handed the parchment back and Scrolls stowed it amongst his other works.

Cole walked a few paces away and took him aside.

"I don't think they know that they are near the Haunt," Cole said.

"What are we going to do with them?" Allred asked.

"Dispense a few coins and keep them around. It's extra hands to carry baggage. Can't let either of them walk off this mountain top until we're finished. The younger one will probably want to, so..."

"A little money. He's more cunning than he looks."

Cole scratched the skin at the side of his mouth, looked away.

"I'll give them over to Stoneburner and tell them they're in the employ of the Throne. It's a kind of true."

He nodded and Cole went over to talk to Stoneburner and the boys.

4

Lookout

He hadn't spotted the explorers coming through the trees. So much time passed without anything happening up here. When something finally happened, he had failed to guard anything.

Lucky for him, the men were friendly enough. An expedition! Real, live Throne-sanctioned explorers and adventurers on Esmer. They had even asked him and Boph to work with them. He couldn't believe his good luck.

The man named Cole, their stern leader, had peppered him with many questions. He did his best to answer them. Boph gave him suspicious looks here and there. That made sense. He was an islander. Esmer did not fly the banner of the Thronelands.

They were an odd-looking bunch of explorers though. A lot of scars. A lot of weapons.

Then again, he had never seen any explorers. He hadn't seen any Throneland officers, soldiers or Throneland anything—just the Attman in his ramshackle room, snoring at his table and spending most of the day at the tavern.

His father had been an imperial soldier, loyal to the Throneland. Other retired veterans and their families, he had seen in the main village on market days. None wore armor, or insignia any longer. They were faded men.

Events were so exciting today. Boph wandered over to him, looking around at something unseen in the trees. He immediately forgot about their squabbling. All the past felt erased and renewed by the arrival of the explorers.

"Do you think they'll tell someone important about us— well, me, if we help them?" he asked.

Boph leaned close. There was no one in hearing range. Cole and the others had set about making a camp for themselves. Boph tended to his donkey and Lookout stood around watching, not sure what to do next.

"No," Boph said, nervously.

"Isn't it wonderous? Real explorers. There are stories about them in the books, too, aren't there? In the legends? Along with the knights and the princes and kings?"

Boph shook his head, "Not as much but some. There are stories of relic hunters. Warnings mostly."

Lookout turned to him, slapped him on the arm, "Isn't it something though? Something new. They probably have news of events far away. All kinds of stories about the Thronelands. I wonder if they've ever had to fight before?"

"They look like they've fought a lot, Lookout."

"Yeah. Well, probably you must fight a lot when you explore for the Throne. It's probably a lot of adventure, maybe even a better life than a knight, you think? Or maybe some of them are knights. I don't know, can you be a knight and an explorer at the same time?"

"I don't know. They told us to stay here. There's something

strange. Something out here," Boph kept looking at the trees around the clearing. "But … maybe you should ask them, if I should go talk to the Attman and tell them they're here?"

Boph made an excellent point he hadn't considered. It was rude that he hadn't offered to send his retainer to bring tidings— that's the way the stories said it—to the Attman.

He hesitated. He didn't like the idea of Boph leaving him up here alone. And what was he looking for in the jungle?

"Are you mad at me? You've got to stay! I'm sure around the campfire they'll tell stories. Your memory is good for legends, so you should hear them told. I might forget. You should stay."

Boph looked uncertain, "I'm just saying that someone ought to tell the Attman, anyway. Something seems wrong."

"I'll ask."

The one named Cole was busy giving orders in conversation with his men. The man wore a heavy broadsword on his back. His hands and part of his face had been burned—the skin flat, devoid of lines, smooth. He was strong but not imposing like the two strange giant twins, but he gave off a heavy presence; as if by walking too near to him, he would be drawn into some course he couldn't break free of except by his command.

"Maybe, I won't ask their leader…"

The one who had manifested above them like a shadow on the tower—sat on the ground smoking nearby. He was the only one that wasn't moving, doing things. That one gave him pause, he did, but Lookout intended to be a knight someday, so he must show no fear, especially in front of his retainer. He marched over to him, grabbing Boph's arm and pulling him alongside with him.

"Come on, let's ask," Lookout said.

"Him?" Boph asked, warily.

The man looked both of them up and down, took a draw from his smoke and blew it towards their faces. He tried to think up a soldierly way of address but now he just coughed out, "What's your name?"

The man remained mute, tilted his head just a little and stared at them both. He was cleaning a small bow fit with mechanics and metals, like nothing Lookout had seen before. The man was taking the machine apart and with a piece of sheep's wool, doused in gleaming oil cleaning each part of the contraption.

"Allred," the man answered and looked back down to his weapon.

"They call me Lookout, and this is Boph. I'm not sure if you heard but I'm the guard. Umm. So, this is my retainer..."

"Retainer," the man repeated.

He held up a small dart and examined it in the sunlight, squinting. The sun caught bright green eyes set in a pale face.

"Yes, a retainer. Like an attendant, a skilled...he decided he wasn't a servant. I was thinking that maybe he could go down the mountain, he's supposed to go back anyway and then he could, you know, tell the Attman, I mean—the administrator—that you've arrived, or—shouldn't that be how it is?"

He was stumbling over his words. The smell of the smoke made him light-headed, and he wasn't so sure the fall he took last night, short as it was, hadn't left him rattled.

"No," Allred said.

That was a simple answer. Lookout forgot about the matter at hand. The strange bow fascinated him.

"I was just thinking though...I've never seen such a machine before, sir. It's a strange bow."

The man didn't answer, his head bent. He wore a leather armor vest filled with sharp things and though it must have been heavy, his whole body looked tight, as if ready to spring up in an instant and put every weapon to use.

"It's a crossbow," Boph said.

Insolent. Annoying to be corrected by your own retainer like that. The soldier nodded his agreement and looked vaguely interested in their existence for the first time.

"My father was a soldier. I've never seen a crossbow before. He said it's better to have a bow. I remember him saying it. Said, you can fire more arrows with a bow," Lookout ventured.

The man put down the wool. Sniffing, he wiped the oil on his trousers and took the redleaf roll out from his lips with two pinched fingers. His hand was a busy map of scars.

"Your father served the Throne?"

"He fought as a spearman. Then he was injured and was made a city watch guard," Lookout said, proudly.

The man considered that, "Spearmen know spears. Less so bows."

Who was he to argue such things, he hadn't even seen a crossbow before now.

"Yes, sir," Lookout said, uneasily.

Boph had taken careful, slow steps to get a closer look at the crossbow. His retainer did exhibit unbound curiosity, it was true. A certain courage even. Surprisingly, Allred took one of the darts, from his vest and held it out. Boph took it as if snatching something from a snake and looked at it closer.

"A small dart for close-up fights," Allred said.

Boph rolled the dart around in his hand and smoothed the fletching with his fingers.

"With a crossbow you get the first shot, all things equal. A bowman has got to draw his bow for his first shot. Kill the bowman before he draws. You can move with a crossbow, ready to fire. First shot wins more often than not. Can't reload it as fast as a bow, in that, your father is right." But, he blew a smoke cloud out. "Can't pull a bow if you're dead."

The smoke cleared. The man looked lost in thinking on the design of his own weapon, or maybe the past. Boph handed him back the arrow. The man stood. Both boys took a step backwards.

"I see, sir," Lookout agreed.

It seemed prudent to agree with this man on such matters. The contraption was intricate, a thing to behold. All dark wood and black metal.

"The smaller darts won't hit as hard as a regular arrow," Boph said.

Allred raised his eyebrows, "True told. It's not a weapon for distance but speed."

"What's the fletching made from?" Boph asked.

The warrior narrowed his eyes. He didn't seem a talkative man.

"I could give you a whole lecture, just like that man—" He pointed to the thin scholarly explorer. "Could talk words all day.

The weight of feathers and how each fly, each material has an advantage." Again, the man gave a kind of far-off look as if he were watching an array of invisible missiles fired across the clearing and judging their arcs. "But I don't want to."

He exhaled a large plume of smoke again and Lookout smelled the redleaf. He had seen it before, though it was a rare enough luxury this far south. Still, traders brought a bale here and there of the dried plant. Men with coin smoked the plant and he had smelled it drifting out of the inn at the village. The smoke hit him in the face. Everything on the clearing, the jungle, the grass, it all looked sharper in the sun-bright, cleansing rays of the sudden sun.

"Exploring is a profitable thing? Redleaf is a luxury here," Boph said.

The man appraised him, "Profitable. Dangerous. Like certain questions."

"That's quite a strong redleaf, sir," Lookout said.

"Who waits in the trees in the shimmering black cloak?" Boph asked, through the haze of smoke.

The question jarred the warrior, and Lookout felt something unspoken, had been aired.

Lookout noticed the figure, too, now that Boph said it out loud. Like a fragment of a dream hovering around since the explorers arrived. A black-feathered bird, watching and singing to itself nearby. A man?

"Huh. Noticed the mage, did you?" Allred asked.

"Yes," Boph answered simply.

"My redleaf is a special blend. Not for everyone. Maybe the vapors opened your eyes a little to unseen things. He's a kind soul but it's best to not bother him. He likes to be alone. Like me. Go talk to Stoneburner—that's the fat, older man. Make yourself useful."

"A fine weapon, sir. Thank you, thanks much," Lookout said and backed away, nearly half-bowing, though he didn't understand why.

Boph turned on his heel and caught up with him, punched him in the ribs, not too hard but hard enough.

"Stupid," he whispered.

"Why?" Lookout asked annoyed and still confused by the thing Boph had said. There was a man in the trees clad in a black cloak. He knew that to be true, had known it all this time. But did he?

"Just are," his retainer said.

He dragged Boph over to the man named Cole. He was speaking to the older one called, Stoneburner. Lookout stood there off to the side waiting until the other man stopped talking and Cole turned and recognized him.

"Yes?" Cole said.

"Um, we were wondering if Boph should go tell the Attman...you arrived, so that if you need anything, then maybe..." Lookout trailed off.

"No. I'm assigning you to this man's command." Cole said pointing to Stoneburner. "He will tell you how to help. You're both in Throneland service until released. Tell me you *both*," he emphasized the word and shot a glance at Boph, "understand what I said."

The friendliness hadn't disappeared from Cole's voice, but the questions weren't questions now, just orders.

"Yes, sir," Lookout said.

"Yes, sir," Boph echoed.

"There's going to be others here, eventually. Those men you don't talk to. You don't even go near them. Do you understand?"

"Yes, sir," they both answered.

"This is Stoneburner. He tells you what to do and when."

"What about the shadow-cloaked one in the trees?" Boph asked.

Cole straightened, "You see him?"

"Yes," Boph said.

Stoneburner and Cole exchanged a silent glance.

"Some are born to seeing." Stoneburner said, smiling. "It doesn't bother you?"

"No," they both answered.

Cole nodded his head. "Good." He walked away to speak with the tattooed man and the scholar, who were arguing over something.

They both looked up to Stoneburner, waiting for what he would say next. He wore a long bushy moustache going to grey that ran long down both sides of his mouth but no beard, short hair, sandy-brown, on a big broad head. He looked like a haggard, friendly, water buffalo.

"Where's the water up here?" he asked.

"The creek," Lookout pointed.

"Let's go start filling up flagons then. Fetch water to cook with," Stoneburner said. He started off in the direction of the creek. He carried a short sword but that was the only weapon on him.

Fetching water didn't seem like the proper role for an imperial guard. He considered protesting for a moment, but the man laid a big hand on his shoulder and pushed him towards the water skins.

"Each of you take one of these," Stoneburner pointed to the ground.

Lookout and Boph scooped them up.

"I can take my donkey down to the creek. He can carry these and then we can carry more," Boph said.

Stoneburner appraised him, "That's the way to think, boy."

"He's a skilled attendant, sir," Lookout said.

Boph looked ready to argue, then thought better of it and went over to his donkey and led it back towards them.

"Noticed the mage, did you? Perceptive of you," Stoneburner said as they walked towards the trees and the creek.

Lookout felt proud, even though it had been Boph that noticed the mage first.

"A mage. Just like in the stories. I can't believe it." Lookout said. "Can we meet him?"

"In time, boy, in time."

5

Allred

Need to move.

He had cleaned his sword, taken apart and reassembled his crossbow, counted darts and smoked. The tips of his fingers were smooth with beeswax and dark with the charcoal he used to coat and maintain his personal arsenal.

Now, he waited.

Stoneburner had established the outlines of a proper camp in the remaining light of day and allowed for space for the Black Boat men. Mage stayed within the treetops for a while. Later he came out and joined the others as night fell.

There was a pitiable little fire pit a few yards off from the tower that Lookout used to cook—built too close to the wooden structure. Allred had seen simple, dumb mistakes like that scatter and ruin camps before. The whole place was ramshackle, the clearing, the tower—the notion this boy, a couple turns lacking manhood was a guard of anything was ridiculous.

Cole broke off from the newer campfire Stoneburner had assembled. It was a proper thing ringed with stones the boys carried up out of the creek.

"Look at that mountain," Cole said.

Between the two trails leading down from the clearing, the ground rose abruptly again, climbing to the last ascent. The true peak of the mountain lay up there. Thin clouds coiled around the rock.

"Another day's march, depends on the trail. Depends on Dhlams, depends on how sorcery-soured the ground grows near the Haunt. Depends," Allred said.

"The old barrier has kept it quiet for the boy. Scrolls says that if we could look down on the outline of it from the air, we would see a giant symbol."

"The kind the winged-things read from the sky."

They had seen the remnants of old barriers before and variations on them around Haunts and Sites. Old wards set to guard against demons and Downside spirits when the last sentries fell long ago.

Allred thought about the giant chalk figures in the hills of his homeland. Figures of old monsters and men scratched in dirt. Some you could see from a distant hill if you found the right perspective. Others could only be seen from heights where no hill or mountain rose to give mortal men a foothold.

"Those Dhlams down the hill must have come around it to hunt us. Must have sensed Mage. The Haunts takes note."

"We're close," Cole said.

Close but they still had to go get the Black Boat men. Lead them up. That would be up to him.

"I can march back, tonight. Alone."

"Alone?"

It would have been easier to use an eye or a magetrick, but it would have cost Mage too much, and they needed all his powers for the Haunt.

An eye would have been convenient though.

Scrolls had explained years ago, while they all still served in the 9th, some of what a fighting mage could do; basics of war-magic, categories of spells and what to expect in proximity to the workings of those things.

Allred still remembered the lectures Scrolls had given the soldiers who would work with Mage. He had spoken of the man who was slouching and pacing in the black cloak as if he were a complicated piece of war machinery of odd design—not a mortal man. Describing the weight of spells, the pressures and wear on a mage's mind was odd to Allred, even back then, especially while the sorcerer stood there listening saying little. There was a cost built into the arcane logic of magic-wielding. The officers weren't expected to understand it all but had to know some of it, the better to use the mage in a fight.

"I move fastest, alone. Leaves you bodies up here in case of attack. I'll take a small-sun," Allred said.

Cole considered it.

"Truespoke."

Allred stretched. He lit another redleaf smoke.

"Bright stars, no clouds. Won't rest or sleep anyway until we're done." He was acting like he didn't mind what command came from Cole, but the truth was he wanted to move. Too much time sitting around was bringing dark thoughts.

Cole had sent him out into the night alone many times before. As the man studied him, he knew he could see Allred's desire to move, too. It had been this way a long time. He nodded assent.

"The Dhlams can get down low on the trail. If you get into trouble and you're far, might have to send Mage. That'll cost him."

"Longer we stay put, the more likely something goes wrong. More likely we run into something more fearsome than our guards over there." Allred nodded to the two boys around the campfire. "Longer for the Black Boat to get spotted. Longer for a villager to wonder up here. Longer things can go wrong."

"Agreed," Cole said.

While Allred adjusted the straps on his pack, Cole explained the commands to relay to Glume. He left Allred leeway to adapt. Above all, get the Black Boat men up the mountain fast. Don't let them rest. Keep them tired out. Keep them away from liquor, small talk and good weapons.

"Heard."

"Fortune," Cole said and turned back to the campfire.

"Fortune."

He slipped away down the trail he had spent the last couple days climbing, back towards the beach and the Black Boat men.

Darkness fell full on him. The trail stayed quiet. Something the size of a dog scurried through the brush. The moon was high and pink in the tropical night and as he descended past the cooler, heights of the mountain, the trees thickened the trail blocking the light. He lit the small-sun he kept in his pack, speaking a magemade word to illuminate it. It fit into the palm of his hand like an oval of rain-smoothed rock. It caught the faintest traces of light, real and arcane and intensified it into an outward-spreading beam.

The light gave up his position, so he moved faster. In his other arm he carried his crossbow at the ready.

Night work. Familiar. When he rode light cavalry for Cole, for the Throne, he often rode alone. In the dark, unburdened, space of night, without the weight of other men's words or thoughts. Without that weight, a man could move quickly.

A shake and flurry of leaves and bent branches was followed by a screech. The Dhlam came off the trail fast, swiping claws reaching for his legs.

He fired once, heard the quick snap of air in the wake of the dart and then the thump of metal meeting scales. He dropped the crossbow which fell to his hip and unsheathed his blade in one smooth motion.

In a killing arc of moonlit metal, the Dhlam's head fell from its body.

He crouched. Waited. Listened.

The only sound was the gush of black blood watering Esmer's ground. Then the sound subsided. He waited longer, listening. Then he plucked another dart from his vest, cranked back the crossbow lever, slowly—each tooth in the mechanism bit noiselessly, like a man creeping up steep stairs.

On his feet and back down the trail.

Three more exploded from the jungle brush, dagger-clawed and screaming.

Step and cut. Slide and cut. Leap and slash. Blood splattered his face. It smelled sour. Felt hot. The moon watched and made no comment.

Nothing again. Silent. The dying becoming the dead. He bid the small-sun dark, again.

There are subtle muscles that warriors, thieves and scouts know. All men have them, but few come to realize those senses connected to such fine tissue. These senses warriors find, recognize, recall and then hopefully forget.

Allred knew them. Layers of thin sensing-skin around the sides of his neck, just behind his ears, growing beside the arteries where blood pulsed. The small muscles near his earlobes shifted under his scalp allowing him to hear better the secret pitches of the night and to accomplish the hunter's soft step.

His ears perked up. He turned and looked back up the trail behind him.

A dozen pairs of eyes stared back. They moved from the jungle to the path, blocking his retreat. If they had swarmed him earlier, he could have turned back. Maybe.

Down the mountain was the only option now. He raised the small sun, spoke it bright, and the beam pierced the trail. Turn and fight, or run?

The Dhlams decided for him. As if by hidden command which only their infernal ear could hear, in a wave, they began sprinting down the mountain straight for him.

So, it's run.

He sent a last bolt into the mass, then cut the line holding the crossbow to his hip and ditched the weapon to flee faster. High steps to clear roots and rocks. One stumble and he would be smothered by scaly bodies tearing through his guts with teeth and claw.

The only steep part of the trail was just ahead. He tried to gauge the distance to the small cliff face where Scrolls had noted the old road beneath.

Not far now. If he took a running leap...He saw the landing in his mind.

The stampede of black-clawed feet churning the trail in pursuit grew louder. The hissing breath of the fastest of the demons reached him, like a tightness on his neck. Without breaking stride, he pulled a dagger from his front vest, half turned his torso and flipped it into the Dhlam's face. It screeched and fell.

He kept running pointing the small-sun in front of him. A beam the same cool shade of the moon's light made clearer the trail before him.

There, the cliff in front of him an all at once thing, demanded an all-at-once-leap.

He launched himself over the rock face, legs braced, soaring out over the hill. His legs mimicked a few steps in midair, nothing beneath him; his body a ground-born thing, pretending flight to fail against the rules binding all no-winged things to dirt.

His boots found purchase on the ground below and he felt the jolt run up his hips into his guts. Near to tumbling over his legs from the speed and distance of the leap, at least his ankles didn't turn, kept braced by his boots. The top half of his own body was too far out over his legs.

Faster, he drove his legs hard to keep his upper body together with his feet. Boots chopped soil like blades in a melee. Sand from the trail flew behind him.

He pinwheeled his legs faster, pumping each step. The palms ahead where the trail turned rushed towards him too fast to slow down he was going to have to—

Slide. Slide. Slide. Sword low. Left face-first and into the brush. He caught at a limb with his free arm to slow down and whipped around the palm on the edge of the trail-cliff and made the turn.

He felt blood and craned his head backwards. He pointed the small-sun behind him and knew then, no matter how hard he ran—Mage would seek him out or he would die.

The Dhlams poured over the cliff face behind him. Dozens now. They didn't slow. Squat reptile legs whipped the night air wildly. Inhuman screams filled the night air. He saw two hit the ground hard at the bottom of the cliff. The others trampled them, unthinking.

Keep running.

No. He had never been good at running and he was tired already, winded from the redleaf and worse; some part of him that frightened him more than the mass of demons surging towards him told him that he wouldn't mind dying in battle, anyway.

Good.

He grabbed a little vial from one of the pockets in his vest, uncapped it and poured the liquid on the small sun. It pulsed and grew so cold it burned his hand but before it could cling to his flesh he threw the thing into the air as far as he could. As it reached the apex it exploded in white light.

6

Lookout

As the sun went down behind the mountain to meet unseen ocean, Cole invited them both, Lookout and his retainer, to sit and share food and wine. The tart warm white felt far smoother than cownut liquor. He wondered what other drinks and food the wider world offered, from places which he didn't even know the names of yet.

He had earned his wine in the half-day since the explorers arrived, working harder than he ever had as a guard. Hauling water, helping Stoneburner prepare food, clearing brush and trees, carrying stones, running chore after chore to prepare a camp for the rest of the soon-to-arrive explorers Cole had called the "Black Boat men."

The two giants felled trees with their axes. Stoneburner had set Boph and Lookout to gathering smaller limbs and broad palm leaves, then showed them both how to weave these things together with thin rope into a kind of mat which they fixed over stumps to create a table for Cole. A big stump served as his chair.

"By the time the Black Boat Men arrive, you'll know a little of what a proper camp should be. Rest well tonight, boys. Tomorrow we'll be digging trenches."

Stoneburner had laughed and slapped him on the back, hard enough to make him stumble. Lookout felt his face flush with pride. He was a part of their mission, now. Yes, the work was menial but throughout the day an idea kept growing in his mind— these men were his chance to leave Esmer. Off Esmer, was the path to knighthood.

He had never really thought past the stories of knights and courts, kings and steeds to how he could be a part of that world. Here was the chance.

His head grew pleasantly warm and light from the wine, while Stoneburner asked him about life on the island—he got the sense the questions came at the bidding of Cole but he stayed quiet. The two giants rolled dice in a tall cup made of what looked like bone and slapped each other after each roll, laughing at each round. Apparently, it was part of the game. The ways of the Green Islanders were strange, Stoneburner said.

Allred had disappeared.

The one they called Mage, too, stayed alone. As night fell, he had come out into the camp, like a stray animal, unsure of its welcome. He produced a round, glowing ball that emitted a moonlike light and sat it on the makeshift table away from the fire and began to talk to it.

The mage was like a figure walking out of the pages of a story. The man stayed aloof, and Lookout felt no threat just a curiosity that couldn't be quenched. When he tried to look at him, he felt that dizzy feeling again; the sense of falling forward from the railing last night or like the half-dreams which take you when you first try to sleep.

The orb illuminated the camp in its strange, crisp light. He had never seen anything more than a taper or torch on Esmer.

Stoneburner had warned him and Boph not to look too closely at the thing for too long. When he asked what it was, the old man just shook his head and smiled and said, "A magemade contrivance."

He couldn't help glancing back to the makeshift table where the thin, bronze-masked figure hunched over the ball of glowing light. Its rays illumined the strange human eyes beneath or caught the light of the odd jewels which capped his teeth. The mage's crooked fingers weaved signs in the air above the orb as he whispered incantations into the milky ball of light.

"You've been up here a year, you say?" Stoneburner asked.

The question pulled him back to the campfire. He took another swig of the wine. He told the explorers everything he could think of about the island of his birth.

He tried to make sitting in a wooden tower alone sound interesting. When his story turned sad, he edged away from those days, so soon he didn't have a lot to say. He spoke of weather, types of trees and wildlife on Esmer. The man named Scrolls made notes on parchment.

It was the first time in his life anyone had ever listened to him for so long about anything.

"How many villagers did you say live in the biggest town?" Lookout told him.

"The boys did well today, Stoneburner?" Cole asked.

Stoneburner said, "They'll do fine."

"Is there a kind of thing I get, a paper or something to show we are commended to—how did you say it? I will want to show the Attman when we are finished."

Stoneburner looked amused and then said, "Scrolls?"

Scrolls stood and leaned his head close to Cole who whispered something short back. A frown crossed the scholar's face. He sighed but he sat back down and took out a folio—real parchment it looked like—and began to write.

Soon enough, "Come hither," Scrolls impatiently gestured to him without looking up. He handed him the parchment. On it was a drawing of an emblem and surrounding it words.

"You did all that just now?" Lookout asked.

"Indeed," Scrolls said.

"When we are finished here," Cole said, and then he paused for a long time, wordless. A gloom passed over his face and the words stopped in his throat, "When we finish our work, I might speak to this Attman in the village. I'll have a word with him and tell him, you did well."

"I understand, sir," Lookout said.

He stared down at the fine parchment, which held a cleverly devised emblem.

In that paper, the future unfolded in front of him. Joining this band of explorers could be the first step. After that, he could win renown in some court...or, something like that. Exploits. That's the word he would need to do. And then he could become a knight for a king...he didn't quite understand how that worked.

Lookout considered asking Cole and the others how one became a knight, but he didn't want to seem ignorant.

"Your friend has some sight," Cole said, gesturing to Boph's sleeping figure.

How could Boph be sleeping? Didn't he know the most important things in their lives were taking place now? That's why he was only a retainer, he supposed.

"He knows some remedies. I think he sees things others don't," Lookout affirmed.

"The sight can make you tired," Stoneburner said.

There was a hint of sadness in his words. The rest of the men grew quieter around the fire. Hortha and Hartha raised their cups in salute to someone or something missing. And the rest of the men around the fire, did too. He decided maybe they were welcoming him into their employ so he whispered, thanks but kept his voice low in case he misunderstood.

He wanted to grab Boph, wake him up, show him the parchment and make him read the words out to him. It would help if he could explain things to him, too.

A sound came from the bronzefaced mage, and everyone startled and turned their head to the table. Far down the mountain, a white light lit the air for a moment, like a tamed lightening bolt, lacking the jagged lines of sky fire. Cole sprang to his feet. Hartha and Hortha stood, conjuring their two axes.

"Ha! Ha! Ha! Allred's in a mess, ha!" Aodlen cackled behind him and Lookout jumped at the man's shrill voice. He'd forgotten he had been pacing around behind them.

Cole dashed over to Mage. Scrolls followed, an impassive look on his face.

"What's happening?" Lookout asked Stoneburner, who stayed put across the campfire.

"Best not concern yourself." He unsheathed his short sword and placed it beside him.

Lookout turned to make out what was happening. There were images on the globe appearing and disappearing as if behind a mist. He thought he could hear sounds coming from the strange object. Cole leaned over it, eyes squinting in the light.

"Hold," Cole said.

Scrolls returned to where the men kept their packs. Stoneburner was on his feet now. He dug out something from the shadows of the baggage and handed Scrolls a small, wooden box.

Lookout stood, comfortably unsteady from the wine. He edged closer to whatever was happening. Boph was awake now, eyes sleep-bleary, looking around.

He felt a wave of weirdness pass over him from the mage. He turned away. It felt like the ground was moving beneath his feet. He sat down hard next to Boph.

"If he goes, he will be weakened for days," he heard Scrolls say.

"Mage, can you do it?" Cole asked.

Scrolls flipped the lid open and the mage laid his elongated hand on it, his face now buried within the cloak, body hunched, his head bobbing back and forth beneath the material of his cloak which seemed to come alive, like skin born without blood beneath, wrapped around his slight figure. With the other hand, he waved at the globe as if feeding air to a fire.

"Allred needs you," Cole said.

Transfixed by the scene, he nearly screamed when he felt Stoneburner pick him up from the ground, "Both of you, up to the tower and wait inside. Big magic might make you sick," he said.

Everyone was leaning over the orb now, besides Stoneburner.

"Allred wouldn't light that small sun if he wasn't up against it, Ha! Stubborn man seeks death, always avoiding my best remedies," Aodlen said.

Cole straightened, looked into the darkness.

"Go and fortune," Cole said.

The mage reached into the box, wrapped his weird long fingers around something Lookout couldn't see.

Unseen forces swirled around the campfire now. The air folded in on itself. Symbols and designs unseen until revealed in the writhing of reality soared through the air. Was the grass beneath his toes speaking? The wine must be strong.

He looked at the flame of the campfire, but the colors weren't right, as if the fire itself had turned grey. Then it leaped into a thousand crowding colors and back to grey again. He opened his mouth to try to speak but nothing came out.

"Uh." Looking up at Stoneburner he caught a glance at the moon and was sure that it stared back at him.

Stoneburner got them both walking towards the tower, pushing them along. Boph was speaking strange words, words Lookout didn't understand. Somewhere, his donkey brayed.

"Up you go." Stoneburner was pushing them both to the bottom of the ladder. "The magic is heavy now. Neither of you are accustomed to it."

He climbed the short ladder and Boph followed. They both pretended to go inside then came back out after Stoneburner joined the rest. Boph was beside him and that made him less scared. They both laid down prone on the damp wood of the walkway, chins propped in hands and watched.

"I had a strange dream. Should we go inside?" Boph asked.

"I want to see what magic looks like," Lookout said.

"You sure?"

The mage stood. His cloak folded and folded again and the air twisted the man and his vestments into impossible shapes. Currents of cold air swept the clearing setting the tops of trees to rattling. The black cloak shrunk, shivered and rippled as if feeding on air from another realm, summoned to this plane. The bronze mask began to melt and shift. Impossible patterns played on metal, cloak and flesh.

Now, the wind died down everywhere. A great vacuum and silence pulled the reality around the mage into a thick oval of dark metamorphosis. The tempest centered.

Lookout turned to Boph, and his eyes were wide-open, "What's happening?"

The cloak where the mage had been now billowed outwards as if caught by another furious wind. It twisted and turned forming the shape of a small dark dragon, the color of shadows. It opened its mouth and razor-sharp jewels sent rays of light racing across the ground. Cole stood beside it and pointed down the trail.

The beast wore the colors of the bronze mask across the top of its bony brow. At Cole's command, it bolted, running across the clearing and then lifted itself off over the trees and took flight. It skimmed the tops of the palms and then plunged down the side of the mountain.

Lookout felt Boph's hand on his shoulder. He opened his eyes. The men below were conferring with one another.

"What did I see?" he asked Boph.

"The big magic of the legends. The kind in the tales."

"Who are these men?" Lookout asked.

"I don't know for sure," Boph answered, turning on his side to stare at him. "But we've got to be careful."

He tried to stand up. His legs were weak. Into the single room at the top of the tower he crawled. In his hand, he still had the commission paper. He carefully placed it with his other important treasures, the figures he carved. It was dark inside the room, and he kept seeing clouds and currents of strange light when he blinked against the comfortable darkness of his room.

Behind him, Boph came in and worked a flint over a fistful of smoking tinder. The flame soared too quickly and Boph exclaimed to himself in his native tongue. The light from the cheap taper filled the room.

"So, that's a real mage," Boph said.

Lookout wanted to answer but he still couldn't quite grasp what he had observed. It was already like trying to remember a dream. He supposed it was the kind of happening a watch guard should record somewhere but he let go that idea quickly.

"While you were sleeping, they made us official explorers. I think."

A man was moving up the ladder. It was Stoneburner. He looked around the little room and saw them resting on the floor.

"Your minds are sound?"

They answered, yes.

The big man studied them both for a moment more, as if unsure. He worked a twig between his teeth and looked nervous.

"There's work in the morning. Sleep." Then he ducked back out.

"I want to check on my donkey!" Boph said, and hopped up, following Stoneburner down the ladder. He heard the man say something with mirth in his voice and Boph answer.

Not long after, Boph come back to the room. The animal was calm and unbothered by the strange sight, he told him, proudly. He wanted to speak more about what he'd seen but already the images faded and the wine's sweet drowsiness came back and he felt the good tiredness of work from the day urge him to sleep.

He kept checking on the taper and assuring himself the natural color of the fire. It steadied and he dreamed.

7

Allred

Allred would bathe in demon blood before they took his soul to meet Alwein. He would present a thousand more heads as trophies to prove his worth. He would paint every prayer in blood.

He slowed his steps, fell to a walk, a skipping turn, a slashing gait as the demons surrounded him.

The arm of a Dhlam fell to the sandy trail. It kept coming at him. He headbutted the thing and a sound like that of an animal escaped him. The demon staggered. He cut. It died.

Another Dhlam, on all fours, slithered over the dead body of the one just fallen. It rose up to two feet at the instant of closing and shoved him with taloned hands. The fight was close work now. He slammed his forearm into its torso, and brought his blade back up, skewering the demon. He kicked once as it slid off his blade. A few more steps backwards. Nearly stumbled.

His end would come and the only thing he felt was out of breath. There was some shame at the mystery of this last moment lost on his own senses dulled by years of war, and if Allwein asked him, he would have to admit he had lost the lust for life which was the great gift of being. Death had become ordinary.

A last smoke would be a fine thing though—

Before he could conclude his last thought, the sound of wings and a thump. The force hit him so hard it knocked the breath from him and he saw a grinning, jeweled mouth before he closed his eyes.

A whoosh, the leaves of the tall ferns parting. The black-cloak spread out, the wings of the dragon. The contours of the bronze mask, sliding metal on dragon-flesh unburned, flowing metal.

A full Battlemage, Nightdragon, in flight carrying him between talons curled in gentle cage.

He took a big breath and smelled chaos pouring through his body—the smell of dragon-flesh dark and cold. Two clawed feet pulled him ever higher into the air.

Cole had sent Mage after him. It would cost them. In his mind, Alwein laughed on his throne, promising a future meeting, delayed.

Up, higher, piercing the night sky above and plunging back again through it—he could see the contours of the game trail below.

He tried to relax in the grip of the monstrous form. Even for him, that much concentrated magic made him feel disconnected from his body and put spinning a thousand images of other realms in his mind. Mage's dragonform wasn't huge, the size of a big horse, nor was it truly the form of a dragon but a hybrid thing—a bat, a serpent, a wolf, a big cat with the sad eyes of Mage refulgent behind the mask which lined its lupine face in bronze-colored tufts of scale and fur.

The mage swooped low farther down the trail and dropped him to the ground without ceremony. He kept his feet and was strangely proud he didn't fall. Mage swept farther down the mountain trail, then picked up speed and circled back towards the demons.

From above the trees, bronze-colored flame ignited the air. The tops of trees became a rushing of embers like gold-colored snowfall beside the trail and already, Allred could smell the demons burning in gouts of fire.

The mage circled once above him and then landed in the tree line near the trail where he stood.

Allred laughed. It was all he could do. He spat, then threw up a little and spat again, still out of breath. Kept laughing because it made Alwein proud and laughing at death cured the Lady of the sadness of the world. He tasted blood and was sure it had not belonged to him. Not anymore, anyway.

There came a stirring from the trees. Out of the darkness, returned to human form, the cloak still billowing and flowing around him, the mage stumbled towards him muttering some verse Allred couldn't discern.

He was still holding his sword in one hand. Crossbow he'd have to collect on the way back up. Shame that. He sheathed his sword as the mage collapsed forward into his arms.

The cloak was still ice cold and the wide sleeve stung his flesh. He paid it no mind and swung the man's thin arm over his shoulder and started back down the trail.

"Curse you, bless you, I might have met Alwein and the Lady, tonight."

He stopped, with the weight of the frail man still leaning against him he lit a redleaf roll from the coal he kept smoldering in his tinbox. The smoke made him feel better and he reconsidered his words.

"Fortune, friend," he whispered.

The mage said something in a lost language in reply. He raised one warped thin hand, the flesh still bubbling and seething over the mishappen bones. Allred handed him the redleaf and the mage smoked between trembling lips, then handed it back to him.

Waves of heat and cold came from the cloak. Allred tried to not get sick at the sound of the shrinking, torn skin over the man's disjointed bones which still shifted on its own accord in the wake of the magic cast.

The price of heavy magic was great. He stopped on the trail. The world was still wavering around him. The two men who had lost most of their souls stood on trembling legs, trembling ground and quietly, without saying much, shared the redleaf roll.

"I suppose the Lady wishes me to stay a while more," he said.

The mage answered in a language like dust.

He wished they had never come to Esmer because he knew they would unleash terrible things here and he knew there were quiet villages somewhere on the island better off for never knowing their presence. Wishing wouldn't get him down the mountain with Mage, and wishing couldn't take him back home, so he finished his smoke and got moving.

After some hours, the sound of surf met his ears. Moonlight dancing in rings and arcs on the black-blue water through the trees ahead. The shadow of the Black Boat bobbing near the strand where it lay at anchor in the estuary.

He whistled the greydown call.

A Black Boat man came forward, looked at the two men and stepped back, stunned by the waves of magic still emanating from the mage.

"Glume?" he asked.

"By the boat." The man pointed behind him.

Allred pushed forward, boots sinking in the deeper sand of the beginning of the beach.

There was fire in the distance. Armed men clattered forward, staring open-mouthed at them both. Waves lapped gently against the wooden hull of the Black Boat. The smell of blood mixed with salt air.

Out of the darkness, near the boat, a gaunt man appeared.

"Been trouble," Glume said. He looked him over. "Looks like you seen some, too. Have a sit down."

Allred sat at the small campfire beneath the bulk of the Black Boat's hull, on the sandy edge of the estuary leading to the sea. The water ran shallow and quick, and the anchorage was still visible from the sea. While the rest of them were up the mountain, the captain had put the Black Boat men to work felling trees and gathering cover to help obscure the ship.

Mage rested beside him in the firelight but his presence didn't bother Glume. A tall, rangy man, he shared a look with many men who spent years on the sea. His skin was wrinkled around the eyes, and he had the habit of squinting at you, when you were near; many sailors do, since they spend their lives looking towards limitless horizon, distances so far away that far away stops meaning anything. Allred had noticed what sun and sea did to men's faces and it was written on the visage of Glume—distance. When he looked at the great nothing of the sea, Glume's face sometimes relaxed long enough to let him smile. Like many of his trade, the land made him nervous and decided him to drink.

The mage had taken his bronze mask off and was cleaning the flesh beneath. Allred felt his gorge rise and guilt for the feeling of it.

"Sorry," Mage said.

He hurried to put his mask back on with his misshapen fingers. The heavy bronze piece slid onto the flesh with a sucking sound. Glume sat across from them, a twig clenched beneath his teeth, hollowed eyes beside the fire with a slight twist of a smile.

Allred drew air in and practiced his breathing. It was an old technique used to calm the spirit. Observe reality around you. Let your eyes light on one thing at a time. Fire. Boat. Wood. Sand. Water. Water. Water. Moon.

The smell of blood.

Mage stood, pulled his cloak tighter around his head. The cloak still billowed and shimmered in the moonlight, catching arcane forces from the stars and hurling them around.

On the hull of the boat behind him Allred saw magic figures of shadow castoff from the cloak. They stole the forms of Dhlams, dancing around their own false fire, the mirror-image of the campfire. They all turned to Allred at once and reached clawed hands to grasp him but could not reach him. Then the shadows pointed to something else, upward. Another shadow, a rectangular hill, high on a mountain.

Breathe in and breathe...Just a boat. Just shadows. He

turned away from it, muttering an old hill ward against untamed magic. Exhausted. Closed his eyes. He opened them and saw the captain holding out a flagon of wine. He took it.

"I should be alone," Mage said and stood. "I'm speaking with the sea for a while."

"Stay close," Allred said.

The dark-clad figure turned back, "Cole says start back tonight if we can."

"Quiet there?"

"It was," Mage said.

He turned and walked down the dark shoreline. A few Black Boat men clumped around whispering nearby nodded and backed away from the figure. Most treated the mage like something akin to a cursed idol, or a minor god.

Allred uncorked the flagon and drank.

There was a feeling of fear and even mutiny all along the beach. The mage and Allred's arrival hadn't calmed anything. The Black Boat men had seen their own trouble while he was gone. It was finally occurring to them, what was in store. A little of it anyway.

"Lost some of them," Glume finally said.

Allred stood up. Needed to test his legs. They worked, so good enough. He sat back down.

"Some water," Allred croaked.

Glume handed him a different flagon. He drank and then asked:

"How many?"

"Ours? Two or three or four depending on who survives their wounds."

"How many Dhlams?"

"I didn't count. I killed. A lot. Lizard-looking things."

"Can the wounded walk?" Allred asked.

Glume shrugged.

He could make out the figures of men standing around the beach. They clutched spears and swords though the attack was past, from what Glume told him. It happened just after dark—a swarm of Dhlams.

Low talking all around the beach punctuated by screams. Some were shaking, some out of breath. A few men danced strange jigs around other fires burning on the beach into which they fed the bodies of the Dhlams.

He knew this mood that swept battlefields after a fight. He had seen soldiers out of control after winning victory, nevermind if they lost it. Good men and bad, out of their minds. Allred saw a man mimicking an owl's call, head turned to the moon.

"They aren't sound soldiers," he said.

"They aren't soldiers at all. Cole knows it."

Cole made plans. He followed orders. He hadn't inquired too closely about this bringing criminals on their next expedition. He just accepted Cole had his reasons.

"Got a bad feeling about it."

Glume sniffed, stared at the fire, spit at it, squinted at him.

"You find the place?"

"Likely."

"Well, there we are."

Allred smelled the dead above the salt of the sea. A corpse close by.

"Other problems?"

"One of them, called me out on my judgement. Over there. Problems? His, I guess," Glume pointed.

Through the low scrub bordering the water of the estuary, the body of a man, headless.

"Slighted you?"

"Tried to bugger one of the others. Night before. Couldn't let it stand," Glume said and spat the twig out from between his teeth. "So, he lost his head in front of the others. Calmed everything down. Then after the fight, they got hold of some bottles. Figured might let them drink, since I thought you wanted to come back and find bodies with heads attached. Eh, well, now, some of them are wild on liquor."

"Damn it, Glume."

"Seemed best at the time." The man laughed. "Keep your eyes open on the march, Allred."

The Black Boat Men were Cole's idea. Glume had made it

happen. He hoped it paid off. Another risk. They were taking more and more these days.

He unsheathed his sword. A lot of demon flesh stuck to it, so he put it in the fire and then cleaned it in the coarse sand. Glume watched him with amused eyes beneath curly black hair.

"You'd be fine leading a column of demons, yourself. Hurt?"

"No much."

"Well, there we are."

He went to the water, dipped the sword in it. Cleaner.

"Burn the dead. Rally everybody together. Get them packed quick. I march on the hour. No rest," Allred said. "I'll push them all the morrow, too, until we reach camp. That ought to keep them tired, less likely to cause problems."

Glume stood.

"Take'em off my hands. I have my crew. I'm taking the ship out to sea when you're gone. Rather wait out there, where I can maneuver. Don't like being anchored. I'll keep her close enough to watch the shoreline."

"Heard," Allred said.

He lit a redleaf from the campfire to cover the smell of the rotting corpse, "Can we get everything up there in one march?"

"Depends. You got a few less men to carry it. Stoneburner got it all set out and organized beforehand."

"I'll march them hard."

"Well, there we are."

Allred scratched his head. Cracked his neck. It was going to be a long walk.

"Torches? I used my light."

"Aye, you'll have them."

"I want the trail lit well. They have some spears and decent metal. No crossbows, no bows. Just blades. Going to wrangle Mage. He's tired," Allred said.

"Heard."

Glume turned and started yelling at people.

Allred walked back down the shoreline.

Out in the sea, Mage stood, water up to his hips. He turned

and walked back through the water when he saw Allred.

"Talking to the sea."

"What did it say?" Allred asked.

"The usual sea things. Nothing to concern the land for now. A long talk it is between the sea and shore. In many years, yes. It's always the same."

"The same?"

Allred found it oddly reassuring to talk with Mage sometimes even though half of what he said didn't make sense. Still, when the man could speak, plainly, or he could discern his riddled language, he enjoyed it.

The mage listened to the waves, the bronzemask had settled back to a solid form and moon reflected off its angles, "It's always the same promise the sea sings ... In time, in time, in time ... isn't that what you hear in the crash of every wave, no matter where in the world?"

The man reached out as if trying to grab a palmful of water from the ocean. He winced at the sight of the elongated joints in his hands. The long curled, fingernails looked like the hand of a corpse.

"How much longer can we Haunt-seek?" Allred asked. He had rarely asked the question out loud.

"We are no suited better for the Downside, friend."

Not the answer he was hoping for.

"Big Haunt up there," he said.

"Spirits set to babbling. People will die on this island. The Dhlams smell the Key. They hear me treading the old roads. I'm weary. I tell them and ask them to stop talking in my ears all day and all night. They don't listen. They went deaf ages ago."

"Right," Allred answered.

The Keys to the Haunts were a special matter, one that Allred didn't understand well. He had listened to the long discussions between Mage and Scrolls about the subject. He knew the finding and forging of the Keys mattered and how certain types worked in certain ways. What he knew for sure was this: Demons could sense when they neared a Haunt. They could sense the ability to open it and they tried to stop it.

"But no. Not longer for you, without living in the temples

where we found the map and the women soothe the maddened. Maybe. You're strong. I like you all. I've been born to it."

"Ready to fly me back up?"

He tried a joke. Talking to Mage was something like talking to a child or a demi-god. Other times it was like talking to an animal, a bird—you didn't expect a coherent response from a bird but maybe some sign of recognition.

Of course, the mage wouldn't use his cloak for such a thing. The amount of power it took from him to save Allred's life tonight had hurt him already and put them at a disadvantage in the days ahead.

"I'll walk like all the other men."

He made a strange gesture with two elongated fingers, mimicking the legs of men going up a hill. For a second, they transformed into human legs in front of him and he had to look away. The aftereffects of the magic were still strong, forming delusion in his head.

"We're both getting old faster than we should."

Mage concealed his hands in the folds of his cloak and stared at the sea.

"Should?"

"Time to walk."

"It's night. I like the night," Mage said.

"Me too."

"The light doesn't work right in my eyes anymore, sometimes."

"Stay close to me on the march back. These men..."

"They are all dead. You know that, yes?"

He didn't know that. The mage grew incoherent.

"Just keep an eye on me in case one of them decides to stab me."

"Of course."

The two men made their way back to the Black Boat in silence. Rows of men assembled on the beach between pyres of demon-flesh. Glume stalked the ranks lighting the torches each man held high from his own. They averted their eyes and hid their surly stares when the captain neared. The fire fell on the hard-faced men, most too drunk to hide their fear. If Allred was right, most were too dumb to plan anything that would be a problem.

Glume finished, stood in front of them beside Allred.

"Well, there you are. Take them," he said. "Fortune. I'll see you if I do."

"Fortune."

He considered giving a small speech, but decided against it. He gave the order to march, in a short bark and the Black Boat men fell into line behind him as he trudged back up through the blood-drunk sand to the Haunt on Esmer.

8

Lookout

Lookout woke up at dawn.

First thing first. He rose from his pallet on the floor, picked up his father's old Imperial helmet and placed it squarely on his head. The inside of it was rough and made his scalp tickle. He should have been wearing it all along, should have kept it in better condition.

He climbed down the ladder. Everyone was awake. He made his way over to the campfire. Stoneburner offered him a wooden mug brimming with an aromatic tea. The liquid was dark and smelled of spices.

"What is it?"

"Kler tea. Better for work than your rotgut liquor."

Lookout sniffed at it, took a small drink. He felt the warmness of it flow through his body, waking him up.

Stoneburner shoved a wooden bowl into his hand, pointed

for him to sit, eat. He did. The two giants sat across from him shovelling down food, the grains sticking in their beards. Worried looks creased their brows, then came and went breaking into smiles for no apparent reason. Cole and Scrolls stood away from the rest, at the makeshift table. The glowing orb was gone, stowed away somewhere. He didn't see a sign of the mage, or the man named, Allred.

A shiver went through Lookout's body, from the tea or the vision of what he had seen last night, he wasn't sure. Boph was tending to his donkey not far away. He felt relief at the sight of his loyal attendant, the only familiar sight about the camp.

The food was good. A porridge he had never tasted, mixed with a sweetener of some kind.

"What is it?" Lookout asked, "I've never tasted such a thing."

"Rue grain," Stoneburner said, "The finest."

He sat the empty bowl down beside him. Maybe he was among the right people. They were roughhewn, perhaps a bit mad, but they had wonderful things, fine grains, sweeteners, wines, and the best weapons. They even carried fine parchments. If they had such things here on Esmer, imagine what they must have wherever they called their home.

"Thank you," Lookout said.

Stoneburner smiled, "Eat as much as you like. It'll be a busy day. You might feel a little odd from the magic last night. Most never see such a thing. Best remember if you get to trembling, that Mage fights on our side."

Our side, he thought with wonder.

"Uh, fights, you say, sir."

The older man looked a bit flustered for a moment, "Well, when things go sideways, exploring isn't always the safest thing."

"Yes, sir, I see."

The grain was good. The tea made him feel sprightly. The blisters on his hands from the digging and carrying of rocks didn't hurt.

Cole walked over and bid him good morning.

"There is an old fence near that trail. It goes around this

94

entire area?" Cole asked.

Lookout had noticed it but paid it no mind. It disappeared and reappeared in places around the clearing. He told Cole so.

"Show us," Cole said.

Lookout hopped to his feet and followed Cole and Scrolls over to the far side of the clearing. He never went that way. It led to the empty side of Esmer. He told Cole that.

"Empty side?"

"Where few build. No farms. The Dragon wash side," Lookout tried to explain.

It seemed obvious to him. The islanders would walk the beach on that side during different times of the season, but the land wasn't used. Some herders might graze there but no one built anything permanent.

They had reached the perimeter where the rusty wrought iron fence stuck out of the ground.

Scrolls began to carefully dig around it. Lookout didn't know why but said nothing. These were explorers after all, so he figured this was exploring.

"Regard," Scrolls said pointing at a bit of the metal uncovered by his hand spade.

There was an emblem of some sort in the iron itself. A symbol Lookout didn't understand. Though he couldn't read any script, it was a script different than the ones in the book Boph owned.

"It is Old Semhel," Scrolls said.

They spent all morning tracing where the old fence appeared through the heavier vegetation surrounding the clearing. Why, he didn't know, but he figured not to ask. He would need to hide his ignorance, be careful about his questions.

Cole used a common short sword for hacking through jungle. The one on his back, did not leave it's scabbard, a huge, broadsword from the looks of it. He thought he could hear the metal growling as they worked, as if it held within it great energy.

Scrolls busied himself with drawing a map, tracing where the fence could be seen and where it all but disappeared. The man swayed from one foot to the other, eyes scrunched and concentrating.

Lookout grew bored, so asked: "Sir, you said something about Semhel script."

Scrolls looked up, irritated, "Yes."

"What is that?"

The look of annoyance left the man's face.

"Semhel is one name for the empire which ruled these lands long ago. Their script is called Semhel after them. One can still see examples of it, though in a much different, mutated form in some of the cult temples on Port Shamhalhan. Its origins are debated in the universities of Mhars. A familiarity with it is most useful when working with texts originating from this part of the world."

That was a lot of words for Lookout to think on. To buy time he asked:

"How do you know all this?

He had never heard anyone talk like this before. Boph was wise, even for a servant and he could read. The Attman, he could read also. They were the only people Lookout had ever met that could read. But a university? In the City of Fountains? That seemed impossible.

"I was sent for education in Mhars. Much of my young life I resided there in the libraries and lecture halls," Scrolls said.

"You lived there?"

He couldn't imagine it. A city famed the world over. Even here on Esmer, he knew of it.

"I lived there—my family estates are elsewhere—and for quite some time, as I just said. Much of my youth I spent studying there before service to the Throne. An indescribable city of beauty. I hope one day to return to it. It's much greater than the capital itself."

It was the first time Lookout had seen the man smile, or at least appear to enjoy anything he said or did. He had a way about him, always looking off to some distance, as if he were impatient in considering some problem.

"You're called Scrolls because you can read. That's why you have the name?" Lookout said.

The man looked a little pleased.

"Our group of explorers tend to use less formal names. Our other names make it difficult to explore as freely," Scrolls said.

"Mhars, the City of Fountains...truly you say it's even greater than the City of the Throne?" Lookout asked.

It couldn't be. He had never seen the capital of course but everyone knew that was the heart of the Throneland Empire itself. Massive and grand and sprawling...Lookout couldn't find the words for it, though it was described in the stories Boph told.

"Greater," Scrolls said, "Greater."

Cole stood among the fallen vegetation, staring out into the jungle.

"Go back to Stoneburner. When we are resting around the fire, Scrolls will tell you more of Mhars," Cole said.

"Yes, sir, I will and I hope you found what you were looking for and I helped."

He made his way back towards the watch tower, stepping through fern and shrub. A cloud of summer crickets erupted from one of the bushes riding the dry sound of sudden wings. The gummy resins of vegetation stuck to his face and his hands were cached in dirt.

Stoneburner sat him down again. Gave him another mug of tea.

"Listen well. Soon, there will be other men here. You've been told not to talk to them, not to be around them," Stoneburner said.

"Yes, sir," Lookout agreed.

He would obey all orders and do his best. He wouldn't mess this chance up. It was pure luck to be visited by men who had walked the universities of Mhars and the Throne city itself. It was like the beginning part of the legends.

"Those men are not like us. You tell Boph again—stay well away from them," Stoneburner said.

"Yes, sir. The other man, Allred, he went to go get them with Mage?" Lookout asked.

"That's right. They ought to be making their way here now."

All of a sudden he blurted out, "Stoneburner, I want to be a knight someday. A real knight. The exploring is good and I'll help you but I can't lie or keep away my true intention because you have been kind to me—someday I want to be a knight."

Stoneburner looked amused at this but didn't make fun of him, as Boph had done in the past.

"Well, I've known some knights in my day. It takes quite a bit of gold, to have your horse and your armor and your land and usually one is born into a House. There are good ones, it's true, but also some not so good."

Not-so-good knights?

He didn't see how that was possible. He didn't dwell on the matter long though. The tea revived him in the high mountain heat and soon Stoneburner put him to task.

Well, the man didn't say he couldn't be a knight, so that was a start.

The first step would be to make himself useful. These men thought differently than others did. He'd never paid much mind to that old rusty fence, never even really considered who had put it there. Apparently, with some digging Scrolls had found out something of importance about it.

I'll need to pay attention to things.

9

Allred

They had marched through the night without another fight. He heard the wonder of the Black Boat men as they stumbled past piles of burnt Dhlams the mage had left in his fiery wake. Wild board had stamped their prints on the ashes, rough mounds where tusks had rooted for scraps of flesh.

The hypnotic sound of men marching. In the night, the bob and blur of bright torches waved against the darkness. Rattling metal, marching feet, the bell and tambourine noise of men on the move trailed behind him. No chance of staying unseen.

Glume had made ready a few simple sleds which the men pulled up the mountain with ropes, arguing about whose turn it was to heave and haul.

One foot in front of the other. He kept everyone at full marching pace. No stop. He was tired beyond feeling pain now. Dawn had come and Mage retreated farther into his cloak.

Allred looked for fear inside himself as if studying a puzzle.

He couldn't find it and that wasn't good. He knew it lingered somewhere within him, hidden in secret warrens of his mind— worse he could feel the fear crawling through muscle and gut.

In the Haunt it's still waiting for us, Allred figured. He scratched his jaw and lit another redleaf roll. His mouth and throat were dry from the smoke. It kept him moving.

Allred knew in his bones they neared a large one. Even if it wasn't, he wasn't certain any of them could bear descending yet again. Overflowing with Dhlams and worse, whatever gate stood at the top of the mountain it led to the ruin of souls.

That meant big treasure. That meant a lot of dead men.

In a perverse way, the Haunts made him feel human now. The most inhuman thing to do, entering those realms inhabited by demons, guarded by curses, filled with tombs. There he felt alive on the edge of doom.

Wasteful thoughts.

"Keep the pace," Allred shouted when he saw the line of men falter.

He slowed and let the back of the line of marching men catch up. He heard some shouting, looked back and saw two men arguing. They had dropped their ropes attached to the sleds and faced-off. One pulled a dagger. The others tottered to a slow stop to watch, an excuse to rest.

He made his way back down the trail, "Problem?"

Both men turned, looked at him. One spit. Daggers vanished.

"No, sir."

"Just a stumble."

"Good," Allred said.

The line kept moving. They had already cleared the small cliff face earlier. The one thing that heartened him—his crossbow he had found where he cast it off.

He returned to the front of the line, head down. The Black Boat man beside him looked tired, afraid but he kept good pace and stayed quiet. He shouldered a heavy pack. A rusty axe hung from his belt loop.

"Drop back. Keep the back of the line in order."

If he didn't have any fear left topside above the Haunt where most mortal men lived and died; then if there is was some portion of fear due to all men, did others carry the burden of fear he had relinquished?

Foolhardy thoughts. The kind of thing Scrolls calls philosophy. Pointless.

One foot in front of the other. Eyes ahead.

He flicked the redleaf roll away from him, pulled from his belt pouch a small wooden plaque portraying the Lady of Allwein. When his thoughts grew confused, he looked at it and rehearsing the prayers he had learned in youth, he offered up his thought to her.

"The Lady of Allwein?" the Black Boat man he had dismissed asked.

"It is," he answered.

"My mother prayed to her."

Against his own feeling, he offered the plaque to the grizzled, thin man. He waved it off but glanced at her from a distance, "It's been too long since I learned the prayers."

The man was a criminal and of the worst type, that Allred knew. He considered answering.

Instead, he just nodded and the man slowed his pace and fell back. Allred put the wooden plaque back into his belt pouch.

They were making good time, not long until the top.

Into the Haunt and out, Allred thought, that's the way to think. Win another victory. After that, maybe talk to Cole.

Something would have to change. Years in the wilderness, in the belly of the Haunts and every single one of them, besides maybe Stoneburner, were living right on the edge of toppling over into a temple for the Haunt-Ridden. He'd rather die than live out his days, slobbering and babbling in one of those places.

They needed to change the plan, but he didn't know how. Cole had the plan, not him.

Revenge drives him. And it's our revenge as much as his.

He dismissed these ideas, like an unwanted sentry. Breathe. Listen to the jungle.

A family of squirrels darted from branch to branch above as

if running a race with the march. Flies and gnats fell prey to green and brown lizards who watched the men from their perches in the palms. Their throats expanded in red flesh-bubbles. They bobbed up and down, hissing at the noise. Cantaloupe-colored blooms drooped from vines burdened with clumps of dry leaves burnished brown by the morning heat.

He's a reasonable man, Allred thought. *But something has to change.*

When they reached the clearing, he whistled to alert any sentry Cole had set.

He felt a lightness as he made his way over the small metal fence, noting someone had dug around the base of it while he was gone. Emerging from the clearing, Cole came to meet them at the trailhead and took charge of the Black Boat men.

They filed past Cole, in his presence all walked a little more upright. They tried to learn something about what would come next from Cole's face.

In the brighter light of the clearing, away from the shade of the jungle he felt the empty desperation of sleeplessness press down on him.

Cole surveyed the arrivals with grim eyes and gave them over to Stoneburner's command.

Mage hovered beside Allred, mute since the beach.

Too quiet.

Either way the job was done. Order fulfilled. And from what he could see, it didn't look like any fighting had broken out up here.

Aodlen joined them. Cole released the doctor on them both.

Cole said, "What happened?"

Allred reported in clipped sentences, in a matter-of-fact way, condensing the entire fight—the beach and return march while Aodlen poured powders and medicines on the wounds he suffered from the Dhlams. It distracted him. His tongue heavy from the lack of sleep.

"I shouldn't have tried it alone. Mage had to save—"

"My call." Cole said and that was the end of it. "No more trouble on the way up?"

Aodlen kept bothering him.

"Ha! Got to patch you up."

In the distance, Stoneburner shouted at the Black Boat men.

"Look up there, yet?" Allred asked, nodding towards the last ascent where the Haunt would stand.

"Not yet. Rest. Tomorrow, we try it," Cole said. "Aodlen and Scrolls will mix the Haunt-potions, now that we know our number."

Before entering a Haunt, every man had to take Aodlen's special remedy. Allred knew the ingredients but most of the names made no sense to him. Aodlen's job. Everyone had a role. Good enough. He turned to the doctor, waived him off, "Make mine double strong, Aodlen."

Gods, he was tired.

"Oh, ha! Allred, I've been doing that for a long while." Aodlen laughed.

"Heard." It wasn't humorous. Probably wasn't meant to be.

Aodlen followed him back to where Stoneburner kept the camp. Scrolls walked past, nodding a greeting and went to meet Mage.

Aodlen didn't look tired at all. As usual, he was excited by his own concoctions. The feeling of being around someone drinking that much medicine wasn't so different than being around a mage. There was a dangerous underlying hum of the spirit coming off the doctor in his twitching restless movements.

Stoneburner brought him food, sat him down, nearly slapped him on the shoulder, then seeing the wound, gripped the other one in a friendly embrace.

"Ready for this one?" Aodlen asked.

"Ready for you to leave me be. Tomorrow, I'll worry about tomorrow," he said, shoveling the rue grain down fast. He noticed the wooden spoon was shaking in his own hand.

"Ha! Tomorrow. Yes, yes, well tomorrow brings its own worries."

Aodlen was reliable, unflappable in battle, but he couldn't tolerate the man for too long, especially when he was tired.

At least it's some respite to have company on the edge.

Aodlen more than most of them looked like he was barely

fighting off the Upside Fever. His eyes stared beyond your shoulder, staring through you and past you at once. Better than meeting his lightening quick glares. Talking too fast, punctuating every thought with maniacal laughter. His breath smelled like old metal, and he sweat all the time.

"I pronounce you fit enough for war, ha."

The tattooing began years back and built up over time. His arms and chest were covered in them now. Recipes for remedies he said, "Got to write them down, in case I forget, ha! My skin is better than some parchment. Parchment gets lost, ha! That could get lost. Lost, yes. Parchment, I'd have to talk to Scrolls, hahaha! If I lose my skin, then I lose the recipes and then we're all in a mess."

The tattoos weren't about Scrolls and his parchment, though the doctor enjoyed needling the aristocrat—Aodlen had cooked up a special ink for his tattoos and it helped him sleep.

Cole didn't say anything about it.

Allred didn't say anything about it.

No one said anything to anyone about it. Each of the Relic Hunters were allotted their own portion of magic to do with as they pleased. No questions were asked.

It was odd though, when he thought about it. Ink helped the doctor rest. Ink helped Scrolls rest.

"You both love your ink," he said.

"Ha! The scout has a more subtle mind than it appears. Hiding behind your little provincial mask, I think. We all hide where we can."

Allred shoveled down the last of the rue grain. Stoneburner brought another bowl and handed it to him. Aodlen chattered on beside him.

People's minds came loose after the Haunt. On the edge together. His mouth full, he stared at Aodlen and felt a weird pang of affection for the man.

"It's going to be big, Allred. I can feel it. Ha! Yes, yes, though of course this is just how one must do things..."

The fast-talking made him dizzy and his hands tingle.

"Can't you see this man is weary, Doctor?" Stoneburner chuckled. "Give him some time to sleep."

Aodlen ceased talking, considered this and put a black, ink-stained hand to his own lips. "Quite right, quite right. Would you like a concoction to sleep?"

We all get by our own kind of way. All tired. Except Cole.

"Don't need it," he grunted.

Aodlen leaped up from the low bench hewn from a palm tree someone had constructed while he was on the march. A small palm trunk cut down the middle and setting on top of two stumps.

"I'll get the doses prepared. Too many. I just realized. Lost men on the beach. Hmm, double doses, I guess! Ha! If need be. If need be. Need to recalibrate. Formulas. Hmm. Expensive ingredients." Aodlen finished talking and then turned and wondered off, pulling his old playing cards from his belt and shuffling them as he paced around the camp.

Stoneburner pointed to the top of the watch tower.

"You can sleep up there by permission of the young, watchman of Esmer," Stoneburner smiled.

Allred handed the bowl back, made his way up the tower. There he found a pallet laid out for him. He started the task of taking out the sharp things he carried all over his body and laying them beside the blanket.

"Yeah," Allred said aloud to no one.

Too tired for nightmares is the right kind of too tired.

"Yeah."

In one hand, he gripped a short dagger, in the other a throwing knife. Outside, the Black Boat men barked and complained and were quieted and it wasn't his problem for a few hours, so he fell asleep.

.

10

Lookout

He watched the Black Boat men file into the camp.
"Stoneburner said keep clear of those," he whispered to Boph.

"They look like explorers to you?" Boph asked.

"No, they look like something bad."

Some appeared sickly and all were weary. They dumped their packs and sleds where Stoneburner indicated. They answered Cole but he could hear anger simmering beneath their words. They wore a collection of motley rags, bits of armor. Most were unarmed but a few carried old spears or rusted sword and axe. Their downturned eyes saw more than they should.

"Stoneburner said stay put until he comes to tell us different."

"I won't argue," Boph said.

For once, Lookout thought.

When the mage returned to camp, Scrolls had hurried off to

look after him. Lookout grabbed Boph's arm, "Let's go talk to the scholar. I want to know how that magic light works, don't you?"

Boph didn't want to budge, "It's high sorcery."

He was growing impatient at the timidity of his attendant.

"He can read and write, like you. I know you're curious. I've never seen such a thing as that light. How do you capture light in an orb? How? Do you know?"

"I've heard of it. They have some of those things in Port Shamhalhan. He doesn't seem like he likes to talk. He's always swaying from foot to foot and his eyes are turned in on himself. The others laugh. He doesn't know when to laugh."

It was true, the man was contained, less friendly than the others. He said little and preferred his scrolls to the company of the campfire. When he spoke, his accent was strange and cold.

He didn't care. He needed to know all these men better, if he would be serving with them. If he made friends with them, became useful to them, they would be the path off this island. His dreams of armor and a powerful steed, the stuff fueled by cownut liquor and lonesomeness— maybe he could make them real. This was the chance and Lookout wasn't going to let it go by. He had to make these people like him.

"Come on. He must know all kinds of tales if he uses writing," Lookout said. Admitting no more delay, he took Boph by the arm and dragged the smaller boy over to where Scrolls sat writing.

"Hello," Lookout said.

The man looked up from the small makeshift table the men had set up.

"Yes?"

"We were wandering how that thing you used last night, how does it cast light? There's no flame inside. It's not a taper or natural fire."

The man blinked at them both. Lookout thought he would just keep staring at them and not speak. Instead, he sat his stylus down carefully and folded his hands.

"I admire your curiosity. Perhaps you aren't just silly peasants, after all, though that's the obvious conclusion to come to upon seeing your wretched state."

"Uh," Lookout said.

"Yes. This makes sense. You would never have seen such a thing on this remote, primitive island. The history and legends concerning the manufacture of—"

Both Lookout and Boph stood listening for a long time as the man launched into the subject, midway into a history he had no understanding of. Scrolls didn't stop talking. He came back halfway through his lecture and spoke of the first accounts of these objects which went by many names—Small light, small sun, Candlefalse, Liar's Lights...

Lookout hid a yawn behind his hand. "So, it's magic?"

The scholar cocked his head like a bird looked at a worm which was simply too pathetic to devour and then went on, ignoring his question.

At some point, during a lengthy exposition on the etymology of the words which were used in ancient texts to describe the lights, his legs grew tired. Stoneburner was still directing the Black Boat men and hadn't called on them. He started to desire work, lifting stones or fetching water to this stream of unending words battering at his mind. He was lost in the explanation. Boph appeared to be following along and that irritated him. It was difficult to keep up with the man's speech. He used a lot of big words.

"They say I'm a taciturn fellow." Scrolls said, when Lookout asked him what *dust-heightened-tallow* meant. "Perhaps, I am. When it comes to the subject of the past, I enjoy speaking on these matters. There is a line from the poet Boephius, you may know— oh, well perhaps you don't—but it can be found in his lesser-known fragments, *The Works of—*"

Lookout listened. Kind of. He stared at nothing, his mind wandering, still no more learned on what could capture the light within the object that dazzled him the night before, but pleased, nonetheless, to be admitted to the scholar's company.

"Now, it is true that one must separate the meaning of the stock-epithets which we find in the sparse documentary evidence we find housed in a lesser-known archive of the Emerald Library at

Mhars from the literal meanings we can document elsewhere. It may interest you to know, I've gazed upon—"

What was a "stock-epithet"...

"And then there is the quite interesting and fascinating possibility that predating even this invention in the age of—"

His eyes began to grow heavy. He jerked awake. One of those little shivers which wake you up for no good reason while hovering on sleep. His father had said it was the tiny sleep—gods who pinched you to keep you from dreaming because the dream world could only be so full at any one time. If the little sleep fairies didn't do their work of pinching and everyone slept at the same time, people would run into each other in their dreams. His father had told him, that's why sometimes you can't fall asleep good.

That story made sense to him. It was a simple explanation. Not like the scholar's talk filled with words that referenced words that referenced words that no one could find the bottom to, anyway.

He noticed Boph sat attentive and listened, eyes open and the scholar was clearly speaking to his attendant now, not him.

"...and so, we cannot truly be certain of the origin of this word, the word which first seems to indicate the harnessing of magic, the capture-process preceding the instilling-of-the-essence-process within a form manipulatable by mortals. What is primary? That's what it comes down to. This I hope has elucidated the matter for you both," Scrolls said.

And then ceasing his lecture all at once, he simply picked up his stylus and began writing again, as if the two boys had vanished.

Lookout leaned closer to whisper to Boph, "So, it's magic?"

His attendant sighed and smiled.

11

Allred

A cool mountain breeze came in ragged gusts against the wooden walls of the tower. The sounds of men digging outside woke him up. Shovels in dirt and Stoneburner barking. It was night.

He sensed no one else in the room and setting each knife down, which his sleeping hands had clutched he dried his sweat-slick palms on his trousers and rubbed his eyes in the room's soft dim.

The Relic Hunters of the 9th had tracked down Haunts in many different lands; around the periphery of the Thronelands and sometimes inside them. After leaving a place, he tried to forget about it. He told himself it was because he needed the space in his mind to keep track of new places but it was because memory was loss and loss hurt and he could only afford so much of that.

Nice enough weather in the southern seas. He yawned. His leg felt tight. He sat up and worked the muscle between his hands.

Ought to light a taper.

He stood-stretched, walked out to the platform surrounding, leaned against the railing and felt the stars singing down from the night sky on his neck.

Everywhere looks beautiful just before entering a Haunt, he thought, *And then you forget.*

Looked like Stoneburner hadn't allowed the Black Boat men to rest after the march. He had them digging a long defensive trench some ways off from the tower. The clearing below was lit by torches, sharp-ends fixed into the ground their fires dancing in the wind.

He studied the lines of the camp. A lot of work but worth it. If they needed to stay, or if they needed to fight, Stoneburner had designed a place that gave them better odds.

He climbed down the small ladder and looked for Cole and found him with the two kids and the donkey.

"Slept?" Cole asked.

"Some," he answered.

"It's near dawn."

He'd slept longer than he thought then. That meant the Black Boat men had been working all night after the march.

Lookout sat watching Cole, admiration in his eyes. He whittled a figurine like the ones in the room above. Little white flakes of wood were scattered around his bare feet. Boph kneeled on the ground, scratching signs in the dirt. The boy kept stealing glances at Mage who stood off alone, talking to his demons. He didn't look away when he regarded him in turn. Mage even stepped over to where Boph was drawing in the dirt and studied the symbols the boy drew.

"Me, you and Scrolls. Up the mountain to see what we can see. The rest remain in camp for now."

"Heard," Allred said.

Stoneburner brought him over a mug of Kler tea and dropped his pack next to his feet. He nodded his thanks, washed it down quick.

"How's the cut?" Aodlen asked, wild-eyed.

"Don't feel it," he said and shrugged.

Aodlen looked suspicious but left him alone. He picked up his own loaded crossbow hidden in the grass and turned to watch the Black Boat men, still digging their trenches.

The sky looked clear as the dark turned to the gentle rose of a tropical dawn. Felt like rain hovering behind the mountain. He lit a redleaf and waited for Cole's order.

Soon enough, Cole gave it. They set out across the clearing to the trailhead leading to the peak of the mountain. The two boys followed them.

"You two have never been up here?" Cole asked the boys again.

Boph shrugged.

Lookout said, "I haven't explored it. I haven't seen any other trails. One leads down to the empty side where you came from, and the only one I've ever used is the main trail down to the village."

Mage moved like a shadow slouching under the sun, trailing them. He had his cloak draped over his entire face. Lookout took an unsteady step backwards at his approach, but Boph just tilted his bald head and watched the sorcerer with his round, curious eyes.

"I guard the approach," Mage said.

He walked a few steps away and huddled beneath a tree near the beginning of the trail, fading into the brush and green.

There was a remnant of the old barrier at the trailhead and Cole pointed at it.

"This works protection, still," Scrolls said.

"Protection against what?" Lookout asked.

"Bad things," Allred answered.

"What kind of bad things?"

"He means the High Place demons," Boph said.

Allred put out his redleaf.

"You've seen them?" Cole asked.

"The stories tell of them."

"Is my attendant, correct?" Lookout asked.

"Go back to camp," Cole said.

The way up might be harder going. This trail was less-travelled and looked steep from the start.

"Let's march," Cole said and waved him forward.

He clicked the safety off the crossbow, wished he'd had another redleaf and set out up the trail.

The terrain was different. The path broadened out quickly but remained steep. The old road broke through the soil, until soon, they were treading the ancient road itself.

"That's what we're looking for," he said.

"Since we are higher to the peak, there is less debris to fall downhill to cover it up," Scrolls said.

Cole drew his broadsword from the scabbard on his back.

They walked on for some time in silence. The air was thinner. The jungle, too. The heights paired everything down and there were less sounds of animal life. Still a few boar tracks beside the stone road. The birds did not sing.

He turned back to look down the trail. He could still make out the camp below above the treetops.

"I want to get sight of what we're heading for," Cole said.

They came to another clearing like the one where the tower stood below but smaller. The dirt was patchy and along the road clumps of green grass grew up between jagged stones, the remnants of ancient signposts, Allred could make out faint writing inscribed in the stones and Scrolls bent over them, lips working old words in silence. Pink and yellow flowers grew in clumps, sheltering in the shadows of the forgotten stones.

"The Haunt will be ahead," Scrolls said.

They walked.

The first wisps of low clouds began to slip around them. It was an odd feeling he never got used to, the faint coolness of clouds on his skin in high places. Soon, they crested a ridgeline past the clearing. He halted. No one said anything for a moment, just stared ahead.

The mountain sloped down into a last valley. The old road was bare now, old cobblestones and he could see it pierce the beginning of a dense forest in the valley. Visible beyond it, the mountain climbed again out of the forest which ended abruptly at the bottom of the last peak. From here, he thought he could make out stone stairs carved into that steep incline and then as it ascended the shape of the mountain took on unnaturally rectangular dimensions where stairs wrapped around it and disappeared on the other side. At the apex, the rock appeared to conform around some structure built long ago.

They had found the Haunt.

"Big," he said, breaking the silence. He lit a redleaf roll, kept his eyes open for attack.

"How many living men have seen this?" Scrolls asked, quietly.

He thought about it, "If the Throne knew about it this island would be occupied."

"No one looks in the correct places. The natives of this island may be primitive, but they aren't complete fools. Their wisdom tells them not to go up to these places," Scrolls said.

Cole said nothing. He leaned on the weight of the broadsword, point digging into the ground as if he were claiming it, warning that a will greater than the evil beneath stood tall above.

"It's not far but will be treacherous. I see the traces of an ancient grove in the forest. And there through the tops of the trees—barrows. I expect foul tricks before we reach the gate. This is guarded and warded land," Scrolls said.

He felt something true and strong when he gazed on these works of ages. A kind of amazement mixed with terror and excitement held him and made him forget the losses. The sheer adventure of treading places unknown heartened him, still. These moments they all lived for—the seeing and taking of terrible things from afar.

"May not have the numbers we need for this, Cole," he said.

"We've never had the numbers we need," Cole said, "Going to change that, someday soon."

"Until we find the gate, we know little. It could appear physically imposing from here but be relatively inconsequential," Scrolls interjected.

"Could sell the map," he suggested.

They could. Their reputation alone could sell it. A detailed map leading to a Haunt like this would sell for a lot of coin to the wrong people in the right kind of market.

But money wasn't magic, although Allred knew most men

disagreed. It wasn't the kind of magic they were searching for anyway. In his mind, he saw the holy face of the mad man who gave them the map in Shamhalhan and knew they were fated to enter.

"Could do," Cole replied, turning to him. His hands were draped over the hilt of his sword and he almost looked like a prosperous farmer, gazing out over a pasture, discussing the crops, discussing the rain, relaxed. Almost. The killing look in his eye wasn't aimed at anyone, on this ridge but it never went away. "That what you're thinking?"

"I'm just trying to talk so I have time to smoke this redleaf, before I got to march more, Cole."

Cole almost smiled.

"I know we're ragged."

"This is what we do. So, we do it."

"Well said," Scrolls replied, sarcastically. "Once your work hunting relics concludes, you'll clearly find a place at some court as chief poet or a teacher of rhetoric."

"You could make a decent jester," he replied.

Cole turned his gaze back out to the Haunt and spoke his words as if answering the valley before him.

"I've seen enough."

They headed back down the trail. It still struck him as odd that even on a sparsely populated island like this, no one would know of that place. Likely some curious villagers had gone up and just never returned.

In the distance below, men were still digging trenches. Boph stood with his donkey and Lookout. The two tiny figures appeared to be arguing with each other. Allred stopped and pointed near the trail to the village.

"Movement, in those trees, you see it?"

Cole put a hand over his eyes to shield them from the sun. All the men below dropped their spades and looked to the tree line in the same place. Hartha and Hortha standing close to the two boys and the donkey, turned to where Allred had pointed—they must have noticed it at the same time. It looked like one of the twins was talking to the animal, feeding it a fruit from his hand.

"Something's wrong," he said.

Mage scurried out of the brush below.

A warning cry went up from the area where the sentry was stationed. It was cut off abruptly.

A Black Boat man let loose an arrow towards the trail. It went far wide of the target. Stoneburner stopped him with a shout. Other men drew swords or picked their shovels up to swing instead of dig.

"Allred!? Is Cole up there?"

It was a woman's voice. Faint and behind the treeline and Allred knew it.

"It's the Rats," Cole said.

"How did she find us?" he asked himself and lowered his crossbow.

"Still a problem. Different type," Cole said.

They made their way down the trail into the clearing.

"Hold fire!" Cole bellowed.

Everything got quiet. Most of the Black Boat men stood peering over the trench they had dug.

"Hold your fire!" Cole said again, then turned towards the tree line, "Show yourself."

"Cole?"

"And?" Cole asked the trees.

"Helga and her Rats," the answer came from the trees, "I'm coming out."

All along the camp, Stoneburner was walking, calming the men, waving his meaty arms in the air. Hartha and Hortha walked forward slowly, grinning.

A blond woman with a round pale face, a black eyepatch over one eye darted out from the trees near the trail leading down to the village. She wore light, scuffed leather armor which didn't hide her pleasing figure. Her tan trousers were tucked in old boots.

"How many with you?" Cole asked.

"What's left of us," she said, striding up to Cole.

"Bring them out."

"Is that the way?"

"Bring them out."

The woman whistled and waved, keeping her one blue eye fixed on Cole. Four Green Island dwarves shambled out from the brush around the trail. They were dressed in a motley style, a mix between fisherfolk, soldier and traveling actor. Ragged and sunburned, each wore elaborate moustaches melding into pointed beards. Whatever path had led the Rats to them on Esmer, it had not been a simple journey.

"Cousin," Helga said, looking at him.

He hadn't seen her since the gathering at Ceardhardt castle. She was still a beautiful woman, but the world was a hard place, and it had traced its troubles on her face. The last time they had met, she regarded him with the same mix of friendliness and the distance of a fortune-teller at a market faire; but then she had regarded him with two eyes instead of one.

"Cousin," he said, and nodded, "You're in a far-flung place."

"Has anyone followed you?" Cole asked.

"No, hardly nothing up this way for half a horse's day," Helga said.

"Stoneburner, see our guests have something to eat and drink," Cole said.

He had been holding his breath and didn't realize it. When he heard Cole's words, he was relieved. No blood for the moment.

Allred watched the Black Boat men climb back over the ditches they had been digging. Stoneburner told them, *back to work* and set out to gather provisions for the Rats. Greedy eyes clung to the figure of the woman.

Another problem. They didn't need another problem.

"Who is that lady? She's your kin?" Lookout asked him, innocently.

"No."

Scrolls interjected: "The people of Allred's remote and savage lands call the members of rival clans, *cousin* when they are not feuding. When at war, they call each other *close cousins*. They are a peripheral people with peripheral ways."

"Yeah," he said, keeping his eyes on the Rats, "We're peripheral."

"Peripheral. I'll remember that word," Lookout answered,

solemnly and turning to Boph, "We are peripheral, I think, me and you. You more than me."

"She looks...fascinating," Boph said, "A woman wearing a sword?"

Children. Now women. Not what they needed a half day's hike from a Haunt, Allred thought. He lit a redleaf roll, then took another from a different pocket, the ones untreated by Aodlen. As Helga approached, he lit it from his own and handed it to her.

"Fortune, cousin" he said. She took it from his hand with a smile.

She inhaled deeply, "Fortune, my cousin."

Cole waved them towards his makeshift table, "Come."

"Quite a welcome," Helga said.

"He didn't order you killed. That's a fortune," he said.

She winked at Allred with her one good blue eye, or she might have just been tired and closed it.

He settled around the table. Helga sat on a stump at his side. He could see what Cole was doing, leaving her there to talk to him for a while before he joined them.

"Why?"

Helga shrugged, "Desperate."

"How?"

"On a boat, just like you," she answered.

"Cole is a hard man, and you know it."

"Well, it's a fishing boat we followed you in, if you must know," she laughed.

Her laugh died out against his silence. A look of anguish passed over her face. She possessed a cool beauty, unmarred by the patch she wore, unbroken but dimmed by some tragedy in her nervous laugh. Her hair was longer than what it had been, last he'd seen her, soft and falling around her shoulders. She wore a simple tunic of dark green, beneath her leather vest, belted, her buckle of copper embossed with an image of a rat. Her boots had seen many miles and they were hard ones.

Cole came over to the table and sat down. He stared at her a moment without saying anything.

"Lost your eye," he stated.

"I know where I left it," she said.

Cole didn't answer. Slowly, he took out his own small tin of redleaf, fit some in his pipe, his action measured and deliberate.

"You followed us?"

"You've been busy looking ahead, not behind you. Spent a fair sum on a magemade mask out of Shamhalhan," Helga said, "I'll make it simple—I got six dwarves, a fishing boat, some banged-up swords, two magefire whips and nowhere else to go."

The mask would have cost a great sum. It was like the feint their mage conjured but stored in an object and called forth later with a sealed-word by anyone who knew it. The magefire whips, if she wasn't lying were costly, too.

Before he could doubt her, she bent down and fetched two short metal rods from the pack beside her and laid them on top of the table in front of Cole. They looked like the real thing, powerful weapons, the type of weapons that could turn a fight in their favor. Cole barely gave them a glance.

"I count four dwarves."

"The other two are back on the boat. Thay and Tym, Staah and Shad are the four who play the Bone Cup game with their Green Island kin."

Hartha and Hortha had greeted the dwarves with merry cheers when they settled around to eat. It didn't take long for the bone cup and the dice to appear.

"Keep talking."

"Figured your mage might catch wind of us. He didn't. I'm guessing you didn't, since you look surprised, Cole. You don't have my talent for acting," she said, "Or do you?"

Cole ignored the small jests, the prodding. He cupped his pipe in his fire-scarred hand and watched her through rings he exhaled.

"I'd likely not be where I am if I could act," he said.

"You going to kill us?" she asked.

He took his pipe from his mouth, studied it.

"What did you see coming up the trail?"

She was displeased and rolled her hand across the smooth

cylinders of the magefire whips, then rolled them back off the table.

"No," Cole said.

She put them back. Cole took them and put them beside him. Her mouth frowned but her eyes stayed pleased, at least he'd taken something offered.

"Worth a sum."

"Yes, they are. Keep talking."

She sighed, pretended to relax. "We came up the village side. Docked the boat there. Told the villagers we're simple traders and entertainers, the travelling sort. The Attman down there, a big fat fellow, he gave us leave to head up the mountain and talk trade for cownut liquor."

"You've been tracking us since Port Shamhalhan, then?" Allred interjected.

"Yes," Helga nodded.

"Quiet in the village, was it?" Cole asked.

Cole was a subtle man. Allred was not. His question didn't let on that they had not seen the village on that side of the island, yet.

"We're in the middle of a big nowhere, Cole. I'm guessing you found a big something in the middle of a big nowhere. Otherwise, why would you be here? Port Shamhalhan wasn't so quiet, though, was it? I heard tell of Optri in these southern islands. Could be just rumors."

Was she lying? Making her own gambit? Helga had made her living as a performer. The Rats were the remnants of her troupe, renowned in their own small part of the world. That was before the rebellion and the war came. Now, she was a nervous woman with small scars chipping at her appearance.

"If Optri followed you here and you bring them down on us, there's a toll," Cole said.

This was the danger. The presence of the Rats could lead others to their location.

"I didn't hear it in Shamhalhan. You put stock in those rumors?" he interjected.

He realized he had just told Helga something that she didn't know before. He hadn't heard of Optri in the southern islands. Then he realized something else. *He* hadn't but that didn't mean Cole hadn't.

He grunted. Word games, mind games—leave it to the others. He lit another redleaf and fell quiet. Let these word-players parry and guard and probe.

"Didn't stay around to find out. We set sail after you. When your ship came to port, you left quick. No one was following us. So, no one was following you—that's how I see it."

"Do you see clearly, Helga of the Rats?" Cole asked.

Helga said, smiling, "A Throneland ship burned in port, just after you left. There were two magefire whips onboard and they were stolen. What do you think that's worth Cole?"

"It's worth knowing."

"That's a start," Helga said. "I have other news, which you may find more valuable."

Cole ignored that, "How did you pick us up in Port Shamhalhan?"

"We watched. Disguise is a skill. The dwarves helped. Most everybody looks at a dwarf once, most nobody looks twice."

Cole would let them live. Likely. They were Rats. They were set against the Throne. They all remembered the 9th.

Around them the sounds of the camp became quieter. Stoneburner had finally let the Black Boat men rest.

"Sounds simple," Cole said.

"Nothing is simple, anymore, Cole."

For the first time, she let some of the weariness come through in her voice, just a slight dropping of the mask.

Cole found a flagon and picked up a wooden cup beside the log where he sat. He poured her a portion and handed her the cup. "Tell me your story. It's been some time, since we last met."

So, that was that. No blood. For now.

Helga downed the contents with a swift tip of her head.

"Another then. Fair trade for a tale. Drinking is a habit actors pick up."

Cole poured it from his own skin.

He could make out the first shimmering of stars in the clear night sky and smell the damp wood of the jungle burning atop fresh-lit campfires. Stoneburner came over and placed a small sun on the table, gave Helga a charming grin, then with a surprisingly elegant bow for a man his size, he left.

Over at the main campfire, Aodlen had inserted himself in the middle of the dice throwing with the Green Islanders. He knew as many modes of wager as he did medicines. Scrolls watched them from a distance, the sorcerer beside him. The two boys still toiled over the pots, cooking the campfire soup.

"If I tried to talk to you in Port Shamhalhan, I knew you would either disappear us, or convince me it was foolish to come along—which it might be. So, I figured I would try following you. Not much choice, really," Helga said.

"You've been around hard magic since last we met." Cole said.

It wasn't a question. Allred could smell it on her, feel it on her. It showed on her face and the dwarves, too.

"When last we met, at Cearhardt's castle, I was married to Harad Swift, just after your leave-taking. He joined me in our journeys—out to the Pits. Harad was the close companion of Scroll's eldest brother—Carther Cearhardt. Harad is dead. Carther has disappeared. Out into the wilderness on the far side of the Pits. And that means, Cole, that your scholar is the presumptive heir to the Cearhardt House. And that's the other tidings, I bring."

Cole didn't flinch just puffed his pipe.

Allred remembered both Harad and Carther. Carther was firstborn, in line before Scrolls who was the second son. If he had vanished, it had consequences for the war, since Cearhardt House controlled the pace of the war due to its strategic location.

"I'm sorry about Harad," he said. "A hard thing to lose a husband and a good man, a named man at that."

"Thank you, cousin."

"Scrolls has said nothing of this," Cole said.

"He wouldn't know. Is that worth something, Cole?"

"Could be."

She wasn't a fool. She had survived this long at her business, granted, lacking an eye now, but he'd known smarter men to lose more. He couldn't help admiring her. How Harad the Swift, a noble under the Cearhardt banner could have stooped to marry this common woman, he understood well enough.

She was a performer, yes. And she didn't know what she had just walked into, true. But she remembered the 9th and for that alone, she was a friend in a world where that was hard to come by.

"Tell your story, Helga of the Rats," Cole said.

She stood and projecting her voice as if on a stage, she stared past Cole. "I'll tell the tale of the Rats. Of Harad the Swift I cannot say much. The recollection of the loss brings sorrow. Harad is why I see half now, no less than that. When he lived, the world was true and large and now my sight is wrecked." She was echoing parts from a famous play, he thought. He wasn't really certain but it seemed like she was speaking the lines of some folly but inserting her own names. "Of Carther Cearhardt, I'll relate what I know. It's not much."

"Then welcome to the wine." Cole recited a traditional greeting of friendship. "There's much to do on the isle of Esmer and I'll judge what part you play."

12

Helga of the Rats

Cole sat on a log behind a small makeshift table made from branches, vines and stalks. On the table itself sat a small sun, emanating cool moonlight.

That's a thing that doesn't come cheap, she thought.

In the City of Fountains, the best of the theaters decorated their halls and stages with small suns. She had never seen them, but an acrobat from Mhars had sworn it was so.

Someday, she hoped she could see it for herself.

Finally, found a place to perform with elaborate lighting, she thought.

This was no theater in the City of Fountains. The chatter of royalty wasn't absorbed by the silk and velvet of rich tapestries; no wealthy merchants sat between concubines clinging to their arms. Just her and her Rats on the top of a jungle mountain, in the middle of nowhere, trying to convince a warlord for a chance to fight with them and likely be buried here.

The wine is good though.

They hadn't immediately killed her. She hadn't thought they would or she wouldn't have risked coming, but she had learned in her years performing, it's a step-by-step kind of life for people like her.

"There's much to do on the isle of Esmer and I'll judge what part you play," Cole said.

A woman and an actress learned to sum up a man fast on the road. Cole had learned how to soften the sound of orders over time but only just. She knew well who held her fate in his hands— Cole, the man who led the remnants of the 9th back from the fiery treachery of the Throne. A man whose name had been feared and admired before the Throne turned against him. He survived its fury. She saw the flat obliteration of the flesh on the palms of his hands as he passed his pipe between them when it wasn't clenched between his teeth. She shivered and cultivated a smirk to hide her fear. If he saw through her, which he did—he would understand her, too much. Nonetheless, a mask can be a greater weapon than a sword, but Cole knew all manner of weapon.

Legends had grown up around each of these men. The last time they met, none appeared entirely devoured by madness or blood. The intervening years had taken a toll, that much she saw as soon as she had entered their camp.

"The truth is it was partly luck and partly genius on my own part. The genius of a Rat, may the Gods keep our outfit whole." Helga began and then lowering her voice for effect, "A bit of desperation, too."

Living in the Pits was a hard thing, especially for a troupe of performers made up of Green Island dwarves, her, and her husband, Harad. But that was much later...

The Rats, well-known across half the eastern plains; renowned in their own lands for acts of tumbling, acrobatics, amusements, the popular recitations of great poets, minor feats of contortion, illusions, displays of fire flowers, illuminations and smoke shows—after the rebellion broke out most of those talents became worthless.

Gold poured into the purses of blacksmiths, shipbuilders,

assassins, mages both free-natural and leased, poison-boilers and those who make their antidotes, masons, fletchers, coopers—all those who can turn their peaceful arts easily to the necessities of war grew rich.

Clowns, fools and actors could not so easily convert their talents to coin.

It hadn't taken long after the 9th was betrayed for rebellion to spread. Helga had never seen such a thing; it happened in a slow way. Not all princes and kings declared at once. Some didn't declare at all but played both sides. In the wake of rebellion brought on by the betrayal, the Throne's armies staggered south in pursuit.

Soon, most of the roads were clogged with thieves or soldiers or men plying both trades at the same time.

Their large carriage decorated with a lively painting of a rat sitting upright on its back feet, juggling with small pink hands, a jester's cap atop the furry head; she parked it amid fields not yet burned to ash. In those first weeks of rebellion, there was an awful stillness about, sealed lips as people waited for what would happen next.

She recalled the day they were turned away from their performance on the border town of Aleton. The Throneland guards met them at the gate, looked over their license to perform acts of circus feats and simply didn't hand the license back.

The Thronelanders were still turning away people from the hill kingdoms, with a confused 'you may not enter the city'. The Throne hadn't yet announced the harshest of restrictions against travel on Throne roads. That would change soon enough. As it was, the Rats were turned away but not imprisoned, and now with no license to perform, headed back into what would soon be rebel country.

Early days.

Early but Helga could smell the trouble. Not just burning fields and tumbling walls from the north— that came later.

Coin ran short. Prices for food increased. When she suggested to the Rats they should try their hand sifting through the Pits, all her troupe agreed at first.

Then one by one, when they thought none of their compatriots were watching, they came to her individually or in pairs, asking for their portion of gold and quitting the company. They made good reason; they were not relic hunters but jugglers and poets, they wouldn't go to the Pits with her. Some tried to convince her she shouldn't go either.

That was the way of actors—most evinced loyalty but wouldn't stick. Actors nearly always agreed to your face. She didn't hate them for it. She was one of them.

A couple of the dwarves spoke of heading to the far north to try their luck in the Ruej ports to work the bale mazes, perhaps. Others gave no hint at their plans. Others said, they just wanted to return to their villages, to wait out the war as best they could.

Few could look her in the eyes (at that time she had both) when they demanded their due and went their way. She didn't blame them and wished them luck. Later in her worst moments, in and around the Pits, she would think them the wisest of the Rats.

And so, Helga was left with a handful of holdouts desperate or loyal enough to stay when they set out to the Pits far to the east. At least it was away from the direction of war bearing down from the north.

The journey to the Pits wasn't particularly treacherous. The lands adjoining were still debating war—half didn't believe it was coming. And in time there were fewer and fewer people, sparse villages in quiet land. She even managed to perform with her limited troupe in a few larger villages on the journey for board and bed at small inns. The eastern part of the rebel kingdoms were the quietest.

Finally, their large carriage, pulled by strong horses from her homeland met the land where the hill country rolled flat, and they entered the free city of Aklion, perched on the western side of the never-ending marred landscape known as the Pits.

There Helga and the Rats became relic hunters instead of actors.

"It's a long story, you tell, cousin," Allred said, "What of Scroll's brother?"

She turned to him— "Patience cousin, in the songs they sing of you, you're a quiet man, who prays steadfastly to the Lady."

"Songs are useful like that," Cole said, puffing another ring of smoke into the air.

She saw Allred flinch at Cole's words. He took his little plaque out from a belt below a vest shining with darts and knives. The man looked a living armory. She remembered before he even joined the Ninth, the legend of the boy at the Battle of the Bales and the story of how he earned his name—

"I don't know how much time we have, Helga," Allred said.

"The Lady decides, her head bent to Allwein's ear, no?"

"As you say," he replied and put the plaque away.

"We prospered as well as anyone could expect, I suppose."

Prospered to a degree. The Pits were huge, unruled—a landscape scarred by eruption, cratered, the legends told, by the onslaught of the heavens. Flat plains plunged into tunnels. Ancient trenches revealed fragments of stone monoliths bewitched with leering demons and worse. As far as the eye could see, an arid plain, pitted with labyrinths.

The only settlement of size was Aklion, a town run by and for outlaws and populated by religious fugitives, runaways, criminals, the unclean. The Merchant Houses of Aklion were armed rival bands and rumor and smuggle were the acts of their government. It was a place where brigandage and robbery had been afforded centuries to crystallize into a set of customs and loose laws.

It had some advantages to it.

Around the fringes, on the rim of the Pits a series of old caves in wind worn mountains housed ecstatics, religious orders, armed cults led by warlords and unbonded mages. On occasion, they warred with one another or clashed with those who scavenged the Pits, but no one quite knew why or what they fought over amongst themselves. It was to these people, the eldest Cearhardt would go.

"But that's later, after we met in the Cearhardt lands?"

Allred asked.

"Yes, that first year, I was alone with the Rats."

Her type they called: Pitdiggers, Vultures, Scavengers—all criminals by the Throne's decree, but in the Pits, decrees from the Throne meant less than nothing. Knives decided the law and the Merchant Houses of Aklion judged by steel and coin, alone.

No one knew how large the Pits were exactly and before she saw them, she thought the scale was just part of the legend. Afterwards, she knew the truth—it seemed to go on forever. Land impoverished and cursed by war between the gods, dry mazes piercing the landscape; warrens housing scanty treasure—a land so crazed and sprawling that the few people who braved living there didn't intersect often. There were tales of another people far to the east, but these were stories.

She spent a year in the Pits.

She lost half her band. A few fell to fights, ambushes and the brutal unexpected melees that can occur when groups of scavengers suddenly come face-to-face in the depths of the tunnels. Some died to the Pits themselves; collapsing old arches, landslides, stone worms, sand pits, bad food and poison snakes.

"I'm familiar with the Pits, the cities of Culan and Aklion, so there's no need to elaborate, Helga, but take your time in the telling of the story. It informs my decision," Cole said.

"Decide what, Cole?" Helga asked.

"On how to answer whatever plea, you'll end your tale with," Cole said.

Well, at least he's interested and I can still sell a story. After all this is over, I can return to my art. Become a juggler for a burned down world.

In the Pits, you gathered what you could find of magic and fine things from the lost ages and then you trekked back to Aklion to sell it.

There in the black markets men traded for anything. She saw certain things for sale that she tried to forget. What the town lacked in law, order, wealth, culture, peace, rule, custom, sanitation and good manners it made up for in extraordinary vice and rumors.

In Aklion, the remaining Rats would shelter in a tavern inn, the best inn in Aklion meant only one sentry need be posted to your rooms, instead of two. One night there she heard a song about the Relic Hunters of the 9th. On inquiry to the bard, she was told there was to be a great meeting soon in Cearhardt lands to decide the next phase of the rebellion.

That night, as she nodded off over her wine, the bard's harp sad and warm and the tavern quiet in the late hours, her companions long retired to their good beds, she decided two things—She was very lonely, so she'd better find a man. That was first.

Second, she would set back out from Aklion and to attend the great meeting at Cearhardt Castle.

"Poor places are often rich in songs," Helga said, "That bard had skill. He made me realize important things."

Allred cut her short.

"Can't eat a song though."

"You can, cousin," Helga replied.

"Poet talk."

Cole cleared his throat, "So, you set out to Cearhardt Castle. I remember you and the Rats from the great meeting."

"That's so. And that's where I met, Harad."

"He followed you into the Pits," Cole said.

"Let me sing my song. I'll tell you of what the bard sang of you, first."

Cole nodded his assent.

Speak of songs. If you cannot sing, you can tell. That night the bard sang in Aklion.

He sang of Cole the mastermind, unjustly exiled and betrayed, exacting vengeance on an unjust throne by delving into the most terrifying Haunts.

They sang of brave Allred, horse rider, dealer of death in darkness, close companion of Cole.

They sang of wise-scholar Scrolls, son of the brave march lord Cearhardt and his holdout house, the greatest mind of the university of Mhars.

They sang of the most famous battlemage in the Thronelands, a name to exceed even the likes of Eion the Just—the shimmering cloaked, bronze face, the crooked-hand, Mage of the 9th.

The rebel bard sang even of Stoneburner and the twin Giants of the Green Island with their shields heavy with victorious names.

"What about me?" Aodlen asked.

He had come over and joined them, fidgeting with his playing cards, listening to her story. She could still draw an audience.

Helga shook her head, sadly, "I don't recall you figuring into the songs."

"Absurd! Ha! Travesty. I'll have a word with Stoneburner. I'll have two words," Aodlen said.

"Aye, you should. What was your name?" she asked, wide-eyed and innocent.

"A travesty! I'll hear no more" Aodlen laughed and stalked off to gamble more with the dwarves and giants who mocked his losses and welcomed him to their fire.

"How did you get here, Helga?" Allred asked.

"I'm getting to that."

She looked to Cole who said nothing. The lines around his eyes gave away no feeling, no indication of her fate.

The Great Meeting lasted weeks. All the nobles in rebellion attended. There were feasts and a spirit of goodwill—hope that the Throne could be stopped, and a truce made. She met Harad the Swift at a dance within the castle, which she had managed to gain entrance to by performing.

"You were there, cousin."

"Aye, but I'm not much for dancing. I remember you on the stage, in one of the castle's great halls during a feast. I remember your beauty. It was talked about, a scandal of the court—the jester-girl, a rude woman from the middle of nowhere, rumored a scavenger of the Pits, a common juggler who stole the gaze of Harad the Swift."

"People say such mean things," she laughed.

"You're right. It's woman-talk. Court talk. Useless," Allred said, "But I recall it, still."

"We spoke."

Cole cleared his throat, tapped the bowl of his pipe on the makeshift table, spilling ash and watched it blow away in a little rapid of wind.

"Your recitation of the poets that night stirred hearts, Helga. We left the Great Meeting before you and Harad," Cole said.

"You did."

Harad sat his own swift horse and rode out beside her and the last of the Rats to brave the Pits together. She sat behind him on his stallion, holding his waist. The carriage was driven by a Green Island dwarf with a scar on his face and rattled along in front of them, giving the two lovers some distance to ride together in the dark.

As they left the castle, behind her a figure stood in the morning dawn atop a short tower at the main gate, leaning against a crenellation. Harad's greatest friend, Carther Cearhardt waved farewell and watched them take their leave.

"I think Carther wished to follow his friend and his friend's new wife to adventure. No matter to him that I was a Rat and a commoner. He stayed. I still see him on the broad battlements in the grey morning, waving to us. Carther is a strange man, a good man and now he is somewhere east of the Pits."

"East of the Pits is nowhere," Allred said.

"Well, that came later, Carther's disappearance."

"You went back with your husband Harad," Cole prodded.

"Yes," she paused.

Why did we go back? Her pride, she thought.

Harad was a noble. He had money and land and a

reputation for valor. True, his joining with her might cause controversy, gossip and a drop in station for him but it would have passed.

No, he was leaving the war by leaving with her in a way. She was taking the prize with her, Harad the Swift, an honorable man willing to leave a land in strife for her.

"Why not just stay. Be his wife?" Allred asked.

"If we stayed, he was Harad the Swift, greatest companion of the heir to the house of Cearhardt. If he adventured with me, he would truly be mine. It sounds wicked but it's true. I would have stayed if he wanted to. The truth is he wanted to depart, not from cowardice, though, not from the war but he wanted to leave something behind. What that was, I never found out. I like to think he wanted to see what I'd seen because he loved me."

They continued their work in the Pits. With Harad by her side, the enemies they met fled or fell. They grew their treasure together and began to build their own wealth. She loved him. He loved her and that made the days speed by and every hour feel a blessing. In love, the scarred landscape even looked peaceful, solemn and calm. All the demons made sense, in his arms at night. Harad took lead of the Rats. They prospered.

And then, Harad the Swift fell.

That was all.

She wouldn't speak of that story.

"I mourn your loss, cousin," Allred said.

Cole smoked, nodded.

"Fortune," she whispered, then brightening quickly she wore a smile too strong for the moment, "Now, why am I'm here..."

When my husband's best companion arrived and found us, he wept by Harad's grave for three nights though he had been buried some time before. I would go and watch him from a distance. His rich cloak, emblazoned with the seals and symbols of his house shook on his shoulders. Night and day, he kneeled. I had done the same. I watched and felt jealousy at his mourning, as if my husband's grave should be only for me and then I repented of the thought and left the good man in his mourning.

One morning, I awoke, and he was gone. There was a purse with some gold, he left for us and a small note which one of my dwarves read. It said not to follow him. It said he was heading farther east, alone, to seek something he wished to find and something he thought could help the House of Cearhardt in the war.

His tracks led off far to the east, that much I can confirm. I saw them before the wind had covered them.

We followed. I became obsessed with finding him. I needed to talk to him, of Harad, of his plans, of anything. I needed some last word with the man, though I didn't know him well. But he was my love's best friend and had known him for more years than I had.

It became my obsession and in the obsession my pain subsided. But after some days, the Rats took hold of me. We neared dangerous lands. They convinced me to go back to Cearhardt Castle and tell his father of what I had seen.

So, I did.

And Scroll's father asked me to find you and to tell his son that his brother is gone.

The King of Cearhardt Castle sends his good greetings, Cole.

"Your message has been delivered," Cole said, "And now what?"

"Now, I ask to join your next venture," Helga said, "Into the Haunt."

Allred said, "Not that."

The warrior put a hand over her own. She shook it off.

"First, how did you find us?"

Cearhardt gave me a paper to hand to a man in Port Coldewater. That was a man named Ghad-Ahl. Coldewater had fallen to the Throne so even carrying the paper from Cearhardt was a danger.

Ghad-Ahl read the paper quietly at his writing table, in his room, near the harbor in Coldewater. Finished, he put his head in his hand for a moment, then reaching up touched the edge of the paper to the flickering taper and looked up at me and said, "Port Shamhalhan," then ushered me out.

"My magnificent carriage remains there. Someday, I'll be going back to retrieve it," she said.

"And in Port Shamhalhan you found us?" Cole asked.

"We did. When we arrived, we walked the city, making inquiries here and there," Helga said.

They had walked the docks and eventually traced Cole and the others. They waited. They watched. Then one day Helga saw entering the port, the large ship carrying the Black Boat men and followed Cole to it.

"We followed you south. We spent our last coin from Cearhardt on the fishing ship, supplies and a few other necessities," Helga said.

"Why not tell me of Scroll's brother in Shamhalhan?" Cole asked.

"Because my husband is dead. I'm an out of work leader of a defunct troupe of dwarves in the middle of a war and I need something else. The Rats, they need something else. I want to join you in the Haunt. If I let my presence be known in Port Shamhalhan, you wouldn't allow me here."

"You're not inept," Cole said, turning to face Allred.

"She doesn't know what she's saying, Cole." Allred turned to her. She could see he was angry. "You don't know what you're saying. The Haunts harrow the spirit."

She ignored Allred with a smile and turned to Cole.

"You saw us. Our fishing boat is like any of the others plying the waters in the south. Our boat is much smaller than yours, at a distance it's easier to see you than the reverse. We used the magemask procured from Shamhalhan's mage-market—I admit, we lost sight of you a few times. Asked the Gods. Took a chance. If all else failed...well, what? Now, here we are."

Cole folded his hands. She remembered who he was, the ugly stories told in whispers at the Great Meeting, the stories not found in the songs.

He had been dedicated to the Throne, the Throne's greatest soldier. It was his greatness which led to his betrayal. That was what the legend was anyway. Rumors built legends though and some of those differed. Some of those were not as kind to Cole. Some said that he found such success in the Haunts because he was more terrifying than the creatures who existed within them.

"You've never been inside a true Haunt?" Cole asked it as a question out of politeness, she knew. He knew she had not. He looked right through her and it didn't make her happy at all.

"The Pits only."

"You understand why the easiest thing for me to do, is the worst thing for you?"

"Optri. Thronelanders. Even another rival relic hunting group—if they found us, then we could lead them to you. But put aside and forget my own tale of woe. I know you can. The war goes poorly for our side. You must know it. Cities and castles falling. There's less and less of us. And now, the heir to Cearhardt lands is on this island if Carther isn't found."

"Did Cearhardt say something else?" Allred asked, suspicion on his face.

"He wants you to return and help him find his son. If not, he wants you to return Scrolls."

Cole lit his pipe. It had gone out in the telling of her tale.

"I see," Cole said.

"We learned a lot in the Pits," she started in again, afraid that the demand of Cearhardt had not suited Cole.

"Cousin, what you faced in the Pits, I swear to you, it's nothing like the Haunts."

She didn't answer Allred. She just stared ahead at Cole.

Cole arrived at a decision, though his face betrayed little emotion. She thought his face would be the same, if he decided instead to cut her throat and all the Rats and shove them into one of the ditches they were digging for some reason up here.

"You can be of use, under my command. Some percentage of what we gain, you'll have. I'll speak to Scrolls of what you said. You will not. You will not say another word about his brother to anyone else. But, a fair warning Helga of the Rats, your cousin speaks true—the Pits are no Haunt. It's likely most of you die here."

She already knew that possibility.

"It's understood."

"No, cousin, consider carefully," Allred replied, "You don't understand."

"I accept your terms, Cole," she said, ignoring Allred.

Cole tapped the ash from his pipe, "Take the night to think. Tomorrow, decide for sure. Regardless, you're here now. You can't leave now until *we* leave Esmer. I'll see you paid handsomely for the message-bringing if you choose not to descend."

It was a better deal than a shove off a cliff.

"I've made up my mind."

The stage was set, the acts to commence, the play to begin in earnest.

Interlude

Scrolls

An exhaustive history of the origins of the Haunts is outside the scope of my current attempt to put down in writing a true and definitive account of the Relic Hunters of the 9th.

However, events have changed this evening. We find ourselves contacted by an amateur band of clowns, led by a one-eyed hill woman of considerable beauty with empty purse and news of my brother. While devoted to the cause of the 9th they have no experience with exploring Haunts. Cole has decided to employ them. They will likely perish.

Now, let me return to the subject of the Haunts.

There is a wide vocabulary employed by those who hunt relics. We call the most dangerous and richest places Haunts.

They differ from what we call Sites, which is a broad term covering everything from archaeological areas, old temples, sacred groves and more. As with all things in this world, the task of classification and speech—the tool we use to construct classification, varies.

It has been noted concerning activities in the domain of the obscure that artisans breed their own vocabulary. Arcane disciplines require arcane words to further those disciplines.

So, to a peasant a Haunt or a Site might simply appear as a place which is "bad" or "dangerous". This is a simple wisdom which keeps these peoples safe from dangers which they cannot fathom.

The Rats now wish to join us in an exploration of a Haunt. They know nothing of the different types of Haunts. They likely have heard of Downside Fever and Upside Fever, Quakenings, Spirit-Filth—the list of words to describe how the Haunts assail not just the body, but the spirit of mortal men is long and varied—but they know little of it in reality.

In the city of Fountains there exists a book by Cryfuss (May the God of Wisdom protect him) wherein he traced the words denoting these places back centuries and the states of being which accompany their exploration. He traced various languages of men from many nations. And in the days well before Cryfuss wrote his expositions on the places we call Haunts (which he termed, Under-Places), a more practical people, the earliest explorers of Haunts devised meditations, prayers and medicine to ward away the dangers to the spirit for those who descend. Cryfuss preserved these works, used the scattered writings and preservations of them as the basis for his study of etymology.

The Rats know nothing of these matters. Have they read of the attrition rates of relic hunters of the past which are catalogued? Those tables should warn away anyone. I have read them, the Tables of Semhelhen. The book begins with this epigraph:

Halve and halve again, those who descend. Halve and halve again, those who ascend.

Cole decides. However, I must speak to this Helga, or perhaps Allred shall convince her and her dwarves not to accompany us past the gate.

And though I am a man devoted to words—what they can convey, what they can teach; I know myself—words cannot prepare them.

I should speak to her, but I write instead.
Cole told me about my brother.
I should speak to her.

13

Allred

Cole stood up, offered his hand to Helga and she grasped it. The news spread; the Rats would join the expedition.

Hartha and Hortha blinked, and both gave a hearty cheer, raising their flagons. Aodlen jumped like lightning hit him and unleashed a long, unnerving string of laughter. Scrolls stood, put his stylus down and gave Helga a look, quiet and frustrated, and gathering his parchments walked away. Mage was still sleeping beneath the trees. Stoneburner just muttered something like, "well, well." The two boys stared big-eyed around the fire. The donkey wore the usual expression on its face and the Black Boat men finally slept.

Helga stood and put both hands on her hips, looking victorious. There were scars on her knuckles and arms. Her arms were heavier with them than last time he had met her.

"You have anything to say, cousin?" she said, turning to him.

"Cole decides," he shrugged.

"Your bronzeface is nearby. Still alive. I feel him. Bodes well for our chances."

"He lives. In a fashion."

"And those two big Green Islanders—just like in the songs. My dwarves will get along well with them. Don't know how you hide yourselves as you travel with such a strange lot. You must have skills in disguise like us."

"A true spoken thing, cousin," he said, falling into the tones of the hills, their homeland.

She smiled.

"And you cousin." She walked closer to him, bent down, stared him in the eye as if inspecting the teeth of a yearling. "Still alive. Not sad to see it but a little surprised."

"Same."

She stood straight again, looked off at the camp.

"I know you think I've done a reckless thing," she said, a note of sadness in her voice, quickly covered. "You've found this Haunt, yet?"

He wasn't sure what he should say. Inside, he was still thinking of ways to convince her to walk away from this and then alternatively, to simply stop caring. Better the latter.

"Got eyes on it."

"You've seen it then?"

"The outlines. Dhlams, demons already came at us hard several times. This clearing is behind an old barrier, tell your people not to wander out of it. And, yes, you've done a reckless thing, cousin."

"I'm out of gold and down a husband."

"You loved him."

"I did, but it was a short season."

"Better than nothing."

"Maybe."

He lit a redleaf. She tried to snatch it from his fingers, and he pulled it away. "Not this one." He lit another for her. She eyed him suspiciously.

"If Cole doubted your loyalty to the 9th, you would be dead. I don't think you know what you've talked yourself into, that's all."

She puffed at the redleaf. Coughed a plume of smoke out. Her eye watered.

"We aren't just actors and acrobats. Not anymore. We've survived rough country, rough roads. It's bad in the home country. You've been gone a long time."

"You already convinced the man that counts. Don't waste your breath on me," he said.

"Truespoke."

He wasn't certain he had the spirit to try to stop her. He knew he should. The Rats were not warriors, he could see that. Survivors, maybe, but not ready for a Haunt. Beaten-up dwarves led by a widow with one eye.

The Rats loitered around pretending not to stare at Cole and the other named men of the camp. He shook his head. Lost.

Helga stopped with her haughtiness for a moment, looked troubled, "You're worried?"

He thought about that. He knew what the word meant but a lifetime of war had burned it out of him, like ash growing damp in the rain after a fire is extinguished.

"Not quite. Not anymore."

She looked to answer then bit her lip and said nothing.

Cole came back to the little table in the dark with Stoneburner in tow.

"He'll help you with camp. Be ready at dawn to move," Cole said.

"I'll show you what's where, Helga," Stoneburner said. She followed him, as she beckoned to the Rats who stood huddled around a small campfire.

He stayed and said nothing. He could feel Cole's eyes boring into him. Scrolls had followed Cole back to the table and was writing again.

"Say what you want," Cole finally spoke.

"You told him?" he nodded to where Scrolls sat.

"Yes."

"And?" Allred said.

Scrolls looked up, "And? My elder brother deserted his

station, deserted our father, deserted the men he led. Now he is lost beyond the Pitlands. That's what I understand. Have you other information to shed light on the situation?"

"Your brother is lost," Allred said.

"Yes, I just suggested that's what I understood. And my father paid Helga to bring this message to me. To us." Scrolls said, looking at Cole. He was digging the tip of the stylus into the parchment, his fist clenched around it, white-knuckled. There was venom beneath the coolness in his voice.

"Well, I'm sorry, that's all," he said, and let it go.

"You had no role that I'm aware of in the disappearance of my elder brother, so I've no need for your sorrow."

"Enough," Cole said, interrupting them, "The Haunt."

"They aren't prepared to walk a Haunt."

"Truespoke. No one is the first time."

"So, she ought not to," he said. Seemed obvious to him.

Cole watched him for a while, then said, "Tell her this. When you finish, tell the boy who wants to be a knight what it's like to ride full tilt towards a line of pikemen. Tell them all the truth."

Allred grunted.

Cole stared at him with hooded eyes in the small sun's light, "People find out what they need to in their own way. No amount of telling them the truth beforehand makes any difference."

"If she led Optri here, it's a problem."

"Won't be changed now. Time isn't on our side. Never is. Lost how many Black Boat men on the beach? We can use the extra hands and the extra packs. The Rats offered themselves for a price. I'll pay them fair."

The image of the Haunt in the distance across that valley passed through Allred's mind. They *would* need more people.

"Heard," Allred said. "I'm going to sleep unless I'm on watch."

"Watch is covered," Cole said and looked up at him. "Convince Helga if you can. We have enough gold. She's for the 9th and she fulfilled her courier appointment. We'll see her paid. My word runs on that."

Cole would do it. If he convinced Helga, Cole would help

her, even without her doing anything else. The Rats would stay close until they walked the Haunt. Cole would tell Stoneburner to distribute them gold back in Port Shamhalhan, or wherever they ended up next.

He shook his head, "She won't listen. I know her because I know my people. You do, too. Stubborn," he said.

"Go sleep."

He got up and without another look back, ascended the tower and went to sleep.

His eyes snapped open. His palm clenched on the handle of his dagger. The sun hadn't yet risen. He'd slept but it was brief and empty.

He started counting heads.

Scrolls was awake, on guard, sitting on the log near the table. Cole, slept on the ground beside him. Scrolls nodded to him and then returned to pouring over his parchments in the lambent glow of the small sun.

Around the campfire of the Relic Hunters, he counted. And those who were not there he counted, awake, at prayers to their gods, alone, in fellowship or still asleep.

Among his brothers of the 9th, nine. Eight, on the mountain. Glume below.

Less the fallen; counted no more among them—bodies abandoned in ice, frozen waiting on the thaw. In warmer climes, compatriots, mummified, sand-swept faces, skin stretched thin over once familiar bones—less the fallen. Now, there were nine left, the marching men who avoided swift pyres and shallow graves.

There was evil ahead. No time to think on those names now. He gestured with his hand away from his face—dispelling the ghosts and the names he honored in his private prayers.

So, nine remained. What of it?

He stepped along the top of the narrow trench where the Black Boat men slept. Some lay within the trench itself, others around the lip of it. A couple of the men were awake and talked in low voices. They saw him, then bowing their heads ceased talking, or lowered their voice to whispers.

He counted.

They had started with thirty Black Boat men, released from the dungeons of Port Coldewater, led to redemption on Glume's Black Boat. One man, he had jettisoned overboard only a mile from shore, so his redemption was cut short. That left twenty-nine criminals onboard, all convinced of the sure discipline of the ship's captain.

They had lost ten at the beach to the Dhlams. Nineteen. Prior to it, Glume took the head of another. Eighteen had marched up from the beach below.

He counted heads. This he had done before every battle and after. It made him calm. He lit a redleaf. Felt the sharp smoke, shake the last blurriness of sleep away and the mystical tang and whine of Aodlen's added magic which was his lot.

Circling back around the clearing, he came upon the Rats. One of their dwarves waived. He waived back. Good. Helga had posted her sentry.

Seven Rats total including Helga—two in the village, posing as fisherfolk meant five had marched to the top of the island of Esmer.

Seven Rats remained. Two pairs of dwarves, Green Islanders.

Above him, in the tower the two boys were still sleeping on the opposite side of the small room, where he had just left. Some sharp pang in his side made him exhale the redleaf smoke in a puff—war had hardened his heart, but he didn't want to see the boys in the sure hell ahead.

My head and heart are crowded places, these days, he thought.

Two boys remained.

And the donkey.

So, here. Now: eight Relic Hunters, five Rats, eighteen Black Boat men. Two boys and a donkey.

Call it thirty-three.

Stoneburner coaxed the campfire with a stick, and he could smell the big pot of Kler tea boiling.

How many would survive, Esmer?

146

Less than that.

Stoneburner handed him a cup, without taking his eyes off the ground. He felt the brew clean the memories that haunted him in the early dawn light. The brimming-over of too many deaths and memories of the fallen. He felt it as pain in his body.

The tea revived him. He walked out the stiffness in his leg in small circles, puffing away at his redleaf.

Cole was up. Orders of the day began to circulate around the morning fires. Today, they would touch the Haunt if all went well. Ten of the Black Boat men would remain at the base camp to guard it. All the Rats would accompany them. The two boys and the donkey would stay at the camp with Stoneburner.

Mage would walk with them today. And he would be scouting point.

A risk to divide the forces. If anyone had trailed the Rats, they would appear soon enough.

The two boys climbed down from the watch tower. He overheard Lookout plead once to go with the group and Cole silencing him with a flat, "no". Stoneburner took charge of both boys, scolding them for sleeping too long and set them to the task of spooning out porridge for the marching men's breakfast.

The boy has some bravery, or he's simply ignorant, he thought.

The two often were interchangeable.

He brushed away the offer of a bowl of porridge. Didn't feel like eating.

The men assembled. Cole formed a loose line out of them. Allred took his position in front, crossbow out.

The air was cool. No rain. Birdsong met the dawn. Animals bounding through the treetops mixed with the jangle of men shifting the weight of packs. The sun was on the sea behind the mountain.

It was a good day to find another damnation.

Cole had carefully distributed a few better weapons to the Black Boat men but kept the bows in the hands of the 9th and a couple of Rats. The Black Boat men would mostly carry picks and spades instead.

"Walk quietly. Follow. Touch nothing. Say nothing. We're bound for haunted lands," Cole said.

The men remaining in camp, watched, wary and wondering if they were safer left behind or missing out on first plunder. A wave of unease and excitement worked down the line when Cole gestured him forward.

It didn't take long to reach the top of the hill where they had stopped the day before. He halted the line, knowing they would stumble and stop at the sight of the Haunt.

Everyone stood staring at the valley below and the ascent across it. Even the dullest of them could see they were looking at some great buried structure in the distance incorporated into the peak of the mountain itself.

Hard men's eyes filled with fear.

Cole made his way up the line.

"We can cross this valley by mid-day. Expect resistance. Fast but you set the pace," Cole said.

There wasn't much more to say. Find the Haunt. Then find the gate. Down and come out again if the Lady willed it.

He headed down the slope of the hill into the valley. For some time, the trees and jungle leaned away from the road as if grasped by an unseen force, treetops tipped towards the barrows hidden deeper within. He could see sky above him. Soon, the jungle closed in tighter. The canopy darkened the sun.

No Dhlams. Nothing.

The only sounds were the footsteps of the men behind on the road.

Bright-feathered birds watched them from the tops of trees. He thought their proximity to the magic of the place added a knowing gleam to their gaze. Beside the path butterflies flickered, yellow and pale green, dancing in pairs among the ferns. Then behind him one of the Black Boat men shouted, "Treasure!"

One of the Black Boat men had spotted what he thought was a golden vessel just off the trail and ran to seize it. Allred noticed it now, too, though its form was already fading. A mistake.

"No! Hold," Cole shouted.

It was too late. The man came back to the road, holding aloft nothing in his hands as if displaying a great prize and the other men began to move towards him in confusion. Then a crashing of limbs and the rush of leaves above him and the barrow trap unfolded.

He looked up just before they struck him, a mass of ghostly vipers fell upon him, wriggling in an ancient death dance, preserved by some ancient magetrick. They dripped down from the trees.

The line panicked. Men crouched. Shovels clattered to the road. Some men lay on the path and looked up, covering their heads. Useless.

The grey serpents swarmed over the man. Hissing fangs speared his flesh. And then as if on silent command, while the man frantically slapped at himself; they slithered down from his body in a sinuous wave and fled into the green beside the trail, disappearing.

He didn't move. All the Relic Hunters kept their feet, watched with practiced eyes of stone.

So, seventeen.

Cole jogged up to Scrolls. A sob escaped from one of the Rats in the line. It was followed by quiet curses.

The Black Boat man still stood there alone in the middle of the ruin of the ancient road. His face swelling, unable to scream from his bulging throat.

Cole walked up to him. Aodlen followed. Curses quietened. A hush fell over them all. Unfortunate. In the quiet, they could all hear the man's eyes exploding from the pressure of the old poison within. The sound would visit him later in sleep. He checked the rest of the trees above him. Just branches swaying in the breeze.

The man tried to say something to Cole, but his tongue filled his mouth. He fell to the ground and lay still.

Cole kept his hand up in a fist, the gesture for halt. Aodlen began to approach the corpse, but Cole shook his hand again. Aodlen drew back just when the corpse began to shake and twist on the cobblestone of the old Semhelhen road.

The body writhed, propelled by internal forces. Bone

snapped and from the swollen blood-wet lips, an alien voice uttered curses in an ancient tongue. Only one sentence, repeated over and over.

Back in the line, Scrolls cocked his head and listened.

At the sound of the voice, all the birds in the trees took flight in a hurry of wings. Limbs creaked in the sudden branches unbowing. The fowl disappeared into the sky. Someone retched and vomited. Another Rat cried out. Helga's shaking voice silenced him, saying, *still, steady*.

The corpse stopped talking. It stared hollow and as if finishing a prayer and sticking out its tongue, slowly bit through the muscle. The tongue fell wiggling on the trail. The thing lurched to its feet and lunged at Cole.

Cole kept his hand high. He didn't blink—simply stepped aside. In one motion, he drew the mighty broadsword from his back and stuck the thing, pinning it at a distance. Hortha bounded forward in two great strides and beheaded the creature with his axe. Then swung. And swung again, chopping the thing to pieces.

There was a rustling amongst the line. Cole moved back through them, steadying them with his gaze keeping the line solid. Hard men stood. They said little and brushed the dust from their trousers. Cole conferred with Mage. The cloak tilted in some affirmation; he couldn't hear from the front of the line.

"He failed to listen," Cole said, then motioned him forward and that was all.

Spirits possessed the areas around them, strange omens from the natural world warned away interlopers and men's minds suddenly fragmented. That was expected as they neared the Haunt.

In the morning, he had seen to it that Scrolls spoke to Helga while they breakfasted to explain such things. He had watched her listen and nod to Scrolls. Then she turned to where he watched her, morning sun lighting her hair and playing around the smile on her face and she pat the scholar's leg, dismissing him, never breaking her gaze from Allred's own.

That had been a couple of hours ago, back in the safety of a camp that welcomed her. Now he could see on all their faces, Rats and Black Boat men alike, that they finally understood something of what they were marching into.

Soon enough the trees thinned out again, the road widened and there was open sky above. In that circle of blue the birds circling overhead sang to one another.

They made the valley in good time. Soon enough, they faced rock stairs cut into the last steep incline of the mountain.

The old stone steps were worn, covered in grass shooting up through breaks in the rock. Slick blankets of curly mosses and lichens coated the stone in streaks where rivulets of water ran.

"One can see the marks of the flint axes these people employed to carve the steps," Scrolls said as he squatted down to get a closer look.

"Yeah," he said.

"Indeed," Scrolls answered, rising, "Expect more Upside Bleed. Tricks of the spirit such as the crude incident with the vipers behind us. I should have liked to study the corpse. I have a theory that chance is not what it seems in proximity to the Haunt."

The closer you came to the gate, the beginnings of the horrors inside manifested and intensified. Wild, untamed spirits troubled the land. No Dhlams, yet. He hoped he had drawn the bulk of them out down the trail and on the beach.

He lit a redleaf, waited, crossbow tucked in the crook of his forearm, while Cole and Scrolls conferred. He made his own observations.

It was going to be a climb. The first real physical challenge they had dealt with on Esmer—one of the most geographically tame locales compared to their past expeditions. Didn't look to need ropes, from down here at the bottom of the steps, but squinting through the redleaf smoke, his head tilted back, he couldn't tell how steep it would get where the road disappeared around the midpoint of the mountain above.

He drew in the redleaf smoke, looked with forward eyes. One bad step could turn into a fall. To the left of the stairs, the mountain plunged straight down deeper where the land fell away. To the right of the stairs, the ground tumbled back down the incline of the Haunt face itself. Small, gnarled trees lined the right side of the steps. Could be useful farther up for handholds.

Cole said, "Straight ahead.

"Move them slow. Steps will be slick," he replied.

He moved one step at a time. Up. There was a lot of space between each, and it was easier to bend forward and half crab-crawl up.

Confirming his own foot placement each time, he touched the stone with the back of his hand to get the feel of the ground. Years of scouting taught him to use the part of his hand less calloused to sense the difference in ground.

If Dhlams attacked, they would have to stand and fight. No retreat. If there was trouble this would favor the enemy, especially an enemy who had no regard or even sense of their own life.

He stopped, signaled for Cole to come up towards him. Cole took the steps like a mountain goat, steady and sure and rested on one of the stones. He leaned in to hear what Allred wanted to say.

"If Dhlams come at us, we die here," he said.

"A light feint will rattle the Rats and others. If they come, Mage will bring fire."

"Heard." He started to climb again. Maybe halfway up now.

Ricocheting off the stone step in front of him a shout. He turned slowly to look. No sudden movements. The steps were narrow now, and one wrong step meant falling.

A Black Boat man pitched backwards below. The man behind dodged his plummeting weight but tumbled down a few steps. The falling man scrambled with fingers that could not find purchase on the rock and the void swallowed him. There was a rapid flurry of sound, the weight of a body rushing through leaves, then the deeper sound of limbs small at first and then larger cracking and then nothing.

Cole was talking to the line straggled out across the cliff face stairs but he couldn't make out the words. He figured it boiled down to—that man is dead, watch your step.

Cole motioned him forward. He kept climbing.

Sixteen.

The steps grew taller and more difficult near the peak. It would be easier going up than down.

If there's a back down *to be had for any of us.*

Cole shouted, "Go low! Hug the ground!" and he felt a shiver run through the bottom of his boots, up his back and end in cold fear in his skull.

He sat flat and fast then turned on the slick step. He saw the line crouching in the distance, hugging the stone face.

Below in the valley, a flock of birds took wing. They began to carve patterns in the air. He watched them, turning sharp in swarm, tracing signs and symbols in the air, that he knew Scrolls and Mage could probably interpret.

He aimed his crossbow as the creatures finished their aery script and dove towards them.

He breathed in. Waited. As they came closer, he saw they were small emerald-bodied things with wings the color of baked bricks. They turned and didn't harry the climbers but settled on the cliff face beside him—old dust and jade and a turning to stare at the intruders.

He waited and watched.

There were hundreds all preening and sharp and sudden. One bird differed from the rest. A small replica of the face of the Black Boat man who had fell below stared back at him with empty eyes perched on top of the bird's body. The rest of the birds began to peck at the grass, paying no attention to the spirit-infested bird which spoke:

"I see a young boy in the hills beneath a blood-wet blade. Son of Aehdor, Caelhy—."

The crossbow dart hit the creature square in the body carrying it off and away down the hill. The other birds fluttered and then took flight, melding back into the canopy of the jungle valley below.

Allred reached for another dart, reloaded his crossbow.

"Problem?" Cole called out below.

"Good," Allred shouted back. His voice sounded ragged, so he gulped back that feeling and said again, "Good. Moving."

Regaining his footing, putting away from his mind the treacherous ways of the reflected dead, the thralls to the Haunt, he resumed his climb.

They wait for the soujourner,
with memories,
in the halls of the dead,
bereft of sleep,
solitude quakes in circles of century,
the driving gyre,
to bring the brave minds
to ruinous deep.

Who had written those lines? Helga or Scrolls would know. He couldn't recall the poet.

His fingers clung to rock. He dug each boot into the moss on the rock before propelling himself farther. Kept his eyes ahead. Waited for death.

Soon the ascent ended at the top of the cliff in three small steps. The road turned sharply to the right, hugging the face of the Haunt and the mountain itself. Up here it was broad and level. He felt the relief of a climber who is admitted to less treacherous ground.

To the left, some trees filled the edge, then the same plunge down the cliff which made the stairs so treacherous.

The rest of the line managed the top without incident. He gestured them forward to keep them from bunching up at the top of the ascent as each climber stood relieved and hesitant.

He glanced once more to the left of the stairs where the road ran out. No way out that side, except back down the steps. He moved a little farther down the road, waiting for the group to assemble.

Cole stood at the top of the steps, herding the ones who paused at the top, their heads inclined staring up at the sheer rock of the mountain which hid the Haunt.

He kept moving down the road ahead of the others. Needed space if they were rushed. Would be a bad spot to get caught up in a fight with the stairs and the cliff at their back.

As he moved forward and took it in, he could see how the long path they had walked all the way down from the beach revealed its true nature here. He was staring at a ceremonial road which he knew in his bones had been used for processions long ago.

To one side of the road, more cliff falling down the mountain into an unknown valley. He went to the edge and saw it was less steep here but still deadly. On the other side of the road was the face of the Haunt itself, the last of the mountain towering above the peek perhaps impossible to reach from here. The road was straight for a long while but he could make out a slight bend to the right as it wrapped around the mountain.

Cole joined him. He had his broadsword out again.

"Forward, slow."

The road cut along the mountain and he followed it. The rest not far behind him. The sun shone on his armor and the air was thin and sweet as if the nectar from the jungle flowers swirled to nest near this peak. Sweat trickled down his forehead and leaping over the ridge of his nose fell onto his upper lip where it tasted sour.

The road ended in a slight expansion and broadening out of the mountain road.

It looked clear to him where the ancients had positioned the gate, at the end of this processional road. That would make things easier.

He waived them all forward and Cole and Scrolls joined him.

"Here it is," Scrolls said.

Cole wasted no time. He set everyone to digging into the dirt and rock that covered the face of the Haunt, searching for outlines of the gate.

"The Key sings," Mage said.

"Take a few men down further with you. Scout it out," Cole told him.

He gestured to a couple of Black Boat men who were staring at the face of the mountain, picks in hand, unmoving and said, "Follow me."

To his right the face of the Haunt remained uniform, a mass of dirt-covered stone with patches of vegetation growing in the dips and irregularities.

To the left more of the same drop down. He walked close to the cliff edge past the brush. The descent, a little gentler here in places. It wasn't a sheer drop down but would be impossible to navigate without rope. There was another valley below. He could see the tops of trees growing from the slopes of the cliff.

The gorge was good for them in some ways, no reason to worry about an attack from there. No way to run either.

The cobbles ran out. A few flung by age and wind slept in the tall grass and reeds but a game trail took its place and widened more and more. The face of the Haunt on his right finally dropped down and met the ground. The trail switched back hard to the right and then scaled the mountain peak in a sharp incline disappearing in brush leading to the top of the peak.

Just before that, where he stood with the uneasy Black Boat men, there was a small mountain watering hole with a few remnants of bricks around it. He watched for a long time. The only motions were the tiny flurries of life around a living water, frogs and lizards and insects too small to be given names.

"Nothing here," one of the men said.

"Quiet."

They watched. Nothing stirred. No movement. He approached the edge of the water. His boots sunk in the mud. He bent down, cupped some water in his hand, smelled it and took a small sip, then flinging the rest from his palm, stood.

"Can drink it if we have to," he turned the men back.

Halfway back to where the rest were digging, he left the two with orders to watch the trail they had just explored.

The dirt was falling away fast beneath pick and shovel and covered the ancient road as the men worked to expose what they had come far to find. Cole stood back some distance, close to the cliff's edge, leaning against a scrawny tree, arms folded, watching. He had allowed himself his pipe.

"The road ends in some water, might be a spring. The Haunt face drops off down there. A game trail leads up higher, maybe. Looks quiet. Nothing else. This cliff face runs all along it. Only way down is the way we came up looks like."

"Good," Cole said, not turning his eyes from the face of the

Haunt.

There was just the hint of some desire in Cole's eyes and it bothered him. It wasn't greed. It wasn't satisfaction that they had discovered this hidden place. It was the look of a man in love with the thing which destroyed him, knowing that it destroyed him and loving it more for it. Worse than that though, because that was at least a human thing—he'd seen that look in the eyes of beggars in thrall to wine when they lingered over the first bottle of the day before drinking--no, worse, the look in Cole's eyes promised to supersede even this, to devour his own destruction and then turn that power to the world.

He looked away from him and squinted at the face of the Haunt. Best to put those thoughts away.

"With rope, grappling hooks and time, we could lower ourselves down off this drop behind us. If need be. Maybe ... It's steeper in some places than others. Can't make out the ground through the jungle, but if we got cornered up here ... maybe. It's not a sheer drop off like near the stairs.

Cole nodded, "Good."

They stood and watched as the dirt poured from the face of the mountain and rocks long hidden from light basked in the sun on the cobbles. In the distance, the Black Boat men he had stationed to guard their flank kept turning to peer down the road at them.

"There," Cole said, pointing with his pipe stem.

The first outlines of ancient stone columns peeking through the excavated areas. Soon they would find the gate to the Haunt on the island of Esmer.

Mage hunched under a tall tree, twisted by wind, its roots growing out and up from the precipice behind him. Scrolls stood behind the Black Boat Men and the Rats, staring quietly.

"Going to split camp or everyone back?" he asked.

"All back," Cole said, "Soon. I want to see the gate before we bring all the men and supplies up."

The sound of metal striking metal rang down the line. Everyone paused. Backs straightened.

"Think ... I think ... think there's something under there," one of the Black Boat men stuttered. He dropped his shovel to the ground, clattering on the stone road and pointed in front of him.

Cole put his pipe away. Allred followed him to the man, who open-mouthed, still pointed as if entranced by what he had revealed. Cole moved up beside him, took his pick, and squatted down to study the place where a dull lead-like metal gleamed in the sun.

The Black Boat man's hands shook without the pick to hold on to.

Cole turned at stared at the shaking man. He handed him his pick back and squinting in the sun said, "The gate."

Few spoke. A bird called from somewhere down the gorge. The men slowly pulled in towards the discovery, like water swirling down a drain.

Cole set six men to digging, exposing more and more of the gate, and put the rest to hacking down the trees growing on the sides of the road near the edge. From those, they would make stakes for palisades.

More men began moving the dirt from the face of the Haunt and shoveling it along a line perpendicular to the old road, building up a short berm of dirt which could serve as a defensive point. Along that berm, he set to burying the palisades. It was hasty but it would serve to slow some things down.

The berm could eat arrows and anyone attacking on foot would have to step over it. He had lived through flurries of arrows from a hip high berm of dirt many times.

The Rats dug. The Black Boat men dug. Helga tried to joke and laugh, among her Rats. The Black Boat men watched her. He saw her pretend they weren't watching her.

Cole had warned them all in the morning that they would see odd things near the Haunt, and he'd explained simply it was best not to speak of those things, that speaking of them gave them more power. The vipers and the possessed, the flock of strange birds and now the sheer power of this Haunt was taking its toll; even the hardened Black Boat men looked more worried than fearsome. As the dirt fell from the mountain face, a strange scent pervaded the road and waves of power poured over them.

The gate revealed itself below pick and axe. Men whispered

to each other—

"Soon, we'll be rich."

"Treasure beyond counting."

"Glad we found something in this jungle."

"All will be rewarded," Cole said, just loud enough no one could remember if he were talking to himself or answering the Black Boat men.

Because we get what we deserve, he thought.

Soon enough the gate revealed itself to the sky for the first time in untold eons.

It was a metal rectangle set in the face of what looked like marble, which in turn rested in the raw rock of the mountain. Along the face of the gate was carved an inscrutable script which he recognized from past Haunts but could not read. He wiped dirt from his hands, checked his crossbow for the hundredth time.

In the center of the gate sat a structure; a slowly rotating disk, powered by arcane forces. It was a seal, blacker than the night sky, a void, glass-like with points of green and white light darting within its heart. In the center of it was fit what looked like a common keyhole but it stretched and breathed as if the metal were alive.

"Forward," Cole whispered.

It didn't seem like he spoke to anyone living among them.

Once the gate revealed itself everyone edged away from it. Many wouldn't look at it at all, preferring to keep their heads down and hands busy. It was as if they stared at some sleeping malignant creature.

Cole gave the order to march back to base camp before nightfall. Everyone would move together on the morrow.

Mage said nothing, standing in shade and shadow beneath the trees. Hartha and Hortha towered and glowered beside him, wordless and mute but for their humming of shield-songs.

Allred watched the sky turn darker, lose light, while everyone stowed their tools, checked their packs, drew from their flagons and prepared to set back out. Down the steps and back to camp.

"Move," Cole said.

Some of the Black Boat men broke out in faint cheers, still nervous about the return march. A few courageous souls attempted laughs. A few stared transfixed at the ancient gate's mouth, then looked away. Helga was one of them. She tried a cheerful mask for the sake of her Rats. He could see the echoing memories of the Pits in their faces.

For most here at the top of Esmer, this was their first look at something older than their own gods.

"You're leading the line. I'll keep them moving thinner on the steps," Cole said.

"Don't let these fools fall on top of me," he answered.

They lost no more men. The way back was uneventful. No Dhlams. No spirits. It was as if in revealing the gate, the Haunt would make no more effort to prevent them from entering.

By the time, they were descending the last of the road the spirits of everyone lifted. He could feel the line yearn to start running, to cross that barrier which few had probably noticed, but all felt gave them protection from the horrors of the Haunt.

Men behind them started to lift their voices and trade whispers of relief.

The sky had turned to indigo nearing nightfall. A line of pink betrayed where the sun sheltered behind low clouds. In the distance, he saw a figure running towards them, shouting, "Soldiers" and then the man fell forward and he could see the two long shadows of arrows in his back.

He called a quick halt to the line. Cole hurried up to him. He smelled blood on the wind.

"Under attack," Cole shouted behind him.

Below them a skirmish had broken out in the clearing. The grunts and shouts of small melees and hand-to-hand fighting issued up the last of the slight incline of the trail. The sky darkened more every moment but, in the gloom, he could see the rust-red of imperial armor.

He aimed at a man near the base of the tower. Let fly a crossbow bolt. The distance was too great, but it drew his attention. He reloaded on one knee. Waited for Cole's orders. The rest of the men were hurrying forward around him.

Scrolls sighted and drew. An arrow cut through the air above his head and soared into the clearing below. It hit a Thronelander and the soldier fell to the ground seeking cover near the base of the tower.

Helga ran up to him, crouched low. An arrow bit the dirt near his boot so hard, a clod of dirt jumped up and struck him in the cheek, "The Rats will follow."

Mage's cloak snapped. War-magic summoning, building on the breath of the mage. Hartha and Hortha brought their shields up high.

"Forward!" Cole yelled.

The line broke into a charge downhill.

Cole caught him by the arm, "Cut off the trail down the mountain. I'll watch the village side. Not a single soldier leaves this place. Take one alive, if you can."

Behind him, a couple of the Black Boat men were less eager to join the fray, Cole screamed in their faces, and they bolted, more afraid of him than what danger lay below. Another arrow whizzed past his face. The air ripped apart in the wake of the fletching, singing a single line from the wasp-song of war and Allred moved fast and low into the fray.

14

Lookout

The hatchet in the man's neck made a wet sound.
He kept hearing it over and over, despite the other noise of battle. He didn't want to look up, yet.

When the fight happened, it wasn't like the jousts and duels in the legends. Not one bit.

I cowered, that's what I did. I ran and hoped no one would notice me because I'm not a real soldier.

It wasn't long before Cole, Allred and the rest arrived and joined the battle. He peeked his head back up and bellydown scrambled over the ditch. Stoneburner grabbed him by the collar and tossed him face down again. In time, Boph found him, holding the reins of his donkey in one hand and a knife in the other.

Shouting and the clash of metal. Swords met armor. Arrows cut across the clearing. He could hear the thump as the weight of them hit the tower. He never knew arrows made such loud sounds.

A short javelin came hurtling through the air from above and stuck in the dirt close to where he sat.

A feeling passed through him, a sure knowing that he was glad to be alive. Boph lived. His donkey lived. Allweln's gift was life and the sudden recognition of the sin of not loving every moment of it clenched his heart.

It didn't feel like his own thought. He recognized the thinker of the thought. He looked at Boph's donkey. The animal stood calmly, then sat down, folding its legs beneath him.

For a few moments, he thought the battle had ceased. A Black Boat man crouched not far away. He could see the man breathing heavily, his shoulders moving up and down.

A soldier came running down the trench fast, screaming, straight towards him. He had never seen a man scream at nothing and everything all at once.

War-frenzy, war-frenzy, war—the term kept echoing in his mind from the legends. The Black Boat man sprung up, then crouched back, a low snarling sound deep in his throat. Then Lookout watched a man die for the first time in battle.

Not far away die, like in the tales, but right there in front of me.

The Thronelander slammed his knee into the man's head. At the same time, the Black Boat man shot his hand out and lodged a small dagger in the soldier's hip socket.

The soldier stopped screaming, which Lookout thought odd since he had just been stabbed.

He swung his short sword down. The Black Boat man tried to back up, still reeling and stunned from the knee to his face. He had lost his knife in the man's body. Now with the distance between him, he couldn't get it back.

The soldier hacked over and over in graceless crippled arcs. The sword came down and across, over and over.

Unlike in the stories the man didn't just die. He took slash after slash of the sword and kept backpedaling on hands and feet through the dirt, grunting, "No. Not. No. No."

Lookout understood something terrible then. It takes time to die.

The Black Boat man grunted and bled. The dagger in the imperial's hip didn't slow the butchery. The Black Boat man scraped at the dirt and threw a bloody handful at the soldier's face. It was a ridiculous thing to see because it worked.

The dirt in the man's eyes slowed him but the sword kept slashing, whistling through the air.

Boph tried to pull him farther away. They didn't get far. More arrows peppered the path in front of them. Then something hit him in the head so hard, it knocked him to the ground. His ear rang on one side. He shouted. Beside him he saw the splintered shaft of the arrow that had struck his helmet.

"Get up," Boph said, "Get up."

He did. He worked his jaw up and down. Still couldn't hear out of that ear and it made him dizzy and off-balance. He straightened his helmet. The impact had knocked it crooked over one of his eyes.

A few men held torches in the near dark. Stoneburner had set about lighting them just before the attack. Lookout had been helping him. It was an eternity ago.

The duel ended between the two men.

The Thronelander gathered himself up, winded from the work of his butchery. Hoisting his sword high, he paused and aimed and brought it down, slicing into the Black Boat man's skull. Hunks of hair and brain sprayed in the air.

They lied in the legends.

The soldier leaned on his sword, tired. He pulled the dagger from his hip and dropped it. He looked around as if confused. He limped forward steady and slow gasping for air, one hand pressing where the dagger pierced him. He was coming to kill them next.

Boph stepped in front of him then, his loyal retainer, clutching the small knife in his hand. He handed the reins of his donkey to him. Lookout took them.

Cole slipped over the ditch behind the Thronelander. He stuck a dagger in the side of the man's throat as casually as if he were digging his eating knife into the ground. The soldier didn't even have time to turn to see what struck him. He reached up towards his own neck. Cole tripped him.

Not how they fight in the legends.

The soldier dropped hard, his hand pressed to his throat, purple blood spurting on the raw earth of the freshly dug ditch.

The soldier dropped his own blood-covered sword and reached up to his neck with that hand, as if checking to confirm the other hand's blood-slick sensation.

Cole bent over the soldier and stabbed him three more times fast—in his back, his side and his throat, then wiped the dagger on his trousers and walked towards him and Boph as if nothing out of the ordinary were occurring. He didn't even bend low to avoid arrows.

Cole pointed at the ground where Lookout already found himself sitting and said, "Stay there. Take this." He handed the long dagger to Boph, unsheathed his broadsword and continued down the trench.

The battle-clamor began to fade. Boph took the reins back to his donkey and sat beside him.

He smelled urine. Didn't know why. The noises of shield and arrow, armor and sword stopped. Someone tossed a lit torch into the ditch in front of him for no clear reason. It landed on the back of the dead Black Boat man. The ditch filled with the smoke of flesh. He closed his eyes.

Was he crying? He couldn't feel it. But why was his whole body shaking. Boph stood above him watching him with wide brown eyes.

"I think it's over," Boph said.

He didn't know how to answer that, so he just closed his eyes again for a while.

At some point, Cole stood above him again.

"Boy, look at me," Cole said.

He kneeled in the ditch in front of him. There was blood on his armor, he could see the slickness of it in the torchlight but it blended with the darkness. Cole put his hand on his shoulder examining his face.

"Was he injured?" Cole asked Boph.

"No," he answered.

The least he could do was answer for himself. The words came out in a shout for some reason.

"An arrow hit my helmet. I can't hear right. Things are wavy like I'm drunk."

Cole turned away, took his hand from his shoulder, "These men are not real Throneland soldiers. They were pretending to be."

The man stopped his explanation, looked down at his pant's leg. Lookout flinched then looked down and saw the damp on his trousers.

"Alright," Lookout managed to say, "I don't know who did that."

Cole looked away again. The man's eyes looked like an abyss in the night. He walked over and picked up the torch still sputtering on the dead man's body. Groans had replaced the sharp shouts of battle.

"It happens to some who see their first battle. No shame in it," Cole said, studying the torch.

"Alright," he repeated.

Cole looked at Boph, "Your donkey lives."

"Yes," Boph answered.

"You did good." Cole winced, tried to smile maybe. "Both of you are alive."

"Alright," he said.

Everything felt far off. The sounds Cole and Boph were making, he knew they were words, and the words formed the language he spoke, but they were faint compared to the other language he had heard for the first time—the rigid and unfaltering grammar of steel on steel. The arguments of swords, each element clear and final.

Everything looked different. True, there were strange men here upon his hill. The hill he was supposed to guard was now full of strangers and the dead. The jungle, the mountain, even the watch tower, a place grown painfully familiar and boring over the year appeared foreign. The air tasted wrong.

"I'll send Stoneburner over soon," Cole said.

Cole took out a flagon of wine, uncorked it and handed it to him. Lookout drank. Some of the wine spilled down his chin. It brought him back to the moment. All the sounds rushed in closer and real.

Cole took the wine back, looked down and winced once more, then a calm took over the man's face and he saw a faint smile curve his lips and then he was gone again.

Two men came down the ditch. They held shovels. Other Black Boat men. They said nothing as they dragged the corpses away.

"Thank you," Lookout said to Boph.

"Yes," Boph said.

Soon, Stoneburner stood above him hands on hips, his mouth crooked and wondering beneath his bushy moustache. Aodlen accompanied him.

"Nobody got to me. One of those Black Boat guys fought one of the...Imperial...looking soldiers," Lookout said to him. He wanted to explain events more to himself than the kindly man or the twitching doctor.

"Imperials, yes! Ha! Maybe—I doubt it can be done, ha! Maybe someone will explain someday," Aodlen said bending down to study him. "Hmm, good. Stoneburner has some things for you. Both rather more alive than not. Wonderful. On to the next corpse!"

Aodlen hurried away down the trench. Scrolls appeared behind him. A Black Boat man, blood on his face, beside him holding a small torch, counted the dead. Scrolls paused, regarded him, then Boph, and the donkey, too, made a mark with his stylus and continued his procession.

"Stand up and take these," Stoneburner said.

Lookout grabbed the man's offered hand and got to his feet, taking the folded bundle of cloth from Stoneburner's hand. He let it drape down. It was a new pair of trousers.

"I'll go to the creek with you. Clean up. The trousers are northern style. They'll be too big. We can fix it up."

Lookout followed the man through the torchlit camp towards the creek. Boph led his donkey to the water with him.

Screams still pierced the night, interspersed with boasts of victory.

Near a fire, the doctor bent over huddled forms lying on the ground. It was ringed with torches. In the low light, Aodlen held a small saw and then lowered it towards a man's leg. Lookout turned away. He almost reached out and grabbed at Stoneburner's hand and then remembered he intended to be a knight someday, and instead covered the ear facing Aodlen's to block the sound of steel on bone.

They made their way down to the creek, turned off the narrow trail where a path of bent grass made by a year of his own coming and going led to water. Here it was quieter, and he listened to the steps of the donkey's hooves whipping through high grass.

A Black Boat man torch in hand, stood by the creek. His eyes were full of fear and he blinked at them, trying to recognize the familiar. Another sloshed onto the muddy bank out of the creek, carrying water for the wounded. He labored under two big wooden buckets sloshing back and forth on the ends of a pole which he held against the top of his neck. They stepped aside and let him pass and then went down to the water.

"Go wash up. Put these on and come back when you're done," Stoneburner said.

Boph followed him down to the creek. Lookout was unsteady on his feet. He had to think about each step he took. The ground felt soft and unsure. The donkey nosed around the weeds of the bank and drank.

Lookout handed Boph the new trousers and walked out into the center of the creek, his feet sliding against the soft sand at the bottom. Now, he was closer to the far bank, and he undressed, tossing his clothes on a flat-rock. He bathed here often enough and it was a familiar place. He cupped both his hands together and splashed cool water on his face, then bent low and sat in the soft sand of the creek and let the water roll over him. He realized he was still wearing his old helmet. He took it from his head and laughed when he saw the place where the thick hide had prevented the piercing of his skull by the arrow. He dunked his face in the water and beneath it a weird laugh broke from him and he felt the bubbles roll across both his cheeks.

He took a deep breath as he came back up to the surface.

Every sudden sound stung somewhere inside him, undiscovered until now, and made him twitch and twist. He didn't take his eyes from Boph and the donkey standing on the shore. Boph had turned away to give him privacy, Stoneburner, too, and he could hear them murmuring to one another.

In the dark, Boph pet the donkey's neck with one hand. Lookout got lost in the play of torchlight on the creek's surface. At the bottom, the moon bright in the dark of Allweln's sky, cast soft white rays on the backs of olive frogs and small magenta fish playing about in the mud his feet stirred up.

He heard another scream from back at camp. The fish and the frogs did not notice the screaming. He longed to be down there with them, whose light was the stars and moon and who knew nothing of the deeds of men.

He splashed some water on his face, put the helmet back over wet hair and waded back to the bank. The mud felt good and sure beneath his toes and for a moment, he wanted to stand there; never leave the little creek in the darkness. He imagined himself a happy spirit watching the years turn in the cool mud of the unnamed creek and was sad that it had no name, so said to himself, "It's called, Goodcreek. That's its name."

Boph kept his head turned away and held the new trousers out for him and some broad fern leaves to dry his body. He wicked the water away with the fronds and stepped into the trousers. They had the feel of new cloth and smelled like something stored at the bottom of a trunk.

Stoneburner leaned down, studied him in the torchlight, "You're rattled. Arrow hit your helmet, shook your head, mostlike. Eh, I guess you hadn't seen a man die before, either?"

Lookout shook his head, no.

"You neither," Stoneburner said, turning to Boph.

"No never," Boph said.

"Course not," he muttered, as if remembering something. The portly man stood straight again, sighed, "Those trousers are too long. You'll grow into them. If I got time, I'll show you how to hem them up. For now, just fold them."

"I thank you," Lookout said.

He heard the unmanly catch in his throat. Would he rid himself of that soon? He would. A knight must not waver.

"Time to eat," Stoneburner said. He stood up after folding the ends of the trousers into cuffs and sticking a small pin through each to hold them.

He took the torch back from Boph. One last look at his handiwork and a satisfied huff and then he led them both back up into the camp. The old man's deep, calm voice made Lookout feel better.

"You caught a Battle-Chill, that's all. It happens to some men who haven't seen fighting before. Seen it take hold of veterans, too. You shake. Nothing seems solid. Your spirit attracts strange thinking. It'll pass in a bit. Listen to me—here's how you can evade it; do simple things, wash, dress, eat, work. Keep your spirit far away from dwelling on blood spilled. That's the way. It'll clear in time."

He led them to the main part of the camp and sat them down. Arrayed around them was a great deal of baggage hauled up the mountain by the Black Boat men. It was this place where they had fought hardest, protecting what things were in these bags, satchels, pockets—sheathed things, locked boxes and food. When the arrows began to fly, Stoneburner had pushed the boys into the trench and told them to stay low there.

A large cast iron pot filled with stew simmered over a fire. Men came and went. Stoneburner served them with a big wooden ladle, then filled two bowls and brough them over to him and Boph.

"For now, stay with me, until Cole tells us what's what. Eat," Stoneburner said.

Lookout couldn't. The food didn't look like anything, didn't seem real.

He wondered about his commission. Had anyone got to the tower? He touched his helmet, making certain it was still there. That was silly though, of course it would be.

Boph ate. Lookout gave him his own bowl. Boph ate that, too. A few times, Lookout started to say something then didn't.

Stoneburner took both bowls and refilled them and put one in front of Lookout again. The other in front of Boph, "Eat. If you're going to be a knight, you must learn to eat and sleep when you can, despite how you feel."

"I keep hearing men screaming."

"Well, that's because they are. I hear it."

Stoneburner went over to his own baggage and returned with his lute. He bent down, one knee to the ground, the other leg parallel and steadying the instrument, "Have you ever played one of these?"

Lookout had heard of them in stories. Usually, they were played by a wisecracking bard, or a truth-telling rogue or by some faceless character in a public house. He had never touched one. The islanders had their own instruments, whistles and flutes made of reed. Drums. Nothing stringed.

He shook his head no.

Stoneburner strummed the strings with one hand and moved his other in complicated patterns on the neck of the instrument. The music covered up the sounds of the night for a few moments and Stoneburner's smile appeared far away in the campfire light. The happy look on the old man's face almost startled him. How quickly the notes soothed.

Another shadow came to the fire and Stoneburner hurried away to answer it. He handed the instrument to Lookout in an off-handed way, "Mess about with it if you like."

Boph wiped his mouth with his wrist and stared at him and the lute. Lookout didn't know what to do with the thing. It sat awkwardly in his hands and on his lap. Was it a fragile thing?

"Would you want to try it?" he asked.

Boph eagerly nodded his head, yes. He handed it to his loyal retainer.

Boph set about immediately hitting one string and letting it ring out alone then the other.

Lookout watched his friend, his head cocked to the side, tongue out in concentration, listen and know each of the strings in turn. He wondered if this was what it was like to learn to read. To listen to the sound of letters, one at a time, and then make them all sing together.

His attendant soon found a three-note melody, picked out

the tune he had discovered and then found it again, quicker.

Lookout lowered his head.

"I have been mistaken to call you a servant in the past. I officially name you my loyal retainer," he said.

Boph stopped plucking at the strings for a moment, smiled and said, "I accept this."

Lookout wanted to lay down, wanted to look up at the stars in the night but he tried it and he felt open to attack laying belly up to the moon.

So, he sat back up and listened to Boph try to play the lute, while Stoneburner cast glances over at them both and waited for Cole to decide their destiny.

Soon enough, Cole came over to the camp. Stoneburner served him a bowl of stew. Lookout watched as the man ate it efficiently, watching both the boys for some time before speaking. Cole tossed some sand into the bowl and handed it back to Stoneburner.

"We were attacked tonight by Throneland soldiers. They are not in service to the rightful throne. You are loyal, both. Tomorrow, we'll continue what we set out to do. You'll follow and help. Do you understand?"

Boph had stopped playing the lute as soon as Cole came into the torchlight. He agreed immediately.

"Tonight, you've seen men die. Shake it off before it stunts you. If you don't, it will shake you and shake you until you fall apart. Do you understand?"

Both answered, yes.

"One came at me and would have killed me, if it wasn't for you," Lookout said.

Cole lit his pipe, leaned his elbows on his knees and watched them in the campfire light.

"No one on Esmer speaks about the wars for the Throne?"

Boph spoke up, "Attman says the Thronelanders are always fighting somewhere and something. Here, it doesn't touch us. It's far away."

"My father never talked about fighting much. He said the

land here is bad but it's better than being too close to the Throne," he put in.

"You did good to stay alive." The smoke slid across Cole's face in the moonlight and obscured his eyes. "Tomorrow, you'll help us carry supplies, our armor and other things. It's good to be of use after a battle. I know you'll do well, both of you, don't you think, Stoneburner?"

"I do," Stoneburner said.

"But which side? I mean, the commission you gave me...us...which side does it work for?"

Lookout couldn't quite figure out the way to ask what he was asking. If there were different sides but they both dressed like Imperials, how should he know what side he was on?

"The right side. But papers and medals won't protect you from men. Only swords do that." For a moment, Cole seemed to be talking to some part of himself that he was trying to defeat once and for all. His words came out bitter as if worked over, again and again, through years of dispute inside his own mind. They were words that had been pressed flat and hard beneath worry. "I found out about that a long time ago. Some men's promises mean less than nothing—they're just what they wrap their lies in. That's not my way."

Cole stood and walked back out into the darkness away from the campfire.

These were the good Thronelanders. They had protected him, given him food, given him papers, and given him coin. He was a Guard of the tower on the island of Esmer. The tower still stood.

He felt anger at the other Thronelanders who attacked them for the first time. What right did they have?

Something about Cole made him less afraid. He had stopped shaking. Boph picked up the same melody on the lute. Lookout started to eat his stew and wondered on what tomorrow might mean, instead of what the day had become.

15

He found the soldier behind a palm, loosing arrows into the camp. When he heard Allred, it was too late. He looked to run but the cold steel of his sword at his neck convinced him to put the bow down.

The soldier was terrified, young, and Allred understood both these things in a quiet way and said nothing to the man while he held the blade to his throat and waited until the last of the fight died down.

In a moment of mercy, he considered killing him there and then instead of bringing him to Cole.

He led the man out from the trees once the fight was over and back to camp and tied his hands with rope Stoneburner gave him. Stoneburner took him over to the table and gestured for him to sit beside the other prisoner, an older man, who kneeled on the ground and wore a ribbon of the Optri around his forehead. *This changes things*, Allred thought.

Cole smoked his pipe at his makeshift table. Helga stood near him, talking to the side of his head, Cole saying little.

Cole spoke to him, "I'll speak to the Optri first. Accompany your cousin away for now."

Both prisoners heard the interchange. The older one understood its meaning and grinned in grotesque expectation. Hartha and Hortha flanked each of the men. Mage stood in the shadows; eyes fixed on the back of the Optri man.

Allred beckoned Helga over and she followed him a few steps away.

"I didn't lead them here," she said.

"No one said you did." He didn't doubt she thought that was true. "Did any of your people fall?"

"No. Nor, did they throw themselves into the fight."

"Good," he answered.

"What I saw today, the vipers, those birds, the things up there—"

"Just the start," he replied.

He took out a redleaf roll and lit it from a torch flickering nearby.

"Those are Throneland soldiers, cousin. How did they find us here?"

If he had been leading their group, they'd never have shown their faces, never would have fought here and never would have died. He would have gathered information instead of trying to gather heads.

"Cole will find out. The Optri man won't talk. If the younger one won't, Cole will make him. If that happens, cousin, I'd prefer you turn away."

Helga looked pale in the moonlight. The weight of the Haunt already had started bearing down on her.

"He'll know if they are lying?"

"Cole has a way of seeing through people."

The look that crossed her face indicated she might finally understand what the Relic Hunters were.

You didn't survive the Pits without trouble. She had known

bloodshed. She just didn't know the many ways it can be shed, yet. He would have liked to save her that, and knowing he couldn't now, he satisfied himself with a smoke and a shrug.

"I'm going to check on my people and the two boys," she said and left.

More torches flared up around the camp. The sound of men pulling bodies through dirt, gathering fuel for a pyre. He saw Stoneburner leading the two boys and the donkey off towards the creek. That was good the boys lived. As Helga walked away, Cole signaled for him.

He unsheathed his sword as he approached. The younger soldier turned towards him. Carefully, he put the side of his sword to his face, turning him to face Cole.

Scrolls appeared out of the darkness behind the table and whispered in Cole's ear.

Cole turned to the prisoners.

"Why are you here?"

"I didn't know—" the younger prisoner started.

The older one was on top of him in an instant, lunging up from his knees, his mouth seeking out the younger soldier's throat, missing it, and biting his ear instead. The Optri tore off the soldier's ear and spit it into the dirt then kept coming at him.

Hortha grabbed the attacker. He tossed him to the ground away from his erstwhile ally, who screamed but couldn't reach the bloody side of his face with his bound hands.

Allred put down his sword, moved forward to help the soldier. Cole didn't blink, simply sat there watching, unstirred.

"Take the Optri over there. If he moves again, cut him but don't kill him," Cole said.

Hartha and Hortha stood the man on his feet and pushed him away into the night. He licked the blood from his mouth and shouted some curse to his dark gods.

"Doctor," Cole bellowed.

Aodlen hurried over, looked at the ear, the blood, the soldier, then retreated and returned with a clean bandage. It smelled like it had been dipped in a distillation of astringent herbs. Aodlen showed the soldier what it was before he pressed it against his head. The physician bade Allred hold the bandage to the man's head and went back to the blankets where his tools were. He brought back some sort of salve and applied it to the flesh where the ear once occupied. Allred could feel the soldier's body shaking beneath his hand.

"Easy," he said.

"What's your name?" Cole asked.

Through some sobbing, he answered "Aacten."

"Who is that man?" Cole asked.

Aodlen gave the soldier a drink from a flagon of fresh water. The young man drank. In the torchlight, he saw his face clearly. It reminded him of friends he had seen scared out of their minds years before.

Boasting in the morning, shaking in the evening.

He turned away. He didn't want to look at his face anymore.

"I don't know, sir. We're a small company stationed a fair ways north of here. We spend most of the time doing nothing." Aacten motioned his head towards the darkness where the Optri man had been hauled off by the two twins. "He showed up and took command, brought us here. He never talks but he's, well, you see what he is, So—"

"You know what the Optri are?"

"I've heard, yes, everyone has heard of them."

"He's one of them."

"Yes, sir."

The Optri were the secret units of the Throne. Spies. Torturers. Diplomats. The military could not control them, though they were forced to work with them. They all swore to the Throne by way of devotion to a particular battlemage or old god. These battlemages often mastered the most esoteric arts of magery, schools nearly forgotten. One of them had taken command of this regular soldier's unit and they had come to trek them.

Aacten didn't know exactly what they were looking for, the Optri had just said, they were seeking unlicensed explorers.

"He's the only Optri with you?" Cole asked.

"They have their own ships, their own ways. We don't even see them, too ... different. Rumor is they have a command ship somewhere. I've heard it houses a mage. I've heard wicked things of it. It was so easy down here before he showed up. Before all this. We just sailed around, show the banners in Port Shamhalhan, never go farther south than the Middle Isle."

Allred believed him. It sounded like standard Throneland work in a neutral area. They would be given a little silver to spread around to local chieftains. They might help with local problems, capture a bandit for them. It built goodwill for the Throne, and it was the way they controlled places they didn't occupy. And when and if the time came, to occupy, well they would have some locals already favorable to them.

"You know who we are?" Cole asked.

"I don't know. I just ... this was a good place to serve. That ... thing rarely talks. I tell you, not a word. I don't think he's even a man. All was easy until he showed up. One of my friends—they're gone now, aren't they? All of them are dead," Aacten said.

"You know who we are?" Cole asked, again.

"My ear is gone."

Quiet had come over him. Bleeding and the realization everyone he had known was dead.

"Yes, your ear is gone. Did anyone from your group escape here?"

"How would I know? I don't know who is dead."

"How many with you including yourself?"

"Ten," the man said.

"The Optri command boat, how far away from here is it?"

"I don't know. I've never seen it. It's just a rumor. The Optri, I didn't even really believe they were real until that man showed up. Our unit, we were the only Imperials down here, almost. There're thousands of islands down here in the southern sea. I'm from the Plains of Alsworn. Never seen anything like this place until my unit shipped here. We landed in the village down there, talked to no one just straight away up the mountain. We've been just going from island to island."

"Expect anyone else to come?"

"I don't think so, but I don't know."

"That's all for now," Cole said, waving his hand. Allred lifted the soldier to his feet.

"Are you going to kill me?" Aacten asked, embarrassment in his voice.

"We are the Relic Hunters of the 9th. We remember. What does the Throne say to that? You can speak honest." Cole said.

Aacten let out a bitter laugh followed by a sob. It seemed the stories they told of their outfit in the Thronelands differed from some of the popular legends at-large.

"Savages," Aacten whispered, "Rebels. Dark magic-wielders. Malcontents. They say you should have all died and if you had, there would be peace."

He smiled at the soldier's honesty. It surprised him.

"And?"

"If you're Cole—they say you've gone mad from living in Haunts and dealing with unclean spirits."

Cole stood, stretched, sat his pipe on the table. Let his fingers linger on it, staring down while he spun it on the rough surface, thinking.

"Tonight, you'll be fed. You'll have fresh water and wine. Our doctor will tend your ear. After he finishes healing our men you've killed and wounded. For that, I don't blame you. You're a soldier and you serve the Throne." He looked up and met Aacten's eyes. "Just like we did."

The man relaxed a little for the first time. Believed him.

In the light of the torches on the island of Esmer, the one charge Aacten spoke rang true enough to him. The Relic Hunters of the 9th had spent too much time in the Haunts.

"Take him to Aodlen," Cole said and waived him away, peering out into the darkness where the twins had hauled the Optri away.

He led him over to Aodlen. The doctor barely looking up from this bloody work, gestured to a tree on the fringe of the camp and told him to tie him there.

He did. Aacten whispered twice, "Will you really let me live?"

"Cole will do what he said. That's all," he answered, and returned to the table.

Now the Optri man was on his knees and Hartha and Hortha stayed close, their axes at the man's throat. The Optri man stared at Cole in the firelight, his face split by a terrible grin. His arms were bound high, his right arm terminated in a still bleeding stump.

Not far away, on the outskirts of the camp, the funeral pyre was lit. The flesh-smoke drifted across the camp. The wind blew the smoke to where they stood, occluding them all, obscuring the Optri man in black banks of it, which he inhaled deeply. All the while, the man's eyes, like rain-wet rocks stared at Cole.

Scrolls came through the smoke, holding a small black bag and put it on the table in front of Cole, who didn't break his gaze with the Optri man.

"His hand was located on the tower above, propped on the railing, facing the camp," Scrolls said in his flat voice, "It contains a living Eye. We are found out."

Worse than he thought. Much worse. When the soldier said there were no more Imperials on Esmer, he believed him. But now, there would be more coming. And first among them would be the Optri.

Cole broke gaze with the Optri man, untied the small black bag and took out the severed hand which belonged to the man staring at him. He placed it flat on the desk, palm up. The flesh was dead but in the middle of the palm something wiggled and squirmed—an inhuman eye couched in the dead flesh. It stared up at Cole. Cole picked it up and sat the stump of the wrist on the table, the eye facing the former owner of the hand.

"Yours?"

A cold smile to rival the Optri man's own broke over Cole's face, as waves of the smoke from the funeral pyre swept over them.

The Optri man's face shifted in the dark and smoke. He breathed in deep, again and again, inhaling the smoke of the flesh of the dead with relish. At the pyre, Allred could hear a few prayers go up among the Rats, low chants of lament. Of the Black Boat men, he heard nothing.

The Optri man spoke slowly, opening his mouth wide. His voice was too loud. Each of his earlobes were missing and the canals filled with some material. Along the scarred skin of his skull, tiny tattooed script ran in the form of a serpent. Each cult had their own strange practices of disfiguration to mark them.

"I have no hands. I have never had hands. That is the Master's Eye. And the master's hand. It serves him. It watches you Cole and what remains of the 9th."

Cole gestured to Scrolls, "On to the pyre."

Scrolls picked up the hand, put it back in the black bag, turned and walked to the fire. In the distance, Allred could see him approach the flames and toss the hand with the Eye onto it. When it met the fire, the Optri man laughed.

"How far away are you?" Cole asked.

"Never far," the Optri man replied in a sing-song voice, too loud. The accent was of the central Thronelands.

"You're just a servant."

"One among many."

He moved around to face him, his sword up and out and pointed and ready to strike him down in case he moved towards Cole. Even with the two giants holding the axes at the man's throat, he didn't like this. They ought to cut him down and put him on the fire now, instead of later.

"How far away?" Cole asked, again.

"Never far."

Through the smoke Hartha squinted, "He's got Doom Root in his mouth, Cole," he said. The giant moved to take it from the Optri man's mouth but Cole waved him off.

"Let him. Give my regards to your master," Cole said.

The Optri man bit down onto the root, which he had kept secreted behind his teeth.

"He knows your aspect," the Optri man said.

"And your worldly master?" Cole asked.

"No," the Optri man said.

The stalk of the plant the man chewed on would soon end his life. It was a powerful poison. Despite that, he kept his blade point trained at his face. He chewed and smiled at him, not flinching and then he let out a terrible, scream of victory and fell to the ground, his mouth erupting in blood.

"To the pyre," Cole said and stood, lighting his pipe.

Hartha and Hortha lifted the Optri man up and carted the corpse to the flames.

They were alone for a moment. Him and Cole.

"The choice. Pack everything, double-time march back to the Black Boat. Leave Esmer, start somewhere else. Or we go," Cole said.

Allred knew already what he would choose. He said nothing. Let Cole talk.

"Figure that Optri man sent our location to the Optri ship with the Eye. We have at least a day's lead, even if they are on the shore, could be they are weeks away."

"If they show up while we're in the Haunt or in Upside Fever, I don't know we survive," he answered.

"If we walk away, we just located a Haunt for the Optri to use and we profited nothing," Cole replied.

"We won't run. We both know it. It's just how we go about it. Force a march back to the Haunt tonight though and we lose more people on the way up."

"Dawn march," Cole agreed.

There was another problem, they hadn't spoken of, "Thousands of islands in the southern sea. How did the Optri man find us in the first place?"

"In Port Shamhalhan," Cole said.

"Helga says she didn't lead him here."

"They saw us, or they saw her. On the sea or in the city. It doesn't matter now. If you wish to speak against going forward, speak now, Allred."

He did not hesitate, "I follow."

Cole nodded.

So, into the mouth of a Haunt with Optri on their trail.

"At first light, we march."

He nodded and looked down at the blood-stained dirt, where Aacten's ear sheltered in the shade cast by the bent low-lit grass where the two prisoners had fought.

"First light," he echoed.

Cole sat back at his table, picked up his pipe and added its

182

smoke to the dissipating flight of the dead.

He made his way to the funeral pyre. The bodies burned, the work done, most had turned away from the sight and smell to their own fires—all but the dwarves of the Rats and Hortha and Hartha. The Green Islanders knelt near the flames, eyes shut and lips shifting and made their prayers for the dead.

He stared into the flames, put his hand on the hilt of his sword, saluted the fallen.

He would have to get a new count of the living and the dead in the morning.

Interlude

O ne night an Optri surgeon had come to him in his barracks, carrying a lantern in one hand, and in the other a bubbling vial so cold the man kept moving each finger from the glass, as if he were holding a chunk of ice. He handed him the potion, marroon, viscous, smelling like sweet clover growing atop a haunted barrow and ordered him to drink.

He obeyed.

When he woke up, both his earlobes were missing. The flesh cut cleanly against his skull, his hair was shaved, and he was deaf in his left ear. The remaining hole on the right, the doctor had packed full of wet clay. He had tried to stand and fell. It was the first time he heard the Optri mage speak to him, the lightest of sounds, calling to him—*servant*.

He wanted to dig the stuff out and he wanted to die.

"Soon enough, you'll understand," the surgeon had told

him.

The clay was mixed with the seed-of-the-orbs and in his ear, it was the conduit for the Crimson One, to speak to him. It took some time to understand. Panic had seized him for days after. He had cried, a grown man, a soldier but he could not hear his own sadness, only the walls of the barracks shaking.

The Crimson One explained in hushed, clear, sibilant tones to him.

Now, he stalked the deck of the Optri ship, and the sea sounded half the same as it had before. Down through the lower deck he climbed, and through the narrow hall to the Crimson One's chamber.

He had given the command to sail to what the map called Esmer.

Coming upon a simple door carved with symbols he still didn't understand and couldn't read, notwithstanding his initiation to the mystery, he did not pause but flipped back a metal slide at the top of the door and peered inside.

The room was bare for the most part with but a few furnishings. It was dim but the wall held sconces where tapers burned. At the far end of the room, a simple altar, the only thing on it, a brass holder and in it burned a single stick of incense.

It was his job to enter the lair and change this incense. Handle it carefully he did, for it was an expensive and holy thing, not the type found in a common temple but a mix of oils and seed-of-the-orbs.

"I serve," Ceph said.

In the middle of the floor of the room, a long velvet bag of red took up most of the wooden floor, pulsing with the writhing within. The Crimson One stirred and in his ear, he heard the reply.

He stood still and listened.

"A servant has found the 9th. A servant has chewed the Doom Root. The men he commanded are dead, except one. The island is named Esmer. I have anticipated your orders to make sail there. Is this your wish?"

The reply fluttered near the high part of his jaw, inside his head, a resounding affirmation.

Ceph eyed the incense. He would return soon, to change it.

He slid the metal back into place. Checked it was firm. It prevented the smoke from escaping into the rest of the ship and pushing the crew into madness. He was accustomed to it and the power of the smoke did not harm him. It was a blessing to be in its proximity.

But that was because Ceph understood what other men did not. It was not madness in the smoke. It was not madness coiling in the cloth. It was not madness echoing through the clay in his ear, not at all—it was clarity; and that clarity could astound.

Interlude

Scrolls

I leave these pages in the travelogue of the Relic Hunters of the 9th. May the God of Scripts and Learning, the Scribe's Arthritis and the elves who guard the bulbs of the Lakefrost flower, the Fine Ink makers, may they all bless these words. Safeguard them against time, weather, war and lies.

On the island of Esmer, the Optri have found us. How far away their forces are disposed, we know not.

The Relic Hunters have done battle with the Optri, previously. My recollection of these fights, I have put down in ink elsewhere.

There is no indication what type or amount of Optri forces are in the area. This far south and with the False Throne committing much of their resources and forces to the homeland kingdoms, it would be surprising if Optri operated in any significant number near Esmer. Yet, they know no borders.

It is impossible to know which Optri mage might be heading

here now. I have noted in the past that many Optri mages are of the One-Path-Clarity school and the markings and emblems on the man we captured indicate it is probable he served them. These Formchangers have entirely renounced their humanity and human form. This school of magic allows for enthrallment. The One-Pathers tend to permanent madness. Powerful but limited in their abilities, they take and retain the form of beasts.

Our own mage, skilled in more subtle arts than any mage under Throneland remit grows weary. He, the master of many arts, the master of his own gentle disposition—has given much to the cause of the 9th, our just cause. With the Haunt on Esmer still before us, an engagement with Optri here could be perilous.

Cole knows this but despite that—

Scrolls sighed, screwed up his mouth, wiped sweat from his brow—far more humid this far south, he longed for the relative coolness of his apartments in Shamhalhan. He scratched through the line above. Firm in his desire not to carry on that line of thought.

My brother—

That too, he quickly gouged from the page. No time for such considerations. A problem for another day. He would not think on his brother. No.

It has been decided to move forward. It is our intention to survive the Haunt, take what is necessary to support the fight against the Throne, distribute it in safety after departing well ahead of any Optri who might arrive. And—

No.

I make this entry in the travelogue for those who remember the 9th, so that future generations may read of our struggles and might understand the truth.

16

Helga

I t came as a surprise to be alive when Helga opened her eyes.

Survive another day.

As soon as she saw the attack, she knew her and the Rats might be blamed for leading them to the camp. She and the Rats had fought little, rushing down the slope of the trail and staying lumped together in a rough circle. They weren't warriors, they were survivors.

Afterwards, she didn't hesitate to speak the words out loud to Cole. He listened and said little. After some time, she realized her protests were not made against his accusations, which were nought but to herself.

She had seen no one following them on the ship to Esmer, there was no indication. It wasn't possible.

If I could elude the Relic Hunters, the Optri could elude me.

She stood up, stretching out tight muscles from sleeping on

the hard ground. Still, hadn't gotten used to it over the years. She felt her own neck. No one had cut her throat in the middle of the night. That worried her in its own way. Seemed Cole simply didn't care one way or the other about her. That irked her and scared her at the same time.

So, another day.

She surveyed her ragged bunch. Tym and Thay were whispering, heads near each other. Thay gave her an uncertain smile. He among them was the least convinced of her plan. Tym, too, was unsure but went along with what Thay said. Staah was still sleeping and Shad yawned, stood and hailed her. He had taken a small wound, an arrow scraping past his waist in the fight but he was sound. Out of all of her Rats on the mountain, Staah was the steadiest, the most loyal. She cared for them all, like only someone responsible for their lives could and she vowed quietly to see them off this mountain safely.

Stoneburner shuffled over and offered her a cup of Kler tea, "We'll be on the move soon."

She took the tea and regarded the older man in the dark. He looked as though he hadn't slept, the lines around his eyes deeper, his mouth pursed tight. She wanted to say something, to tell him something but she couldn't manage anything but, "Thanks."

He hesitated for a moment, stood there looking at her.

"If Cole thought it was your fault, you wouldn't be having tea this morning. Put that thought away. We've been followed before. If you're intent on following them into a Haunt, you've got more things to worry about."

"You're not going in?" she asked, thankful for the conversation. Out of all the 9th, Stoneburner seemed the most human.

The burly man shook his head, "No. I've been in them before but not anymore. Well, if Cole said so, yes, I'd follow him but he knows I don't ... it's not an easy thing, Helga. If I know Allred, I imagine he's tried to tell you already."

"He has but I know what I have to do."

"You don't, Helga," Stoneburner gave her a sad smile and left her with her tea.

They ate quietly, the Rats, saying little. The dwarves had grown taciturn on Esmer. Usually, the Rats were prone to jolly talk, recitations, even the Pits hadn't broken their spirits or joy in antics. Now, they were quiet, gathering their packs, close around their own campfire, stewing over what they had seen at the peak of the mountain the day prior.

The ashes of the funeral pyre still smoldered.

Cole soon formed them all up in a line and readied them for the march back to the Haunt. Everyone would go today, even the wounded would manage. The camp would be left vacant.

Cole and Allred marched in front with the younger prisoner captured in last night's fight. The Optri man was dead. She'd seen his body cast into the pyre the night before. She brought up her Rats in a group behind the 9th. In the back of the line marched the Black Boat men.

The two kids and the donkey, packed heavy, stayed near them. Both boys stole glances at her. They were young and probably hadn't seen a woman like her. She knew the effect she could have on men of all ages and it made her feel a little more certain she could survive the day. Even with her eyepatch, she still turned heads.

It was quiet today and the march, uneventful. She kept her eyes open, and her neck craned to the treetops, the nest of vipers from yesterday's hike still on her mind. She watched the donkey, sure-footed and steady, climb the steps to the Haunt and took solace in its sure gait.

No one dead yet today. Maybe the worst is over.

With the Haunt in front of her now, she admitted that she wished the attack last night meant a change of plans. She couldn't help thinking about backing out, leaving Esmer.

Still, it wasn't the fear of Optri, or the heavy magic of the place which made her consider this—it was how easily Cole accepted the fight, burned the dead and carried on.

His eyes had betrayed nothing the night before as she stood telling him, she was not the reason for the attack. What bothered her is the absolute indifference she saw in his face.

Survive another day.

Soon, the sheer monumental size of the Haunt loomed above her. Down the road, where they had revealed the passage inside, she swore she could hear the gate a thing of metal, inert, sing some repetitive refrain—a force as indifferent as Cole.

That is what had shaped him, perhaps—the going in and out of such places. Soon, she and the Rats would learn the song of the Haunt and she knew it would change them, as it had the Relic Hunters of the 9th.

She stood and waited for orders.

17

Allred

As they marched down the ancient causeway to the Haunt, for a moment he could see this same place as it was so long ago.

The ancients stood in a line on each side of the road. Men and women held their children near, watching the procession, heads bowed, solemn and murmuring blessings. The Haunt's face stared across the valley at the bottom of the mountain towards a volcano on the far side of the island, which they had not explored. Wind whipped the tops of palms, the forefathers of the same trees, which today waved in the wind of the cloud-covered peak. The people went willingly into the Haunt. Those ancient faces beside the path did not revel in the line of flesh fed to the Haunt.

Allred shook his head. Just visions. Dreams. Enough. So far, the bad spirits had limited their attack—the man-faced birds speaking from beyond the grave, clumps of vipers—two malevolent signs from yesterday—their kin had not appeared on the march today. It had been uneventful. No one fell from the stairs, though they carried much more equipment today. Even the donkey navigated the stone stairs easily enough.

He had to stop thinking and start doing. He turned to the two boys, waiting near the top of the steps with the rest of the Rats. Helga had gone on down the road with Cole.

"Stay with Stoneburner," he said.

"I'll watch after them, Fortune," Stoneburner said.

"Fortune."

With that, he set out to the gate to catch up with Cole and the rest.

He almost knocked the bald boy over the gorge when he scurried up and grabbed at his hand, "Hey." The kid didn't know well enough not to come up behind someone like Allred and touch him.

"What did you not understand?" he snapped.

The boy flinched, retracted and took a step back but then jut out his shallow chest and scrunched his eyes up and pointed at him.

"Les Ament told me I could watch the gate. He spoke to me in the night. Told me I was to watch and understand. That's what he said. Ask him if you don't believe me."

Ahead, Mage crouched beneath the shade of some palms near the precipice, huddled in his black cloak, talking to himself. The wind was picking up, the weather turning weird. Gusts of air shook the shivering trees. Odd that the boy had used one of Mage's hidden names.

"If you lie—" Allred said.

"I swear it," Boph answered.

The boy took one last look back at his donkey. Lookout held its reins, while Stoneburner fussed with the pack on its back and glancing at Allred, shrugged. Lookout stared at them open-mouthed.

"It's your concern, then," he said.

A few paces away, he realized something and turned to the boy once more. He bent down, looked him in the eyes. Studied his face. The boy didn't blink.

"You never use any of the mage's true names like that, you understand?"

"I didn't know … I dreamed it, I think—"

"Listen. You saw what happened to the man who didn't listen to Cole. Just don't. Someone might explain to you why someday but for now, just don't."

"Heard."

He stood, sighed.

"You've been lucky so far. Do you know how lucky?" Allred asked, squinting. He felt his lip pull over his teeth in an accidental grimace which must have looked like a snarl to the boy.

"I think so, yes" Boph said, "Yes."

He believed the boy. From the beginning, this one understood the situation better than his friend.

"How old are you?"

"I don't know for certain. Not yet, a man."

He thought no more than ten turns, likely. The other was a bit older.

"You're young. Go back down the road. Don't involve yourself, you don't need to."

"Yes, but I know my own kind of art, something like what Mage can do. And I want to see what is really happening."

He didn't shy away from him, and most did. People didn't lie about Mage. Most people didn't even talk about him. And when the fight happened last night, he'd heard from Stoneburner that Boph had held a hunting knife to defend his friend.

"You didn't get as rattled about the blood last night as your friend. That means you either got evil in you or you're thick-skulled. Either will serve you well if you want to see what war is like … your choice then. If Cole shews you away—run back double time."

"Fortune, Allred," Boph whispered.

He couldn't help a snorting laugh at that.

"Fortune, boy."

"It's Boph."

"Remember what I said."

As they passed the crouching mage, the bronzeface uttered

a greeting in an ancient tongue and Boph repeated it and went over to his side.

Again, the vision hit Allred like an arrow square on the breastplate.

Men like Mage, cloaked, wearing similar bronze masks gathered at the gate at the end of the procession. The grass, the dirt, the cover didn't hide the structure of the Haunt those centuries past. Columns soared to the sky in perfect geometry holding aloft a wood-roofed temple-face jutting out from the mountain. From the black, square pit of the gate pulses of heat and smoke emanated outward, obscuring the ancient mages. They breathed the fumes of the Haunt through the holes of their masks and exhaled smoke-laced spells in dialogue with the forces within.

He shook the vision from his head. At the gate now, the usual human kind of evil. Some of the Black Boat men jeered at their Throneland prisoner.

Allred walked through them, told them to shut their mouths. They did.

Cole spoke: "Today. You shall know your reward."

The Black Boat men looked at Allred for permission. He stared down at the tops of his boots.

Cheers broke out at Cole's words. He said nothing. He realized he was standing in the Imperial style—as if on parade before the Throne—his left palm resting atop the hilt of his sword on his left hip, his right arm crossing his torso to rest his hand on top of his left.

Sudden clouds devoured the sun's light in a quick-paced shadow which swept across the mountain. It felt like rain soon.

"The gate is before us. Do not jeer at this prisoner. He is a Throneland soldier and fulfilled his duty. He may be an enemy now but that will not last. Someday, when the Throne remembers the 9th. This man will have served that cause."

This confused the Black Boat men. There was some muttering and a trading of suspicious looks. Allred said again in a hoarse voice, "silence."

"While the first trial of the Haunt is performed, you'll be stationed to prevent disruption. Prepare yourselves. Once the gate is open, we can expect ... a struggle. That's the Ninth's concern. You'll only be called on to gather the treasures within. Go with Allred now down the path and wait," Cole said, "And say what prayers you have."

Odd. An odd turn. He corralled the men down the path out of sight of the gate. They were muttering, nervous, greedy. Criminals so they figured they were always being fooled. He could see the Haunt straining their nerve.

"Don't move from here until you're called, or you'll die," he said and turned smartly on his heel back to the gate.

He jogged back to Cole. The young soldier stood in front of Cole, bound, silent. Helga watched the soldier, then looked far down the road to her Rats.

"Shouldn't be here," he said to her.

"We're going in with you," Helga said.

Cole raised his hand, turned to her.

"She stays," Cole said.

Helga still seemed to think something was left undecided. Allred motioned her back towards the cliff edge.

"What we do is not the same as the songs tell."

Her mouth bent to an irritated frown, "Speak plain, man, in the language of the hills from where we hail."

"The Pits are dead temples, graveyards; it's treasure-hunting this is—" he tried to explain. Then he stopped, "So be it, cousin. Watch."

She looked confused at his words. Her face set hard. He couldn't argue anymore. The landscape around him was changing and he fended off the interruption of past visions onto the place around him. He needed to stay alert.

"See what needs to be seen," he said.

"You didn't tell me that," she replied.

For a moment, her eye was there, the patch gone, her face fresh.

"What?"

"Did I misspeak? The air feels heavy. It's a confusing place," she said.

He studied her smooth pale face, the delicate blue veins

around her good eye, the rose tint to her cheeks which hadn't faded. When last they met, she looked at him with both eyes and they had been merry and softer. She had seen doom's way since, yet she hadn't trod the path to its culmination; he wanted more than anything to save her from that in this moment.

This was different though— this was Cole's way.

"Try to be quiet," he said.

"It's hard to concentrate. We've encountered geists in the Pits—"

"Do you know where geists come from, cousin?" he almost screamed.

A pang of shame. He'd allowed dread to guide his words. She looked scared there on the mountain beside him. A scared woman with a long knife and one eye and she was far off kin, so he was ashamed at the crack in his voice.

"It's not always a proud thing this work," he said, quietly.

The calm inside again. The placid faces of the long-since-dead. The damned marching in holy procession. The temple glowed. The marble covering shifted and the shrieking abyss grew even louder. That black-green-milky eye peered out and the old people shouted. He heard the prayers in that old tongue, days ancient, spewing from the gate and the mages in conference with the spirits within.

Helga fell quiet. He saw her staring at the prisoner's back. Today he wore a rope around each of his arms, one around his torso, and two around his ankles. The ends of these ropes Hartha and Hortha attached to stakes they hammered in the ground with the flat of their axe heads.

"What is this deviltry?"

"Is there no poem that tells of it?" he asked.

"All things abiding in ancient places and around. Man before Allwein's creation, simple to behold, stand in open-mouthed awe, before the first calendar. Beneath all skin—skin of stone, skin of man, skin of moon, skin of sky—boils blood. Only blood and flesh, past skin and sky and sun," she recited.

"Nothing is simple and poets lie," he said.

"No," Helga replied and folded her arms. She set her jaw

and watched with her one good eye, "But what are those ropes for?"

"I told you to go."

Cole beckoned Mage who came towards them—the shadow of a panther, of a sleek thing on human feet clouded and cloaked. Green chaos-smoke flowed from the eyeholes of his bronze mask now. The island boy sat watching, crouched on the ground, arms wrapped around knees pulled up to his chest, rocking back and forth but witnessing all the same.

The soldier tried to say something, but his mouth made no words.

Mage stood in front of the prisoner now, facing the gate and reached into his cloak. In his hand, he held a shining key. He turned to Cole and said something in an ancient language. He saw Helga's astonishment when Cole answered Mage back in the same language and pointed to the gate, holding his finger firm. Mage watched Cole and beneath his mask, his eyes were watery. He said something short and sharp again and Cole answered with one guttural bark.

"Cole speaks that old Mage tongue?" Helga asked, "That's what it is. I've heard it before—bits of it in ancient poetry."

"He speaks it," he answered.

Speaks it well, in fact.

Mage embraced the prisoner and the young man fell into the arms of the cloaked man for a moment. Then the sorcerer uttered some other spell and offered the metal of the key up to the soldier's face who kissed it.

Mage turned with the key in hand. He thrust it forward into the mouth of the gate. The metal came alive, like a hungry dragon's mouth snapping onto the key. The sound of metal grinding against stone. The echoes of screams grew louder from within, faint ripples from the past merging with the present.

The first drops of rain kissed the old Semhelhen road.

The gate did not swing open, it retracted; top, bottom, left and right, four parts sliding back into the cliff wall. Dirt and rock spilled down from the upper lip of the hollowed-out cavern revealing a yawning blackness. The center portion of the gate hovered there, alien to the walls of itself, the Key spun inside the lock and then the Key and the mechanism floated down and to the side of the threshold.

Aacten required no push, or blade to the neck. He edged forward as if commanded by something unseen. His red tunic faded into the abyss, dragging the ropes through the gate.

The rain came down on the ancient cobblestones, revealing them. A thousand soft drumbeats ringing up through his boots. Helga touched his arm, pointed back along the edge of the cliff, "The rain brings those blooms. I've never seen such a thing."

The low bushes lining the cliff were heavy with green buds. When the rain touched them, they erupted into colorful flowers of purple and ruby, hungry splashes of color.

Can a man see too many lands before he loses his footing? he thought.

Children were picking those blooms, darting between the cloaked mages, while the procession moved forward. They cast them at the feet of those who fed the gate.

No. Dead. Gone. Ghosts. He must breathe and stop the visions of the past from obscuring the task at hand.

The ropes attached to the stakes pulled taut, like the sound of a whip. He turned away from the blooms. A scream sounded out above the rain and then the ropes slackened to heaps.

Cole started pulling those ropes. Scrolls stood beside him like a curious fishermen watching another man hauling in a catch. At the end of one the ragged, still-bleeding torso of Aacten tumbled back through the gate.

"Oh," Helga uttered, turning from the vivid flowers. The rain dripped down from her forehead, and she wiped it away.

One other rope returned what remained of a leg. The bone there stood out raw and white in the thin mountain air. The rest of the ropes returned nothing.

Aodlen and Scrolls both crouched down to examine the body parts.

Helga turned and gagged. Rising from her half-fold, she took leery steps towards the blooming plants, brushing through them, then vomited. He laid one hand on her back and kept hold of her, so she would not fall. She brushed him away, spit dripping down her chin.

Boph stood a few paces away, face smooth, stolid, like rock but Allred saw one of the boy's eyes twitching as the rain pattered on his bald head and dripped down his nose.

"My words won't reach certain ears," he said.

He wasn't sure if he was talking to Helga, the boy or himself.

"My head is light from this strangeness, that's all," she said, wiping her mouth. "He was a foe, right?"

"Poor luck. What can we know of his fate? You, an actress should know that. Don't the plays and follies say the same?"

He took out the small coal-carrier from his vest, careful to guard the little warm coal from the rain and lit a redleaf roll.

Mage turned the Key again and the gate closed. Scrolls took out his magnifying lens from his belt pouch. Aodlen bent down beside the torso studying the marks on it. He dipped a rag in one of the deep gashes soaking up what blood remained. He sprinkled a powder over the leg setting the leg to dance on the stones.

"This is what you do?" Helga asked.

"People think war is a simple thing. For some it is," he said.

A bit of the redleaf stuck to his tongue. He spit it out. "He was good as dead when captured."

"And we are to fight whatever ... entity, did that?"

"They are studying patterns of the bites, length of the jaw, such things, and pouring whatever powders they use to see hidden things. I know nothing of those arts. They'll match the world they divine, to the world written in Scroll's parchments. The soldier's remains are a map to what we'll have to face."

"Allred?" Helga asked and she touched him on the arm.

He looked at her. Kept smoking, wishing he had slept better the night before.

"What if Cole hadn't captured that man last night?"

He didn't say anything.

"Me? That boy?"

"If you die here, it won't by our hand."

The Relic hunters stood talking to one another. Scrolls took out from his pack an old folio, the cover fashioned of a rough leather fraught with small dimples. Bending over it to shelter it from the rain, he pointed to text and images in the pages.

"Best just to come and see," he said, and Helga followed him over to the huddled group.

Scrolls turned pages, each revealing an illustration of some demon, demi-god or beast. Names of things men had forgotten and only recalled in the garbled language of nightmare—things unthinkable came to life in the dried ink of oils and berry, madder and rust. Those images entered the eye and found little purchase in the spirit, and so when the pages closed each of the images of the unclean things grew difficult to recall.

Scrolls stopped at a page and pointed, "Likely, a Minor Leatherwing, not Major, I should think, no. They tend to live in groups. All will be in order if we proceed according to the plan."

Helga turned to Allred, "Plan?"

He didn't say anything. The men took up the ropes, began to coil them up. Cole cut loose flesh from the knots and tossed the torso over the gorge.

Aodlen covered the pools of blood with hasty sweeps of the sides of his boot, hiding the gore the rain had not washed away. "Ha! Ha!" And the rain kept coming.

"Proceed," Scrolls said.

"We're going in there to fight whatever did that?" Helga wouldn't stop talking.

Cole ignored her.

"Just watch and be quiet, cousin."

He turned to her and did a strange thing. He took her in his arms and gave her a gentle hug.

"I was wrong," Helga said.

"Yes."

He let her go. The sky stood heavy and grey like the leaden face of the gate itself.

Steady. Breathe.

Cole stalked down the trail, calling the Black Boat men up. Axes out, swords ready, they marched towards them. Allred had positioned them far enough down the road, that they couldn't see the fate of the prisoner.

"You can go back to the Rats now," he told her as the men clattered down the road.

"She'll stay," Cole said, glancing over at them both.

"I'll stay," Helga said, quietly. She tried to hold Cole's gaze but could not.

In the brief moments it took Cole to go gather the Black Boat men, Aodlen had pulled out a few pieces of gold and silver from one of the many satchels on his belt.

"One for medicine, one for wealth. Ha! Ha!"

The shrillness of the man's laugh fit the day. He had tossed a few of the coins around the entrance of the gate.

He lit another redleaf roll with the end of the last. Helga gestured, her fingers mimicking holding one. He lit another for her.

Greed filled the faces of the Black Boat men. They jostled one another near the gate at the sight of the precious coins near the entrance. One thin man knelt behind the rest of the group and scooped up one of the coins.

He did nothing to stop it.

"The path is clear," Cole paused, dramatically, "Never seen a richer Haunt. Hoards of gold. I'm not sure we'll be able to carry it all away."

The Black Boat men cheered again.

"It's been a long voyage. From the gaols of Port Coldewater to this devil-infested island. Some of you have fought and died already for the 9th. Mage will lead us in first. No need to raise a shield. We leave our weapons here at the mouth of the gate. Fast now. Grab as much as you can, then out again," Cole finished his speech.

The men cheered again. A few were wary of parting with their swords, but most dumped their weapons, at the mouth of the gate.

Allred went along the line, unsheathed his own sword and dropped it on top of the rusted weapons of the Black Boat men.

Helga opened her mouth. Stayed standing, doing nothing. She closed her mouth.

"What about us?" Helga asked.

"The Rats were last, so they'll follow last." Cole answered.

"Your lot will have the scraps of what the Black Boat men can't carry."

The men laughed. A couple ventured gestures at Helga fit for a back alley. He ignored it because he understood Cole's plan.

Then without further ado, Cole walked up to the front of the line and signaled to the mage, "Take what you've earned, Black Boat men."

Mage opened the gate with the key again and Cole led the way forward with the sorcerer following. The Black Boat men crowded in behind them, shoving each other.

He laid a gentle hand on Helga's arm to stop her from following.

In the moment after the last Black Boat man disappeared into the gate, Mage and Cole appeared standing on the threshold they had seemingly crossed.

A simple feint.

"They followed a mirage," Helga mumbled.

A brief silence, then, the screams and shouts of many men emanated out from the Haunt. Mage turned the Key, sealing the gate again.

Scrolls handed Cole a parchment. Cole walked over to Helga and handed it to her, "Read. I know you can. Then go with Allred and bring your Rats here."

She took the parchment in shaking hands and turned away from Cole. Allred knew exactly what it was.

"I see names. Beside the names a list of crimes. Murder. Rape. Brigandry," Helga said.

"That's who entered the Haunt. They're dead or will be soon if they're lucky—and if we're lucky. Criminals from the homeland. Cole's plan. Instead of hanging them back home, they shipped them to us. In their death, maybe they're redeemed. Or perhaps not."

Cole had spoken of the plan before to Allred once long ago. Their numbers low, one night he began formulating the idea around a campfire. How could they neutralize entities in Haunts, and punish their enemies at the same time?

Helga said, "You sent them straight into death?"

"Worse than that. The Rats will ask you where they went.

Tell them the truth or don't. Make up a better tale, if you like, since you're skilled in storytelling," Cole said.

Helga handed the parchment back to Scrolls. Cole lit his pipe, cupping the bowl to keep the rain out. He puffed, then took the parchment from Scrolls and the lit the edge of it on fire.

"The Rats serve the 9th and the rebellion," Helga said, looking out over the cliff.

"I believe you. You serve yourself also which isn't unwise," Cole said, puffing away calmly on his pipe. "You'll do well enough."

He took her by the arm.

"Walk with me, cousin," Allred said.

They made their way slowly back to the steps.

"Cole tells the truth?"

"Yes. He can afford to. He controls judges in Port Coldewater even though it fell to the Throne. The Black Boat men were tried there for crimes in the rebel held lands outside the city. The Throne must arrest them, or it looks as though they don't maintain order, but they don't prosecute them."

Cole's plan had been brilliant. To see it fulfilled, that was another thing. However, now what beasts had been satiated by the Black Boat men might leave them alone. It would buy them time.

"So, the judges offered them a deal. Serve on a ship and avoid the hangman. They took it. The ship arrives in Port Shamhalhan, and they see the Relic Hunters of the 9th. They don't care because they see a lot of gold coins, too."

He shook his head, after the sacrifice the visions of the old road had receded some, as if the Haunt was distracted with something besides torturing him with images from the past.

"We aren't cruel men, but Cole won't be stopped now, cousin. He's ... without any doubt. Truespoken."

Helga said, "We remember the 9th. You believe me?"

"Remember the 9th. I believe you. There's a time to give and take orders. Go and gather the Rats and meet us at the gate. There's no guarantee we live past the end of the day."

"Truespoken," she said and went on unsteady legs down the road to gather up her Rats.

He watched her speaking to them, gesturing. He saw their

heads nodding in agreement. The sound of pledges. He turned back down the road. He lit another redleaf. Gods, he was tired.

Cole, Scrolls and Mage were pointing to an area near the gate. Aodlen measured something out.

Cole walked over, meeting him halfway down the road, "She'll hold?"

"Yes," he answered.

"If all goes well, they'll be glorified porters."

"It never goes well."

"No," Cole said.

The boy, Boph, stood near the gate beside Mage and the other Relic Hunters.

"The boy is accustomed to the mage. He watched all that and didn't make a sound."

"I've taken note. Going to leave the two outside with Stoneburner. It's no real defense but we'll move fast, then depart Esmer quickly."

"If Optri show..." he started to say.

"Allred, I think I prefer northern climes, cooler weather. Many rich merchants of the Thronelands retire to villa cities around Port Shamhalhan but I don't care for the heat." He wiped his brow of the rain which had slackened. "Too humid in the south."

Cole did this before fights or entering Haunts. He would make small talk once plans were decided. Completely relaxed, jovial. He'd seen this strange change come over him, sunk to the knees in blood and mud amid a hail of arrows, smiling and making note of this or that.

"I haven't thought of where I go after it's all finished," he replied.

18

Lookout

He could admit, standing near the precipice, by the winding, moss-covered steps—that he wanted to return home.

Not to the tower. He tried to imagine staying there alone; the explorers finished and gone, drinking himself to sleep. That was the past. He wanted to go home to the farm, to his father's house. He couldn't do that either.

Lookout had heard tell of the bad magic up here, last night, when men settled into sleep around the campfire. He'd spied on the conversations the Black Boat men had of snakes falling from the treetops and devouring a man—worse the vipers had possessed the corpse with unclean speech.

Esmer had no venomous snakes. He had said nothing.

The rain began to fall and the Bahm shrubs opened their blossoms to drink.

Why was Boph conversing with Mage?

Boph abandoned him, chased after Allred, leaving him to

hold the reins of the gentle donkey, who unconcerned, turned its head up to the darkening sky, smiling with bared block-teeth at the mild sun dimmed to a chalk white behind the gathering clouds. The cool rain fell on its dun-colored back and the smell of the wet animal brought some familiarity to the terrible mountain peek.

Stoneburner stood with him waiting, working a twig between his teeth, counting and considering the packs and throwing glances down the trail. The dwarves stood about, too, chattering low to one another in a strange tongue. They were small but not too much shorter than himself. He had learned they came from the Green Island, a place where many children were born either small or quite large and where twins were common. It was good to learn of the world. The Rats seemed friendly enough and Helga—she kept coming to his mind, unbidden.

Afraid to follow, afraid to lead, this isn't how the knights think in the stories.

When he thought about it, the stories didn't tell you much about how knights and heroes thought, just what they did. They acted. They slayed dragons, they rescued princesses; sometimes they made speeches, but only in some of the stories—most tales didn't tell what was in the hearts of those men.

Stoneburner kept his eyes on the steps. Instead of a lute, he now held a crossbow and he wore a short, sharp sword slung from his hip.

The fighting last night, he still couldn't understand. It wasn't like the legends told. In the legends, the enemy didn't hide in trees or attack you while you were making a campfire or stab you in the back while you relieved yourself or shoot arrows at you while you raised a wooden spoon full of stew to your mouth. In the legends, men lined up, they *arrayed*—that was the word Boph used— for battle and they wore uniforms and held pendants and prayed to the proper gods.

What he had seen was this—men hacking at each other, half ducking away in ditches to hide. And when two men clashed and no one fell fast, it turned to wrestling, gouging.

Nothing made sense. And this place, wasn't helping Lookout order his mind. A lot of sitting and waiting and then suddenly arrows and edges, death—then sooner than you thought, the world grew just as quiet as before; birds sang in treetops, whistling their tunes above men screaming below in agony. Their songs unchanged.

He tried to explain what he was thinking, in quiet whispers to Stoneburner while the grizzled man kept his eyes on the steps below and the donkey nibbled clumps of grass growing beside the old road.

"It's part of war. Maybe you should consider the work of a bard instead of a knight. If you stick with us, I can show you some chords on the lute," he said.

"We're at war?" he asked.

"Somewhere, always," Stoneburner said. The older man looked nervous, more so than he had ever seen him. That made Lookout feel better in a way. At least he wasn't the only one disturbed by this strange place.

"What do you think, sir? I'll be taking today how, or rather, am I supposed to...what am I supposed to do?" he finally asked.

Out of all the explorers he had the kindliest face. He had taken care of him and Boph after the fight.

"You don't need to call anyone 'sir' here. We aren't aristocrats, except for Scrolls, I suppose. Either way. Cole gives us order ... If I had to guess, me and you and Boph will be doing a lot of sitting around and watching and waiting and hoping nothing bothers us while they're in the Haunt. Guard the baggage while the rest go into this thing. Hoping Cole won't ask me to go in. Lately, I don't but ..."

Lookout saw a look of fear pass over the man's face, and he loved him for it in that moment. Even one of the Relic Hunters was afraid.

"I want to go with the explorers," Lookout said.

He wasn't quite sure that was so but why not offer the thought out loud and see what Stoneburner would say? In some way, he did wish it.

On the other hand, they weren't what he thought explorers were really like. In the stories, explorers were usually grand men from grand houses. They wore rings and jewels which they had found in obscure and far-off places. They rehearsed stories of adventure and fabulous places, where often they met a beautiful daughter of some tribe.

Scrolls seemed a bit like that. A bit. He told of things obscure, but he rehearsed them in a flat, cold voice, a series of facts, locations, times, and dates.

Stoneburner laughed low.

"You were rattled by what you saw last night. There's no shame in it. What's inside that mountain is a hundred-fold worse, truespoke. I remember how I felt the first time I saw one of these places from the outside. Wonder, yes, true. I went in with all the rest. I'd do it again, if I had to but it's not the same in there as it is out here. The whole place comes down on you. The Upside never looks the same after."

"Upside?"

"It's what we call everything around us. But you don't think of it like that until you go into the Haunt. Nothing seems the same after. It wears off in time. For some people. Never really leaves you, though." Stoneburner threw the twig he'd been chewing aside.

"How'd you start to explore? Seeing all different kinds of places and people. Better to do that, than stuck on a small island like me, isn't it?"

"You just fall into certain jobs, I suppose," Stoneburner said.

That sounded like something an old man would say. It may be true, but he didn't like it all the same.

"I think, I got chosen for something when you showed up. It won't be as easy as I thought. I'm not from a royal house, it's true. Still, I have my own visions of things. I can't turn away from that. It's true those visions come to me mostly after I've downed a full bottle of cownut liquor, but they show me I'm destined to be a knight."

"That might be, boy," Stoneburner acknowledged, glancing over at him while fussing with the straps of a pack. He didn't seem happy for it.

A thought occurred to him then.

"I forgot my commission," he said.

"Your what?"

"My commission that Scrolls gave me. The official paper. I was thinking if the bad Imperials were to find me, I could show it to them and maybe—"

"I imagine Scrolls can muster up another one for you."

No. How had he messed that up, too? How did he mess everything up? Couldn't even guard a piece of paper.

"It's not good. If you leave us here and other Imperials, come and I don't have the commission to show..."

He left off. Unease began to shake him, maybe the change in weather, sudden and odd, or strange sounds he heard echoing down the road, which he preferred to ignore stoked the feeling.

The Rats who had huddled several paces away, shot worried glances at him when his voice rose in frustration and panic. Stoneburner stopped fiddling with the packs. He came over and pat him on the shoulder.

"It's alright now, boy. I'll ask him about another for you when this is over."

"I could go back to the watch tower and grab it." He realized that was the dumbest thing he'd said out loud for some time. Half a day's hike through an evil forest for a paper, where if all went well, they would return to anyway. "It wouldn't take long." He added, defeated by his own dumb thoughts, then to his great embarrassment he realized he was crying, the last sentence coming out in a hiccupping slobber.

Stoneburner gripped his shoulder tighter. With his other hand he kept the crossbow trained down the steps. His eyes were soft and sad in the rain.

"You're in with us now, boy. Don't worry. It's this mountain and the Haunt that's getting to you. Mage, too, sometimes—well, he can't help it—but he gets to normal folks." The man bent down now, came face-to-face with him. "I won't lie to you. We're in for some real trouble for a good long while. Don't go running off by yourself. You'll get your commission, don't worry. And you just, listen now, don't worry."

"Why are you kind to me and Boph?" he asked, quietly.

"You remind me of someone else, someone good. Now be quiet."

Stoneburner put on a brave smile and Lookout knew it was on his account and he thanked him in his heart for it. A scream echoed down the cobblestones. The donkey brayed and the Rats shivered in their huddle, but Stoneburner just kept smiling as best he could until soon enough Helga and Allred came down the road for them.

19

Helga

She had learned to adapt early in life.

A juggler drops the ball, turns it into a jest for the amusement of a crowd—a thing purposeful. An acrobat misses a tumble, but instead of seeing the stumble the crowd witnesses the genesis of a jig. They laugh. A singer forgets the next line, so holds the note, new songs spring from lapses in memory, the never-ending attempt to recall.

Above all, buy time. Keep the audience on your side.

The landscape turned in directions she couldn't describe as if it were crawling, sliding around itself. She felt something watching her, something large and inhuman in this mountain. She had become an actor again, unwitting, in a play which she didn't direct.

She had seen a little too much, a little too fast. It was catching up to her and the Rats. As she approached the stairs at the end of the trail, she read it on their faces.

Allred had tried to warn her away from the work of relic hunters, the effects on the spirit even this distance to the Haunt could have; and because he had, she trusted him more and wouldn't leave.

Like in a performance, if the audience sees the actors under their costumes, the audience is displeased. She had seen under the costumes of the Relic hunters of the 9th. She decided to not speak of the Black Boat men's fate to the Rats.

The Rats, the ones that were left would follow her no matter what now.

No way back.

The Rats looked up eagerly. To Stoneburner she spoke.

"I think they're ready."

Stoneburner nodded, moved off towards the gate with Lookout and the donkey. Now, she was left alone with her people.

"My cousin has told me, true—this will be a fraught thing. He says some may die—well, seems sure of it. Those that don't perish will suffer a disorientation of the spirit after." As she spoke the words out loud, she realized maybe she should have listened to Allred and Cole and stayed out but she continued. "We've been in the Pits. We know a bit about that. I've always told the truth to the Rats, honest tales of the way things run. None of you must go if you want to stay outside. That's what I have to say."

By heart she knew the poems of Estarte and had recited them, standing on her head in the center of villages while simpletons and boys tried to glance up her dress. Pay the silver, see the show—while her dwarves tumbled about her, she could sing the songs of the hills with a voice clear and cold as crystal.

Now her voice sounded tired and unsure.

"Come this far. I won't turn back," Thay said.

Shad looked sheepish, stepped forward with his hands up as if pleading. "I'm staying out, Helga. Decided it. I'll keep a look out but the Haunts not the place for me," Shad said.

"You may be the wiser for it," she said. For a moment, she wanted the rest to say no, to sway her to say no.

She wished they had all refused her long ago and drifted off like the rest. They could make their way in this world, hiding in free cities, make some silver at faires, markets and inns.

Her head was swimming already and the rain brought out the smells of the old leather she wore. She was sure it was silly but she would give all the gold in the world for a warm bath in a quiet inn.

> ...the hard rain, reckless, soothed survivor's steel in the
> hearing,
> unlike the slain,
> mud-drinkers, blood-spillers,
> above and below, ears sealed to the merry sounds,
> the rain cares not where it falls,
> free-rain plunges out of hard sky, time

Was that the poet's words?

One big run with these killers. That's what they were. It wasn't as if she didn't know it before. It's easy to hear of the killing men do when you share loyalty with them. It's a different thing to see it done.

She adjusted her eyepatch with trembling finger. The cloth felt cold and damp. One less eye to cry tears.

Trying a smile, lopsided and cocky, she pointed up at the inhuman structure.

"Looks like nothing we've seen in the Pits. That's for sure. Won't be scavengers anymore."

"Fortune!" Staah answered.

"Then, follow me."

The poet Boethius would have been ashamed of her taciturn speech. But then he had never had to face the Pits, or a Haunt and lived a life ensconced in velvet and silk inside a palace.

The Rats followed her to the gate. Shad traded quiet talk with Staah, then fell behind and went over to speak to Stoneburner. She wondered if the others knew he wouldn't go before she did.

Stoneburner was handing around various armors, secreted away in the baggage and the men of the 9th were armoring and arming themselves with different weapons.

Scrolls draped a delicate chainmail over his thin frame. It was so fine it looked like the webs of a spider—magemade, certainly. It cast a mysterious light, each link cold and precise and proud.

"Rats, listen," Cole said.

As he spoke, he slipped heavy spaulders over each of his arms and Stoneburner helped him fasten them to his lighter leather vest. Inset within the metal of the spaulders flashed dozens of Small-Suns. He would be able to light the way in darkness with it. She'd never seen such a thing or even imagined it could be made. The cost would have been enormous. Winding around each piece of magic light, a thin script was seared into the metal.

"Once we enter, we close the gate. You couldn't leave anyway if you wanted. The spirit cannot survive a quick coming and going between the gates. That's why it's profitable for me to have your extra hands to carry out as much as possible."

Helga began to say something, but Allred cut her off with a gesture and leaned in close to her and whispered.

"We move together. Listen and obey, and you survive."

He turned back to Cole, and Stoneburner handed him a light steel helm. It was a plain thing but ancient looking, scarred with symbols she could not read. Then Stoneburner fitted a bracelet of old hemp with three jewels hanging from it to the swordman's wrist.

"You'll all have one too. Mage and Scrolls designed them. They help keep the mind intact inside the Haunt." Stoneburner whispered.

He rushed around the gate, pulling weapons, armor, and strange objects to outfit them all. He came to her and her Rats and carefully fit the small bracelets on their arms almost tenderly, "Be careful with them. They will bring luck within."

Cole continued.

"Scrolls believes this is a part of a large palace and tomb complex of a servant to a high mage called Calthor. If there *is* a tomb complex, we want to seek it out."

The spaulders were fit to Cole now. He donned no more heavy armor. He lit his pipe once more to smoke.

"We'll encounter at least one Leatherwing on entering. You are not to fire at it, or fight it, nor should you look too closely at it. That goes for everything inside. Unless something attacks you directly, or you're ordered to fight just listen and walk. If I keep my voice low, you stay silent. If I talk, you talk in a whisper. Scrolls?"

Scrolls stepped beside Cole and addressed them.

"It would be foolish and unprofitable for me to attempt to explain to uneducated entertainers the story of Calthor or the methods by which I have discerned the likely architecture of this structure. It suffices to say, that dialogue with Calthor's servants is discouraged and will lead to madness. With any luck, we will not encounter Calthor's servant as I expect him to be far deeper inside the Haunt than we intend to penetrate."

The scholar cocked his head as if listening to his own thoughts for a moment, "You'll acclimate to the Haunt within the first moments on entering. Or you will not. If you don't, you never will and you'll be removed, hastily before the gate is sealed, though that's a desperate measure. However, if you were to lose possession of your spirit, you become a distraction, so we will take that risk. With the protecting charms you should be sound. You'll drink a tincture of our own design as well. Doctor?"

Aodlen hurried around to everyone except the two boys, Shad and Stoneburner, reaching into his satchel and pulling out small glass vials, pressing them into the hands of the Rats.

"Ha, ha! A tincture of ingenious design! When you enter a Haunt, most mortal people need only a few drops. The Haunt works on the spirit. Who knows why the gods cast our souls in their peculiar way, their fragile molds? If you feel your soul tempted into chaos, you may drink half of this vial at once and no more. No more, no matter what! Exceed my recommendation and you'll perish, ha!"

Aodlen put on no special armor as he handed them the vials. The odd, thin man had fitted himself out with a charm and his belt was heavy with pouches and satchels and lined with small saws and knives meant to work on flesh. He had tied a brilliant, orange scarf around his forehead over his mad and feverish eyes to keep the sweat from pouring down his face.

"What is it?" she asked.

"A fine recipe. Don't bother yourself with the ingredients," Aodlen replied, "Eases the toll. Now, dear girl, dear Helga, dear Rats, one and all—take your medicine."

She turned to Allred and wanted to scream, "Is it poison?"

He shook his head, no, and raised his own vial and drank from it. She watched the others do the same and followed. It tasted bitter and the smell rushed from the back of her throat up into her nostrils. She sneezed.

The mage suddenly manifested beside her, silently, the faintest swoop of his cloak. She jumped back a half step and tried to smile at the man but failed.

"Apologies. My step can be quiet," Mage said, sheepishly. It broke her heart a little.

A feeling like soft lightening rippled through her body. Mage smiled his sad smile beneath his mask. Cole stretched his neck, slapped the metal of the greaves above his shoulders, pulled tight a leather strap.

She noticed that he alone wore no charm.

"You'll hold our Eye, Helga of the Rats," Cole said and though it made no sense, she almost felt like he had read her mind and heard her observation about his lack of a charm and chose her as a punishment. Chose her for what, though?

"Allred?"

"Do not be afraid," Mage whispered.

The words Mage spoke formed in the air—drawing, slithering scripts before emanating from his mouth. He drew out a dagger from his cloak and took her hand. The jewels in his teeth flashed and he smelled like incense and a wound.

"It is a burden and heavy magic, but it will not harm you, cousin," Allred told her.

Mage studied Helga's arms and hands.

"She's right-handed," Allred said.

"I am," Helga agreed.

The mage took the curved dagger and traced a pattern above the flesh on Helga's arm. Beneath the tip of the blade the skin turned dark but there was no pain. She bit her lip and said nothing, refusing to shudder or scream.

The Rats watched. Tym reached for his dagger, but she stayed him with a look.

"Look at the wall near the gate," Cole said.

She did. Traced there beside it, staring at them all was a drawing matching exactly the design the mage wrought on her arm.

Aodlen explained:

"When we go inside the Haunt the Eye will ... ck, ck, ck," He clicked his tongue, adjusted his scarf and paced about the road, talking loudly but not looking at her. "Let's say, let's say it will illuminate the flesh. Ha! Ha! No, not comforting. Do no harm to it or your own flesh which feeds it. It will allow us to see outside here, like a portal, yes."

The mage stepped back, "It's a heavy burden for me, my lady. This way if the other flames, bad flames, good flames any flames come-a-flicker flicker flickering, you'll see, we'll see. You'll see too much. Alas, after all this time. I will take it away. I have taken it away. Your shiny arm grows shining again," Mage laughed.

The note of high chaos in the man's words kept climbing with every syllable. His language started to break apart. She knew then for sure; these men's spirits had flown to pieces from their work.

The bronzeface began to sing. A dirge, no words at first, only a melody. The wind rushed through the trees and the day grew darker and then the Key was in his hand again.

She muttered, "I see."

Then she laughed. Aodlen looked up surprised and cackled. Allred snorted. She could have sworn Cole almost smiled. Hartha and Hortha raised their weapons as if hailing the sky above, shouted something to their short Green Island brethren which she did not understand and lumbered into place on each side of the mage. Each were fitted with heavy armor now, which the Black Boat Men had carried, atop their heads, steel helmets with metal horns. Each man appeared a fortress.

Her Rats approached her to study the odd design and she showed them her arm. Aodlen covered the Eye with a bandage, mild and damp with a sort of undiscernible grease. She thought she could feel the design beneath feeding on it.

Cole explained, "You've heard of an Eye before?"

"In legends."

"High magic. Once inside, it will open. Do not remove the bandage until you're told to."

"Heard," Helga said.

She mimicked Allred's voice, low and smoke-scratched.

Her Rats laughed and for a moment, she thought she discerned that trace of a smile on Cole's face again but then it was gone.

"Fortune, Helga of the Rats," he said.

"Protect Mage. He's the center of our battlegroup. Without him, we die," Allred put in, then threw the end of his redleaf behind him.

"In the main, you and the Rats will stay together and guard what we bring inside. Water, some food, specialized tools and weaponry which you're not to touch. Stoneburner has prepared the packs you'll bring in and the empty ones, you'll bring out. It's that simple. If something goes wrong inside and we need to stay longer, we will need those things. You don't touch anything unless you're told to do so. Touch the wrong thing and you die."

"Heard," she repeated.

Cole turned to the dwarves, they mimicked her.

Stoneburner smiled, "Here."

He fitted the pack onto her back, checked the bracelet again on her wrist and patted her arm. He extended his hand in the tradition of the hill country, and she grasped it.

The two giants were speaking their own language to each other, rousing each to war, making pledges of blood. She could understand much of it. They put thicker torcs on each other's arms which shimmered and hummed with power. Hortha had reached into his pack and draped a long copper necklace over his thick head. It was adorned with dried ears of various creatures, some human. His brother did the same and Hortha caught her staring at him and grinned.

"One of my ear necklaces. For fortune and luck," he laughed.

"One of them?"

"Aye, I've got an unlucky one, too but that wouldn't help, Helga."

She didn't know if she was supposed to laugh but then Cole turned to the Haunt.

"Remember the 9th."

Everyone straightened at his words. She felt braver at the simple phrase. Hearing it from the mouth of Cole, the legend of the City of Flames, she wouldn't forget.

Cole signaled. Mage fed the key to the gate. The metal hidden within the cliff shifted and shuddered and she could feel another world yawn before her. It held the old scent of blood.

One by one, they walked into the darkness.

Interlude

Stoneburner

S omething has changed."
 Stoneburner's back hurt. He stood straight, stretched his arms to the ceiling, his hands heavy with gold pieces. He emptied his fists on the large oak table, the coins clattering, settled heavy on its surface.

Allred sat smoking in the corner of the room, ensconced in the soft folds of an ornate chair. The rough warrior amongst rich surroundings was an odd sight. Southern light poured through the closed window near him, falling on his knees and boots and catching the hilt of the dagger he wore; the top half of his body reclined in shadow. Beside him a low table held a silver goblet brimming with ruby Coldewater wine. He had barely touched it.

"I said, something has changed," Stoneburner repeated.

"What?" Allred answered.

The man wanted to say something to him, but wouldn't come out with it, that much he knew. He'd knocked on the door, poured some wine and sat there in the corner, smoking, then standing and gazing out of the window, then sitting again, saying nothing, pretending to drink the wine.

It was no easy thing to get the man to speak.

The Relic Hunters were spread out across the city. Safer that way. Cole had directed him to purchase this place years ago. Half of the palaces were sinking into the water of the harbor and most of the wealthy families who once had inhabited the quarter had since moved to higher ground. A long passage at the bottom of the palace, behind a hidden door, led out to the harbor itself, through a dim, old aqueduct milling with bugs. It allowed for the coming and going, the stealth, they required. Unfortunate. The front door of the palace was a beautiful ornate thing of heavy old wood and bronze ornamentation and he didn't get to use it as much as he would like.

He kept the bulk of their treasure and records here. Down the hall, Scrolls had filled a room with trunks of parchments. Allred took residence down the hall, in a small, unfurnished room.

Even though he slept near, it was the first time he had shown up in his suite of rooms. At night, Stoneburner could hear the man's boots as they echoed across the empty halls.

"Cole. Something brewing in his brow."

Time to say it, plain.

Allred didn't answer. He picked up the goblet, raised it to his lips, hesitated.

"Cole doesn't change," Allred said, setting the wine back down. "We're between places. Nothing new. It's the waiting that wears on us. We don't belong around ... people the same way, anymore."

Stoneburner slid the coins around with the tips of his fingers, rearranging them. There was no pattern to find there, just gold.

"There's this Black Boat business. I've known him longer than you and I say something has changed. Not completely, you hear? But all the same."

"Could be," Allred offered.

The warrior rose, turned, walked to the window, his glassy

green eyes lit by the sun. He stood studying the empty inner courtyard below, where rain-blackened leaves clung to one another. The waves of the harbor lapped against the crumbling sea wall not far away. There'd been a mild squall earlier and now the skies were painfully clear. Thick clouds pregnant with rain still hovered, undecided as to move farther out to sea or make landfall once again.

"If it *could* be, what *would* it be?"

Allred said nothing for some time. Peeked through the lapse in the heavy drape over the window and watched the bay.

"Too many named men are dead. Friends. We're thinner. And there's war."

They fought and died but that wasn't new. Less and less of them, true. They were down to the last few of the named men of the 9th. But that wasn't it.

A cloud shifted outside. The light through the window touched the gold basking on the table before him, lit the jewels accompanying the coins, and reflected on the orb-infused steel of a dagger worth more than many a rundown palace.

"Cole's figuring something," he offered.

"Could be."

"Something's changing in him."

"Could be."

Stoneburner threw his hands in the air, "If all you're going to do is 'could be' me all day, then finish your wine and out the door with you. I've got things to arrange here, boy. Speak plain."

Stoneburner called all of them boy, except Cole when he was frustrated. He was older by ten turns than most of them. He was feeling his age, lately, too. Too much moving around, too much lugging this and that. Too much death on top of all that. He had children of his own, near enough Allred's age, though Allwein willing they would never look as hard done as he.

Allred didn't budge. Let him rant a bit, let the old man shout. He let out a sigh and it turned to a cough.

"Could be is all he says."

He picked up the spectacles that Scrolls had made for him. Better to see the loot, to count the numbers. He fixed the wires over his ears, slumped on the bench in front of the treasure-heavy table. The coins grew clearer. He saw the suggestion of old blood on the dagger. Blinked. Maybe not. Maybe it was only the southern light of Port Shamhalhan.

"The plainest words are unspoken," Allred said, "That's what I've heard said."

"You're a damned poor conversationalist."

"I can go do something useful, pull Aodlen out of the tavern."

Stoneburner snorted, "You knocked on my door."

Allred walked back to the corner, looked to leave, then slid into the chair again, wincing and stared back.

"Bones bothering you? Shouldn't at your age."

"Not bad."

"So then?"

Allred took out a small whetstone from a bag around his belt, slipped his dagger from its sheathe and began to sharpen the weapon. He eased the metal down the stone once, twice, three times, sheathed the dagger and lit another redleaf roll.

"We're losing," Allred finally offered, "Years in the Haunts, got a treasury bigger than most kingdoms even after what we've sent off, but we're losing all the same. The Throne won't need many more seasons to win. The Marchlands will fold, Scrolls' father is already in a half-truce with the Throne, says it's for our good though. Feels like we're losing in all sorts of ways."

"Finally, he says something."

He half stood, situated the bench under his girth to face the taciturn man and leaned his left elbow on the table, where the cold of coin-metal pressed against it. He unstuck one of the gold coins from the fleshy part of his arm. On its face the image of the king stared back at him. He cursed it, remembering the fire.

"There's that but that's not what I mean," Stoneburner said. He tossed the coin in a pile with the rest.

He thought of the war more than most. His elder son, fought for the Throne and his second son in the rebellion. The last he had heard, his eldest was far away still. Every single night he prayed he'd stay far away. He couldn't bear the idea of facing up against his own son someday, if it came to that. Couldn't. Wouldn't ever do it.

"No, that's not what you mean, so why don't you speak clear, old man," Allred said.

"Something in Cole," He gave up on the thought. There was something there, but he couldn't consider it anymore. He turned the conversation back to the simplicity of war. "You think we ought to go back and fight? Is he considering it?"

Allred spun the goblet around slowly on the table.

"The gold from what we find in the Haunt ships a lot of swords, feeds a lot of soldiers, buys loyalty from a lot of lords. We do more in this work than we could on the ground fighting. Same time, there's nothing like being there. What do you mean about Cole?"

Three turns in Haunts on the rim of the world. The Relic Hunters of the 9th were likely among the richest relic hunters in the land; even accounting for the massive wealth they handed off to middlemen and spies to keep the rebellion brewing.

"You think he's planning on turning us around? Take the fight to the Throne?" he purposefully misunderstood the warrior's query.

Allred blinked, stared at him.

"I think Mage is worn down. Not just him. Don't know how many more Haunts we can run. Hartha and Hortha are good enough, still. The rest of us will be lucky to end our days in a Temple for the Haunted. I don't think we even have that kind of luck left. And, old man, I think that's what you're trying to say, not whether I think Cole is going to turn us around to fight. What I want to know? Something I can't get my mind around—why don't the Haunts devour him like it does us?"

That was what he was wondering himself but he wasn't sure he wanted to know the answer. He'd heard some people could go to the Dowside with no consequences but he'd never met them. Rumors. And there was the magic the big relic-hunting expeditions employed, terrible stuff, to make those who descended forget forever, turning them to slaves or simpletons. Mostly, there was a middle ground of nightmares, sudden violence, spasms, hallucinations that all the other relic hunters he'd ever talked to experienced. Eh, some just went mad straight off. The first time he had entered one, he had a moment like that, as if some cold void was just under his feet, starting to work its way through the bottom of his boots to his head. He had felt like he was about to fall through into nothing.

"Well?"

Allred blew a smoke ring, looked back out the window.

"Ask him?"

He laughed, started coughing again.

"Maybe he's just built that way. Never saw him flinch in a battle either. Maybe that's Cole."

"Could be."

Something else though. And it was that something else that had been bothering him and Allred both, like a bug that lands on your neck and starts crawling and then you swipe it away but you keep feeling it there.

"Me and Cole found another map. Haunt-crazed man in the temple. Cole already has Scrolls looking over it. So, I think we're headed south."

"How far?"

"Some small island no one's heard of. South. Island called, Esmer."

"Well, that answers one thing."

Stoneburner had been inside, like all of them. Unlike most of them, he had been left outside the foul places mostly after the first year. Left to guard baggage, to wait and watch, sweat or freeze around lonely campfires and watch his friends exit the gates, hollow-eyed and unclean, the ones who were lucky and made it out again.

"And there's the prisoners coming ... that's a different type of thing Cole has planned. That change, I'm trying to figure in him. I don't know, boy. I'd just prefer to go back and have the fight and be done with it. That's all I'm thinking," Stoneburner said.

But they were Haunt-bound and would be setting off soon enough. If they found another map, Cole would come to knock on the door of this room and tell him to prepare. Buy stores for a ship, outfit the men for whatever weather they would face, make trades, count coins, hire porters, bribe this man and that one, and leave no trace they had spent their time waiting in Port Shamhalhan.

"I've thought the same," Allred agreed.

"You think Cole thinks it?"

"Ask him," Allred replied, "He answers every question a man asks."

"Thought maybe you had. Could be, I will. Thing is Cole somehow makes you not want to ask a lot of questions. Like he has the answers but their heavy and he carries them for us."

"That's why we follow him," Allred replied.

"Could be," he said and laughed.

Finally, Allred scooped the goblet off the table underhanded, drank the wine down in one draught, set it lightly back on the table and made to leave. Walking softly across the huge room the warrior came over to him, paused at his side and put a hand on his shoulder.

"We don't ask because we don't want to know, Stoneburner. It's easier that way."

"Just wondering how much longer we can do it," he said.

"I don't know. With Aodlen's medicine—long enough for us all to die in there."

"We're damn near all dead, already. I'd just like to fight mortal men again."

"Likely we'll have our chance."

"I remember the 9th."

"Aye."

The hard look on Allred's face fell away.

There was just the man standing before him in the center of an undecorated room. The young fighter from the hills. A man Stoneburner had seen fell hundreds with his blade but who wouldn't taste meat anymore. A man he had seen weep over a fallen horse but who had slain more men on the battlefield than any warrior he knew besides Cole and a few other legends of war.

And in Stoneburner's time, he had known a lot of warriors.

"I follow Cole. His hands gave the proof. That's enough for me. But what you say isn't wrong and I'm glad it's been said."

"Truespoke. Cole, I'll follow to the end. But I'm older now, someday I hope you get cursed with that problem, boy."

Allred nodded, looked to leave, pressed one hand against the door and then without turning—

"It's good to serve with you, Stoneburner. That's what I came here to say. Not to figure out anything else. I stopped trying to figure anything out. It's heartening to see your fat old face waiting when we come out of the Haunts. You're a good man and that's all I came to say."

Stoneburner opened his mouth to answer, but Allred slipped out of the room before he could reply. The warrior's boots echoed on the stairs, down the hollow, bare halls and faded.

He took his spectacles off, rubbed his forehead with fingers thick-knuckled and stiff. Surprised, he saw on the table two or three circles the size of raindrops appear. Hurriedly, he set his spectacles down, wiped the moisture away with a small burlap bag beside him, heavy with gold coins faced with the man who'd tried to kill them all.

In the quiet of the room, a melody suggested itself to him. Another song.

"Just getting old, that's all."

He leaned back on the bench, looked around the room. It was filled with wealth and weapons, notes, documents, real and forged, stamps of all kinds, coins, maps and gold.

Along the walls, standing tall, as if on parade, the packs of the Relic Hunters of the 9th stood. Some were for the living, filled with useful things for a quick escape.

Others marked the dead, the personal things of the fallen which he would not consign to pyres but brought back when he could. Those packs he kept. Someday, he believed he would return them to their kin.

They had set there for some time. No one spoke to him about them. No one talked about them. They were like mortuary stones marking the dead. Even the ones waiting for the living.

He stood, refilled his own goblet with wine and drank it down. Standing in the center of the room alone, he said, "Could be."

Part 2

The Haunt on the Island of Esmer

20

Allred

Back again, a return. A different Haunt, a different time but the feeling of familiarity all the same. The fear reached into him. His neck was stiff with it, his back rigid and his hands were numb. He stood in the narrow, short tunnel that was the gate's throat. It was tall enough that he didn't need to bend over and the stone walls were splattered with bits of blood, sheets of skin and blasted bone. The imprint of hands, memorialized briefly in blood, trying to clutch the ground—the sweep of fleeing bodies dragged through their own purple gore to the Haunt. A castaway dagger had landed in a peculiar position, tilted upward against the curved wall. The air was close. Just beyond, the warm smell of viscera wafted through the tunnel on ancient air.

"Keep moving. It'll either come down on us hard or not at all."

Cole stopped in the tunnel behind him, his back against the wall of rock, shepherding the rest inside. He'd summoned a soft light from his spaulders on entering and he looked like a cruel angel sent down from Allwein.

Allred crept forward through the narrow hallway; crossbow raised. At the terminus of the tunnel an unreadable script was chiseled into the stone lintel. It glowed a faint green as if illumined from the flesh of the mountain beneath.

He kept the line moving.

Behind him, the gate stood open. The light from outside soft and cloud-dampened still lit the tunnel. He heard the slide of rock and the light dimmed. They were shut in now, no turning back.

He stepped out, past the tunnel. Beneath the lintel he felt the hair on his neck stand as if the script above noted him, recognized him and his entrance. One small step down and his boots splashed in blood gathered in puddles at the mouth of the tunnel. Before he realized it, he let go a low whistle of amazement that stuck in his dry mouth.

Ivory columns, each the width of a horse and chariot, towered in the darkness. They finished in elaborate capitols of carved stone high above. Great wings gathered the still air and the sound bounced off the alabaster columns and sped across the stone of the floor, reverberating out into unseen corners. The weight of ancient predators peering down from above pressed on him and made his face itch.

The columns formed what once would have been a magnificent courtyard to a great temple complex. The roof if there was one had disappeared and now the columns plunged into shadow, holding nothing, falling short of the innards of the mountain top which pressed down above, carved out by nature or man he could not tell.

The entire space was dim but not pitch-black. Torches burned along the walls to the left and right, disappearing forward into rows of pinpricks of light. They burned in the thick air, green and yellow. He had seen these things in other Haunts, even come upon the creatures who tended them. Half substance, half fueled by foul magic, like much of these lands.

232

The darkness above the column tops shifted as if unseen clouds floated at the apex of the Haunt obscuring ancient stars. Where the tops of the columns disappeared, he could see gentle lights, dimming, then brightening and blinking, like fireflies in a summer field after the rain. From above, issued the sound of wingbeats and above that another, in the background—like a thousand dead voices holding a single eternal note and it bade him think on the color of bones.

There's nothing to kill yet, he thought.

He had seen the unnatural wonders of many a Haunt and so the spectacle did not overwhelm him. The wooden handle of the crossbow creaked as he squeezed it.

Behind him, a cry and a shout was aborted by a hand slapped over an anxious mouth. The rest of the group stood gathered at the mouth of the gate now. Helga and her Rats carried mundane torches dispensed by Stoneburner just before entering. A torch was on the stone floor, its flame wavering where the dwarf named Thay had tossed it. He started to breakdown straight away at the sheer weird of the place.

The dwarf was on his knees laughing and weeping both. Helga bent over behind him, holding her hand over his mouth, pleading to him to stand in reassuring whispers.

She fished the vial Aodlen had given him out of the dwarf's vest, uncorked it and put it against her compatriot's lips. He drank and his body went slack, leaning against her legs. She looked up, unsure of what to do next.

The rest of the Rats stood in various postures of quiet confusion. Waiting for someone to tell them what to do. Aodlen went to them, to reassure them. Cole ignored them, making his own survey of the place, then came forward and stood beside him. His boots sloshed through the blood. It reminded Allred of the tunnel beneath the palace in Shamhalhan, always filled with murky, warm sea water from the bay—a temporary home, yes, and some would find it haunting, a half-empty palace housing damned men and cursed treasure, but he missed that place desperately now.

Something big moved through the courtyard's gloom ahead. A deep black, more subtle than the shadows, slid behind the base of one of the towering pillars. Dust and the bodies of long-dried vines cascaded from the column as the beast brushed against it. The air rushed full of dust which danced in the torchlight.

Everyone braced. Hands sought hilts and hafts in the scramble of metal across sheaths. Scaly footfalls, claws the size of broadswords scraped across the stone floor to answer.

Mage stepped forward.

"Do not fear." he said.

His words were simple and clear. His spirit aligned with the Haunt, his mind free from the turmoil of the Upside; though the Haunt pressed on him as hard as any other, Mage could often speak clearer in the below-world.

The sound of wings. Something large shook the ground in the thrusting scamper leading to flight. The beat of leathery wings ascended and descended, and the shape of a beast drummed away the unknown lights above.

The shouts of a Black Boat man came down from some hidden eyrie atop the columns or built between rafters in the far-off heights of the Haunt.

Then the scream died out and the high, haunted hymn of note like bone faded to silence.

"Hold," Cole whispered.

Nothing. Everyone held their breath and then a hunk of flesh fell to the courtyard splattering on the stone floor—a naked arm torn from an unlucky torso, ragged with gnaw.

Another Rat cried out to an unfamiliar god.

Allred heard the faint pop of someone opening another vial, followed by the wet sound of another piece of flesh falling to the ground. As his eyes adjusted to the dimness, he could see arrayed in front of them, the bulge and shadow of other body parts. The puddles of blood fed from feasting above.

Wings wrought of flesh and steel rushed down. The double pulses of winged things in flight. He sensed it pressing down on him. He didn't move, just stood tall and still, refusing to crouch. He felt a suppressed war-scream buried in his throat and reveled in its power.

The beast skidded to a halt in front of him and Cole, missing them both by a horse-length. In its onyx-beaked mouth it grasped the leg of one of the Black Boat men. It threw its head back and swallowed it down a spasming gullet. The green eyes on each side of its narrow head did not leave them as it ate.

Scrolls had called it a Minor Leatherwing.

Its face was half bird and half feline—all green and rust and grey and old, with the faintest outlines of what could have been an old bronze mask painting the short plumage above its mouth and below its eyes. It regarded them. Its eyes were not human but sheltered some keen recognition. Feathers sprouted on its neck, each one pointed, sharp, a knife, a crest and fan of magic-wrought sword-shaped feathers.

Mage raised a hand. Blood and flesh dripped from the Leatherwing's jaws. It cocked its head curiously, staring back at the sorcerer.

Behind him, Helga and the Rats were stomach-down on the ground, in attitudes of near-worship in their fear.

One of the dwarves lost his nerve, got to his knees and loosed an arrow. Helga slapped the bow from the dwarf's hand. The arrow missed. The Leatherwing turned its head to the source as if curious about another fellow-flying thing and uttered a half-hiss of contempt.

Cole said again, "Hold."

Mage offered his hand to the Leatherwing. Outstretched, broken fingers beckoned in crazed patterns. The beast shuffled forward with sinuous steps, paused, moved forward, sniffed, then walked backwards; shy, half-disappearing behind the nearest column it stood peeking out from behind it.

Mage spoke a spell. Grasping the fingers of his left hand with the right, he shifted the knuckles there. The sound of the bones grinding spoke their own calciferous code, blending with the words crawling from the bronzemask across the gloom—the minor art of the knuckleshifter, the language of living bone.

Allred had grown accustomed to the dark art long ago. He'd seen much higher the toll of different schools of magic but not so the Rats. One of them puked behind him and that roused from the other dwarf new rounds of laughter and crying on the ground.

The Leatherwing's green eyes blinked at the sorcerer, the blacks of the pupils were spinning whirlwinds inside jade—a terrible recognition there. The Leatherwing rubbed its trunk around the column and the sound of a thousand knives cutting stone screeched. It blinked again and opening its mouth, a high, handsome sound-word, questioning emanated from the beast and the word was old as the foundation of the world.

Mage began to sing in answer.

The Leatherwing sat back on its haunches, curious, wrapping one bladed wing around its body and the other below its face, rubbing its muzzle there. It grabbed something behind the column with its beak-like mouth and nudged it forward to Mage. Half of one of the bodies of the Black Boat men it offered.

A rough-orange tongue scraped flesh and bone from the carcass.

Mage's song did not waver.

"Hortha and Hartha. Accompany. Slow-pace," Cole whispered.

The two brother-giants eased up to flank the mage, who finishing his song fell silent. Mage pointed above. The Leatherwing crouched, lunged and soared off with the same half-jesting, half-contemptuous call.

Fed and sung to somnolence, the first danger seamed passed.

"We sang to each other. She will not harm us. But, she will grow hungry again," Mage said.

"Well-done," Cole said, as if what they'd seen was an everyday occurrence. "Get to your feet, Rats. Allred, forward."

He felt the first wave of Downside Fever hit him at Cole's order. He bit his tongue softly, let it wash over him. He felt dizzy from the sight of the Leatherwing. Its spinning eyes were looking out from inside him for a moment and he felt the weight of ancient things grind against his guts. He tried to step forward but the muscles in his back were rigid.

A heavy hand fell on his shoulder, "Allred?"

It was Hartha's hand, bringing him back to the present.

"Don't look at the Leatherwing, too long." His throat felt

tight, "Don't look at its eyes, too long."

"It's gone now, brother, forward to glory! Cling to the clean-spirit-staying," Hartha said. He wore a good-hearted grin beneath his shaggy blond beard. The familiar face grounded him.

"Fortune."

The giant slapped the leather on his shoulder again and moved back beside Mage who stood staring up at the blackness—a faint trail of green smoke drifted from his jewel-heavy mouth in the wake of the spell. The gemstones flared and flashed in the gloom and the mage's smile spoke of a salute to forces Allred could barely sense.

Everyone was on their feet. The Rats huddled behind in a circle. He brushed off the Downside Fever and stepped through the blood and over the corpses and setting his sights on the base of the first ivory column ahead, he marched.

21

Helga

Maybe it itched, maybe not. She tried not to think about the Eye on her arm but kept glancing down to avoid the enormity of her surroundings. The corrupted flesh still felt like escape from the Haunt around her.

Her flesh moved. Outside the bandage, she could see it darkened. Beneath it, worse. Staah shuffled near to sneak a closer look and begin a jest, to feign disgust, then snapping his mouth closed decided against words.

Thay had started reciting poetry in a low mumbling voice as they followed the Relic Hunters forward. She shushed him with a *hsst* and a warning finger to her mouth. At least he was on his feet and moving. When he started to break down at first, she feared she would have to risk sending him back.

She had shepherded them all in the past and she would again. When walking the lonelier stretches of Throne-roads, between the safety of town and city, places where before the war there lurked common brigandage, she led them. Through dusk-dark hill passes thick with wolves, she led them. Through the Pits and out, they survived.

She longed for the old fears of tooth and claw, the daggers and slings of the common criminal, even the Pits. The old fears felt small now in the Haunt and she hated the place for that. It was different than any haunted place they had journeyed in the past. It was the torches that bothered her. In the Pits, there were wicked creatures and spirits, yes; but here was evidence the Haunt was inhabited even though it appeared empty. She ventured inside the world of some other power and it was not abandoned. It was guarded.

Ahead, Allred glanced back at her. There was fear in her cousin's eyes, then the gloom and dim and his quick pace consumed him in the shadows ahead.

They kept moving towards the white columns ahead. Soon, the smell of blood and viscera gave way to the dry chill of the great open space again, and the sound of the Leatherwing's swoop and song faded. Even the screams of what she assumed were the still living Black Boat men—stowed away meat in the high places above, fell quiet.

She kept hearing Allred's warnings repeating in her head. He had tried to keep her away from this place.

Remember why you're here.

Had she said that out loud? Her Rats turned to her, heads cocked in questioning. The short swords they held shook in their hands. Their packs, mostly empty, slouched on their small shoulders. She felt something atop the flesh beneath the bandage shift, burrowing deeper into her flesh.

"Helga?" Staah asked.

"I'm sorry," she whispered back.

The dwarf looked confused, ran his hand down his pointed beard and said nothing.

All loomed over her, the massive walls of rock defining the courtyard leaned inwards towards their small group making their way over these ancient floors—the work of foul giants she could have understood, but intuition told her this place had been built by thousands of human hands. The courtyard pulsed with centuries, the impossible architecture strong-stoned with bitter rage and behind it, some terrible geometry of ancient mages, a purpose she couldn't comprehend. A hollow place, yes. But even in the darkness she thought she saw treks—inhuman prints swept by low-hanging cloaks trailing in the dust. They were not alone. Old blood prevailed.

The anger of a forgotten sentry and an air of sacrifice drifted in the air. Something was summoning the Dhlams and demons from hidden places below.

The faint sounds of a crystalline music accompanied by old reed flutes. Then gone. Did the others hear it? Harp and lute, songs from past performances. She made to cover her ears. The music sounded louder, and her right hand was heavy with her short sword. As she brought it up, unthinking, she nearly cut her own face.

She dropped it with a clatter. The line halted. She picked it up, her fingers brushing against the stone.

This place works on the spirit.

Straightening up, her sword in hand, her arm possessed, she resolved to survive. Then, ahead, she saw her, peeking out from behind the first column—a small blond girl watching her with two blue eyes. Her hands pressed against the opposite round of the pillar; she wore a simple sack dress. She ducked behind the column when Helga noticed her and disappeared.

A geist. Nothing more.

The girl looked like the child she would have borne to Harad. She had his kind eyes.

She stifled a whimper.

22

Allred

One foot in front of the other. Listen to Cole. Let Mage weave his work. I've been here before.

The Downside Fever rushed over his spirit in increasingly quick waves, threatening to overwhelm and confuse his senses and force him into error. With his free hand, he fiddled with the doctor's vial once, twice, then pushed it deeper into one of the pockets of his vest.

Not now. Last resort.

He hadn't needed medicine this fast since the first Haunt he had led them into years ago. He harbored pride in that. Just like Cole. He pretended indifference to the Haunt and though the last years wore away at that illusion, he had kept it up, well enough.

The first column reared up in front of him, dwarfing him, mocking the mission of the 9th and their goals, what was left of their humanity. These ancient places made their purpose seem folly. Cole's vengeance which propelled them around this world, their rebellion, their work. The Haunt laughed at them.

He kept his finger on the crossbow trigger. That was a real thing. A thing which walked with him, up or down. Mage floated nearby, flanked by Hartha and Hortha, shields held high and ready.

Scrolls walked absent-mindedly, sketching out a map of the Haunt as they walked. His hands held no weapons only a brush and paper, to record and remember. A map to sell, a map to barter and a map to guide them back to the gate if the Downside Fever broke their spirits and warped their mind deeper within.

He halted at the base of the first column. Scrolls put a finishing flourish to his sketch and then looked-up as if in a trance, waiting, pale hand hovering over the parchment.

Prefer a real fight to this warped magic.

The Haunt worked his spirit and he wished to bring out the plaque of the Lady to look on her but couldn't bear the idea of even exposing the image of her to this place.

Here and there, grey faces dipped in and out of the murk as if draped in a mist. The burned faces of the City of Fire, mouths open in silent screams, geists.

In his nightmares he saw these same faces. In Haunts they appeared again, so Allred recognized them, and it was a remembering of the dead, he supposed he owed. They did not speak, their mouths buried beneath their own stretched flesh, reshaped by the old fire magic the Throne's mages had stormed down upon them and the innocents of the city. Mishappen lips sealed mute imprecations. Sometimes, their faces transformed while they stared at him, demanding vengeance—pale white to ash. They did not blame him; they simply asked the same question Allred had asked himself when first stumbling out of the City of Flames—who will avenge us?

Cole.

"What?"

"Nothing," he said, confused.

"I thought you called on me," Cole said.

He shook his head. Walked on. He said nothing, focused his breath. The faces retreated. He leaned his back against the column and closed his eyes a moment.

He opened his eyes again and the rest of the Rats and the 9th gathered, waiting, looking at him.

Get out alive. Let the past soften and recede in plumes of redleaf smoke around another campfire.

Cole stood directly in front of him now, staring at him. For how long? Just an instant surely. Something shifted in the distance to their left.

"I didn't call a halt. Column to column. Keep moving until we've mapped out the perimeter. Steady," Cole said.

Cole's face didn't twitch or move, his features as quiet as the stone of these ancient walls. Certain and unmoving. He studied Cole's coolness for any crack. None. He drew strength from it. Cole surely had seen the same faces.

"You see the dead here, too?"

"Geists. I don't just see them here," Cole answered, looking at the handle of his broadsword. "Drink if you need to."

The flat mute skin on the right side of Cole's skull, he could make out below the hair that had grown over it. Doctor Aodlen had done his greatest work, putting Cole back together after the City of Flames—Where was the doctor? —There just beneath the hair, which had grown back, the scars. Cole had told him, "Leave my hands be. Leave them marked."

A promise. There are lesser reflections of the dead.

"Drink," Cole said again, squinting at him.

He would not shatter here under the Downside Fever. If he had to fly apart, above it would be, in the Upside. A drop of sweat fell from his brow into his eye, blurring all before him for a moment, and then resolution and he stood straight.

"Heard."

He turned seeking the wall to the right which he knew was there from the torchlight which flickered in the distance.

Skyward, nothing—a starless night, faint patches of violent and grey appearing and blinking in and out above and then he noticed his feet weren't moving again.

"Allred?" Hartha asked.

"Yes. Good. Just looking," he mumbled.

Hartha tilted his head and with his axe hand, made a motion

like drinking back some medicine from the vial. He shook his head no. Kept moving.

Mage walked stately, as if in a procession, buzzing with spells. Strange syllables dripped from his lips. Heat emanated in waves from the front of the bronze mask. Even from this distance, he could feel it. Through the eyeholes of the mask, wisps of green smoke trailed upwards into the darkness.

Stop feeling. Start looking. Judgement of the hawk. Look.

The Downside Fever ebbed as they neared the base of the second column. From there to the third and then a fourth and fifth. How long had they been walking?

He heard one of the Black Boat men laughing behind him, turned. Nothing there. Voices of the damned. But were they certain all the Black Boat men perished?

Finally, they neared the edge of the courtyard ending in a sheer wall which defined it.

This is just the beginning.

Cole motioned for them all to sit down against it. Cole squatted in front of him and leaned in whispering, "You're under it and stretched."

"Big Haunt. Big Fever. Keep it."

Cole studied him. Allred had seen that look. It reminded him of when Aodlen surveyed the amputation tents back in the army. He knew he was being judged and that sparked a cold fury.

"I'll ride it out," he said again and Cole nodded.

Aodlen hurried along the line, judging them for indications of Downside Fever. He felt relief that the doctor's eyes didn't linger on him long. They got to their feet again when Cole called for it. They marched deeper into the Haunt, keeping the wall to their right and the expanse of the first courtyard to their left.

Torches lit the way here, fitted into the stone. He knew entities attended them, eternal flames always witnessing the horror of eons. The scout in him saw light and the confusion it could bring to approaching enemies.

The bright ivory of the columns continued through the entire massive courtyard; they passed them by.

Were they built of marble or bone?

This thought dissipated at the sound of the pounding tread of the first demon. He dropped to his knee. Pointed his crossbow and shouted, "Dhlam!"

Leather trousers scraped on the floor behind him and the bang of the bottoms of shield and hilt as the group went to ground at his signal.

Out of the darkness ahead a Dhlam, twice the size as the ones in the Upside--stronger, taller, faster came hurtling alongside the wall. He saw it in the short, ragged moment it broke through into the light of the nearest torch.

He loosed a dart. The Dhlam ducked, falling to its belly in one smooth motion on all fours now. It's muscled arms and legs propelled its sharp reptilian snout towards his chest.

He dropped the crossbow with a clatter. Unsheathed his sword. Crouched, stepped back with one foot and held the blade to skewer the Dhlam. Just before it reached the blade, it stopped, the limber, loose joints of its stubby, muscled feet turning and banked its body sharply, climbing straight up the vertical wall to his right. Claws dug stone and scattered debris in his eyes.

Fire enveloped it as it scaled the wall. The Dhlam turned back and away from the blast of mage's fire. Too late. A raspy-throated scream loosed across the courtyard. The monster let go and plummeted, skewering itself in a twisting mass on the pointed end of a torch.

All waited in silence for a signal. Cole gave it. Then passing next to Allred's left he pulled him up to his feet and went to the wall where the demon's corpse writhed.

The torch had pierced its torso. Its clawed feet still scrambled and scraped against the rock face, throwing up dust and stone. Cole shielded his eyes as if looking far away at the horizon.

The Dhlam's flesh still burned with the mage's flame. The skin crackled. The smell was intolerable. Mind-crazed-making, burning still, the thing looked at them with hatred and it wasn't just the mindless rage of a beast.

"Cole?"

Cole watched, his face not an arm's length from the demon who spat and stared and swiped. Cole's face, calm, watching. He raised his broadsword and cut the thing in two, freeing it from the torch and wall.

It fell to the ground, both pieces still moving, arms and legs seeking two directions. And then it stilled in some second death and dark-blood pooled below the flame.

"Forward," Cole said.

He retrieved his crossbow, reloaded a dart, walked on.

They reached the end of the wall at a plain corner of masonry which turned sharply to the left at a right angle. They were on the other side of the large courtyard space.

He leaned against the wall for a moment. He felt the grit and grime of the stone rough against his boiled leather armor. He swayed a bit as if itching his back. His magemade helmet, something he could only bear to don for a short while, he banged softly against the gritty stone to cover the scream he felt boiling in the bottom of his guts.

The Black Boat men lived in that wall. He felt them reaching out to him, wanting to pull him in. It was quiet there in a way. There was no more guilt in the wall. No orders or plans or faces of burned children, no leering demons; and he turned and saw their shadowy faces there in the traces and movements of the torchlight— cleansed of the weight of their past.

They welcomed him, jolly skulls of clean bone, grinning.

He felt the sting of the slap across his face after he heard it.

Cole stood in front of him again. He had been talking to the blank wall in front of him, standing face to the corner. Cole spun him around, hit him and pressed him to the ground with two hands on his shoulders.

"Drink."

Aodlen stood beside him, an uncapped vial, held out to him in shaking hand. "Ha! Allred you're talking to a wall, man!"

"My spirit remains fixed," he answered.

"Not my diagnosis, no. Ha! Ha! The Downside Fever has you. Geist-Rot and worse and we've just begun."

"Cole get this madman away from me."

"Drink it down and steady up. I'm beside you."

"I'm solid—I think."

He insisted but his voice sounded weak to him. He heard the voice of a younger man at war just before the first charge. Couldn't be his voice? He had never been young, though. Allred, the name given to him by his father in the clan wars. Well, he was younger than the boys outside when—

Aodlen shook the vial in front of his nose. Allred snatched it. He nipped at it. The taste a mildbitter on his tongue. Cole watched him. Waited. The stuff would steady his spirit but he knew it would make him slower, less acute and he hated that. Aodlen denied the medicine brought on this effect, but Aodlen was a liar.

"Alright," he said and stood, "I'm in it. Fine."

The medicine worked as soon as it hit him and he knew they were right. He had just been talking to dead men's shadows in a wall. It *was* Geist-Rot, a symptom of Downside Fever. He took another small sip, handed the vial back to Cole.

"Good, let's move," Cole said.

"Heard."

"My medicine will ward it all away. Ha! Don't know why some of you fear it! Ha!" Aodlen stepped back stowing his vial away, retreating into the murk just like the ghosts which had been appearing. He could hear the man's long dirty fingernails against the glass vial like a spider skittering over a web.

"This wall turns sharp left ahead. Move faster across here, so we can get the width of this courtyard," Cole said.

"Heard."

That's what they did. Allred felt steadier yet removed after drinking Aodlen's cure. That dullness could get him killed. He suspected Aodlen's cures made the Upside Fever worse, too, but the doctor wouldn't admit it and none of them asked him to.

No time to think of it now.

They found the first door leading out from the courtyard on their right. It was a large metal door, embossed in curses and leading to some fresh despair deeper within. Exactly what they were looking for.

Scrolls marked it on his parchment.

The head of the door was framed in flesh-colored material and rose far above them as if designed to convenience creatures of greater height than humans.

He waited for Cole's command. Forward to fix the length of the courtyard to their map or faster into the Haunt? The door stood slightly ajar beckoning.

They listened. Scrolls noted. Cole approached it. Allred rolled the smooth wood of the loaded dart of his crossbow between his fingers testing the delicate balance of the dart in its saddle.

Cole nudged the door further open with his left shoulder and shined the light of a small sun within which he held in his hand. He had lowered the light on his spaulders with a fixed incantation as they moved through the darkness.

What will this lead to?

Cole motioned for him. He edged forward through the door. It opened into an empty, plain corridor. It was narrow, the width of three men standing side-by-side, and lined with a few torches.

"There," Allred pointed it out to Cole.

Ahead where the hallway curved, something squatted low in the shadow. The light of Cole's small sun swept towards it but could not penetrate the shadows it gathered around it like a cloak. It stood the size of a large hunting dog and regarded them with two glowing intelligent eyes. It turned, shuffled away, unhurried, the patter of hooves on the stone floor and then disappeared down the hall.

"Back," Cole said.

Cole shut the door behind him as Allred stepped backwards out of the passage way. Cole looked for a lock and found none. He signaled for them to move on.

They continued along the wall passing two more doors like the first.

As they neared the next corner of the courtyard, he sensed a weight dropping down fast on top of him.

"Down!" he screamed.

He fell to the ground aiming his crossbow above. He pulled the trigger, blind to the target.

He felt the rancid scream of the demon on top of his neck just before its weight drove him into the ground and knocked the breath from him. Gasping, he could barely breathe beneath the weight. Jaws fixed on and savaged the boiled-leather armor near his neck. He felt the heat of his helmet flare, hot and scald the flesh of the demon, but it wouldn't let go. Fangs scraped on his steel gorget seeking his throat. It sent shrill sounds of gouged metal ringing in his head.

Claws brushed his face, just shy of blinding him. He squirmed beneath the weight of the Dhlam. He could hear his own panicked gasping. His arms pinned to the ground couldn't pull a dagger. Mage couldn't use fire. The flame would spread and consume him, too. If the thing got to his neck his life would spill out. He kept twisting beneath the Dhlam.

He heard the signature of Cole's broadsword cutting the air. A sound he knew well, each sword swung, a note, a song only a warrior can recognize.

The Dhlam's body buckled and spasmed on top of him and the weight shifted just enough to free his hand to grasp the small dagger on his waist. He wedged his hand between his own body and the floor the stone scraping the flesh from the back of his hand. He felt the wooden handle, pulled the dagger, twisted and slashed half-blind with the weight of the demon flesh still atop him. He felt blood cascade over him. Claws punctured his armor seeking his flesh.

The dagger's steel met nothing. He would have screamed if he had air.

He nearly sliced Hortha's tree-trunk ankle with his dagger. The edge of the blade just brushed the tough blue-leather of the Emeral Islander's boot. The giant hurled the demon from his body. In that instant he heard the calling up of Mage's flame and felt the heat on the side of his stunned cheek from the magework.

Aodlen hurried forward. He took stock of the wound, shook something foul-smelling into it.

His crossbow dart had pierced the demon straight through the head. Attacking from the darkness of the wall where it clung, it fell on him. Murder missed by moments. His flesh burned beneath the wound on his side where the claws cut through his armor and found flesh. He felt the gouged metal in his gorget, little ripples of ravaged steel. It had just held against the demon's bite. His helmet cooled and he ventured a touch to the metal, feeling the wreck of fang marks in the ancient work.

The medicine cleansed and closed his flesh in the chill air of the Haunt; flesh sang an old song.

He blessed the demon as it burned beside him; the attack shook him back out of his thoughts and back to the business of killing and dying.

"Sound?" Cole asked.

"Not dead," Allred said.

"Good."

Hartha and Hortha took a few steps back. Cole pulled him to his feet.

"To the middle of the courtyard. The Dhlams cling to these high walls like lizards," Cole said.

He felt the last of his torn flesh sealed beneath the powerful magic of Aodlen's costly remedies. He set out beside Cole now, then regaining his breathe took the lead again.

After passing through more of the bone columns (for now, he was certain that was the materials of their construct), the courtyard changed. The columns were no longer plain white but adorned with splashes of bright, colorful paints, gums and glues. The stone was lambent with frescos depicting atrocity in a style he had seen before in other Haunts.

Scrolls would know the name of it.

The decorated columns grew slender. Soon, they discovered the first tomb to promise treasure.

A white marble sarcophagus sat dead center in a slightly tapering oval depression of the floor. Red and purple streaks veined the white marble of the tomb glowing with bright-bone-mimicking light. Allred had seen the same material ranging from the Haunt in the Plains of Absolution to the Ice Caverns of Qar.

Cole moved up with Scrolls beside him. He signaled for Allred to stay on the higher ground with the rest to wait and watch as they troubled the tomb.

A series of shorter columns ringed the center of the place. On the faces of the columns were painted ancient battle scenes in tints of ochre. Sentences were carved in the ash and verdant green of forgotten forest adorning them. Most portrayed humans in cowering clumps of flesh, eyes upturned to the powers of titanic creatures menacing above them.

He grew dizzy looking at them, so turned away. Aodlen uttered a relieved sigh beside him, piercing his own flesh with an orb-dipped needle, working on a design of letters with each pinprick on his flesh.

"Adding to the recipes. We'll need them!"

Scroll's stylus picked up the pace—drawing, and writing, growing frantic, the tip nearly piercing the parchment, sketching all which Allred looked away from.

From the stone of the inner columns protruded burgundy-colored branches of a living tree, reaching up and outward towards the center of the recessed oval. The branches formed a canopy above the tomb, threading and weaving together their thorns and leaves, joining, dry twisting over the sarcophagus itself.

The limbs displayed red and yellow leaves, the colors calling counterpoint against the pale bone of the tomb with its thin matching veins. Some of the leaves had fallen atop the sarcophagus, counting centuries unseen by human eyes.

Now at Cole's approach, the leaves began to fall swiftly. As each fell from the stems, the sounds of screaming children echoed across the tomb. Unborn things lamenting in a language used before birth filled the courtyard around the terrible tree. He could not understand the words, but it spoke to him still, familiar to the living in the muscle of his guts.

He held down his bile. He saw the look of horror in the Rat's eyes. Helga wept silently, her shoulders shaking at the sound.

Scrolls, unbothered, bent down and picked up one of the leaves, examining it.

What looked like the patterns of butterfly wings played across the surface of the leaf. Looking closer, the veins formed the impression of distended faces. The faces of innocents agonized and frozen in the evil-tempered Haunt. Evil magic had preserved an ancient ritual.

Scrolls, with his aloof heart, set the leaf gently to the

ground, instead of dropping it, showing respect. The scholar's hand wavered as he rehearsed on parchment the vision before him.

The tomb was fitted perfectly with a marble cover. Cole stepped down into the slope of the floor to look at it. He traded unheard words with Scrolls. Mage joined them, appearing to glide, his feet hidden beneath the shimmering cloak. He reached out, hesitated, and did not touch the marble. Turning, he whispered to Cole.

The men turned back and ordered everyone to wait. Scrolls stepped carefully around the tomb and the cursed arbor's leaves. He moved from column-to-column sketching, recording the bizarre battle sequences depicted on the columns.

Allred turned to the dark around them, waiting for the rush of the enemy. He glanced over at Helga who stood with the Rats at the lip of the oval, visibly quaking, but standing firm, sword by her side, shield at the ready. She caught his eye.

Men aren't meant for such places, Allred thought.

"What?" Helga asked.

Had he spoken that out loud? And how quietly she moved when she wanted. She stood beside him now when just a moment, she was a few paces away.

"I said, pay attention on the Eye? Or…"

The Haunt was fogging his mind, making his speech slurred.

She leaned in closer to him. He could feel her breath on his face, "Cousin, have you seen a young girl hiding around the columns? She has blond hair. She looks … like me."

Allred shook his head, "No. Ignore the geists. Visions, distorted. Ignore them. It's Downside Fever."

Helga nodded. She would understood now inside the Haunt, why he'd tried to warn her away. He didn't find her at fault for not believing him before. Beyond them in the gloom, the faces of the burned came and went about the business of the dead.

A deep feeling of protection came over him for Helga then. He wanted to shield her as best he could, his cousin, even if he had failed to convince her to spare herself the agonies of the Haunt. At least he could do that, couldn't he?

And that sentiment too, he shrugged off as soon as he felt

it. Good. Watch out for her, yes. And the Rats, yes. They are useful. Hands to carry treasure, hands to carry magic.

Coldness, he must not set aside. It would mean death.

Cole and Mage made their way out of the mild cavity of the tomb's floor.

"When Scrolls is finished recording these things, we move back to those doors," he said.

There was a quietness to his voice that hadn't been there before, wasn't there?

"No treasure within that...abomination?"

A voice pierced through the stone of the marble sarcophagus lid in reply. Muted by the weight of the cover. The words spoke a slavering-speech worked by inhuman jaws sealed below. The sound of it gripped them all in its command and he saw every one of them stiffen and shake, even the two giants. The dark magic began to pull them physically, down to the tomb. Each stumbled, taking sidelong steps, as if the entire Haunt was tilted on its side.

"There is nothing within that tomb but death," Cole said, loudly and his voice seemed to block the malign influence of the demon summoning them.

The voice fell silent for a moment and then began to call forth again.

Scrolls scrambled up the incline. Hartha and Hortha grabbed him pulling him forward. It was as if they were dragging him over a cliff, though the floor had not moved. The remnants of the pull of the voice held Scrolls, as if each word shot silvery web to reach him.

"Move. Now. Away," Cole commanded.

Cole shoved him away from the sarcophagus back in the direction they had come.

He set a quick pace as eager as any of them to flee the magic. He could feel the pull lessen as the unholy voice of the entombed one faded behind him. Soon, he was staring at the same door where the hooved beast had shown itself. The rest of the group formed up around him.

Cole said:

"Me and you in first."

Cole now used his Haunt-fashioned spaulders. With a touch and a rehearsed utterance, dozens of tiny small-suns illuminated, inset within the heavy metal of the armor, casting a wide light before him. He could feel the warmth of the light on his back as he moved forward.

After the first curve in the corridor, it straightened again and led to another turn ahead. At the foot of that sinuous turn of stone, again, the beast stood watching them, always ahead. The small sun, that Stoneburner had fixed near his crossbow's end caught it this time as it turned. He touched the small sun with his bloody finger and uttered the one-word incantation which strengthened the light.

He caught the glimpse of a boar, but the head was not proper. Something wrong there. It hovered at the corner, turned away from him, then disappeared.

"Trap?" he whispered.

"Scrolls?" Cole asked.

"Servant of the one who rules this region."

"It watches," Mage added.

"It?"

"Yes. It watches."

"Watches us?" Helga had joined the front of the line.

"Not who but for what—an opportunity," Scrolls answered. Mage did not object.

The corridor's narrow sweating rocks stifled the sound of their footfalls. He relaxed for a moment while they conversed, rolled his head on his neck working out the stiffness. The low ceiling in this tunnel pressed down on him but unlike in the courtyard, he could worry less about death from above.

They kept moving forward. It grew darker. Less torches lined the wall. Cole summoned more light from his armor; behind him Aodlen lit and hoisted a mundane lantern. The warmth of the natural fire bounced off the walls in time with his steps.

The ceiling sloped lower and lower until all had to bend and crouch to walk. Hartha and Hortha had to angle their shields in the lower places to fit them through. The ceiling soon tilted up again. At each curve in the tunnel, the boar remained ahead, moving deeper into the Haunt.

The hallway ended at another open door. This door could have stood inside any humble inn or temple, a simple wooden, unmarked thing. There were remnants of whitewash on it.

Cole said, "Forward."

The door swung open on smooth hinges, soundless revealing another large room.

It was lit by the same torches. The walls were rich with more horrific frescos. Below those paintings, were several chairs of wrought metal. The chairs were not built for men to rest. The metal glared in the horrid light, like the carapace of a crawling thing. Thorns of steel erupted from the armrests, meant to pierce the flesh and hold the occupant fast.

"A demon-bearing place," Scrolls said. He pointed to the high ceilings. "I need time to study the designs above. It's unclear what we face ahead."

Allred craned his neck upwards.

On the ceiling, a terrible figure stared down at them in a triumphal pose, a man with the soft lines of a eunuch around its pallid jowls. It wore the regalia of some forgotten infernal empire over a mage's cloak. The face the artist depicted was grotesque in its power, the head hairless, the features androgenous; two black eyes pierced them, staring into some abyss below the floor.

Scrolls made a copy of the figure above them on his parchment in quick slashes and strokes and the sound reminded Allred of a bird searching for grubs in tall grass.

"It's still there."

Across the chamber, the boar let loose a laughing bark from the far side of the room.

Its body was that of a common boar but not its face. The neck shifted and deformed. The muscles beneath the briars of its flesh merged with a man's throat and face— two tusks poked out from bristle-covered cheeks. Squinting yellow eyes studied them and Allred swore there was a look of amusement on its deformed face.

At the sight of the thing, one of the dwarves let out a crazed, clipped sob and stifled it with their free hand.

"Impossible," Helga whispered.

It made no move. Even when he raised his crossbow at its body; it just watched. Finally, snorting out a half-boar, half-man sound, it turned and disappeared through another passage beyond the room.

"Scrolls. Where are we?" Cole asked.

"I need to confirm something," he answered.

The scholar swung his light pack from his back and laid it on the floor. Reaching within he withdrew the same heavy book he had consulted at the front of the gate. He pointed to the sketch of the painting on the ceiling and then referred to his book.

"It depicts one of the Unspoken Rulers. His name I shall not utter here. That does not mean, we are inside his palaces itself— no; I speculate this is a temple-palace of one of his servants," Scrolls said.

"The Haunt is heavy," Cole said, though it didn't appear to press on him.

He closed the book and looked at Cole. "We are not, I do not think, within a palace of the Unspoken. No, I think not."

"Certain?"

Aodlen blurted out behind them, "If he's wrong. Ha! Ha, ha … that means—"

"Certain?" Cole asked again.

Scrolls returned the book to his pack, inserting between its pages, several sheets of parchment filled with the maps and sketches he had made so far. Pursed-lipped, he said nothing while he arranged his work, then stood with a look of defiance.

"Scrolls, are you certain?"

"Certain of what? What are Unspoken—" Helga began.

Scrolls interrupted her inquiry.

"Certainty is rare. The signs point to the likelihood that I am correct. This is not one of the Twelve palaces but the abode of a servant in thrall to one of them." At this, Scrolls made a gesture of banishment. That was rare to see the scholar perform such a thing and he gripped the handle of his sword tighter. "May its names be unspoken. Wearing similar regalia as in my...let me see...it's the List of Vestments of the Old Empire, I think … That's the source we have for the regalia the Unspoken wore ... It matches the painting above."

"We do not survive, not in our...ha!—um, state, let's say our current condition. No, we do not survive proximity to one of the Unspoken and that's my professional opinion."

"I don't understand," Helga said, again, "And what is that creature watching us?"

"Not all the palaces of the Unspoken are known, true. Of course, it's only rumor that the Throne sets above one." Scrolls was lecturing now, forgetting the danger around them, caught up in his own thoughts. "Hmm, no, I think we are simply in an old Haunt, likely a provincial part of the whole. The magic is rich, yes but so far little in the way of Dhlams. That being said, they will come as they are summoned, I should think."

"Everything is connected," Aodlen said, looking at Helga as if answering her earlier question.

"What?"

"The Haunts," Aodlen said, "Of course. Ha!"

"...yes, the Downside Fever is strong in this place but are we inside one of the Palaces of the Unspoken? No, Cole, no, I think not. I think we would be struck down if that were so. Even with you leading us," Scrolls said.

The Unspoken ruled in unknown Haunts. That was the legend. Scrolls had explained the roots of that legend to them all in the past. Most relic hunters knew the outlines of the myth. No one knew the truth, or if they did, they were either dead or of the ranks of the highest scholar-priests of the Throne and guarded the secret well.

It was believed by many that two of the Unspoken's Haunts at least lay in the Thronelands itself. Sitting below the two most powerful cities, Mhars and the City of Thrones. Far to the east, scholars said there was another, sunk in sands, driving forces which the Throneland armies warred against during the battle which ended with the betrayal of the 9th.

Others disagreed. Some said zero, others twelve. Some said there were no Unspoken. The debates raged between scholars and the half-crazed men who did Relicwork and Hauntmarching in a hundred, hidden taverns where relic hunters gathered to trade.

No one knows anything, Allred thought.

"What is the scholar saying?" Helga asked no one in particular.

Allred turned to her, "He's trying to guess if we are going to die quickly or less quickly, cousin."

"Regardless, we'll not go empty-handed. Not after what we've spent," Cole said."

"We should hasten to check the other two corridors leading out from the courtyard. Equidistant to this room, we might find similar rooms which provide a clue to what we face. I have observed this pattern of symmetry along with *others*."

On this last word, Scrolls regarded Aodlen with an accusing stare, indicating some dispute the two men had on the subject of the architecture of the Haunts, "Many of the ancient palaces adhere to a symmetry of design."

"Move then," Cole said. He turned to Helga, "But first, let me see your arm."

23

Lookout

He was wet with sweat and rain, damp all the way through, and his body was sore from the march and the work Stoneburner put him to.

They had made their camp in front of the terrible portal in the mountain face. The dwarf, Shad, kept watch at the stairs. He could see a small torch far blinking in the night where he was stationed. A brave dwarf to be alone down there, he thought, he would have liked to question the man about where he came from but there was no time.

Stoneburner busied himself with going through the discarded packs of the Black Boat men. It seemed clear that they weren't returning but he said nothing of it and Lookout didn't ask. He stacked them on top of the berm of dirt they had fashioned, and the old man said nothing. When Lookout tried to help, he waived him away from the task.

The rain had slackened and ceased as the sun hid behind

the volcano in the distance and night fell on the camp.

Stoneburner lit no cooking fire, but after some time handed out dried meat and hard bread.

"How long will they be inside?" he asked.

A crossbow in his lap, eyes narrowed in the darkness, he had told both the boys, to keep their knives close. Lookout had gripped his own small carving knife, the one he used to whittle and then finally, when no enemy attacked, let it set in the rain-hardened clay beside him.

"Could be hours, could be days," he answered, "When they come out, they'll be sick and unsettled."

Boph had grown quieter. He said little and Lookout wished he would say more—even if it were something impertinent—he didn't like the quiet watchfulness of his friend. Boph might have a way of untangling this confusion. He shot him an expectant glance, but the One-Bead boy did little, sitting near, his back against the belly of his sleeping donkey.

He didn't understand most of what had happened in the last few days, and he didn't understand this. The more questions he asked, the less he knew. The world had grown bloody and complicated, and he was sure no one was telling him the entire truth.

"Sick from what?"

"From the nearness of an evil place. It will pass in time...somewhat. Don't worry. When they return, just stay away from the ones who are most ill until I tell you it's safe." Stoneburner peered past the berm of dirt down the road towards the steps as if searching for something in the dim. "Not Cole, though, Cole never changes."

He had been told to stay away from nearly everyone. The Black Boat men, which for all their surliness must be brave men, as they were inside now, too.

"But what is it?"

"An old place. Best not to worry, boy," Stoneburner answered. "Just keep your eyes open."

He picked up his whittling knife and stood it blade first into the ground and spun it around in little circles feeling the drag of the land on the balance.

"If I'm going to come with you, I should know some things, shouldn't I?"

Something stirred in the ferns beside them near the cliff. Stoneburner jerked his head up, stood, pointed his crossbow into the darkness and stared at the place where the sound came from.

Lookout stood, too and picked up his knife. Boph did not move.

The moon was near full. They needed no campfire in its light. This high up, there were no trees to shelter them from its rays. They could see so much in the night.

"Just some small animal, I think," Lookout said, and Stoneburner tried a smile and sat down again. Far above them, near the top of the mountain which capped the Haunt a nightbird screeched in answer to some other beast's trilling. He did not recognize the calls. They were higher up in the world than he had ever walked.

Stoneburner sat back down. He did, too.

"I've been alone in the tower for a long time, guarding it."

"Your family lives far down the mountain, do they?"

"My father died this turn not long after he found me my work guarding the tower. My mother died when I was just a child. Just me now. No other kin."

Boph had brought him the news of his father's death not long after he took his post at the watchtower on the island of Esmer. He had brought a few things up from the farm which neighbors had found along with his father's body. There wasn't much to inherit. He made immediate use of one thing—a large bottle of cownut liquor. Boph had stayed at the tower while Lookout set out alone (his attendant had asked for nothing in exchange) to watch over the body with an old village priest.

"Oh," Stoneburner answered, "No other kin here, you say?"

"We were colonists. Father and mother and me."

"You have the land to tend to?"

"It's worthless," Boph put in, drowsily.

Normally, he would chastise his retainer for such an observation. Tonight, he was happy to hear him say anything.

"Boph speaks true. The land here was never good for farming. The grove is leased to a neighbor but the coin I earn here is worth more."

"I see."

He shifted on the ground. On it Stoneburner had spread some canvas to help keep them dry.

"So, that's why I say, I figure with the commission I've been given by Cole that I'll probably join you. I'll ask the permission of the Attman. There's really nothing else to be done, you see, sir. I'll never realize knighthood here and there's not anything for me besides."

Stoneburner nodded his head. He looked tired up here, tonight. He started to say something, then closed his mouth and scratched his chin.

On the mountain, near the gate, sand fell around the drawing of the Eye the mage had made. The carving transformed beneath the moonlight, became liquid and took on the aspect of flesh; it moved under the moonbeams.

"Look," he pointed.

"High sorcery," Boph said. He was wide awake now, leaning forward and the donkey stirred, baring its teeth and then reposed again.

Stoneburner groaned as he lifted his bulk from the ground, again. He approached the shifting symbol, enlivened by the magic of Mage. It moved back and forth just like an eye. Stoneburner gave some sign with his hand. The eye stilled, regarded them all once again before fading into the common elements of rock and chalk.

"What was that?"

Stoneburner turned back, sat again, "The mage's work. Letting them know all is quiet here."

These were the mysteries Lookout felt he should come to learn. To make a drawing on rock come to life was some wonder from the legends.

"So, if you give me a good recommendation to Cole, I can set out with you wherever you go next. Boph will follow me, even if he says now, he won't—I know he will." Boph made a dismissive clucking sound with his tongue and returned to drawing in the dirt beside him. "Would that be good?"

For some dumb reason, he choked back a sob. Weren't they going to take them with him? Hadn't they said as much in so many words?

He looked around and the bad magic of the high place and the bright moon made him feel lonesome. Stoneburner had offered no wine tonight, just water.

"Cole makes all those decisions, but I'll put in the best words for you, boy. Don't you worry about that. If nothing else, seems we could take you off the island. But Cole decides."

Now, he made sure to control his voice before speaking. He brushed aside some tears, pretended to sneeze, hiding his worry. This was no way for a knight to act.

"I figure I should know something about your quests so I can serve. Isn't that what a knight does? Isn't that what all the stories you tell, say, Boph? A knight serves. But what?"

He left the question hanging there in the night. Neither Stoneburner nor Boph answered it, but the donkey raised its head and yawned at the moon with crooked teeth and regarded him for a moment before nestling its long face back into the dirt and falling to sleep.

24

Helga

Aodlen delicately removed the bandage from her arm. She felt the thing leap. The flesh itched all around it. She watched the Eye's painless, circuit.

The mystery of the thing had been a kind of relief—a real worry to take her mind from the horrors of the Haunt and the vision of the girl, who she knew was the geist of the daughter she had never given to Harad.

The dead don't even need be born in this place.

Cole studied her arm while Aodlen held it. Her dwarves stood near around them, and she almost laughed to see that they held their swords a bit higher, ready to protect her.

"Easy, if he wanted you dead, you'd all be buried long ago," Allred said.

She thought this was her cousin's way of trying to make a joke. She preferred to assume that.

Surprisingly, Allred looked the most unsteady down here. Of

course, she might, too, if she had survived the two attacks from the beasts within and had to lead the group. She had a feeling it wasn't the simple violence that made Allred look so shaky. What geists did he battle with?

She'd always been the kind of girl to look at what she was told she shouldn't.

"How is this thing?" she asked.

The inhuman eye stared back at Cole. It was a thing of flesh and magic and art and followed Cole's conjuring gestures. Reflected in the middle of it, instead of a pupil, a picture of the world outside the gate. She could see the two boys and the donkey with Stoneburner. The lute player signaled something with a hand gesture, and recognizing it, Aodlen covered the Eye.

Luckily, when she pitched backwards in a faint, Cole caught her.

"Drink," Aodlen said, holding the vial near her lips. He tilted it back and she tasted the bitterness of the stuff. Her head cleared and she felt a weight shift from her.

She was sitting against the wall of the terrible chamber where they had stopped. Around her, Staah crouched studying her with a worried look.

"I fainted?" she asked, incredulous.

"I told you, not to bother looking at the thing, Ha! It's too much magic for your clownish spirit to take," Aodlen laughed.

Allred stood behind the doctor watching her. Did he smile with a warmth foreign to his face?

Gone. A vision. Her cousin's face was the same blank, killing-stare she knew well. He stepped forward and offered his hand. It felt clammy but oddly soft, as if so much blood on his hands had made the skin tender. He pulled her to her feet.

"No danger outside. The longer we stay here the heavier the Downside Fever. Forward," Cole said.

"Heard," she said, mimicking the way Allred answered.

She could not tell if it was the Haunt warping her mind, but she thought she saw the trace of a smile on his lips before turning.

25

Allred

Hurrying now with fleeter foot, he led them back to the courtyard, along the wall and the other door. The boar always just ahead.

Another door like the last one. Another breath held and a going-through. The same tunnel, the same march, their footfalls faster grew dim to his ears. They arrived at another room with the same painted face leering down at them from the ceiling. The chamber was like the first one in all but one respect. This one was occupied.

The room was brighter with bewitched torches. A chair here ran wet with blood and gore. A Black Boat man had survived the Leatherwing and fled. It would have been better for him, if he hadn't.

"Must have run," he said, staring at the still writhing figure.

The Black Boat man's eyes were hollow and inhuman, lips moving beneath a bloody foam, seething with curses. The possessed body jerked as if trying to lunge at them but it was pinned to the chair by thorns of metal. Allred raised the crossbow but preserved the bolt.

Scrolls ventured near the man. The thing snapped with bloody teeth, pulling forward. He could hear flesh on metal. The slate-faced scholar bent low to listen to the curses. After a few moments, Scrolls stood straight, turned to Cole and said, "I've heard what I must."

The body leaped again from the chair; the iron legs of the contraption scraped against the smooth marble floor of the room.

"Cole?" Allred asked.

"Mage?" Cole asked.

"Nothing more," Mage said.

"End it," Cole said.

Allred pressed the trigger. Dart met skull with a wet slap. The Black Boat man's head bounced into the metal of the chair and then rested.

"Can that happen to us?" one of Helga's rats asked in a quavering falsetto. He hadn't bothered to sort their names out.

Allred took one step towards the corpse, grabbed the dart, twisted and pulled. The metal tip was bent and the magic-laced poison dispersed, "Yes."

Helga stared at him; mouth open. Her frightened face saddened him. He wished others didn't see the horrors which had become commonplace for the Relic Hunters of the 9th. Even the atrocities of this place couldn't remain a private matter, shared between those who had endured them but now others who held them in high regard saw them at their work. She looked away from him.

"Don't waste anything in a Haunt," he said. He bent the tip back straight brushed away a bit of the skull bone which clung to it, then inserted it point down into his belt beside its unused mates.

He reloaded a new dart while Scrolls sketched the ceiling. What looked like the same figure leered down at them; he could have sworn, the shape of the mouth had grown more pleased, as if the tortured man had thrilled the spirit within the painting. Just the Downside Fever, likely. Looking away, he decided it didn't matter.

Nothing moved. He wanted demons. He needed something tangible to fight.

Scrolls set to drawing again, punctuating his labor with little, 'ahh yeses' and 'of courses.'

"Done," he said.

Cole motioned them back into the corridor. Scrolls spoke.

"We are not, in my opinion inside a Haunt of the Unspoken, instead a simple prince serving them. Look at the sketch."

Cole and Mage gathered around the book.

"The painting differs in slight ways here. This I think is the tomb of *a servant* of Calthor, Calthor—the etymology, quite complex...quite interesting. This isn't the tomb of that king—it's his servant who honored him by mimicking his regalia and manner. Whoever dwells here had these paintings done to imitate his lord. Like a court official copying the style of a king and his court, verifying his allegiance and vow of service. Now this is proof of something I've speculated upon many times—"

"Good enough, save the rest for later," Cole said. He turned to Allred, dismissing the rest of the scholar's lengthy dissertation, "Let's go."

"I'm fine," Allred said and then realized he had not answered any of his companion's question.

Mage studied him behind the bronzemask, raw human eyes blinking against the tendrils of chaotic magic emanating from his quiet, unsinging mouth.

Cole turned to the dwarf who had spoken earlier, "Yes. It can happen to us. Downside Fever broke that man," Cole said. He gestured to the corpse of the Black Boat man. "Move. Faster.'"

"Where's the treasure, asking kindly, Cole of the 9th?" the dwaf asked in a scratchy voice.

Cole ignored the question. Helga bumped the dwarf with her leg, silencing him.

Scrolls stopped his incessant writing and looked at the dwarf, "Your name is Thay, yes?" He bent down as if talking to a child and gestured for the dwarf to come forward. Thay ventured two shuffling steps forward and then stopped in front of the scholar and said, "It is." Aodlen raised his lantern, bathing the two in a circle of light.

"The map I'm creating, the designs I'm tracing, the weight of which makes my heart most burdensome—*these parchments*—" Scrolls drove the stylus down with his writing hand on the top parchment, smearing ink on it. "To the right buyer, these drawings are worth more than one hundred Green Island mud-hut villages from whence tiny monstrosities like you spring. So, kindly shut your mouth and try to survive while we do our work."

Scrolls pointed his metal stylus at the dwarf's face. His hand shook. Hartha stepped forward between them, one slow, clomping step, "Scrolls" he said, gently.

"I didn't mean anything by it," Thay muttered. He stepped back to join Helga who stared shocked at the sudden rage of the scholar.

"Oh, of course not," Scrolls said, "But I meant everything I said."

He began to sketch again, his face quiet and blank. Hartha turned to the dwarf and spoke a few words in the dialect of the Green Islanders. The dwarf shrugged and the giant returned it.

Scrolls was right; a map of a newly explored Haunt drawn by a renowned relic hunting outfit would bring a lot of gold. They could sell it on to one of the large-scale relic-hunting groups which operated under writ of the Throne.

But Allred didn't care about that. The unpleasant thought occurred to him that he was not the only one losing his bearings under the Haunt.

"We don't have much time left," Cole said and turning to Allred, gestured further into the Haunt, "I'll walk point for a while. Behind me. We're not going back to the courtyard. Straight ahead."

Cole wouldn't have turned around even if the quiet scholar had buried his stylus in the dwarf's neck and started ranting in the same wicked tongues of the possessed Black Boat man. They would only stop when they each carried a man's weight in magic, relics or gold out of the jaws of this place.

That's what we do, after all. The Relic Hunters of the 9th.

Across the room, he noticed the boar-thing. It must have been sitting, watching them. Allred thought he heard the paint crack above him—the dead mage smiling—flecks of it came down, glittering in the torchlight on their shoulders.

He didn't look up. They marched. The boar turned and led Cole and the others further into the Haunt.

Door after door led to empty rooms. Indeterminable stretches of wet tunnel. They descended deeper. Nothing barred their way. No demons attacked; but always the shadow of the boar leading them forward. He could smell it now, the deep earth-scent of its bristled flesh and the slick scent of slaver-speckled tusks.

Cole called a halt to the line. Outside, night had come a long while ago and they had not stopped to rest.

"Drink. Eat," Cole said, "Don't lean against the walls. Stay close. Don't wander off."

Stoneburner had given the Rats flagons of water to carry and tight-wrapped little square bundles packed with dried meat and dried berries. Hartha and Hortha carried water, too.

Allred took the flagon of water from Hartha and drank and handed the water back. He fetched a coal from his vest and lit a redleaf roll. Stayed on his feet. Waited. He wasn't hungry. He stuffed a handful of berries in his mouth and chewed anyway.

"This isn't a Haunt for sleeping," Cole said turning to him.

"No."

"Push on and out. Sleep when we leave."

He just nodded.

The Rats whispered among themselves. The men of the 9th didn't speak, each alone with their thoughts, preserving their strength. Even the babbling of Aodlen ceased as he walked among them, studying their eyes and actions for the signs of the Downside Fever. He came to Allred and looking over the wounds on his body, verified that the hard-healing medicine he had used was successful. The doctor stuffed some food in his mouth with ink-darkened fingers and stared at him, as if looking at one of his experiments. When it annoyed him, he stared back and something in his eyes made Aodlen smile and retreat away from him. Cole's order came quick enough after they finished their meager meal.

"Follow me."

He started walking.

Besides the press of the Haunt on their spirits, they neared the edge of exhaustion from physical exertion. He could feel it like a numbness in his legs and feet and it worried him. He'd seen men so tired from forced marching that they lost control of their legs, stumbling and breaking their bones. He saw a lot of that on the march back from the City of Fire.

It would only be a few more hours until dawn outside. When had he slept last?

He didn't even notice they were moving again, lost in his thoughts and he slapped his own face to wake up. Cole led now, taking the burden from him. There was just the dim of the tunnel, few torches now but Cole's armor pierced the darkness and lit the way. Ahead there was a different light.

Cole called a halt. The light was gold before them. It rendered the finality of the tunnel distinct. Here there was no door, just the naked mouth of the tunnel, a square of damp, dripping stone leading into a torchlit room. He could almost taste the difference in the light ahead—the smooth, oily light of golden things basking.

Behind, the lantern of Aodlen and the small-sun's light melded together. Aodlen put the lantern on the ground with a clatter as they all filed into the room behind Cole. Excited murmurings from the dwarves. Hartha slapped Hortha on the back and pointed.

Along the walls, sconces in alcoves gripped torches. Others held no torch but silver and golden idols instead. Statutes watched them with orbs of magic where inset eyes should be. Below these statues, ornate tables held urns brimming over with ancient metal coins. A treasure room, Scrolls would know the names and the why of it—its purpose in the rituals of the past. He did not.

"Magic," Helga whispered, "Pure."

In the center of the chamber stood a heavy stone altar. On it was piled various offerings. Gold chains lounged in gem-studded bowls which shared the space with the bones of creatures which Allred could not place in the world above.

Scrolls walked over to one of the low tables. On it a book lay unopened. His hand lingered above it.

"Not yet. Don't touch anything. See what's just ahead before we decide our take," Cole said.

A short corridor of only a few steps led to another chamber—this one far richer than the last.

Allred's throat was dry from the redleaf and the marching. He felt relief looking around. The room was so rich, they might be able to turn around from here. This could be the destination.

Here was a circular room with walls of curving stone. Fitted equidistant into the wall itself, orbs of pure magic glowed and hummed. Each the color of lime chalk tinged with salmon and porphyry and worth incalculable amounts. Ensconced in circular cut outs snug in the stone—

"There's enough raw magic in this room to rule a kingdom" Helga said.

And he felt like the room was watching them, as much as they were watching it. A quick count. Twelve in all. Each orb about the size of a man's head.

"Careful, friends," Mage said.

This much magic could make their own bronzeface into a weapon to wipe out an army—if he could bear to use it.

In the center of the room stood another altar carved clean in white marble. On it stood a statue of a boar with a human face, a large thing of common wood. He had not seen the boar since the light of the rooms appeared to them.

"Calthor's servant's tomb?" Cole asked.

Allred aimed his crossbow at the statue. It didn't move, yet it grinned back. The brown-bark face wrought with skill was a wise-man's face stretched into a delirium of evil.

"Perhaps," Scrolls stood admiring the place, studying it and started sketching again. "Be careful. There's a surfeit of magic here."

"Tricks and traps!" Aodlen said.

Behind them, Allred heard a shriek echo down the corridors, bouncing from stone to stone. Beyond another closed door leading to unexplored passages, crawled the sound of clawed feet summoned to the march.

"You hear that?" he asked.

Cole shook his head.

Orb after orb of it waiting for the taking. Untouched for time beyond reckoning. Perfect and preserved.

Still, that sound.

"There's something coming," he said.

"Calthor's servant wishes to speak," Mage said.

The door opposite the tomb room rattled, once, then twice and shook again. It sounded like a furious animal throwing itself against the door. Allred looked back at the altar. The statue had it shifted, the wood itself changed? The same leering grin of the archmage's face met him, mocking him.

Scrolls looked up from his drawing to the shaking door. His lips moved as he read the old script surrounding it.

"What does it say?" Cole asked.

"Much. I'm committing it to memory," he kept writing, "In the years of foul harvest, the mage Calthor under the service of the principality of—"

"Summarize, Scrolls," Cole said.

Allred moved his crossbow from the statue to the door.

Scroll's lips kept moving silently for a moment, "The script reads, 'these'... and then there's an old word for what we call orbs—'hold in place powers long buried' ... this isn't the tomb but just an altar leading to it. Ahead, 'Calthor does not sleep'."

"Scrolls, shorten it—"

The scholar shot Cole an irritated glance, "It basically says, don't touch Calthor's orbs or he'll kill us. So, I suggest the bellows."

"The demon's servant wishes to parlay," Mage said again, pointing to the door which held fast but shrieked at the impact of whatever crashed against it.

Cole didn't hesitate.

"Packs off. Bags out. Gloves on. Hartha and Hortha—the bellows. Aodlen, assemble it. Now," he turned to Helga and the Rats. "Don't touch anything. Allred, keep eyes on whatever is behind that door."

They quickly moved at Cole's command. They had worked out the basics of the bellows idea in a former Haunt early on when displacing a small orb from a wall had brought that wall down upon them.

Certain relics when removed signaled long-established consequences inside the Haunts. Ancient traps prevented the removal of the magic orbs. Allred understood it. He had laid traps for enemies many a-times.

Cole had heard tell of how the large Throne-sanctioned Haunt miners had used a clever trick, which sometimes prevented these traps from initiating. Scrolls and Aodlen set to work designing their own version at Cole's suggestion.

A bellows, a small one—carried into the Haunt was attached to a leather bag full of a mixture of lightly magic-infused clay. This led to a hose fitted with a metal nozzle. They had paid a man handsomely to forge this piece, a blacksmith trained in magecraft, since the metal had to be alloyed with the magic itself.

"What do we do, Cole?" Helga asked.

"Just watch the door with Allred," he answered.

The Rats watched as they began to work on the first orb. Cole fit the nozzle carefully into the small space where the orb fit against the wall while Hartha pumped the bellows sending the clay mixture behind it. The pressure of the clay slowly formed around the orb, easing it out of the area.

Cole has a plan, Allred thought, *Always*.

He fumbled in his vest and lit a redleaf roll and watched.

All the torches in the room expired in a whoosh, as if some great demon watching them had taken one agitated inhalation.

Now only the illuminated orbs lit the room with Aodlen's modest lantern and Cole's armor shining. Small suns were lit, the sound of steel in worried hands silvered the sound of the darkened chamber. Someone coughed.

The door rumbled again. In the dark, Allred could see bits of masonry tumble to the floor, whatever lurked on the other side grew insistent. He worked the redleaf smoke between worried fingers, held the smoke in his nose and blew defiant rings of it towards the door; his eyes narrowed, squinting in the lambent light of the chamber.

Going to be a fight.

26

Lookout

Night had come heavy on the mountain and the hours passed. Lookout figured none of them would sleep.

Boph spoke less than usual tonight. He would stand and walk along the face of the Haunt, near the gate but not touching it, studying the designs and scripts on its face, hands folded in front of his chest. He stood below the thing Stoneburner called an Eye and gazed into it.

He took another drink of water but no matter how much he wished it, it wasn't wine.

"Often, my retainer there, helps pass the long hours by telling me legends," Lookout said.

Stoneburner nodded. His eyes had grown heavy in the night. Without a campfire, the man looked older, worried, the moonlight playing on the wrinkles of his unhappy face.

"Stories are good that way," Stoneburner said, quietly.

He did not start a tale, though Lookout thought he might

coax him to it. The donkey snored, the stars blinked, and lucky for him, the sky cleared and the rain of the day swept past them in silver and purple clouds out into the sea.

"Where do you hail from?" he asked Stoneburner.

"Someways on the outskirts of the Thronelands where many of us from the 9th were born. The house that rules the land is called Ashspring."

Lookout had never heard of it. Most of what he knew about the world outside of Esmer came from stories his father had told of the Empire or what other veterans told of it. The legends Boph told were of a time past.

"Do you think the House of Ashspring needs new knights?"

"Every house needs good men but they're made by birthright. War can mint more and gold, too, but it's blood for the most part."

A problem he knew he would need to overcome. His name meant nothing to the wider world.

"Ashspring. It's a good sounding name. Do you miss your home?"

Stoneburner smiled and said, "I do. It's been too long since I've seen it. I have three boys of my own, and girls, too. They are grown now. All grown and the boys, they're men now and took up the sword."

"You get to go back and see them sometimes, when Cole lets you, or however it works like that?"

Stoneburner smiled sadly, "It's safer for them that I stay away for some time. So, that's what I do."

This seemed a tragic thing to Lookout. This man looked strong but some way past the age where fighting and marching and exploring made sense. How did the world work? Shouldn't he be allowed home?

"You've explored for the Throne a long time with Cole and the others?"

Stoneburner thought on that question for a while and Lookout wondered if the man had forgotten what he asked. The night had grown gentle and there was a soft song of night birds in the trees. He imagined them sitting in their nests, bathing in the moonlight and listening to the two of them speak.

Boph had turned back from the gate and joined them. He sat on the ground, his back against the small berm of dirt. He pulled his legs up near his chest, folded his arms around his knees and watched Stoneburner, waiting for an answer, too.

"It seems to me, on nights like this, it was a life ago since I joined the Ninth. First there were many years of fighting for the Throne."

"Years?" he asked.

"Many," Stoneburner answered, "And these long nights waiting take a toll. It's a heavy toll on all who remain."

"Fighting was harder, or exploring? You were a knight, yourself?"

He wasn't sure what types of duties a knight might be called on to fulfill, so he figured he should know what was more difficult.

Stoneburner waived towards the face of the Haunt and the gate and said nothing, "Most fighting men aren't knights. This work is the most difficult. But, like I said, I don't go within anymore."

Fear ran through Lookout then because in the moonlight, the older man turned his head away from them, pretending to study some sound on the cliff behind them but Lookout could make out a silver tear sliding down his face.

"Who is hunting you?" Boph asked.

Stoneburner turned back towards him and smiled. Lookout thought maybe it was just the heavy magic of this strange place that had tricked the mind. He saw no sadness in the man's face now.

"Who isn't?"

That was a different story from the one the explorers told at first. He cleared his throat.

"So, you mean...the Throne doesn't exactly—"

"There's a war. Cole is in the right of it but there are many who don't see it that way."

"The Throne?"

"There's dispute," the man said, "Tell me, you've been transfixed by Mage, quite a lot. He has spoken to you?"

Boph looked down, and studied the tops of his hands, "I

don't understand everything he says. But I think he sees the future and the past and that's why he can't make sense in the present. I believe we will join you. I believe Lookout will become a knight. I believe I'm fated for the life of a mage."

He had never heard his retainer say that. Lookout could hardly believe the words leaving Boph's mouth. He was at once excited at the prophesy but more fearful than ever. More than anything, it meant Boph would go with him.

"Was it some prophecy Mage spoke to you of?" Lookout asked.

Boph shook his head and turned to him, "Maybe. We don't have a choice. I think we'll go with these men. I'll bring my donkey; I know that much. I won't leave him. Not ever."

Stoneburner took a deep breath.

"Cole decides these things. Few join us but there might be some place for you."

It sounded like he was conceding something grim, and Lookout just couldn't understand this. A way to leave Esmer, a way to the Thronelands—it sounded like a dream come true! This island had nothing more for him, no kin, no trade.

He smiled, satisfied, and looked over the cliff face. Beyond the tops of the dense jungle below it, and down, down, down the mountain's face to the sand of the shore, past the lip of the sea-kissed beach lay island after island with their own sandy shores—beyond, those though he knew no maps—Throne lands and beyond those other lands of legends; and surely, somewhere in this wide world there was a House where he could pledge to serve.

"Are you very old, sir?" he asked.

"Compared to what is inside there, no."

Boph jumped to his feet, eyes bulging, Stoneburner stood, too, stared towards the steps. Lookout gripped his knife.

"What is it?" Stoneburner asked.

"Something is on Esmer," Boph said, staring past Stoneburner. His eyes were wide and he could see the reflection of the moon within the black pupils.

"I heard nothing. Did you hear something, boy?"

Boph shook his head, "Not with my ears. Something

touched the ground of Esmer. I feel it running through the land. It's a twisted thing."

For the first time in his life, he saw Boph more scared than himself. He was trembling and in some sort of half-trance. He always suspected his attendant had the powers of witchery about him, but he'd never seen him in a state like this.

Stoneburner stood staring down the empty road. Lookout went to ground at Boph's alarm, his left hand on the top of the dirt berm, he peered down the road. All along the sides of it, he thought he could see whisps of geists, images pulsing in and out of the shadows of the trees and then they faded.

"Boph?"

He was still shaking there and Stoneburner had gone near him but stayed back a pace or two, as if wary at the power inside him.

Stoneburner lowered his crossbow, "The power of the Haunt can get to you, even if you're not inside."

Boph insisted, "Something red and ruling comes. It used to be a man."

"Has he showed the power of this sight before, Lookout?" Stoneburner asked.

"Not like this, but I believe him when he speaks. He can make potions to heal, that I know and I've seen him reading the stars some nights but he doesn't talk to me about such things."

"You talk to the stars, boy?"

Boph had regained a little composure now. He looked at them all as if he'd been gone for a time and then raising his hands, he formed them as if holding an invisible sphere. He spoke a word and then another. He shook his hands as if frustrated. Nothing happened and Stoneburner began to relax.

"I can read stars, yes. When I saw Les Aments, I knew my fate—"

His eyes went wide again, and he sang another phrase and gestured again. Then clapping, a spark soared up from his palms, hovered in the air, quaking. He uttered another word, and it fed the fire and the light which he had conjured. It reminded Lookout of the sphere Mage had peered into when Allred went down the mountain.

"So, he has it," Stoneburner smiled.

"I ... I've never seen him do such a thing." He was in awe now of his friend. This was true magework. A mage, Boph was a real mage! His friend could wield magic and he saw in that light the future for the briefest of instants—He *was* a knight and his truest friend *was* a mage.

Light sprang up above Boph's hands and steadied and for a moment there was an image there which Boph described.

"Men moving up the mountain, carrying a covered thing with something inside. Inside it is a terrible thing. "The wind, you felt that gust? There it is, a moment later, riding down the mountain. It is brushing against some material which is draped over the thing. Four men hoist it on their shoulders. I can see the raw flesh beneath the wooden poles. There's others in the wake, jerking as if dancing or in fits—"

Boph shouted and jumped as if something had struck him. The light extinguished and he looked up at them both, his hands now empty. The skin of his palms glowed as if infused with the magic he had conjured.

"A hissing sound blasted the curtain. It saw me looking at it, I think. There's an abomination drawing near. It looked back at me. It knows you're here. It knows you."

Stoneburner stared at his retainer for a long while without breaking his gaze. He bowed his heavy head and put his hand to his mouth as if trying to hold in words that would frighten them and said, quietly:

"Lookout, fetch the small torch I prepared. Light it with the fire in the coal box and bring it here."

Stoneburner began to search for something within the pack he kept near him.

Boph still stood staring at his own hands, surprised at his own ability. So, it wasn't some power his attendant had kept secret from him. Lookout knew then that this was the first time Boph had accomplished a real spell.

"My friend is a mage," he whispered as he fetched the torch. He found the coal burning still and he held its fire to it. The flame came to life and it was simple fire, the yellow, warmth was a relief after the strange light Boph had brought forth. He carried the torch to Stoneburner.

"You don't sense it? Do you believe me?" Boph asked, still staring back down the road.

"You might be a bit touched, but that was magecraft of a sort, no doubt. It makes sense. Even if you're destined for magery being near a battlemage can confuse even those taught and trained for it. I've even seen men who had no magic, do strange things around him. You're telling me true, you've never done such a thing before as just now?"

Boph just shook his head.

Stoneburner stood thinking for some time. Then cursed beneath his breathe. "I had hoped it wasn't so. For your sake. No. It looked like real sorcery. Too old to lie to myself. Optri likely coming. Going to let Cole know."

In his hands, he held a stylus. He dipped it in some ink and began to write in the torchlight words Lookout could not understand.

27

The room filled with dust, magical and mundane, which grew dimmer with each orb they pried loose and stowed inside their packs.

"There's enough gold in the room behind us to buy an army," Thay whispered to her.

She stood staring into the treasure room. The temptation to sit was strong and her legs felt weak.

Helga, my love. Where are you now?

His voice. Harad calling to her from somewhere behind her. She had left him in the Pits and now he had made his way back to her. No.

"Helga? What do you see?"

"I see it," Helga whispered. "Yes, there's a lot of gold."

Shaking her head, she tried to rid herself of the voice. Thay was looking up at her with a far-away wondering look. Tym joined him.

"I can't stay here, Helga—tell them, just tell them. We should just—let's take the idols and leave. Go back. These men, they don't need us," Thay whispered.

They kept working, the room growing darker as the orbs fell into their packs. She calculated the space they had left, the weight they could carry. Even with the orbs and every precious statue in the antechamber, they could carry more.

"Just wait. After they take the orbs, we'll take the gold," she answered, "Do you hear Harad's voice, Thay? You knew him. I know, it can't be … but if anything can happen here, maybe something good could, too?"

Thay's hair was damp with sweat, pasted against his pale forehead. He smelled like fear itself. His eyes darted back and forth from her to the statues smirking in their alcoves. She thought they had all moved, since she first saw them, turned slightly to face the chamber of the orbs as if watching them.

"No. Not Harad, Helga. It's other voices, I think. Why aren't we leaving? These men are mad. This place is killing us," Thay said.

"We listen to Cole. He's survived this long."

"Thay's right. Cole is unclean, a demon, himself," Tym whispered, "Look at them all. They're all unclean."

"It's so much gold. We never saw this much in the Pits," Thay uttered in awe, entranced by the fanged-idols watching the orb-laden room. "We're fools not to grab what we can and turn around now."

"I trust Cole," she mumbled. She believed it but it sounded like she didn't.

"It's too much. I keep seeing images from the past. Not real," Tym said.

It was Tym who had nearly lost spirit on entering. He had been quiet ever since but there was a lost look in the dwarf's eye she didn't like. At least Thay was talking some sort of sense.

"We just need to listen to what they tell us and we'll survive it." She couldn't afford to believe anything other than that now. She watched the Relic Hunters working at prying loose the orbs.

"I want to go. Never come back. This place makes the Pits look like a warm inn."

It was true in a way. In all their time out there, they hadn't dreamed of this much pure magic.

"I'll never escape this place, Helga, no matter if my body leaves whole."

She grabbed Thay and pulled him towards her, "That's what they tried to tell me. If Cole is a demon and Allred why would they try to warn us away? Hold. We've come a long way and survived."

"Have we? What happened to the Black Boat men, Helga? He fed them to this place. And that soldier? Never saw him again" Thay answered, looking at her as if surprised how obvious the truth was and unsure how she couldn't see it. She slowly let him go, ashamed of her actions but more worried at the fact Thay hadn't flinched when she grabbed him, hadn't cared or felt it at all.

"Take a drink of that vial Aodlen gave you," she said, standing straight.

Staah stood across the room, watching them all, biting his lip. She nodded to him and he returned it.

Her skin crawled beneath the bandage on her arm quicker, the eye shifting, alerting her. She ventured a look at the Eye. Stoneburner stood before the face of the Haunt gesturing at a parchment. She nearly fell backwards at the weirdness of the mirror crafted from her own flesh. Tym steadied her and she heard Staah move towards her.

"Deviltry and abominations and you let them put it on you, too," Thay said, turning his back on her.

"Thay?" she said, as he turned away, "Need to tell Cole."

She took a few steps deeper into the orb room, gripping her sword, trying to keep her voice steady.

"Cole, there's something … Stoneburner is doing at the gate." Her throat was dry again and she looked away from her arm.

Cole leaned over the bellows that Hartha worked. He came over to her, grabbed her arm and looked at the Eye. He brought it closer to his face.

Allred watched them both from across the room with narrow eyes, bloodshot with smoke.

"Well done to notice it," Cole said and giving some signal to the Eye she could not discern, he gently let go her wrist. "Nearly finished here. How are your Rats?"

"What of this treasure?" she asked gesturing to the room of idols.

Cole looked back into the room where Tym stood. Thay was kneeling before the idols, drinking from his vial. Staah had joined them and the three circled around each other arguing in their native tongue.

"Your dwarf falters," Cole said and took a step forward towards them.

"I told him to drink," Helga said moving in front of him, "There's voices we hear. Don't you hear them?"

"I only hear one thing." Cole looked down at her, studied the dwarves a moment more and firmly shoved her aside to talk to the dwarves. "It's the Downside Fever."

Allred had shuffled backwards slowly across the chamber while they talked, holding his crossbow trained on the opposite door the entire time. It still rattled, insistent.

"Did someone take that idol of the boar?" Allred asked them both.

"What?" Cole asked, turning from the dwarves.

"The statue on the altar in the center of the room. It was wooden, ugly—the boar who wears the man's face."

Cole stopped, thought and left Allred with her, "Let me ask the physician."

"Did you take it, Helga?" Allred asked, a hint of accusation in his voice.

He didn't meet her eyes. Sweat pouring off his forehead, down his nose; he smelled sweet and burned like the redleaf he smoked.

She didn't know what he was talking about.

"I don't think so, cousin." She looked back at her Rats. Thay was grinning at the idols now, staring at one, while the other two dwarves flanked him, arguing and trying to pick him up from the ground. He crawled towards the nearest statue and she swore, it turned on its pedestal to the dwarf and opened a hook-toothed, golden mouth and spoke back. It looked like he was bowing to the figure, daring glances with greedy eyes between each anxious prostration.

"Allred, this isn't good," she said.

Across the room, Aodlen was busy guiding the tube that secreted the clay concoction behind the last of the orbs. Cole whispered something to him and the doctor reached up with gloved hands and the orb drifted down from the niche in the wall, softly, as if composed of feathers or dust bound together—a hollow thing, far lighter than what its size signified. He carefully placed it inside a shielded bag at his feet, wrapped it and placed it into a pack.

Scrolls stood motionless in the middle of the dark room. He had been like that for some time. Helga looked at Allred again. She could see the same evil working in his mind. She felt a surge of fear again.

Cole came back.

"I'll hold your bow while you drink," he said to Allred.

Her cousin looked confused, "I'm keeping it trained on the door that's shaking."

Cole reached up slowly and put his hand on the middle of the crossbow, lowering it, "Prefer you take up the sword after you drink."

Allred almost let the crossbow go, each finger unwrapping from the grip one by one. He stepped to the side and raised it again towards the door, turned to Cole and said, "We've tracked a boar with a man's face through most of this Haunt?"

"Drink, Allred. The Downside is heavy. We are breaking under it. We've been here before. Drink. It's an order."

Her cousin looked down at his vest, where she supposed he kept his vial and looked back up squinting across the dim room, "Cole, something is wrong."

"Yes, it is," Cole said.

Allred shook his head, emphatically. He raised the crossbow to aim across the room.

"You've all seen the boar with the face of the man?" he shouted to everyone in the room. "Leading us. But you didn't see the statue of it?"

Cole lowered his voice as if soothing a dangerous animal,

"Yes, but drink. Look at what Scrolls has drawn of this room," he said and put a parchment on top of the crossbow, facing Allred, who looked down at it.

Helga could see it, too. The scholar's rendering was swift and accurate of the room in which she stood. He had sketched in light ink a realistic drawing of the place, outlines and shapes with a minimum of ink strokes.

The altar in the sketch stood empty.

"There is a geist ahead of us but no boar statue."

"You're wrong," Allred spoke, plainly, tipping his chin to the parchment, hands still on the crossbow. Cole took it back. "Scrolls is wrong. The drawing is wrong."

"You remember collapsing back in the courtyard?" Cole asked.

"When the Dhlam fell on me? Yes," Allred admitted.

"Prior to that. Downside Fever. It's getting worse."

Mage spoke then, "Cole, there is tide and swell of Fever in the room. We mustn't tarry."

Cole turned to Helga as if bidding her to agree and she did with a simple, 'Aye' because Cole demanded it. She didn't know what was true. She closed her eyes and tried to keep to her feet. She could hear Harad behind her, felt his hand on the back of her neck, where he used to place it when they lay together beneath the stars.

From behind her, she heard Tym crawling around the room, talking to himself. His brother asked him something she couldn't hear.

"Drink a drop to calm yourself." Cole reached into Allred's vest and pulled out the vial, uncorked it and offered it to him. "Ready to move forward soon. Not far. Then we double back, take the treasure from the antechamber here. Then out."

"How do we go forward with that thing shaking the door ahead," Allred asked, ignoring the offer of the vial's contents.

Cole's brow creased, the smooth flesh on the side of his burned face failing to wrinkle, making his face appear half frozen.

"At the door, a tide," Mage hummed.

She was confused, too. There was no rattling of a door. The

only other door in the room was still and closed. Behind it Harad stood, holding her daughter in his arms, waiting for her to join him. He rapped upon the door with one skeletal hand, drawing her ... But that ...

"There's no rattling door, cousin," she said. "Cruel tricks."

Allred looked at her. He took the vial with one hand from Cole and drank from it. She could see his body relax.

"It was there," Allred insisted.

"Finished, Cole," Aodlen said walking over to them, looking at Allred, "Fever on you hard, I hear? Ha! On us all. On us all. Ha! Ha! I just ride the waves of it now, all the time."

Allred handed the vial back to Cole, turned to the doctor and for a moment, Helga thought she saw the pupils in his eyes turn to black diamonds, the eyes of a hunting thing, a killing thing. She blinked and they were the same worried, light green eyes as before. She shook her head and took out her own vial and nipped at it.

"On us all, I think for a long time now," Allred answered. He took one quick step to Aodlen. He did nothing and did not point the crossbow at him, but the speed of his move made Aodlen throw up his hands and cackle and step back.

Cole stepped in front of Allred and the crossbow now. The dart pointed straight into his chest. If Allred pulled the trigger at that range, it would kill him dead. He didn't waver. The light from the small-sun speckled spaulders illuminated her cousin's face in the dark of the chamber. Pale. Hollow. His eyes were the eyes of a hunting thing, but Cole barred him from some deed. Allred didn't move but blinked, "Cole?"

Cole stepped even closer. He let the tip of the dart press against his own armor, and reaching across the weapon, laid a hand on Allred's shoulder, the crossbow between them. He pulled her cousin's face close to his and leaned forward, his forehead touching Allred's and looking into those murderous eyes asked, "Whatever waits in front of us, we face it together. I swear it to you, Allred."

Allred returned the stare but the killing look left his face and he lowered the crossbow. Cole slowly released the warrior from whatever power he held. She couldn't understand it but she felt it from across the room—the absolute stillness of Cole's oath.

"Yes," Allred answered, as if in a trance. Then a terrible cold smile broke out across his face, "Yes, let's march further, Cole. Let's never stop."

"Good," Cole answered and turned to her, "It's only Fever."

Helga realized everyone, the Rats and the men of the 9th were watching them. All but Mage and Scrolls who stood in close conference near the altar. Behind them, now she saw the door was open.

"Listen up, we go some ways farther then—" Cole addressed the entire room, who had gathered nearer to the two men, listening.

"Cole?" she pointed at the door.

Everyone turned to look.

The boar with the human face stood inside the threshold. Its mouth puckered and spat syllables which raced across the floor. She could see it for the briefest moment. Then it turned and walked back through the door.

"Yes. I'll watch the gate. I'll start back," Thay screamed behind her.

Turning, she saw him push his brother away, reach up and grab one of the statues and wrench it down from the pedestal.

The base of the thing came away from the wall. Rock began grinding against rock. She thought she saw the warm metal of the mouth of the idol sneer.

Thay screeched in victory, hugging the heavy idol to his chest. Dropping his dagger, he began running towards the entrance. Staah lunged and tried to grab his legs but missed and fell to the floor beside Tym who was still on the ground weeping. Hortha lifted his axe as if to hurl it at the dwarf across the room, then hesitated and turned his blocky helmeted head up into a flood of dirt and dust cascading from the ceiling and screamed as if challenging the very rock.

Cole moved fast, grabbed her and held her as the floor of the orb chamber fell downwards with a one long crash like thunder lingering over hills. They were all plunged into a racket of darkness and dust that drowned out the mad exclamations of Thay dwindling down the Haunt's tunnels.

28

Allred

He saw the geist. He saw the dwarf snatch the idol and run. He admitted he felt a little vindicated at the sight of the boar and in the brief instant of weightlessness and the dropping down, a smile twisted his lips as rock and wall and floor plunged down cloaking him in a shroud of grime.

He was still smiling in the gloom and at the fact that his bones weren't broken. A short drop. Not dead. Yet. He'd have to change the count, though. The dwarf who'd sprung the trap was likely gone. Thay was his name, he thought, but he hadn't bothered to learn the dwarve's names since he took them for doomed.

"Allred?" "Cole?"

Helga's voice came from somewhere nearby, weak and dust-choked.

Belly down, he rolled in the darkness and sat up. He had kept his grip on his crossbow and he felt the weight of the dart still within. Now, he laid the crossbow near his feet, useless in the pale dust of the room obscuring his sight. He reached for his short dagger at his belt. Best for close-work in the blindness of the room.

He waited patiently listening to the surprised shouts from the others in the room. He rubbed his dust-filmed eyes. Edging forward, the toe of his boot met rock.

There were shouts and Helga calling their names. Ahead, through the settling dust beyond some heap, he glimpsed a figure lit by a penumbra of foggy light.

"Cole?"

"Don't move. Let the dust settle. Let me hear names. Hartha, answer." Cole called all their names, one by one. He heard each of the 9th answer the roll call.

The floor above in the chamber had collapsed. Everyone in the room had plunged with it to the level below. Not a far drop, luckily. He could make out the edge of the room above, the lip of the pit where they now stood. A man standing on another man's shoulders could reach it and pull himself up.

"Allred?"

Helga's voice again to his left. He stood and began to shuffle slowly towards it, sliding his boots against the stone-littered floor.

"Cousin?"

"Over here," she answered.

He found her, still sitting on the ground.

"Can you stand?"

He saw her hand through the dust, grabbed it and pulled her up to her feet.

"Your Rat has not answered," Cole said.

"I think Thay ran," she said, dust and guilt in her voice.

She called his name. No answer.

One of the Rats called from the lip of the pit and said, "Thay touched one of the statues and fled."

The dust settling, Allred could see well enough now. The light from the small suns instead of making more obscure the chamber, illuminated it in the settling air. In the center of it stood a pillar which supported the central altar above. It had not toppled with the floor. Heaps of human bones were stacked around the pillar. Lining the walls more bones jutted from piles of fallen mortar and stone that had once been the floor. Skulls stared with an accusing look, as if their eternity was disrupted.

"Form up around me," Cole said, standing near the altar.

The room filled with tired groans, the doctor's yipping, barking laugh, and the slow unsteady steps of exhausted men gathering in the gloom to heed Cole's command.

"Look! The lantern survived the fall, Ha! That's fine quality, fine quality, yes. Only the best for the Relic Hunters of the 9th!" Aodlen held the lantern aloft and turned in slow circles, grinning. "Let me look for bumps and bruises and the broken things."

The physician made his way around the pit, fevered eyes exploring. All were sound enough to keep marching. Hartha, falling had turned his ankle. He could limp along.

The creep of exhaustion numbed him. He put his dagger back into his belt, held his crossbow pointed at the ground and waited for Cole to decide their next move.

After mustering the explorers to the center of the chamber, Cole took stock and then retreating across the room examined another door.

"Everyone still has their packs?" he asked.

Assent all around.

"Hortha, retrieve the two dwarves," Cole ordered.

The giant made his way across the room. He set his shield against the wall of the pit, stretched his hands upward and commanded the dwarves to jump down.

"Don't know about that," one of them said, uneasy, looking behind him.

"Follow or stay," Cole said and turned back to examining the door leading out of this place.

"You Greenies are excellent at tumbling. Wasn't that your work before this? Perhaps, Thay will find us but best to listen to Cole," Hortha said, laughing but there was a sadness in the giant's voice.

The two dwarves scoffed at their large kinsman and spat out some Green Island curses. One threw up a sign with fingers pointed upwards.

"What about Thay, Cole?" Helga asked.

"Gone," Cole said, not bothering to turn to answer her.

"What do you mean?"

Cole said nothing.

Helga didn't press him but joined Hortha and coaxed the other Rat to lower himself over the lip of the pit where Hortha could grasp the bottom of the dwarf's feet. Then, with a powerful shrug he pressed the dwarf a few inches into the air, sending him flying and caught the Rat like a child in his arms, lowering him with a laugh.

"We aren't at a festival, green-man-tall-folk, stop your guffawing," the Rat said, brushing dust and old bone from his tunic.

"You've tumbled before at market faires, green-man-short-folk," Hortha answered and slapped the dwarf on the back so hard, he stumbled over to Helga.

Cole consulted with Scrolls near the door leading up and out of the pit.

Helga whispered to Tym, "You saw what happened?"

"He started talking strange words, grabbed the idol and ran."

"What now?"

Allred didn't answer.

She persisted. "He said he would go back to the gate."

"He's good as dead," he said.

She blinked, wiped away dust from her cheek. Tym and Staah turned away, studying the blank face of the pit where they stood.

"Well, he's mine to find—" Helga said.

"It's not that. What's done is done. I mean, he's dead. Not because Cole will strike him down. Even if we find him—gone."

"There's a chance, though," Helga insisted, "He might make it back there."

"Could be," he agreed. He was tired of talking.

He made his way over to Cole, turning away from Helga. It would sink in with time. No use wasting words on it, now. She followed him.

"We're going forward," Cole said, turning to them all.

"Can we?" he asked.

"Yes."

Beside him, Mage stood silent, hands folded in front of him.

"Cole, it was I think, the fault of my man who pulled the statue and—"

Cole watched her with a blank face.

"Yes. We're going forward," he said again ignoring the beginning of her apology. Cole didn't care. He just kept moving. She hadn't understood that, yet.

Allred felt a sudden desire to shout *no* but he couldn't be sure what he wanted to say no to now.

Cole turned to them, sensing the weariness and fear and fever on them all.

"We go forward."

"I'm sorry, Cole. That's all," Helga said.

"Just turn your back on it, cousin," Allred said to her. He watched his words pierce her like arrows.

"Weapons ready. Don't touch anything. You're beside me, Allred."

"Heard."

The door was not barred. It led into another corridor, that quickly climbed up to the same level above. They made their way through it, reaching a set of stone stairs that switched back in a tight narrow curl. He was looking back down at the floorless room, where they'd just been. There were prints of a boar in the dust.

They turned around. Another tunnel led deeper into the Haunt. He walked it, small sun lighting the way, Cole beside him. Soon the way forward became confused with more and more doors lining the damp-stone tunnels. Each ended in small bone-bare, unadorned rooms or down other hallways they had no time to follow.

"Marking the way," Cole said to him.

From his belt, Cole untied a drawstring fitted around a small sack of cloth. Pinching magecrafted sand between his fingers, Cole sprinkled it on the floor where they stood. When the light of the small sun lit upon it, it glowed incandescent blue; otherwise, it looked like common grime. One more concoction Mage, Scrolls and Aodlen had invented for their work. The materials costly, the devise useful. It let them see the trail, without giving it away to other eyes.

He marched along with Cole in the dim bowels of the Haunt. Time was kept by the echo of their boots on the tunnels and nothing more. He could see the tracks of hoof prints leading them further into the Haunt. As a scout, he knew the game; he knew they were being led forward.

Cole knew it. Those behind felt it—the Relic Hunters of the 9th marching in stoic silence and the mutter and whisper of Helga and her Rat. Cole never paused in his pursuit. Like he said, "Their packs were only half-full."

"It's leading us," Allred whispered.

"Yes."

"Trap?"

"Not if we suspect it."

It went like that for some time. The elixir did its work. He felt steady but adrift. He lost his sense of how long ago they had descended into this place. The corridors turned in arches of stone and Cole marked the crossroads. Down unexplored tunnels, strange hymns sung by strangled voices echoed and the sound of hidden mills and subterranean foundries came to their ears. No one spoke of it. They creeped and mapped, and after everyone had fallen quiet Cole asked:

"Do you feel fear?"

Allred studied the man's face in the penumbra of light his breastplate cast. His armor was filth-crusted, magic-coated, battered and worn but strong. The smooth, burned places on his face and hands glowed eerie in the light. All of the dust and cuts and hurt on him, and the years and he kept walking beside him; his leader, still marching.

"I drank some wine in Port Shamhalhan. Good quality. Stoneburner's stock. Ruby something, can't recall. Tasted like nothing. I'm emptied out. Something besides fear crowded out the way I used to feel. I don't want to believe it, but I think it's a quiet madness and the only time I don't feel it is when I'm fighting."

Cole opened his mouth, looked to say something, closed his eyes for a moment, then without breaking stride, took his flagon from his hip and drank the water he carried.

"If someday, we can't find a way out of a Haunt. If we get truly lost, or can't win, we'll be faced with unthinkable things."

"Could be."

"I'll dwell on the unthinkable. You don't have to shoulder that burden, but Allred—" He turned his gaze on him in the dark. "You may be the man I must to ask to do unspeakable things."

Cole rarely talked like this. The Downside Fever might be reaching into him, too, but he didn't believe it. He wanted to ask him why the Haunts didn't shake him the same way and nearly did, but he knew there was no answer that would satisfy him, no answer Cole could give, so he kept his mouth shut and his feet moving.

Finally, after uncountable steps, he said, "Yes." Just ahead they found what they were seeking.

Interlude

In the night they beached the ship and hastened up the mountain to punish the wicked.

Emanating from the curtained palanquin, one slithering syllable twisted in Ceph's head—the Crimson One calling a halt to the line. He gestured, the master's will his command to give. The four slaves bent knees and lowered the master's shelter to the profane ground. The silk whisper of the quiet parting of a yellow curtain he could not hear. The scent of the incense which pleased the master issued into the night as the Crimson One crawled to make his own survey.

Ahead, there was a break in the path and beside it a scattering of a few palm huts. A dog barked from behind one and then fell silent.

"Bring them to be Wyrmdancers," his master whispered into his ear.

He signaled the Optri forward. Swords out, they shouted for

the villagers to leave their domiciles. Wary eyes appeared in the moonlight from doorways. The Optri pulled them from their houses and threw them into the mud of the mountain path. The soldiers went inside the huts and brought out those who tried to hide with the others where they quaked at the power of his master's call.

Perhaps a dozen would be blessed. Some children, some adults. If it were up to Ceph, they would bring more to the fight against the Relic Hunters of the 9th but it was not up to him and these dancers would help fill out their ranks.

He bowed his head in thanksgiving. These peasants would be given the rare opportunity to serve, to feed this master's power by drawing hidden power with their dance.

In the cold light of the moon, his master rose up, climbing upon the strength of his own pert coils. The serpentine jaw dropped, distended and the master drawled out the spell to instruct the peasants in the Wyrmdance. He could feel the syllables wash over his naked back, each segment of the spell hesitating in his own guts, squirming there and then moving on.

Ceph held a spear over them but they were already beginning to transform. At the last moment, one tried to run. A boy pushed away from another he sat beside. His feet dug into the mud and splattered it on the peasant beside him who was scratching at his unworthy flesh revealing it to the wisdom of the charm of his master.

He hurled his spear. The point took the boy in the back, the weight of the thing knocking him to the ground. The blood bubbled from the wound but none of his fellow villagers went to him or paid him any mind now and soon the boy lay still.

The rest reached to their eyes as the master spoke, and they moaned in the ecstasy of servitude. From their eyes sprouted the writing bodies of a hundred red worms, swaying to the tune of the Crimson One's hymn.

Now, in thrall, all at once, the peasants rose and ceased weeping. Blind to the false world now their true path was clear, and their step was graceful and sure as they lined up to follow the master's plan.

"Proceed," his master whispered in his dead ear.

The palanquin curtain waved in the mountain breeze and the Crimson One took his place within. The Optri men heaved it upon their shoulders. A dozen new servants followed their path up the mountain. The dog came out and licked the face of the fallen boy.

Some ways up the mountain, there was a light in the distance, peering at them from the forest. He heard his master curse at it, dispelling it and then the night was dark again.

29

Lookout

B ut what do you sense? You've never said you had a knack for magery?"

Whatever Boph had told to Stoneburner, the old man hopped quick to tell the others through the symbol on the mountain face.

"I don't say everything to everyone. I keep my mouth shut. You ought to learn that, Lookout. Anyway, I don't know. I've felt it stronger since Mage arrived."

"When certain people get close to a battlemage it awakens all kinds of things in them," Stoneburner said, returning.

He gripped his crossbow tight now. After setting down the paper with the message he hadn't let it go.

"Who is here though?" Lookout asked.

"Another mage with his men, most likely. I'm hoping what you saw was far away, maybe even on another island. It's possible," Stoneburner said, nodding at Boph. "But...we ought to figure Optri are on our trail with a battlemage of their own. Likely. No..." the old man trailed off.

"Who are they?"

"Men sent to kill us."

"For coming here?"

"For doing what we do."

"So, like the others?"

Stoneburner scoffed, then something made him sullen again, maybe the thought of the prisoners they had taken, "Those were common soldiers led by one low-level Optri. If Boph is right, this will be different."

"Well, what do we do?" he asked.

Stoneburner thought. A tired smile creeped over his face. He sat back down.

"Cole decides. We wait. We have a head start on them. I've prepared the camp well enough. But if they catch us out in a fight. You two listen to me now. If the Optri come, you both run. No matter where. Run."

30

Allred

A bare archway stood ahead. Cole turned and called a halt. "Me and you," Cole said.

Allred nodded in the darkness and moved forward.

Small-suns cut the gloom. Lines of light pierced a vast open space. There were the same torches, ever-burning, but the lights faded each into their own small globe amongst the expanse of the place. Water dripped down from high above.

He pointed his small sun up. There was no visible ceiling. The walls he could see were fashioned of common stone blocks, damp. Even in this dead place there was the crawl of insects fleeing the light. A white lizard affixed to the wall watched them with empty red eyes then bolted.

The water dripping from above created puddles where the floor had fallen and caved in places. Slurry darkened the patches of stone and marble. There were traces of footprints, the dragging of debris, streaks of movement paused in mud. The smell of things both dead and between life greeted his nose. He studied it all, making his own map in his mind, gauging the when and the if and the how of attacks to come.

"Something here," he said.

"There's no end to it," Cole replied, but the answer was to some unspoken question of his own reckoning. He saw the two orange eyes just before the demon hit Cole low in the knees. He unloaded the crossbow bolt into the back of the creature. Felt the weapon buck against his arm. The magic-tipped dart whistled. The demon twisted and turned, dragging a clawed hand down Cole's leg. In one motion, he dropped the crossbow and drew his own sword ready for the attack.

Cole swung striking the wounded Dhlam down and finishing it. It writhed for a moment more, then Cole stabbed down with both hands and there was silence again.

Blood welled up on Cole's leg where flesh parted beneath his trousers. Allred stayed still, then reloaded a dart. He kept his eyes wide open while Aodlen rushed forward.

"Hold," Cole called through the arch.

The footsteps of the rest slowed and stopped at the mouth of the tunnel where it spilled into the cavern. He went to Cole and felt him sag onto him for a moment, as he shifted the weight to his good leg.

He kept his eyes trained on the darkness as Aodlen tended Cole's wound.

"Work is without cease, without cease, ha!" Aodlen said, dousing his potions on Cole's leg. The smell of flesh-forming, wound-curing magic filled his nostrils.

"Be quick," Cole grunted.

The demon still twitched. Its mouth worked on its headless snout then stopped.

Cole stood straight. He made no grunt of pain. Silent. Allred could still hear his skin boiling. He took a few halting steps in a small circle, testing his leg.

"It's good."

Aodlen looked up, his lean, ravaged face and bright eyes

assessing Cole and his handiwork. All around now, the scuttle of claws from beyond, echoed through the cavern. The splash of a foot in a puddle far-off, the slither of demon flesh against darkened stone.

All three heard the sounds building and Aodlen, his head cocked said, "I'll be busy. Ha!" The doctor cackled and stowing his potions away he picked up his lantern from the ground and drew his own short sword.

Cole called the rest of the band forward.

"Move slow. Eyes open. Weapons out. Going to be a fight," Cole said.

Allred started forward.

It looked like a half mage-made and half-natural cave within the mountain. The manmade stones of the corridor floors upended and ceased in a jumble ahead and revealed damp, grey sand.

The rest of the group joined them through the mouth of the corridor, staring in wonder.

"Treasure-taking time," Hortha said.

Allred kept walking, crossbow up. Ahead, there was a small underground pond, like the one above. On its surface, a few drops of water fell. More of the albino lizards were arrayed around the waters, staring at him with their bloody eyes.

They had encountered these "mirrors" in Haunts before. Reflections and echoes of the land; the Haunts remembering the world above before they were sealed. No one understood these things. Were they the dreams of the damned laborers who created these places alongside the archmages? Were they memory of the world—preserved and distorted and enduring down here?

Could just be a pond.

He picked up the boar tracks in the dirt around the lake. He followed those. They led around the water and on the other side of it he saw the chalk-white of standing stones, gargantuan rocks arranged in circles in the shadows.

The monoliths were sinking into the soft ground, some crooked with age. Side by side, some remained flush and partnered, obscuring what lay within.

"There," Cole said, pointing.

There was an entrance inside the stone circle formed by an opening where two rock slabs were capped with a lintel. On that lintel, carved in the stone was what looked like some map of the night sky.

Scroll's stylus scratched his parchment. The sound of the enemy in the distance had not ceased. The sound was tricky in here. It could carry from far off. Not far enough off.

Cole gestured to him to wait outside. Before he could protest, Cole ducked through the doorway, his way lit by his armor. He disappeared inside the ceremonial structure, the darkness covering him. A moment later, Cole's voice beckoned him forward.

"Just you."

Facing him just inside the passage was a smaller, tighter inner ring of standing stones and he winded around them to the center of the place, following Cole to the central chamber. There was no roof to the structure. He heard what sounded like claws on stone and brought the crossbow up. Both froze. Nothing.

Cole stepped aside and let him through. There, in the center was a simple altar. Atop the altar was a handsome gold bowl and inside it set the single largest orb Allred had ever seen. It pulsed a sharp thin light vertically into the darkness of the cavern through the roofless stone circle.

He heard someone behind him weeping outside the standing stones, but he could not be sure who it was, except that it was no one in their party.

The orbs light was akin to the light of the small-suns. It felt to him as if the light held something above with a great strength and that it had been there for ages beyond reckoning. Upwards it shined, as if holding the burden of the darkness itself but illuminating nothing, nonetheless.

Cole stood before the treasure, quiet. The cities of the Throne burned in Cole's eyes, and he saw his own image striding beside him through ash-blown miles. And with him, the 9th, resurrected, renewed.

But the army they lead were not the men he had known in life. And though they walked with him, he knew they could not feel anything but the fire they brought with their steps. A trail of destruction which led down, down into the deepest Haunts and then back above to vengeance and an empty throne. In his vision, Cole stank of fire and his face had become a flat inhuman mask.

"Need to get out. That much magic is making me think twisted things," he said.

He blinked. Cole stood before him again staring at him. His eyes were two black stones. He felt the cold edge of steel against his throat, and he tipped his own chin to the darkness above, offering it to the knife. Black claw struck stone above, showering sparks. The orb danced and swirled on its pedestal. Above and below, a jagged laugh pierced the cavern.

Breathe in. Breathe out.

"Take another drink," Cole said to him, softly.

He felt Cole's hand on his arm, pressing down gently and then looking down saw the dagger at his throat was in his own hand.

"No," he mumbled.

"Drink," Cole said again, steadily, "It's a lot of magic. Heavy."

Allred drank, sheathed the dagger, "Don't have much more time, Cole." His voice shook.

"No, we don't."

The man's eyes were normal. His face dirt-streaked and yes fire-scarred but the face of a regular man. "I'm taking this. Get out in case something goes wrong. I can smell the Downside fever on you."

"I hear a fight in the air."

"The blood and clash will bring clarity if nothing else."

Allred turned his back on Cole and walked back out of the old place, ashamed, staggering back around the winding circles of stone. They felt cool on his hand and for a moment, he stopped walking and stood alone, his forehead pressed to the rock, regaining himself.

The 9th were staring at him when he re-appeared.

"Big magic inside. Cole's going to get it."

Hartha and Hortha had drawn close to Mage, nearly obscuring him from sight. The black cloak whirled and snapped between the two heavy shields. Two long deformed hands rested upon each brim of the shields that protected the sorcerer. It looked like some demon trying to hoist itself from a sepulcher but he reminded himself it was only his friend.

"Scrolls," Cole said from within the stones.

The scholar moved forward, finishing his sketch of the map on the lintel. Allred followed him back in. If Scrolls could tolerate it, he could.

"You're under a strain, Allred. I see it," he said, slowly making his way through the winding tunnel.

"Yes."

He stopped, turned and regarded him, "You'll hold. You always do." Then he turned and kept walking.

Effete, maybe, but a good man.

Inside, Scrolls examined the orb with the coolness of a market maker or auctioneer in the Twisted Shadow Bazaar.

Looks like a tax collector, Allred thought, bitterly. *But an enlightened kind of tax collector.*

The scholar's face broke and lit up with wonder at the sheer weight and size of the thing before them. A child's innocent curiosity suffused the scholar's face and brought a smile to his thin lips.

He's not so bad. Even if he is—he's the 9th.

"Appears to be free-standing. A reasonable way to proceed would be for us to leave this enclosure, and for one person to pick it up—in case I'm wrong."

"Take the bowl, too. Gold. Going to be heavy. I can drag it out to Hartha and Hortha," Allred said.

"Bring Mage," Cole said to him.

He stepped back out, gestured to the giants who smiled at him, "Cole wants you all."

The two giants escorted the mage to Cole's side and parted so that the bronzeface could stand staring at the orb from within his hooded cloak.

He chattered to himself in some dragon-tongued verse. The words called the stone to crawl around them for a moment and then turning to Scrolls:

"A city-destroyer."

The scholar bowed his head, looked away.

"All of you leave here, in case these walls fall when I take it," Cole said.

"I should. Can't afford to lose you—" he started to protest.

"Go," Cole said, and that was that. "All of you."

As they filed back out Mage whistled like a bird and said, "I'm afraid there is much blood on the way. But we all knew that."

No one answered. Outside again, Helga asked:

"What is this place?"

"We should find a treasury of the priests nearby," Scrolls answered from behind him. "Our journey will end here one way or the other, I am certain. We couldn't press much farther."

Allred could feel the entire place alive with a fury at their presence, the sounds of claws were growing to a constant scuttle. Within and below, he felt something calling the foul ranks of the guardians of this place to fight.

As he thought that, the light shining up from the center of the stone circle dimmed and went out. Shrieks echoed across the floor in protest. Cole had taken the orb.

He joined them soon enough, wasting no time. On his back, the orb barely fit within his pack. The canvas and leather glowed. The gold bowl in his hand, he went to Helga. He set the thing in front of her, "Yours, carry it how you want."

Her mouth was open in amazement. She scooped it up. The dwarves gathered about her and admired it.

"Cole, I believe there will be a reliquary of the priests nearby," Scrolls said, "Likely so."

Cole turned to him, "Find it."

Helga heaved the golden bowl into one of the dwarve's pack who tottered on his feet at the weight of it.

They soon came upon a cleared-out space where the ground turned back to stone. This gave way to white marble streaked with veins of purple. In the center of this marble—a circular pit.

Around it, urns, each the height of a man and nearly as wide, brown and purple painted. Emanating from each, the shadows of geists, drifting upwards like smoke to disappear into darkness above; and on their contorting mouths they called to something below. Each plume warped and wrapped upon itself, turned towards the Relic Hunters of the 9th, accusing wisps of fingers pointing then dissolving.

Helga swore and her dwarves spat protective curses. Scrolls made busy his stylus, while the two giants brandished their upheld axes in defiance.

He approached the pit slowly, Cole beside him. A narrow staircase spiraled down into the gloom.

"You hear it?"

"Aye," Cole answered.

He had hoped Cole would say no. He had hoped Cole would have told him, he was in the Downside Fever again. This time, he didn't.

The sounds of clawed-feet marching, upwards. Not a few, hundreds and they marched in time.

"Quickly now," Cole turned and set off.

They began to run deeper within and passed by more stone temples like the last, but many were toppled and tormented by time or the hands of past bands of relic hunters. They soon reached the end of the cavern. The wall shot straight upwards. A single set of double doors, closed, stood before them, a torch flickering on each side illuminating the Sem Hel Han script carved into the stone above.

Cole turned to Scrolls whose lips moved silently, translating. Then answered Cole's silent question with a nod, "Yes."

"Me and you then," Cole said.

The sound of the marching grew with every moment. Now he heard shrill calls of the Dhlams. It sounded as if they were singing to one another.

"Weapons out. Everything," Cole commanded, "Allred with me."

He shadowed Cole, close to his back, crossbow trained over his shoulder. Cole pushed the doors open.

Mummified bodies lined the walls of the burial chamber. Two torches cast undying light within. Patterns of filigree falling down from the ceiling to the walls framed each body, metals flowing and dancing. Gripped within the desiccated hands of the dead priests were daggers. Each handle was laden with magenta gems, bloodstones ensconced in handles of silver. And beneath the malformed feet of each priest was arranged in some forgotten ritual pattern gold plates heaped with coin minted by forgotten kings.

"Come!" Cole shouted behind him.

They stepped into the room. Helga's mouth was agape at the wealth and weird of the room.

"Fill your packs with the mundane things, you and the Rats." He told Helga. "Scrolls work on the relics," Cole said.

"There could be traps, Cole. I could study this room to—" Scrolls said.

Cole turned to the first priest, drew his broadsword and swinging it in a short arc cut the hand holding the dagger from the corpse. It fell to the ground with the sound of a sack of sand and Scrolls bent beneath the blade studying it before depositing it in his sack.

"What...what is it?" Helga asked.

"Grab the damn gold, cousin," Allred said and went back out of the room, "Cole, it's coming."

Cole looked up from his grim work. More dried hands fell to the floor, "Let them."

In the center of the two open doors, Mage stood, his back to them watching the cavern, staring at the pit. His back was shaking, and Allred knew the terrible truth—Mage was laughing. He turned to Allred, and the chaos of the smoke leapt from his tongue and danced about his bronzemask:

"They come."

Allred breathed in. He set his crossbow beside his foot and with his free hand made the sign to the Lady but could find no words to pray. Instead, he gripped the hilt of his sword. The sound of steel sliding from the scabbard was his proper prayer.

Barreling through out of the darkness came the first dozen demons sent to stop the theft. The largest they had faced, yet. Some looked like a cross between a boar and the lizards they had so far fought.

"Cole," Allred called.

Cole kept hacking at the hands, freeing the daggers from the dead priests. The aromatic odor of the embalmed flesh filled the tomb and the dust of old skin and bandage, dried fine as a mist choked their lungs. Helga and her dwarves were shoveling gold as fast as they could into their packs. She looked up, scared eyes beneath her sweat-soaked brow and dropped the gold from her hands at the sight of the Dhlams running toward them. She let out a small chirping sound, too fast to hold the fear in and kept scrambling to fill her purses and packs with coin.

"Cole," Allred said again.

Mage was still laughing but now he raised his hand and uttered syllables, disturbed. The air before the charging demons ignited. The Dhlams stumbled through the blanket of fire, screeching, then tripping and hurling over themselves. By the time they reached the ground, they revolved in screaming whirlwinds of half-flesh-and-ash.

Undeterred more demons, charged over the burning bodies of the dead.

Mage uttered another dirge and twisted his fingers. Five turned to heat, then smoke then nought. The two giants tapped the handles of their battle axes against their shields, counting each kill.

Helga and her dwarves were hauling out their heavy packs and setting them against the cavern wall.

"More coming," Allred yelled behind him.

"Big light up," Cole yelled back.

Allred dropped to one knee and plucked a particular dart from his vest. He put it into the crossbow, replacing the other and aimed into the darkness ahead and fired.

The bolt soared across the cavern and disappeared for a moment then exploded in a golden halo above the pit. It was like freezing the power of a lightning bolt in place. Everything stilled in the great bright of the magic-coated dart—the power of the small suns on its tip.

A collective inhuman shriek answered the light. Gathered around the pit, he could now see what faced them.

"Good," he said and reloaded.

A small army of Dhlams stood in ranks facing them. Their eyes shrank in the light and they fell from two legs to four and set up a great howl, jaws straining. Behind them, near a fallen monolith, there stood something else. In the moment of light, he could see the figure of an inhumanly tall, cloaked man beckoning the Dhlams forward with twisted hands.

In the ever-upwards span of rock wall that shaped the cavern, individual Dhlams clung like lizards, staring down at them, ready to lunge and fall upon their prey from a dozen different angles.

He put down his crossbow. He felt nothing now but a calm, clear will as the light began to fade.

"Move up away from the wall behind us, so the things can't use it," he said.

In a lockstep like a dance, Mage strode further forward, and Hartha and Hortha moved with him. They raised their two massive axes in the waning light, shaking them to the sky and screamed challenges in their Green Island tongue. Behind him, the two dwarves answered it.

Another surge forward, of the shrieking things, fast galloping now, on all fours, low and fast, they came in clots of claw and fang.

The mage turned more demons to ash scattering the first waves. Raw magic built currents of air, small tornados of heat spoke destruction. He conversed with the powers he summoned in the sound of shifting bone and Allred knew that across the darkness, he faced another battlemage from the past who led the Dhlams.

Behind him, Cole strode from the chamber, assessing the battleground, then tossed his own pack to the ground. He pointed his sword at the figure near the pit in challenge. He smiled and there was no rage or anger or torment in it, the smile of an innocent at peace; he bowed his head, gallantly.

His sword he had not named but others singing of it knew it and called it *Judgment*.

Two more Dhlams sprinted down the wall, headfirst

towards Helga and the Rats. Helga cut with her sword and the Rat beside her hacked, too. Black blood splattered across her pale face and she screamed out the challenge of her clan which Allred knew from long ago.

Hack and stab and then silence, the demons came. They were testing them. The sound of some dark tongue met with a hundred screeching Dhlams.

"Calthor?" Cole shouted.

"One of his servants most likely, a mage behind them," Scrolls said. He had dropped his pack and parchment and stood firing arrow after arrow into the enemy ranks.

"Rest," Allred called to Mage.

Two more demons came sprinting forward. Allred strode forward to meet them.

The demons pulled up short of him and stood on their back legs. They stared at Allred, forked tongues darting in and out of slavering jaws.

The demon on his left thrust its claw-bunched hand forward. Allred didn't move, didn't respond, just watched as the claws missed his side. The demon drew back. It lunged again. He swung his sword in soft wheels of death.

Steel bit flesh. The demon's arm dropped to the ground. Head followed arm.

The other darted forward. He stepped towards the fallen demon, opening space. He turned his back to the attacker and whipped his sword behind his shoulder. He felt the deep thud of the blade run through his own arm, when it sunk into the demon's skull.

He wrenched it free of bone. Turned and swung. Edge met armored flesh. The impact ran down the body of his sword into the pommel and through his own body and he felt whole and certain and solid in the warring.

Another command from the servant of Calthor and then the first red wave of the flood came.

He laughed now, too, body shaking like Mage, and he glanced behind him, to see his friend behind a veil of smoke. For a moment, the fearful bronzeface peaked through and he saw the animal form of it grinning out of the fog of chaos at the center of the giants. Already, there were piles of demon bodies stacked to their knees.

They fell from the walls behind them, trying to encircle them. The bulk were in front and he met them with a smile on his face.

He could dance now.

A demon passed beneath his arm. He dodged. It kept running towards the others. He swung and the head of another fell. Another. Soon all around him, they came, gathered to bring him down, to pull him into death. Some scrambled wide past his soaring, singing blade and died in the ranks behind.

His sword screamed now through the dead air of the cavern. Metal and man took momentum and with each swing, he launched himself from the ground, boots lashing out, blade spiraling through demon flesh, hacking and hacking, his sword unslowed by the death he brought down on his enemies.

He couldn't stop. There was no outside anymore, just a shroud of black heavy with blood and it felt like rest until finally the corpses could not compete against his blade and he slowed and slowed and stopped among the writhing dead and the ending of the first wave of attack.

Behind him, the demons slammed into the giant's shield wall. Hartha and Hortha, grunting, singing, flung them back broken, mauled by the flurry of their twin axes describing death. Adding lines to the legend inscribed on their shields, digging lines into the memory of their progeny, they did battle.

Now, the shrill doom-songs of the geists met the low tones of the mummified priests behind him. Rotted mouths on handless torsos sang a dirge but did not move.

The wave broke. The battle waned. The ranks subsided, silenced by one dark syllable echoing across the cavern from Calthor's servant.

Allred held his sword in front of him, hypnotized by the flow of black blood and gore on it. He felt light and free of his own body; filled with the simplicity of war. His mind disappeared beside his allies, the ones still alive, the remnants of the 9th and he rode waves of blood back to stand side-by-side with the ancestors of his clan. The men of his line rejoiced at his coming to them in battledream and their spirits bathed in the holy blood of those opposed to him which he offered.

For the first time since stepping on the island of Esmer, Allred smiled like a child.

31

Helga

S he might survive it.

The Rats heaved the baggage onto their backs, took them outside the room and leaned them against the wall. She could hear Allred say something and his voice sounded calm for the first time since they had entered the Haunt.

Cole hurried from the room, "Don't touch those daggers, or you'll die," he warned. They listened. Those were true-relics and she could feel a dark pull around each of them, as if by even glancing at the old ceremonial weapons, she might be sucked into them—flattened and disappeared beneath the weight of the silver, or entrapped inside the blood gems which adorned the knives.

Scrolls filled his pack methodically, moving as if strolling through a market exclusive for the highborn. He held his hands behind his back, perusing, plucking a votive candle holder he found on a shelf which lined the burial chamber.

"Here," he pointed and Tym struggled under the weight of a

piece of the wall, which Aodlen had loosened with a small chisel.

"That's not gold, Scrolls. That's just a bunch of writing on a stone," she said to him, smiling. And smiling, she knew for a moment she looked mad. Her teeth bared. There was a bit of spittle wet on her chin. She wiped it away and the smell of old metal coins filled her nose. When she laughed, she sounded like Aodlen.

The aristocrat turned to her, his hands folded behind him. She thought she saw some light in his eyes and then it was gone. He nodded with a sad look, "We could trade this one stone for all the gold lying about this floor. You've a thief's mind, wretched in its simplicity, yet alluring for all that." He made a brushing gesture, as if sweeping dust from a table towards her.

She laughed again. To him, she was just a porter or servant and perhaps it was so—a commoner.

A rich one, now at least.

She laughed a second time because outside something terrible was forming and it was coming to kill her, but she didn't feel fear anymore. The wealth and glory and weird of the treasure chamber had her in its grip. Still, outside the air was filling with fire and she thought it harder to breathe in the old chamber. The sound of Allred's sword cutting the air crept into the tomb. She laughed and let herself laugh, because on her knees among the piles of treasure, she had finally done it.

She wasn't just a Rat in the Pits anymore but a Relic Hunter, no matter how the aristocrat sneered at her, it was so.

Scrolls considered the weight of a magemade pediment adorning the top of the entrance to the treasure room. With a disgusted shake of his head, he decided against trying to remove it.

On the shelves of stone lining the room there were vials and dried herbs and the things the ancients used to accompany the dead and to do the work of mummification. She figured that's what the vials held but didn't know. These Aodlen studied in the light of his lantern and with a gloved hand, took vials of this and that from the tomb, piling the ancient tinctures into the bags on his belt. "Research, ha!"

Cole stood. At first, she thought he had been putting the

daggers in a pack but she saw that the dead hands still clung to the blades, so he had slung a light chain harness over his magemade armor. On that chain there were hooks and, on those hooks, he had skewered the mummified hands of the priests still gripping the daggers. She gagged, then laughed again and shaking her head, wildly, looked away.

It had only taken a few minutes and their packs were filled with more than they could carry. Cole looked at Scrolls, "Full up?"

"Yes," he answered.

The sounds of the fighting grew more intense outside. Helga stood looking at Cole, coins spilling one by one from her hand as she stared out of the doorway.

"Cole?" she asked, pointing.

Outside light filled the cavern and streamed inside the chamber where they stood, blinding her for a moment and exposing an army of demons outside, packs of which broke off the main body and burst into flame or died on the sword of her cousin and the axes of the giants.

"Time to depart."

Cole turned, calm, as if what lay outside was no great matter but an obvious thing, a fate, and what's more—a fate he commanded. The smooth, fireswept flesh on the side of his face glowed like the marble of the burial chamber and though she had never seen it, she thought perhaps the Throne itself was made of something similar.

He walked outside, tossed a sack to the floor and unsheathed his broadsword. The blade looked common steel but she felt the Haunt shrink back for a moment as if the entire demonhold wandered at its glow.

"He is not quite a man," she said to Staah, who still knelt beside her, scooping up coin.

"No, but I'd follow him even for that," he said.

"Yes. I will, too."

She carried the last of the loot to the chamber door and the dwarves heaved their packs and followed. The chaos and clash of magic and sword rang through the cavern. Cole joined her cousin as the first big wave of Dhlams poured over them. Aodlen and Scrolls were readying their own weapons, and both took a moment to smile at her. Here was the famed 9th fighting in front of her. A legend unfolded and she wanted to remember it. She would recite a poem one day of this trial, if she survived it.

Dropping the last of the treasure, she drew her own sword.

32

Allred

To fight, to flee and do it all over again.

Another city, another ship. Maybe the village outside Shamhalhan. To rest.

Behind him, he heard Cole and the rest forming up behind him. The whole cavern rocked with his heavy breathing. He wiped the blood from his sword on his trousers. He felt no pain from wounds.

The war-spirit held him. He shouted a challenge to the void ahead. He pointed his gore-soaked blade into the darkness.

Near him, Mage fought with slithering syllables riding mounts of pain. He worked his fingers in patterns made possible by exquisite self-torment. A lifetime of learning to deal death in a thousand hidden passages that ran through his heart; an unbearable heart for the mage was the kindest among them. The bronzeface's spells warped and twisted the air and Elaohir, archmage of the 9th, stood spitting fire between his loyal giants.

Cole came up beside him. On his chest, hands hung from hooks each still clenched the daggers they held. He could hear each certain step, heavier with the weight of treasure. Judgement in hand, Cole regarded him and the quiet fire in his eyes portended more blood as he called across the cavern:

"Calthor's servant, stay your hand. We will go. We've taken our lot. Send no more of your brood against us."

No answer.

On the edge of the shadows which enveloped the cavern, red eyes stared across the floor heavy with dead Dhlams. More and more began to appear out of the pit. Facing them, eyes glowing, none moving, forming in masses. Soon Allred could not count the number of eyes.

Mage sent a wide, weaker blanket of cold flame across the cavern. The Dhlams took a few steps back and the battle waned.

The small suns were dimmed by a spell sent from behind the Dhlams. The cavern fell into a darkness profound. Hundreds of eyes drilled into their hearts across a darkness which was more than the absence of light. All the eyes dimmed at once and there was only void.

Calthor's servant spoke.

A thousand eyes opened again and blurred in the dark as they surged forward.

"Brace," Cole turned.

A line of fire devoured the ground ten paces in front of him. He heard Mage shout guttural commands to the spirits who hovered over the geometry of the inner dimensions where he tread, summoning, coaxing and compelling magic, bringing it forth to this world.

They answered. His fire rose and he swept it forward with spear-words, crawling crafts forbidden to man.

The demons ran forward crazed. The line of fire the mage summoned held, made the first wave split. Allred stepped forward a pace.

He held the sword out and let the first one spit itself. It slid off and down. Before the weight of its body left his blade, another came in low. Allred spun and whipped the back of his boot around in an arc knocking another to the ground.

Two arrows sped past him. Two more fell.

The demons fed the fire and he thought he saw them dancing there in strange jigs of death as more of their brethren swarmed over them. Even the ones in flames, ran towards him seeking to consume him in his own mage's magic.

One of the Rats had joined him toward the front of the fight, waving a short sword. He stabbed and took a demon down but another rose and leaping forward on back legs, grabbed him in a death embrace. Its jaws bit down on the man's arm. Hartha reached across, grabbed the demon with one hand and hurled it away from the dwarf.

"Tym-goed, flee," Hortha yelled.

Allred ducked, flipped a demon over his back. Desperate eyes met his own.

"Get back."

The dwarf scrambled back with a furious grin, screaming and holding his arm. The bodies became thick on the ground and he picked his way over them, delicate steps across writhing corpses.

Cole swung this broadsword in great arcs, eating demon flesh in clouds of blood, around him they fell. Jabbing, hacking. Wordless, Cole struck. Hartha and Hortha bashed bodies with their shields and butchered many.

Not enough—

Too many now and the mage's fire came down, dampened by the sheer weight of the flesh it consumed.

It made him feel curious for a moment as he lashed out with his sword. To die here. He saw the grey horses running across the frost coated fields of the hills of his home.

Then another slammed into him and another on top and another and he went under the wave.

Fire broke out around him, Mage's spells close, dangerous, and necessary. He felt jagged tooth in his arm tearing into him. He struck out, bucked beneath the demons freeing himself but the weight grew heavier as they swarmed him, piling on top of him. He tried to keep his eyes open, but he was on his back now and he could see nothing but the swarm of snapping jaw and ragged claw all around. He would die under the press of the weight of the things before being torn by their claws.

Then a strange sound. The swoop and beating of wings.

He struck out, wild to regain his feet. Punching with his sword hand, his other found the short dagger and slashed. He felt a deep gash on his side and the wet warmness of his own blood inside his leather armor. He rolled over his own crossbow, still attached by the band and the machine bit into his leg.

"Leatherwing!" Hortha shouted.

Another wave came crashing forward. He caught a glimpse of Cole nearby fighting to try to reach him. He went down beneath the demons just as Allred had.

He felt the doom of something massive and unknown above him. Death finally come to take him to the halls of his ancestors. Through the pain, he smiled and in smiling tasted the blood of the demons which bathed his face. It was bitter.

The Leatherwing crashed to the ground nearby, fell upon the backs of the approaching hoards. Mage crouched under the shadow of Hartha's shield, turning his bronzeface to the beast. He was on one knee as if winded from a long run. He spoke words like burning iron to the Leatherwing. The mage smiled in recognition beneath his mask at the unholy creature.

He hurried to Cole who writhed and wrestled on the ground with the Dhlams. They bit and lashed as he peeled them off Cole's body. His hand shot up from the ground. Allred grabbed it and pulled him up. In his other hand, he held aloft one of the magefire whips.

"Use it if it comes to it."

He stuck the handle in his belt. The coldfire within it ran up his arm and he could feel the power of the weapon pulsing.

The Leatherwing fought in front of them on the ground now. Dozens of demons surrounded it, slashing at the beast.

"It fights with us," Mage croaked.

"Rally to it," Cole shouted.

Demons swarmed over the Leatherwing. One had sunk its claws beneath the armor of its scaly haunch. Another had hold of its neck, teeth digging into the flesh of the beast. They were like a pack of wolves working to bring down a bullock in a spring meadow.

The Leatherwing snapped and bucked. Its wings shot outwards, the sharp feathers slicing the enemy; but weighed down, it could not regain flight. It pierced another demon's skull with its dagger-shaped tongue while a dozen more moved in for the kill.

Allred fired. The bolt pierced the demon stuck to the Leatherwing's side. It slid off.

Now, the beast sprayed golden flame from its mouth in gouts of destruction channeled through its iron-fleshed throat. The fire burned bright from its innards, lashing out and venting through unseen small holes around its head. The flame formed an aura of light in the cavern where the battle grew the most fierce.

The grand beast fought—worthy death-dealer, creature of eons.

Allred wouldn't see it downed. He'd prefer his own death to that of watching the mystical creature destroyed by this hoard of common demons. There was no terror in the eyes of the Leatherwing, only vengeance and Allred recognized himself in those hard diamond eyes.

I was born to this alone.

"Mage!" he shouted.

Far behind him, he heard the answering chant.

He cast aside his crossbow, sheathed his blade and pulled the magefire whip from his belt. On the handle he pressed forward a small indentation, the panel revealing a symbol chiseled into the metal beneath. He pressed his thumb onto it and it leaped and bit onto his hand. Across the cavern, Mage shouted a single syllable and he felt the letter leap. A fiery-blue whip spilled from the handle, bucking and snapping, a short killing chain of magic infused fired. He spun the short whip around his head. With a prayer to the Lady, compressed by the strain of battle to a few grunts, he leaped forward onto the Leatherwing's back as if mounting a wild horse.

The beast did not throw him. It coiled beneath him, its head snapping, tail bowling over two more demons. Allred cut and slashed with the whip. It sliced through the demons with no effort.

He kept his balance, careful to not let the whip touch the beast or his own body. The demons sensing the weapon screeched.

The Leatherwing gained its feet and stood. Then just behind his legs, a sound like a metal fan unfolding, its wings spread out and the body beneath him shivered with a few fast steps before launching upwards to flight.

He dug his free hand into its neck and found purchase in feathers hard as steel. The beast swept upward with a quick beat of the wings.

The Leatherwing soared into the air, then turned, half-circled and he could see the maw of the pit beneath him filled with the ranks of the demons and the mage in white, deeper down within it beckoning them, directing them to war. He took a deep breath, kept the whip spinning, just as he had in his youth while riding with a lasso to gather enemy clan's cattle. The beast's wings ceased their motion, folded in tight to its body. They plunged. His stomach flew into his mouth, his body weightless and a laugh of fevered joy escaped him as the creature dove to deathing.

The beast turned upwards hard as it neared the floor, its belly nearly skimming the hard stone. They broke through the ranks of the demons surging in line after line over the 9th. The Leatherwing scattered bodies with its speed, like riding in a cavalry charge. He leaned to his side and slashed out with the whip. The blue light blazed and the demons ran red down the ranks. The whip devoured row after row of the enemy, in bursts and splatter of lightening flashes, the enemy perished. His arm became inhuman, distant, unfeeling, a grume-drenched instrument to slay the foe. Those who escaped the magewhip's fury, the Leatherwing smashed in its charge.

Allred and beast brought death to the cavern.

Mage's spells wrapped and weaved, scattering the remaining demons and the Leatherwing ended its charge and pulled up again to soar into the heights of the Haunt. He felt the world turn, upended. He leaned forward and squeezed his legs against his mount.

Below him, the wicked smile of Cole's sword seared the dark. He thought he could see a grim smile on Cole's face but it was dark below. He dispatched a final demon with his broadsword, cleaving the monster in half and then looking up through the dimness of the dome to where he flew, Cole raised his sword in salute.

Hartha and Hortha raised their axes to him and shouted, from below, "Remember the 9th." The chaos-smoke of Mage's spells looked like little puffs of cloud from on high and he never wanted to go back to ground. To never return, to ride up and up and on into the dark and be done with the world of man. To swing in spinning circles among Allwein's children, the stars silent companions, eternal and it would always be night. The magefire whip was possessing him with wild ideas and he sensed the danger of it. He could feel the cold sureness of it working itself down his arm and to his heart, calling him to some glory which he would seek no matter the cost.

"Fortune beast."

The air buckled beneath him in the swoop and awe of the Leatherwing's great soaring. In the heights he could make out warrens and mazelike tunnels worked into the mountain stone up here. What treasures to discover there? What demons to face and slay? What glory to win. The hellish world of the Haunt revealed itself to him in all its awesome age and doom and riding high, he felt equal to it, sure and certain. Because he and Cole and all the rest of the 9th were more terrible in their fame.

And then it was over.

The Leatherwing glided down and down and contacted the ground of the cavern on unsteady, shaky feet. Weary and injured, the beast hissed and bent. He swung one leg over its barbed head and dismounted but then leaned against its body for just a moment.

He could feel it breathing. The heat of fire in its guts vented through scales and warmed him. There were footsteps coming from everywhere. He sagged against the beast. It turned and looked into his eyes and there was a long promise, a cold vow playing in its swirling irisis.

Cole made his way to him. The beast eyed him suspiciously. The Leatherwing moved its head, the muscles of its bleeding neck rippling beneath scales, then lunged at a corpse and fed. It lapped at its blood. It looked back at Cole and Allred, cocked its head at the light of the whip and appeared to forget about them both.

Slowly, he found the metal and pushed it back covering the symbol and felt a foreign word lodge in his throat as if the Mage spoke through him. The whip screamed in protest but retracted back into the rune-covered cylinder and he felt a presence leave him. Cole sheathed his sword, held out his hand. For a moment, he didn't want to give away such power but Cole took it from him and he felt the relief and weariness as his arm began to warm.

The battle had ended.

All around him, the work of the 9th. Uncountable rows of demons fallen. Heaps of ash. He could make out the tops of Hortha's and Hartha's helmets from behind a pile of corpses smashed against the shields. They pushed through the flesh now, heaving mangled bodies out of the way. They were covered in savage claw marks but stood tall and firm. Aodlen was already working his vials over them. Between them, Mage chittered and spat tiny streams of fire in a frenzy. He'd been pressed hard here and for too long. The fingers of his distended hands were purple, the flesh torn and bubbling.

Allred looked away.

In the distance, a figure in a white cloak manifested atop the stone monolith near the pit, surveying the scene of battle with cold regard. Beside it in the darkness stood something much greater. Naked ivory flesh, a torso of a creature on bent, muscular legs. The topmost of the body disappeared in shadows but two red eyes stared back at them from the height of five men.

Mage said something in an old tongue.

The white cloaked battlemage swept his hands upwards and dozens of demon corpses suddenly slid across the floor. Their dead flesh was blown about, ripped and re-arranged in a flurry and Allred ducked from the awful display. The bodies melded into each other, into a crude oval of heaving skin and bone. This abomination grew misty, transparent and within it, a reflection of Calthor's servant alongside his grotesque giant which he had kept back and not set against them, yet.

Mage approached the portal of dead demon flesh and Cole with him. Words were traded with the image. Scrolls joined them, taking notes; he looked untouched and he envied the man his choice of the bow as he felt the spikes of pain shooting up his own arms. The scholar wrote while Cole spoke in the same old tongue that the mage used and then the thing in white responded. Cole said something once more, sharp and then turned away.

Mage raised his mutilated hands in a gesture of leave-taking.

Calthor's servant raised his own distended hand to Mage. The dead bodies fell away from one another, no longer fused and the image disappeared. Far off, Calthor's servant vanished into the gloom with the beast in his thrall. The last sounds of the battle were the dragging of the heavy chain binding the mage to its beast and the grinding of stone against stone issuing across the cavern as the pit closed and the Haunt's guardians retreated.

33

Helga

How do you fare?" Scrolls asked.

It confused her, the scholar asking such a common question. During the fight, he'd stayed in the back, near her and Staah, launching arrow after arrow into the enemy and when a few got to their back line, fighting with his own short sword.

She was embarrassed that she could only find a single confused word in answer, and a lie at that, "Yes."

Aodlen pointed to Tym, "This I cannot heal here."

In the fight, the Rats had scattered around the packs and baggage. Tym had ran forward to fight. Both were alive, somehow.

"Oh, no," the gentle Staah said.

Tym's body was unharmed, besides a few small wounds, but his mind was clearly askew. He wallowed around in a pile of fallen demons like a dog roiling in the scent of a corpse. "Is he possessed?" she asked Aodlen.

Tym's face distorted, twitched. The bones in his face were moving beneath his skin. Blood issued out of the side of his mouth as he gnashed his teeth. One broke off. She could hear the ivory-snap and he spat it into the air and laughed.

"Haunt-ridden," Aodlen answered, squinting at the dwarf and keeping his distance.

"What?"

"Some don't come out with their soul, ha! Most! Despite my vials, despite my toil."

"Tym's got a demon?" she asked turning to Staah as if he would somehow be able to answer her more clearly.

"He *may* recover once we depart," Scrolls offered.

The dwarf had dropped his sword next to the dead demons. He slithered across the corpses, licking at the open wounds on their scaly flesh. He reached out, as if swiping with claws he did not have.

"He thinks he's one of them," Helga said, understanding.

"Worse. Maybe. Worse? Yes. I've seen it happen before."

"Some texts say, the Haunt-ridden transform but I don't believe it's so," Scrolls said, standing beside her, "I wouldn't trouble yourself on that. However..."

"Wouldn't trouble myself?"

She called Tym's name. His head snapped towards her. There was a hint of recognition there but sealed beneath the demon reasoning crystallizing in his mind.

"Tym!"

Nothing.

Scrolls looked at Cole who had rejoined them, beside him a staggering Allred, blood-soaked as Cole—twins of war.

"Go, gather the packs, Helga," Cole said.

"He's my people," she said.

"Aodlen?" Cole asked.

Aodlen withdrew a pin from his apron, dipped it in one of his brown glass vials and stepped carefully forward. Allred with a weary sigh, unsheathed his sword and followed. She grabbed her cousin's arm, "No. No, cousin. If this is done, I'll do it."

She drew her own blade.

Helga circled the dwarf—her friend. She had to remember,

his name, Tym. Shame hit her as she feared nearing him. She dragged the tip of her sword in a circle on the cavern floor against the blood-soaked rock. It felt heavy, like holding ten thousand swords and she nearly let it fall. Little sparks jumped from metal on stone.

My friend.

Tym eyed her. Even through the fog of the Haunt, she could see him smiling, playing tricks in market lanes; or bedded down beside his friends in the soft hay of a friendly farmer's loft after a day's hard travel. An easy spirit, even in the Pits, even after she had lost—

She dragged the sword in another circle, then raised it to strike and put her friend out of his misery. She closed her eye and swung with a whimper escaping her mouth.

Allred parried the blade casually.

Aodlen jumped into the air at the sound, "Allweln's balls, woman! No. Ha! I'm glad you're not my physician! I'm going to put a heavy dose on him, that's all. Tie him with rope to your waist to lead him. He'll walk. Put a pack on his back, too. No reason he can't lug it, even if he thinks he's Dlahm. I can learn much from observing him."

"Yes," she said, again, too tired to talk.

"Ha! Yes, perhaps but not the sudden cure you had in store."

"We need out, Cole," Allred said.

Aodlen leaped forward and stuck Tym in the leg with the pin laced with his medicinal. The dwarf's body relaxed and he stopped babbling in imitation of the demons. Aodlen fit a small dowl, attached to a bandage around the man's mouth. It reminded her of a bit inside a horse's mouth, but it would prevent him from biting his tongue.

She felt too tired to be sick anymore. She wanted out.

Aodlen tied a loop of rope around her waist as she hauled her treasure-laden pack over her shoulders. At the other end stood the drugged, Tym. Aodlen burdened him with a pack and the dwarf hissed and spat but made no other protest.

"Safest for us and him if he's carrying a heavy load,

perhaps," Scrolls said.

The attitude of the scholar enraged her, though she knew he was trying to make the fact palatable. It was as if he were trying to apologize but couldn't find the right words.

"We move quickly," Cole said, "Leave behind what's not necessary."

"Didn't you speak to the demon, Cole?" she asked, wearily.

Cole ignored the question. He drank once more from his flagon, then poured the water over his own face, washing the blood from it and discarded the flagon. The blood streamed and washed across his breastplate forming intricate patterns, as if searching to coalesce in some text which would make sense of itself.

Cole turned to Allred and gestured. Allred loaded his crossbow and stepped through the corpses, craned his head around in a circle and with a deep sigh that turned into a laugh, he set out the way they had entered.

She followed.

The Leatherwing followed them back through the cavern to the tunnel near the monoliths. Behind her, she heard it take wing. Her cousin, stopped and stared as the beast disappeared in the darkness.

He walked on.

The creature had fought with them. Why, she could not fathom. Perhaps, awaiting another sacrifice. There was something more, secrets to these places she could not comprehend and the vision of Cole speaking with the entity which sent the demons against them kept coming to her mind. She let the mystery roll through her mind. It kept her distracted from the horrors and the terrible feeling that a small hand tugged at the hem of her tunic, as she followed the illuminated Cole.

"You're not here," she whispered and was ashamed at the venom in her own voice.

As they made their weary way back, they met no more enemies. The Haunt allowed their retreat, seeming to welcome it in recognition of the bloody battle fought. She kept seeing the hand of the enemy mage, Calthor's servant she assumed, and the recognition between it and their own mage, maybe the entire 9th.

The small girl watched her from darkened doorways, silent.

"I'm sorry."

"What Helga?" Staah asked.

"Not to you. Well, to you, too but I was talking to my daughter."

"You've no daughter, Helga."

"I know."

Staah said nothing as they walked on.

A few times she had to tug on the rope behind her, leading Tym on the makeshift leash. It—no, he—he was still alive though transformed; he bit down on the dowel in his mouth, the only sound from him. A few times he went to the ground, walking on all fours. She pulled the rope. He stood. She tried to believe there was something human left in his eyes, but the light was dim and her head swam and she couldn't quite make herself believe it was so.

In the light of the Upside, she would know.

She kept her head down, neck burdened by the weight of the treasure on her back and followed, too exhausted to mind much, if a demon sprang from a wall or some hidden crevasse and took her down. That too was a lie. She wanted life and felt guilty for it. The gold on her back was heavy.

The march back went faster, and they didn't stop or waver. She might have slept while walking, a thing she heard soldiers did but never believed. Closing her eyes, she sensed the pulse of her own steps but opening them, she found herself farther along than she thought possible. A few times, she raised her weary eyelid and called, "Thay? Thay?"

She walked behind the limping giants sheltering the mage. She couldn't draw too near. Emanating from the bronzeface, was too much magic. It boiled around him in a visible aurora. He spoke no human words now, but his muttering was punctuated by shadow-smoothed shouts. His two guardians said little, but on occasion, she saw one or the other lend a heavy hand to the sorcerer, urging him on.

The mage could fight a thousand more battles with the orbs they carried out with them, Helga knew. From looking at the ragged man, she did not believe he would survive channeling that much magic.

There's a lot I don't know. A lot I should have preferred not to know.

She knew this—they carried the firepower of a great army on their backs and enough treasure to hire enough mercenaries to fight the Throne.

The figure in the black cloak staggered forward. She followed.

They had taken losses. She hadn't the time to feel the hurt of her own yet but with every step, felt unbidden rage welling up. At every turn and doorway, looking for Thay and afraid to find him, she staggered forward.

Soon they reached the courtyard of columns, and the gate was just ahead. Cole fell back and walked beside her in silence for a while, as they made their way through the center of the room.

"I should have listened to you, Cole," she said.

She barely recognized the bitter voice that came from her own mouth. If it didn't heal, she'd never sing again.

Cole said nothing for a moment. Up ahead and above, the heights welcomed the sharp pinion whistles of the Leatherwing's return. It had taken some route back through hidden, high tunnels and now landed before the gate ahead, blocking them. It let out a piercing hiss. She felt no fear, wondering if it would attack them now, hungry for the last human flesh it would see for eons.

Cole looked at her with his stony eyes, his pain-flat face, "I have led men to death. You have, too. Survive the day, Helga of the Rats. Our trial is not ended. The Upside Fever will be on you soon." He drew his blade once more.

The Leatherwing pawed the ground and waited as the Relic Hunters came approached the gate.

Mother?

The girl called out from behind one of the columns. She turned away from it and a sob escaped her. She wanted to grab the sound of her own crying from the air, snatch it from him, stow it away, not allow Cole or any other hear her weakness.

Cole stared straight through her with hawk-eyes, "Geists. Things that have become and then perished. Worse, things which never became."

"I might hate you, Cole," she said but couldn't say exactly why.

He said nothing. Then she understood it.

"I hate you for not killing me before I saw this place, I think."

Cole didn't blink. There was still blood all over him, the cruor of demons not washed away by water or walking or however much time had passed, "Give me your arm."

She did. He waved his hand over the Eye. She saw Stoneburner watching. He turned and gestured to the rest of the group outside, as if preparing for something.

"Give me your sword," Cole said.

She didn't argue. Unsheathed it and considered sticking him. She saw him recognize her own murderous thought and he did nothing but wait. She handed it to him, "Get us out."

He walked past the Leatherwing, not bothering to even glance at it.

"Open the gate."

34

Allred

When they reached the column crowded courtyard, Allred saw the Leatherwing. He would not do battle with it, no matter what the command.

Cole gathered them near the gate and beckoned for Mage to come forward. Allred kept his crossbow trained out into the darkness.

Behind him, a herd of grey horses were running between the columns, a rush of bodies, all around him. It was a vision, and he knew it and he indulged in it. The silent hooves beat against the ancient courtyard, and then Cole spoke through Scrolls to Mage who brought out the Key from beneath his cloak and put it in the lock.

The raw lively air of the Upside rushed into the narrow hall where they gathered. The last of the evening light came rushing to meet the weird of the Haunt and he could see Stoneburner and the boys standing in the mouth of the gate, ready to help each man through, meeting them with medicine, unburdening their packs, taking their weapons. They didn't look real. The Haunt was real. The Upside was just a place to tarry in the sojourn. His steps were hell and his soul was behind, back there. The horses broke to gallop, retreated back into the heart of the Haunt.

Mage conversed with the Leatherwing in twisting tongues of fire. Cole looked at Scrolls.

"The Leatherwing wishes to leave," Scrolls said.

"What's Mage say?"

"He's trying to convince her that the world outside is worse than she can imagine. That she has forgot the horrors of men," Scrolls said, looking down.

Cole said nothing. A shallow smile like a single thorn split his face.

Allred handed his crossbow to Cole and approached the beast. It blew two streams of fire from flaring nostrils and turned its head. He reached out a hand. It took a step forward.

"We owe our victory in part to the beast," he said.

The Leatherwing waited and he knew there would be another fight if Cole tried to bar its path.

"Go," Cole said, gesturing to Helga and her surviving Rats. He turned away from the Haunt-ridden one with a shiver of disgust.

"What about Thay, I can't just—"

"Gone," Cole answered.

"He is my friend, Cole," Staah, the quiet dwarf said.

"And he is dead," Cole said.

"How can you know?"

"I asked."

The dwarf hesitated, looked ready to fling himself at Cole. Helga bent down, wrapped an arm around the man and whispered something in his ear. Behind her, the other dwarf snarled. Staah answered her in Green Island dialect and taking one last look behind him turned to the gate.

One by one they all went through the gate to the Upside. Hartha and Hortha hesitated but Cole waved them on. He went to Mage and let him rest on his own shoulder.

"So?"

"Free it," Cole said.

Allred turned to the Leatherwing and spoke a word he didn't understand and had never learned, as if a bit of the old tongue of the Leatherwing riders had seeped into his heart. The beast gently eased its head into Allred's trembling palm, like a horse nuzzling a feeding-hand holding a pert summer apple. The beast looked up to the dark of the courtyard crying out a leave-taking, which was answered from above, by a cacophony of shrieks.

The Leatherwing folded its wings close to its body, laid its bladed neck fan low and slinked through the gate. He followed it out, his left hand on its back.

Outside, Stoneburner and the boys stumbled backwards at the sight of the creature. Hortha assured them. The Upside buckled as the Leatherwing emerged into the world. In the distance, a spout of orange fire rushed up from the volcano on Esmer, blending with the rage of the setting sun.

Cole followed behind. He heard the strange sound of Mage feeding the Key to the gate and closing it. A cloak snapped and the mage fled to the shadow of the tree line, blinking in and out of a pulsing, uncontrolled, Feint.

He felt the lightness in his body. Staggered. Kept his feet. The Upside Fever came in waves.

The boys stood open-mouthed. Stoneburner held a crossbow, an arrow knocked, pointed at them as they came out of the Haunt, just as he was instructed to do, just as he had done in the past. Allred remembered a painful day when Stoneburner had needed to fire on one of them.

Outside, the sun was slipping faster behind the volcano than it should. Each second felt like a stone around his neck, weighing him down but time moved faster for the falling.

The Leatherwing reared back once, on two back feet and twisted in the air, diamond eyes glancing against his soul once more. His hand fell away from the beast. It ran through the trees on the side of the cliff which bent and broke before it; then leaping out, over the cliff and plummeting over, vanished.

Just for a moment in its falling swoop did it disappear. Then atop the jungle canopy beyond, it rose on unseen currents. Curling, wings and tail whipping, mastering the sky beneath it, the Leatherwing circled back, heading towards them.

Cole said to Stoneburner, "You can put the bow down."

"That's what you always say," Stoneburner smiled keeping it trained on them, "What about that dwarf gone mad?"

"Aodlen's got him fixed for now."

Something shifted inside him. The colors of the sunset looked wrong. The sun itself too large. He knew the Downside was leaving him and the Upside greeting him. In the dirt, Helga was on her knees wailing and the Doctor did a strange jig along the trail. Scrolls stood watching the Leatherwing, his face twitching.

Some other ancient word escaped his mouth again and he felt the others turn to him. He raised his sword in salute as the Leatherwing bore down on them all. No one moved or tried to flee, even the boys. Stoneburner trained his bow on him, nodded and smiled, then turned to look at the creature.

"What do we do?" Stoneburner whispered.

"Salute the beast," he said, "It has survived and it seeks vengeance. Just like the 9th."

All around him, he heard steel unsheathed, all raised their arms to the sky in salute to the Leatherwing. Even Helga turned her face to the sky and reached out toward it, as if trying to touch the beast.

The Leatherwing swooped low, armored belly stripping the leaves from the tops of the trees lining the cliff's edge. It flew down the old Semhelhen road, over their heads, tracing the ancient road of sacrifice as if trying to remember the place from long ago.

It mounted the air again, circled above them, playing in the heights, curling and diving in the pink-tinged clouds of the setting sun. And then, turning south, it disappeared.

For the first time in a long time, Allred felt something like what prayer meant. He still couldn't recall the words of the religion of his homeland, all he had was the little wooden picture of The Lady, but he found himself on his knees searching for the portrait with numb fingers. He nearly stuck himself with one of his own crossbow darts in his frantic pursuit. Where was the portrait?

The Upside Fever fell on him. He wasn't sure if it was

religion or the wound in his side that brought the darkness, but he saw Stoneburner smiling down at him, still keeping an arrow trained at his face and when he woke up, he was lying flat in his camp pack and it was night and the stars of Allwein twisted above.

How long he had been half-asleep in the throes of Upside Fever, he couldn't recall.

Two small fires burned in front of the gate. The sounds of laughter and weeping, tangled with the surprised gasps of sleep interrupted by nightmares. The usual madness.

He knew it to be true, expected it, all of them were used to it. Helga and the Rats would not be.

Aodlen was moving around in the dark with a "ha!" punctuating his every other step. Allred squinted in the darkness. The skinny boy, Lookout was trailing him. He held open Aodlen's leather valise, filled with bandages, vials and magic-dipped, herb-dipped, prayer-dipped needles and peculiar quills.

He couldn't quite focus right. His side hurt but his head was clearer than he expected. There was something cutting into his palm, and he looked and saw he had been clutching his plaque of the Lady in his exhausted sleep.

Staah walked by, staring at him with bulging eyes, pointed at the sky, "Leatherwings, he called them! I saw it myself."

The dwarf laughed maniacally, a note of pure hysteria and then sat hard on the ground, like a drunken man at the end of his revels. He stared at the light of the small campfire, frowning, and confused at his own mirth, "My brothers are lost."

Aodlen steadied the man up, "Drink."

He gave him a wooden spoon full of something. The man made a face like a child smelling a poultice but drank it.

Along time ago now, before he descended his first Haunt, Cole—or was it Stoneburner—had tried to explain the Upside Fever by telling him of the divers off the coast of Port Coldewater.

In late summer, the waters were warm enough to swim for a short season. A certain tribe made their living at a dangerous trade—swimming out and hunting for the pearls that grew inside the mushy guts of the mollusks which thrived in the inlets. If they weren't savaged by sharks or swept out by currents, they still had to be careful—after the depths there was the surfacing.

He had never seen that tribe or their labor, no. A story told inside an inn. Had it been Scrolls who told him? No, it must have been Cole.

He couldn't remember. He felt around in his vest for redleaf. It had survived the fight at least, though the leaves were crumpled and he thought he tasted demon blood on it. He spat. He groaned and standing, stumbled over to the small campfire.

He sat down and put his face near the flame, redleaf gripped between his teeth. The fire singed a stray hair on his head and burned away old sweat. The smoke hit him full in the head. He exhaled it and the taste of it made him dizzy.

The pain would pass. The redleaf helped. Squatting, peering into the fire, he inhaled the good smoke and then relaxed and tumbled backwards softly from the fire and sat back up in an anxious slouch.

Upside Fever twisted time. Men heard voices and noises. Your eyes didn't work right. An adjustment. There was heaviness to the Downside Fever but the Upside Fever felt more like a terrible lightness of spirit, as if the senses were unpinned, the spirit leaped off a cliff and just kept hovering.

It passed for most men in teeth-clenching moments or hand-wringing hours. Sometimes it took a night or two of restless slumber. Other relic hunters through the centuries had left lore and rumor and recipes for potions to help cure it. These Scrolls had dutifully studied. The doctor dispensed them.

Reverberations of the Upside never truly went away though. They had woke him up in a cold sweat, years after his first Haunt. At least he told himself it was that—just the waves of the coming and going from cursed places.

He sensed a face leering at him, studying him from behind plumes of smoke.

"Fever hitting Helga and the Rats. Ha! Of course. How do *you* fare?" Aodlen asked.

"Sore. Creaky. Cuts the demons left, you healed well enough."

"Yes, I worked on them while you slept. You've been asleep for hours, ha! The wounds are deep but will heal in their own way."

"Sir," Lookout said, nodding to him.

"You're still here."

"Yes, sir," Lookout said, smiling nervously.

"How is my cousin?"

The answer came on the heels of his question. She came straight at them, hair frazzled, and face smeared with dirt and grime. In the low fire of the camp light and the broken blaze of furious stars she looked like a demon, and he reached for a dagger at his belt, which he always kept hidden and nearly threw it.

"Not particularly well, ha!"

Her steps were fast and unsteady, unbalanced like a cripple. There was a deep purple ring around her one good eye, and he could smell the Upside Fever washing off her.

Lookout backed away. Aodlen put out an arm to shield the boy.

"Perhaps some help," Aodlen warned.

"You saw what they are, kid? Or were you too busy drinking your island liquor to notice?"

She had stopped, staring at them, as if trying to choose which one to vent her anger at.

"Helga, you lost men," Aodlen tried to intervene, stifling the bitter chunks of broken laughter which usually peppered his words. "It's a terrible strain, you see. Not recommended for artistic temperaments such as yours, hmm. Everyone feels the Upside Fever—"

"Even Cole? Does he feel it, Aodlen? Allred? See, I have this idea he doesn't," she pointed down the darkened trail behind them, where he assumed, Cole stood watch somewhere. "You're monsters but he is worse. Do you know what I saw? My unborn daughter, that's who. Harad's child."

The boy looked to run but stayed near Aodlen, hiding behind his leg. Allred got to his feet with a heavy sigh, still smoking.

"Ha! Myself, I feel it too, yet, I have a job to tend to—" Aodlen reached for something in the medicinal bag hanging from his belt.

Lookout still held the larger satchel where the Aodlen kept his other vials.

"Tending to work?" she moved quick, gave Aodlen a shove and snatched Lookout's arm and held him, pulling him closer to her. The boy snapped closed the leather case with both hands and managed to hold on to it.

He moved towards Helga. She shook the boy, "Do you know what happens inside?"

"I'm going to be a knight. I didn't kill your friends. I'm just going to be a knight. They'll teach me, too."

"Oh, please get away from these men, get away from us when you can. It's not what you think."

"I want to be a knight."

Helga punched him once, hard straight in the face. The boy went down to the dirt. Almost like an afterthought, she turned to Aodlen as if confused by what she'd done. The doctor grabbed her. She slipped under him, dumped him face first on the ground.

"Hold, cousin. Mercy of the Lady. The boy didn't do you harm."

Her fever was raw and contagious and swooped down on him like an axe. The Upside Fever could spread. The panic taking people like a cavalry charge that breaks a line. He'd seen it fly through camps before.

She slapped the boy again. Lookout held the satchel up to block it.

His legs were still weak, and everything was sideways, but he stumbled towards her.

"The boy is innocent, ha!" Aodlen said from the ground, scrambling to get up.

"That's what I'm trying to tell you. That's what I want to tell him before it's too late for him," Helga shouted.

Allred reached her. She whirled on him, eye wild.

"And you? You're already gone."

He got hold of her. She struck out at him, once. He didn't bother to block it, let the punch land on his shoulder. He wrapped her up tight in his arms and eased her to the ground.

"The undead. Unclean spirits. I saw him treat with it. You

made me a murderer. Should have cut him down when you found him. Should have cut us down when we arrived," Helga sobbed in his face.

Allred said nothing.

"I saw a face grinning at me in the firelight but on a boar's body...I thought, but maybe not," Lookout stammered. He held one hand to his cheek where Helga had slapped him.

"Why are we here?" Helga asked through the sobs.

"I'm sorry for your friends."

Allred knew she wasn't talking to anyone besides the geists still resident inside her heart. The boy's eyes were filling with tears, in the lambent light of the camp's fires. Around the gate, a few small-suns arranged about, brought some light, warding off Dhlams and the dark. He could hear Stoneburner sorting through the bags, deciding what they would carry and what they must leave behind.

He pushed her away from his body then, holding on to both her arms and looked her in the eye.

"You chose your path, cousin. We chose ours."

Aodlen moved in and pricked her arm. The Eye had started to retreat into her flesh, with the cleansing of the symbol near the gate. Mage would have erased it there as soon as he could. Her arm wouldn't ever be the same, Allred knew. The same scars dotted his and Cole's arms, too. Most nights you couldn't notice, but some nights you woke up screaming, staring back into an eye watching you which held the image of dead friends beckoning.

Aodlen quietly collected his vials and knives and all the bad tools of doctors and barbers, brushing them off, cursing lightly. He pricked his own flesh with something.

Down too far, too many times and we can't stop. So be it then.

Aodlen's face relaxed when the pin met his flesh and reached his blood. His cousin was quiet now, the storm of the fever subsiding in the tow of Aodlen's cures.

The volcano far off spilled its orange fire and the stars cast mute patterns. Around them, the sounds of the night on a lonely mountain clifftop—chirping and the brush of leaves and things that glowed and hunted or slept.

Someone shouting down the road brought Aodlen back to the moment and he whispered a small laugh, "Ha!" and the same maniacal smile cut his face.

"With me, boy! On your feet. More to fix up now," Aodlen said.

Lookout watched Allred with wide eyes. He nodded to him. The recognition gave him some heart. He clutched Aodlen's case tight, hugging it. "I'll help," he said and wiped his eyes. They both moved off into the darkness, Aodlen rattling away some instructions and observations to his little helper.

Allred sat on the margins of the campfire rocking his cousin back and forth. He'd seen mothers do the same with children. He'd seen grizzled veterans do the same with fallen companions after battle, when they lay dying and even after they died. The sound of brass mourning horns crawled up the skin of his neck, recalled him to the field. There was a burning city and he was mounted and most were not. They were shaking, sobbing and he could feel the middle of his foot through the stirrups as he shifted his weight and looked away. He wouldn't break, not now, wouldn't go back to the past.

"Thank you, cousin."

Helga breathed low and steady now. Her body shook with the occasional nightmare.

"I should have stopped you," he whispered but Helga had fallen to sleep and didn't hear him.

So, he sat with her, another haunted one. He sat and watched the wet palms drip rain and the stars—untrustworthy things in the hallucinatory night sky, shift and dip and dive—some came plummeting to the ground singing through the indigo air above Esmer.

He listened to grey horses gallop on the beach below. It was not horses, or the herds of his clan, just the sound of a restless sea.

He laid Helga down on his own blanket. Casting one last look at her, assured she slept, he lit another redleaf and went off to find Cole. One thing Helga had got right. Cole didn't suffer much from the Upside Fever. It was as if he belonged down there.

But he didn't want to think about that.

He needed the plain, cold logic of Cole to help straighten out the night.

Aodlen was tending to the wounds of the two giants who had wandered to the campfire nearby. Allred made a gesture, his head cupped against his hand to signal Helga slept.

"I'll watch her," Aodlen said, looking back at him from the swollen ankle of Hartha.

The two giants wore wine-painted grins, swilling toast after toast to each other's glory in battle and the Ninth. They were riding through the Upside Fever valiantly and getting very drunk.

"Fortune, Allred!" Hortha said.

"Triumph, Allred!" Hartha said.

Beside one another, their eyes gleaming in the fire both still covered in blood drying dark, they held high their flagons and poured wine down their throats and into the fire, offering it out to the fallen.

"Fortune," he said to the two jovial giants. Nearby the dwarf who hadn't gone under, sat watching them all with fearful eyes, an uneasy smile plastered on his face. He clutched the bone cup and tossed the dice into the air, then rattled it about the cup.

Pure hearts, Allred thought, *purer than some, anyway.*

"Allred!" Hartha said, again, looking up from another long guzzle of wine, as if forgetting he had just spoke to him.

He rose and nearly knocked the doctor over into the fire. He embraced him in one huge arm, "You've been asleep! I'm thinking I'm mad at you. I should wrestle you! You're a greater warrior than us! How can this be! How can I let it stand!"

"Woah," Allred said, as if reining in an excited horse.

The man nearly crushed him in his forgetful hug. His silver neck torc shone bright under the stars. His ear necklace smelled foul. His brother watched them both with a broad smile on his wine-stained lips.

"Sorry. I am the strongest, see! Isn't it so good to be under the air? I can live with being the lesser warrior under this mountain air." He let him go from his grip, backed up, looked down at the other dwarf and the smile was chased away by a thought. "It's bad about your cousin's dwarves. They're dwarves, yes, but still Green

Islanders. You were wise, Shad, not to go, I think."

The dwarf named Shad, nodded, looked down at the bone cup and said nothing.

"Aye but the losses were lesser this time than they could have been," he said and slapped him on the arm.

He grabbed him again in a crazed bear hug, "Many losses."

The giant's cheer brought him solace, even while he nearly crushed him in his drunken embrace.

He asked him where Cole was and Hartha looked confused for a moment, then stopped pressing him so hard to let him speak. He asked again, laughing, and Hartha then let him go and staring hard into his eyes, replied:

"Back in the dark somewhere, watching. Near the steps. Cole, he's always watching things, isn't he, Allred?"

"Aye."

The giant sat back beside his brother who saluted him again with his wine. The doctor went back to tending the big man's ankle.

Allred stepped over the crumbly bank of the ditch the Black Boat men had fashioned. The dizzy feeling took his head again. He felt with each footfall a kind of memory in the stone of the road, of men and women and children, all walking into the maw of the gate, heads laden with garlands of wildflowers.

Breathe in.

Cole sat alone in the darkness where the curve in the road gave him shelter but he could still see the steps. He held his own crossbow on his lap. The moon shone down from the sky strong, casting half his face in shadow. The cool light illuminating the half unburned.

"Been asleep. Helga's not good. Doctor calmed her down. What happened?"

Cole filled him in on what he knew between puffs from his own pipe.

Allred had collapsed after the Leatherwing flew. Aodlen had attended him, fixed up the worst of the cuts and wounds and laid out a blanket for him to sleep on. The Upside Fever takes a few minutes or even hours to set in. Cole had planned for it as he always did with Stoneburner keeping watch over everyone.

The Rat who lost his mind, they tied to a runt palm near the cliffside.

"She doesn't understand it fully," Cole said.

"You got scraped up down there."

Allred saw the long red line running through the already slick skin of the burned side of his face. He could smell the stuff Aodlen doused on their wounds and could still hear Cole's skin knitting under the strong potions of the doctor.

Cole dismissed it with a wave, "You were under the press of the Downside, hard. Thought I lost you a few times."

He took another puff and Allred could smell the redleaf he smoked, a different blend from his own, mixed by Aodlen.

"Well, there's actor's paint. There's masks and costumes."

"I suppose there is."

He fumbled in his vest for another redleaf roll. Cole handed him his lit pipe and he lit his own from the fire in the bowl. He passed it back. It was a simple pipe, a thing of heavy wood, well-crafted and down the pipe stem, gold leaf covered it.

"Always admired that pipe," he said.

"I found it long ago in the City of Thrones."

"Might want to pick one up myself there."

"Likely have the chance."

Both sat smoking, watching the night. He had come to tell Cole; he was at the end. To say plainly, he would not go into another Haunt. To argue, that they all teetered on the line between half-mad sometimes, and forever living their lives out in a Temple for the Hauntridden.

But he didn't. He simply sat under the fat moon and smoked and looked into the darkness and the stillness of it made his spirit gentle and he knew he'd follow Cole most anywhere.

One of the smoke rings, climbed the air, wrapped around the volcano, the moon.

"Could be."

Cole shook the ash from his pipe.

"First light we move fast. Stoneburner says the bald boy has some magic in him and senses Optri here. If so, best we dodge that fight."

"Aye."

They weren't in any shape for another fight. Cole knew it. He felt it. He said nothing.

"We'll split after we reach the tower clearing. Then you go back to the Black Boat. The other group, I'll lead it down to the village where the Rats have their fishing boat. You bring the Black Boat and her crew to the village side. I'll secure the village itself. Spoils are divided already, Stoneburner's been working on that."

"And then?"

Cole turned to him, looked him square.

"We have to rest. We'll try to make our drop to some agents outside of Port Shamhalhan, get news on the war, then back in the city I'll find someone to help the mage and we'll recover."

It wouldn't be easy. A mage-surgeon was a rare thing, like many of the professions surrounding relic hunting—there was no sanction for them outside the Throne's remit.

"Without him—"

"He'll be healed. As best he can be."

To find someone who could help the mage would cost a great deal. Double or triple that sum given who the mage was seeking the help. But he knew Cole was good on his word.

"The boys?"

Cole looked down at his scarred hands.

"Stoneburner says, they want to sail with us."

"You'll allow it?"

"Mage as far as I could discern, backs up what Stoneburner says—Boph has the makings of a mage. Could be useful." He shook his head. "Besides, if we leave them here when Optri arrive they'll look to put questions to them. No need to let that happen. We have room in the ship."

Cole had already decided to do right by them.

"Says he wants to be a knight, Lookout does. Helga went at him back there," he tilted his head toward the campfire.

"You can teach him to ride then," Cole said.

"The other one, the witch-boy?"

"I got some ideas."

Good. He didn't like the idea of leaving the two kids on

Esmer to fend for themselves. And Cole was right. The Optri would show up sooner or later.

"What did we find down there? You taken account?"

"Those daggers are blood-guzzling, god-smiters. The orbs are enough to supply a dozen battlemages if we can field them. It was a heavy haul and Scrolls is still documenting it all. It'll take time to move some of it in the markets."

He hadn't been able to keep track of every relic they'd found. For the short time spent down there, it was one of their richest takes.

"Truespoke."

"Go sleep. I'll keep the watch."

"I'll sit for a while with you. More peaceful out here on the edge."

Cole picked up a flagon from beside him and Allred could hear the wine slosh against its side, half-empty. Cole handed it to him. He uncorked it and took a drink, then another, replaced the cork and handed it back.

"We all feel it," Cole said, "Some more than others."

"You don't, though, do you?"

"Not the same way."

"Why is that? I never asked, always noticed it."

"Born in fortune, I guess."

Cole took a drink, then placed the flagon between them. Allred smoked and watched it duck in front of the brightness of the moon, fold onto itself, curling and tumbling up into the dark.

He knew Cole was lying but it didn't bother him much.

Most had shaken the worst of the Fever by the time the first rays of light broke. Allred could still see it lingering on them all, the hollow eyes hovering on ghosts dissipated in the light, watching too long nothing visible, an unsteadiness in responding to common questions, as if the world was a secondary place or some forgettable waypoint where they lingered, uncertain. Those who descend and return are never quite sure which world is the truer.

The Rat who had lost his spirit in the Haunt had not recovered. Someone, Aodlen probably, had bound the man's hands to keep him from harming himself.

Cole stalked the little camp, checking on his men, consulting with Stoneburner, glancing at parchments Scrolls foisted in front of him. He hadn't slept.

There was no time to eat, no time to do anything but march as quickly as possible. The weight of their treasure-brimming packs, mixed with the still unsteady visions rattling in their heads would make the march slower.

Cole didn't waste time explaining the plan he had outlined to Allred the night before. Mage kept looking at the gate—the forces within sealed for now. Stoneburner hurried among them all, and everyone helped hoist heavy packs on each other's backs.

Helga said little but kept casting glances back at the Hauntridden dwarf. She likely didn't remember much of her own words from the night before. Lookout kept his distance from her, staying near Boph and his donkey.

"What's his name?" he asked, pointing at the fevered dwarf.

"You don't need to pretend you care, cousin."

"I ought to know."

She sighed, "Tym, it is. Ready?"

She had the dwarf tied to the same rope as yesterday. The man was gnashing the dowel to splinters but looked well enough to walk. He tottered under a heavy pack whose sides bulged with the geometry of old coin.

He nodded, "If we can get your dwarf back to a temple in Shamhalhan there's a chance—"

"Don't tell me lies in the morning, cousin." With that, she gave a tug on the rope and the dwarf sneered at her but looked as ready to march as a mad man can.

He took one last look at the gate, standing bare in the belly of the mountain. An entrance to a kingdom of demons, but for some reason he felt the sweet-sick feeling of departing home for a long voyage. The strange fondness for the gate wasn't new. He'd had the feeling many times around the world. He never understood it. At first, the thought it was the dread of leaving the dead behind, which they'd done when necessity dictated but that wasn't quite it.

"Move," Cole said.

He bent down and lit a redleaf roll on a still bright coal in the cooling campfire and rubbed some of the ash on his hands to dry the sweat.

He strode past the Relic Hunters. Aodlen slapped him on the shoulder. The Rat named Shad stepped forward and walked beside him.

"I'll walk with you. I can't bear to look at Tym," Shad said.

"Better you fall back. Shouldn't be up front."

He set out down the Semhel road, boots soft on the rock, crossbow out. The redleaf felt good early in the morning. The dwarf fell back a few paces. After the road curved to meet the steps, a motion in the light brush on the cusp of the cliff caught his eye.

"What is it, Allred?" Shad asked.

"Go back," he whispered, waiving him off.

He lifted his hand in a fist and heard the halting of the line behind him. He smoked. He watched. He waited. He squinted. He felt his stomach clench. Everything quiet until it wasn't. Then the sinking feeling when the crimson of the uniforms grew clear in the morning light.

"Optri! Back! Back!"

The Optri foot soldiers burst out from the light cover of trees beside the steps down the road. Shirtless, earless, and wild-eyed—they grinned at him from afar waiting for an order. Behind them, a barrage of half a dozen arrows let loose and flew over their backs.

He turned to run. An arrow hit his side, but his armor repelled it. The shaft splintered and the impact spun him around. He fell to the ground facing back towards his own men and shouted again, waving them back to the trench. He turned on the ground, aimed and loosed one shot from his crossbow. The dart arced over the road and caught one of the footmen square in his bare chest. He saw the rise of blood, a distant dot of purple, in the man's mouth before he fell.

"Back," Cole was shouting from behind him.

The Optri mage revealed itself then. A crimson beast in the shape of a serpent. Its scales were bright, casting strange patterns of light from its body. It reared up on its coils peering down the road and even half unwound, stood twice the height of their giants.

"Optri mage! Formchanger! Counter spell!" he shouted.

A small village-worth of men and women and children staggered out behind the beast. The Optri mage had mastered them somewhere. Even from this distance, he could see the writhing bodies of serpents, snaking out of the holes where the human eyes once were. Each of them walked as if in a slow dance, or like puppets in the wind.

The Optri mage lunged forward, opened its huge jaws. A high whistle issued forth from its maw. A black, forked tongue jutted and waved, spinning and concentrating the spells it summoned. The Optri foot sped forward, spears raised to earless heads.

He scrambled to his feet and started to run.

The crimson serpent saw him retreating and pushing its head forward, leaped from its coil into a massive slither. It barreled towards him down the road in slinking curves that ripped the stone from the road.

It raised its mighty head from the ground. Opening its mouth, it uttered a curse and wind swept down, lifting him from his feet, slamming him against the cliff face. The air gathered itself as if in a giant bellows and rushed back towards the serpent's open mouth. The archmage propelled it back down the road at him, leaping and dancing with sparks of white and red fire.

He bounced off the hard rock of the Haunt's face, the magic meant to stun him, slow him, so the great serpent and his minions could close the distance and hack him down.

Where was the arrow from Scrolls?

Hugging the weedy line where the road tumbled into the rock face, the rushing crackle of another spell missed him, bursting in patterns along the road. Fields of raw magic sparked around his body.

If they didn't do something to stop the Optri mage, he'd die on this road soon enough. The red and white sparks fell to the ground, their crazed dance ending in a transformation of the air into the steely flesh of small serpents. These two, coiled, turned, stared at him with beady black eyes and chased toward him.

Justin A.W. Blair

Scroll's arrow answered the attack from his line. The heavy magic-tipped arrow exploded near the Optri mage. A puff of grey smoke went up. Scrolls had launched it just in time. The arrow would dampen some of the Optri mage's spells—a common enough weapon in war. A similar arrow answered that one, speeding over Allred's head and landed near where he guessed their bronzeface stood.

The small metallic looking snakes reached him. The last few feet away, the two leapt from the ground. He reached out, grabbed one midair, and slammed it against the hard face of the mountain. It shattered like glass. The pieces cut his palm. The other one found his neck and began to twist around it.

The foot soldiers were gaining ground on him. Their steps thundered in his ears as his vision began to blacken from the other spell-snake choking the air from him. He dropped his crossbow, grabbed his dagger, cut the body of the thing. The flesh was slippery and hard and the blade wouldn't bite.

Panic as the thing wrapped around him a second and third loop. He could feel the hard scales cutting into his throat. He stopped trying to breath. Exhaled. Calmed himself and moved deliberately.

Still on the ground, he crabwalked backwards to the Haunt face and slammed his back against the rock. Dirt and moss cascaded down on him. He slammed his body again as hard as he could tolerate. The snake loosened its grip. A sharp stone jutted out from the Haunt face. He lunged forward and used the rock to cut at the snake's body. Another arrow plowed into the dirt over his shoulder. The shaft exploded into a hundred tiny splinters. Blood ran down his cheek.

Finally, he worked the snake-spell off his neck. The body spasmed, gave a shrill, rasping scream and fell limp. He hurled it over the cliff side.

The Optri mage hissed. Its jaws unlocked, the giant bones unhinged and it sounded like a waterfall terminating to steam in a conflagration. It ducked its head down and curling paused in its pursuit.

Allred rolled against the face of the Haunt, sticking close to the rock. He scuttled backwards and choking and gasping for air saw that Shad had stumbled or taken to ground in retreat. Leaning against the Haunt face for shelter, he kept moving back to his own line. He half crawled, one hand cradling his crossbow, stumbling to the dwarf and then saw the arrow in his throat.

Shad was still breathing but the blood flowed from the wound fast. He looked up at him with eyes filled with fear. Tried to talk. Only wet syllables of blood came out. Allred had heard those same words enough to know what they meant.

He got to his feet. Another arrow soared by. The Optri foot soldiers would reach him soon. He needed to get back to the others to stand a chance.

Through the bottoms of his boots, he felt the ground heave and boil, caught in the magic of the Optri mage and the press of the counter spells Mage hurled down the road.

"Lady help us."

He leaned down and grabbed the Rat's arm. He swung the dwarf over his back atop his own pack. Blood splattered over his face. He felt it running down his neck, warm and thick.

One hard sprint back.

The Rat blew bubbles of blood from his mouth and tried to pull the arrow from his throat.

"Don't touch it. Aodlen'll do it right," he yelled.

He waved backwards over his own neck with his free hand. He dropped the crossbow to his side, letting it hang from the short strap that secured it and kept running, jumping over discarded packs, gold spilled. A statue of a leering demon discarded in the dirt mocked him. A statue with a boar's head.

"Knew it."

More arrows split the air around him. Several rattled off the mountain face to his right. He leaped over the berm. Another arrow thumped into the dirt, upended, and spun off tearing through the brush and tumbled over the cliff.

He nearly stuck his leg on one of the crude palisades they had built. Missing it, he blessed it and laid Shad down on the road before the gate.

"Aodlen!"

He looked around. His vision was still dark.

Cole was in front, calm on his face, broadsword unsheathed but casually laid across his knees. He turned against the small berm, stealing glances over the dirt. Hartha and Hortha had taken positions on top the rise, standing tall behind their giant shields. The enemy arrows rang against them. Mage huddled between them, working the joints on this hand and muttering spells, keeping sight of the enemy.

"Tell me," Cole said.

"Small village worth of mastered-ones. At least a dozen Optri foot, spears, swords and closing. Earless ones, looked like. Can't tell how many archers in the back. Maybe six. Optri Formchanger looks like a damn big snake," he said, between gulping breaths.

Aodlen was pushing bunches of cloth against the dwarf's neck to stop the bleeding. He could see the dwarf breathing fast. Dying faster.

"They stopped, Cole," Hartha said, looking down at them from behind his shield, "But the people … the things are dancing."

"Dancing," Hortha echoed, "A terrible display."

Cole snuck another look over the dirt.

"Their foot stopped. Feeling us out. He'll close after he sends the first forward. You're bleeding," Cole said.

Aodlen looked up. Tossed him a cloth. Allred put it against his face. He was starting to catch his breath. The sky began to darken. A guttural song winded down the road from the Formchanger's drum and the mastered ones.

There began one of those strange, unexplainable moments in a battle, small or large … the arrows stopped. The press of magic slowed, both mages working against the grey smoke which still drifted across their positions and the other's own spells. The air smelled sharp and clean. Small spells sought each other in silence, tangling on the road. The initial battle cries faded. Allred had lived through many of these moments. Everyone waiting for the other to move.

Aodlen scuttled behind the berm and beckoned for Helga to come near. "Keep this pressed against his neck."

"He's alive?"

"For now."

Helga bent over the dwarf whispering a prayer or cursing the 9th. There was no difference in a way.

Allred realized he still had half a roll of redleaf in his mouth. The leaf paper was dry against his lips and stuck there. He puffed it. Still had some fire, the ember came to life.

Optri spells couldn't put out my redleaf. Couldn't kill me.

He puffed, his back against the dirt, watching Cole beside him, waiting for orders. He fit another dart in his crossbow while he smoked, working the lever back.

A voice came down the road in a perfect high-Throne accent.

"All Haunts belong to the throne by writ. The Optri require your surrender. We know it is you, Cole of the 9th."

Cole squinted, ignoring the soldier shouting down the road, "They'll charge or not," he said to himself—looking up at the mage: "Let them come to us."

Allred peeked over the little ramp of dirt. The Optri mage ran impatient circles along the road, then came barreling toward them, stopped, reared back up again, as if in challenge. The last of the morning sun through the clouds bounced off the crazed-markings of its skin. He had to look away from the sheer wicked majesty of the thing—a man once, willingly subsumed for eternity in the form of that monster. For a brief nauseous moment, he understood the full commitment of the mage.

Around the creature, the villagers danced quicker now and writhed in ecstatic trance feeding the magic. They sang dark consonants. The rhythm of their footfalls sped up, their grotesque movements gorging their master with power. The snakes nesting in the cold goo of their eyes leapt and writhed, snapping at the air before their blind eye sockets. The same Optri man who had spoken his challenge to them, stood near the Optri mage and beat a drum. He quickened the pace of their dance, faster and faster, until Allred could see the mastered-ones had lost all sense of proportion. Their limbs snapped, flung far and wild; ligaments tearing, and their blank faces showed no pain.

There were children dancing among them.

Helga had turned to the scene as the drum grew louder, looking away from her fallen Rat with tear-streaked cheeks, "What? Cole? Allred? What new horror is this?"

She glanced back at the bleeding Shad. She scrunched up her eye, looked sick.

"Surrender, Cole and the 9th. Return to the Throne. Live in proper service to it," the Optri drummer called again over the beat he kept.

Helga crawled forward up to the berm. She handed the bloody rags to Staah who now held it to his brother's throat.

Behind them, he saw the Haunt-crazed Rat, Tym, screaming and running, trying to climb the Haunt face itself. Boph had been sent to tend to him and was whipping the dwarf with the rope to which he was tethered, as if trying to control a wild bullock. Stoneburner stood back, halfway between Boph and their own line, axe in hand, watching.

"What is he talking about? Surrender?" Helga asked. "What is wrong with those people and their ... Allwein's promise and the Lady's lies, man, what is that?"

"An Optri mage, Formchanger, with his drum and deaf soldiers. He's mastered some unfortunate villagers. He will use them to sing and dance in thrall to him. It increases his powers," Scrolls answered, "We should eliminate them swiftly before it builds and target the crier. That is my suggestion, Cole."

"There's women and children—"

"There was. Isn't anymore," he said.

"Cole of the 9th, surrender—"

Cole didn't bother turning. Looking straight ahead at nothing, as if into some personal void, he bellowed to the sky—

"I'm going to bury you. I'm going to bury your mage. I'm going to bury your king."

The Optri crier turned to the mage. His drumming slackened for a moment at the answer and Allred could see dismay and fear on the man's face. The skin of the drum didn't look like that of a common animal and he knew it was not.

The Optri mage understood Cole's answer. It opened its

mouth, pouring forth foul spells. The foot soldier each leaned back and hurled their spears towards the trench. The magic caught the spears in their arch and the spears turned to the same steel scaled serpents sent after him before.

The air around them burst and shrieked in crimson works of wind, tearing holes into the air. Mage shielded them as best he could; one exploded near Allred. He felt a shock and a ringing in his ear and then a dull pain like needles pressing lightly against the skin of his scalp. Helga screamed. The serpents landed and made for their pit.

The mage brushed most away in a wave of roiling green shadow. The spell covered the arrows and then hurled them all straight into the sky, then sideways, slamming them against the Haunt face where they shattered, spilling bits of jagged glass-like metal into their trench.

One made it through.

Allred leapt to the berm, took aim over the pit. The serpent jumped. The dart caught the thing in midair and it shattered. He ducked as the bits of steel bit the dirt in front of him.

Everyone stayed behind the berm, hugged the road. He could smell the old blood shed here in the grit and dirt which bound the cobbles of the Semhel road.

"Put some arrows in the villagers," Cole said.

He reloaded while Scrolls leaned over the berm and poured arrow after arrow down the road. Behind him, Stoneburner let fly, too. The Optri mage conjured serpent shaped shadows in front of the arrows which swallowed the shafts and then vanished in the air. One got past. A villager fell dead.

"He's keeping them blocked, Cole."

The drumbeat increased. The bodies of the villagers were a whirl now, each digging out of space a cocoon of spinning shadow, feeding the Optri mage. The serpent let go another spell, surging down the road, a thousand miniscule serpents, each hard as glass. They impacted the giant's shield, and he saw them take a step back. The snakes exploded over their head and he felt the shards burn and cut his neck.

A powerful spell. He felt the wounds in his flesh burn.

"Those cuts are poison," Aodlen shouted. He was running now between each of them, pouring the liquid on their cuts. The liquid cleansed them, "Get this on the wounds, now! Rub it in! Ha!"

"Cole?" Helga cried.

She had jumped over the body of the wounded dwarf to shield him from the spell. Aodlen was pouring a vial over them both.

"Let's have done with it," Cole said. He grabbed his broadsword, pushing his back against the dirt, then got to his knees. "Mage. Everything is required of you."

The bronzeface looked down at them. He stood tall on top of the berm, impervious to the arrows and un-afeared behind the shields.

It was the first time he'd seen the mage close-up since they left the Haunt. Weariness that made him sick peered back at him from behind the bronze mask.

It's time. Time to do what we are fitted to do.

"It is strong, Cole, the Crimson One is committed. To defeat it, I'll leave you for a time. Afterwards, I'll be of little use, only a burden."

"I'll carry you, Mage," Cole whispered, "I'll not abandon you."

The mage nodded and he smiled, the red lips cut across the pallid hue of the mage's face. It would have looked like a monster smiling if it wasn't one of Allred's best companions. He realized Cole was asking him to push past the brink, to where he might never return.

"We can't let him die," he said.

"We won't." Cole stared him down. The drum was growing more insistent. "I won't. After the first wave, we press them. Can't wait them out. If I fall. You lead. Kill them all. Let not one leave this place."

"You'll not fall."

"At my side, Allred. Hortha. Hartha. Feign advance, draw them in."

The twins straightened in unison. The mage drifted down to the road from the berm. The giants tracked close, conforming to every shift and move of the cloak, bashing the flat of their axe blades against their shield with each heavy step.

The serpent slithered back and froze, waiting. It issued a command and the Optri foot stood still. Through yellowy-eyes alive with old intelligence it watched its adversary—Mage strode into the road to face it.

Now the drum beat peaked, and the magic grew so intolerable, Allred thought the entire road might collapse down the mountain side.

The villagers twisted and spun, broke themselves on their own wicked exertion.

As Mage walked forward his cloak fluttered with each step. A wind washed over the road. It coaxed the small conflagrations burning in the ferns and brush around the old Semhel road—fires set alight by wayward spells. Clouds closed in fully on the sun like a serpent squeezing prey. Darkness fell in one sweeping shadow. The two archmages faced each other.

The moment arrived. The true violence the mages let loose in front of the gate on the Island of Esmer would be sung of in ages ahead.

The Optri slave-soldiers, covered in the marks of their allegiance, crimson trousered, gripping short daggers lunged straight for their position at the command of one hissing syllable.

They ran past Mage and the giants, ignoring them leaping to the berm—determined, suicidal in their rage.

"Take them first, then forward with Mage."

The first soldier Cole caught on the point of his broadsword. The Optri slashed at him, spit and blood flying from his mouth. Deaf screams came from the Optri foot as he slid down the sword's length towards Cole, each slash of the sword nearing his face.

He could smell the burned flesh around the man's guts as the soldier's breastbone slid down the blade's edge. Allred moved in and struck, lopping the soldier's head from his body. Cole turned the great blade and the body slid off. He spun, bringing the heavy sword around with both hands, and Allred dropped to avoid it. The edge barely missed him, slicing into the next Optri hurling himself into their position.

The Optri soldiers wore no armor, only their red trousers. The dye of their clothes squirmed, as if the red were made of real pits of blood where serpents swam. Their earless heads wrapped tight with thin leather helmets, smelled foul, cured in unclean concoctions.

All down the narrow road now, the Optri came in a rush to kill and die, as the two mages faced each other on the road paying little heed to the mundane world of sword and steel.

The twang of a bow. Scrolls put an arrow through an Optri's skull. The impact broke the man's neck before the point bled him out. Scrolls pursed his lips, pulled another arrow from a quiver, and sent a second into the Optri man with the drum. The arrow took his life. The drum fell. The villagers dipped in and out of oval shadows, froze, quivering and screaming.

Mage moved. The Optri mage answered.

Hartha bellowed his war cry. Hortha took it up—a duo of blood-soaked hymn in the harmony of war. Both men charged forward, shields held high. Two of the villagers hurled their already broken bodies at the shields and were smashed to pieces on the steel. More, snake-eyed, lost souls, the twins scraped from the ragged path of the living. Optri and Mastered, alike, perished in the fatal sting of the giant's cold-forged axes.

The battle leaped to fast frenzy.

Helga was screaming. Tym broke his leash from behind and came running down the road and Staah tripped him up, grabbing his feet. The Haunt crazed one dug fingers into the throats of his friend and the dwarf kicked out. Allred turned to cut him down, but Helga shouted, "no" and got hold of the crazed dwarf.

The light had turned to grey, and the grey had turned to blood, and he felt holy war fill his veins.

Another blast of magic. The skin on his neck burned. The light and fire dazed him. The world was dragging, spinning. He slashed at the legs of an Optri who stood above them stabbing down at Cole from the top of the dirt.

His sword cut above the boot of the Optri man, opening a gash. He fell back behind the berm.

The crimson mage reared and swayed, towering over the

tallest palms beside the road at full height. The serpent wore a hood like the poisonous serpents the two-Bead Shamans entranced for copper coins in the bazaars of Port Shamhalhan.

Hartha and Hortha advanced in two wide steps. The eyes of the Optri mage, yellow and black, set deep within the serpent's snout watched them—a cold, insane intelligence.

Mage sang deep song-spells and the cloak shimmered and shifted, dancing in wild patterns. He shifted and as if plummeting down a deep well, fell within the folds beneath his magical vestments and then, emerging, giving birth to himself, warping the weave of the world around him—formchanged again. Fangs beneath the bronzemask lashed out behind the shields and struck at the crimson mage who dodged the green-tinged claws and savage snaps of the Nightdragon.

The crimson mage retracted, bobbed, and wound itself around the bronzeface, once, then twice. Nightdragon bit down through the scales of the crimson beast, tearing loose snake-flesh in plumes of blood and a shower of meat.

Green fire burst. Red fire burst. Yellow fire burst all along the road between the jaws of the mage and the forked tongue of the Optri mage. Tooth on tooth, claw on claw scraped and the power of the two mages made even Hortha and Hartha stumble back. Both men raised axes high and leaped to the kill.

The sky shook as Hartha and Hortha battered the Optri mage with ax and shield. But the Formchnger had wrapped around the bronzeface, and the giants could not strike strong blows for fear of hurting Mage. It would not loosen its hold no matter how much flesh the giants tore from its body—squeezing harder—the sound of a rib cracked across the road. The Nightdragon shrieked.

Rain fell in sheets, warm and strangely serene. The thunderclouds burst above, and it began to pour on mage and man on the old Semhelhan road.

Allred looked at Cole. Cole met his eyes just for a moment.

Another Optri, flung himself towards him. Cole swung his forearm against the man's head. He went down. Cole slammed his foot on the man's throat. He died.

"Hold this line," Cole shouted, "Take a shot if you can. I'm moving up."

Broadsword in hand he leaped over the berm and waded forward through the Optri and the last of the mastered villagers— swinging his broadsword, like a scythe threshes the autumn fields, Cole harvested all before him.

Allred found his crossbow beside him. He laid stomach down against the berm and took aim at the Optri mage.

A bloody hand reached out from behind the berm, grabbed at the dart on the crossbow and wrenched it down, dragging it from his grip. He let it go, throwing his enemy off balance. He grabbed his short knife, scrabbled over the berm and hacked down through the Optri's collarbone. He sunk the knife deep. Wedged beneath bone, he plunged it deeper into veins and muscle, then wrenched the blade up, snapping the bone. The soldier glared at him in death-maddened rage, hugging the crossbow to his chest as if gripping some treasure to take to his grave.

He struck again and again, butchering the soldier against the ground. He wrenched his crossbow back, and ducked back behind the ditch, with a push of his foot on the chest of the dead man.

He fitted his dart once more and took aim at the Optri mage.

The rain came down in sheets now, but it could not extinguish the flames of the raw magic around them. Allred closed his right eye, found his site. The crimson mage crushed Nightdragon in its embrace and now both bodies glowed with the heat of the space-warping magic. Hartha and Hortha stood back, helpless.

Allred let loose the bolt. It found its target, digging into the scales of the serpent at the edge of its mouth. It lodged there. The jaws froze in loose-letting curses and conjuring of spells. Four ivory fangs wet with magic-frothed saliva, the forked-tongue jeweled and flickering wild. The beast slackened its grip on Mage.

Screaming in Cole's face, an Optri soldier left his guts on his broadsword. Cole punched the soldier twice fast and he crumpled to the ground. Cole flipped his blade and drove it down into the soldier's throat and hurried towards the heart of the battle.

The Optri mage screeched, a high, piercing tone that called forth the last of the Optri archers. Allred counted five. They loosed another barrage of arrows—magemade points impervious to the spells of the bronzeface pierced Nightdragon's flesh and transformed to writhing serpents which bit and tried to burrow into his body. They cast down their bows and rushed forward with knives while Mage shook off the spells.

Hortha crashed to one knee. One of the arrows caught him in the leg, the shot ricocheting from the ground, turning to a serpent on contact, then slithering beneath his shield.

The big man lurched, driving the bottom of his shield into the stone road and shattering the serpent arrow, then stumbled. Hartha reached over to steady his brother, turning. As he did, the crimson mage unwound itself from the bronzeface in an instant. Slinking beneath him and swinging its diamond-shaped head, it lunged at Hartha.

Jaw unhinged, gaping wide, the Optri mage struck, batting the man's shield aside, clamping down on the giant's exposed leg. Four fangs sheared through the giant's heavy trousers. Bucking and swinging its head, the Optri mage tore the giant's leg from his body. The flesh came apart at the man's knee and for a moment the leg hung in the jaws of the Optri mage who swallowed it whole.

Hortha fell from his brother's embrace.

Mage, now freed, slashed with claws at the Optri mage's body trying to protect the giants. The archers rushed forward with blades and suicide in their eyes. Scrolls felled one with an arrow. Two more, Cole devoured with his sword. The last two archers rushed towards the giants trying to skirt around the mage. The bronzeface opened both wings like blades and lashed out decapitating both. Two heads rolled in front of the Haunt of Esmer.

The crimson mage retreated, coiled, wrapped itself around itself, slithered back down the road in a sidewinding retreat. It called again and summoned forth yet another wave of Optri foot, kept in reserve. Scrambling forward, arms pumping, waving curved blades above crazed eyes, they closed.

"Allred, press them. No one leaves alive," Cole shouted.

Aodlen was sprinting forward to the giants, his satchel in hand.

Called forward, he joined Cole now. Readying his sword for

the close work. The mage lunged forward, quick flaps of darkened wings in the rain and seized the Optri mage in his own jaws. Clawed feet bit into the raw flesh of the Optri mage and pinned him to the ground, preventing his escape.

The scales grating against the ancient road, generated cascades of sparks. The bronzeface bit down again. The crimson mage shrieked and snapping its heavy head outwards like a whip, battered the bronzeface dragon.

Hortha was trying to drag his brother back. The bronzeface stayed atop the Optri mage, unrelenting, trying to keep the beast pinned. The Optri mage screamed but held the ground, and loosed another spell. Another blast of magic turned the fast-falling rain to boiling water, burning the groaning giants wallowing in the mud and blood of the maelstrom.

Allred saw as if from a distance, it might be their end. He squinted, searching for something inside and felt nothing but the desire for vengeance—to make the Optri feel his sword's steel. The Throne had burned them, hunted and hounded them, trekked them, and above all betrayed them and now they would perish. The enemy foot closed in, and he thought of the Lady with a peaceful smile as he strode forward to fight.

The Optri troops ran past the still struggling mages, buying their master time in the struggle.

Allred braced himself. Smiled. Sensed something on his right. He moved to strike but turning saw Lookout standing there, quaking, a short sword gripped tight in his hand.

35

Lookout

It was death all along the road. Chaos of the tumult. The dwarf gone mad. Boph running. Blood and then more blood atop it making copper-colored puddles along the path. The twisting terrible dance of the villagers, he could not bear to look at; some he thought he recognized from faire days.

It didn't matter now.

The last wave of soldiers plunged forward. He kneeled near Helga. Trying to help the dwarf. He couldn't watch her crying. What could he do? The bandages were wet with rain and blood.

"I'm not going to die a coward," he shouted to no one. But Helga was near and thought he was talking to her.

"What?"

He grabbed her sword. She had laid it down in the dirt while tending to her friend. Her friend was dead. Had been. The eyes frozen, looking into the sky. Rain didn't make the dead blink. She didn't seem to understand.

"No," she lunged at him, trying to stop him.

He ignored her. If she wouldn't fight that was fine. She was a woman. She shouldn't be here anyway.

He scrambled over the berm which had turned to mud. One of the red trousered men, dying grabbed at his feet and he skipped over him but couldn't bear to turn and strike him with the sword.

From behind he heard Stoneburner yell, "Stay here, boy! Lookout, come back!"

He slipped in the mud, banged his knee hard on the cobbles, nearly stabbed himself with the blade as he wiggled through the mud and the corpses and scattered and shattered body parts on the road. There was so much blood, none of it looked real. A crazed, wicked thought came to him—maybe they were all actors, like Helga the clown lady, and after this was over, they would rise and take a bow and that would be that.

An arrow whipped through the air. Missed him by an arm's length. It lodged in a corpse behind him, and he whimpered and his body hurt already and he kept trudging forward.

Another of the earless men, grasped at him as he made his way towards the beasts and the giants and Cole and Allred. This man got a hand on his ankle, and he fell again. The stone knocked the breath out of him. The man was weak, near dead, no ears! But he tried to drag him towards him. He took the sword and bat the hand away with the flat edge. No use. The man clung to him. A mist formed near the man's eyes, blinding him but still he hung on.

Pausing, and then tentatively, he stuck the point at the man's face. It bit into the cheek, and he felt it press through the flesh and the tip met jawbone. He pulled it back, sick from the feeling of the bone running through the metal to his hand.

He made it to his feet. Ran. He did not turn back.

Run. Because now Stoneburner was coming over the berm to grab him, to pull him back. He turned, "I must fight. Protect the dwarf and the gold and things."

"Back now."

The command in the big man's voice almost brought him to his senses.

"No!"

He turned. Ignored him, ran forward to the fight.

Far back, down the road, he saw Boph who had retreated, standing with his donkey in the rain watching him.

The two giants were bleeding on the ground. One missing a leg. He was dying. Someone called the doctor forward through the rain, but he couldn't see who. The rain came down so heavy it was hard to see ahead.

And then he was there. Inside the battle. Beside him, Allred. He looked down at him, nearly struck him when he saw him, then opened his mouth in surprise. He shoved him back to make space to swing his sword. More soldiers were coming straight at them, the last of them, he thought.

"Fool!" Allred called, "Go back."

A red trouser man came crashing into Allred and it was a blur of steel and rain, and he stood there waiting, looking for a chance to poke the sword forward into one of the men who attacked his friends.

A sudden gust of wind and rain soared across the high mountain road. It tasted like blood on Lookout's lips. He spat, shrieked. The sword was heavy, even for a small one. The point sagged down unless he tried hard to keep it upright.

Another red trouser soldier came through the rain from the side.

He swung his sword. So heavy. The soldier in front of him didn't do what a man should do. A man should stop before running into a blade. This one didn't. He just threw himself towards Lookout with his upraised sword and he was going to die.

The blade flashed and came at his eyeline. Before it struck, Allred came twisting and turning in front of him, as if he were of the wind itself. The red trouser soldier's head disappeared in a burst of blade and speed—neck a mist of blood. The man's sword clattered to the ground and Allred spun away back into the rain. Two flashing swords he could make out through the din and dim, Allred, and Cole, dealt death.

He kept moving forward, slower now. He could feel the roll and weight of the two beast's bodies in front of him.

Cole hit a soldier in the face with his sword. The man's teeth exploded out of his mouth and the bottom part of his face fell to the ground.

And still beyond them, the two beasts writhed. He could feel the strange heat. The smells of the magic were like sacred things that should not be known to mortal men. It made him feel sad and elated and overwhelmed and alive at the same time.

Pressed hard they were. Lookout realized all at once he couldn't breathe. He looked down to check, no blood, nothing touched him, but his stomach was hard like a rock. The spells kept erupting in the air. Stray colors skipped across the road, the air made heavy and weird by the magic.

Were they to lose? That was the thing he couldn't quite understand.

The red snake thing had broken free of the beast with the bronze mask, the mage transformed just like a few nights before.

Now, the enemy moved towards them. The last of his soldiers flanked the beast. They crouched, slinking forward on human legs as if mimicking the step of their serpentine master in some strange rite or dance. One had taken up a foul-looking drum which he had heard earlier but had then been stilled by Scroll's arrow shot.

In a strange dancing march as if summoning and gathering the magic of their master to their choreographed step—on both sides of the serpent, empty hands on the scarred scales they came to kill. Only Cole and Allred stood fighting, hands clenched on blades, waiting for the end.

They were being backed up against the cliff's edge, pushed off the road as the earless soldiers circled with their backs to the mountain face. The bronzefaced dragon creature was crawling back towards them, in unsteady steps. It—he—still spoke in gouts of green flame. It's spell-speaking sounded exhausted.

The enemy half-circling pressed them towards the cliff, still stomping and feinting in time with the wicked drum.

He stood at the edge now, half-sheltering behind one of the runty palms growing at the edge of the cliff.

"Boy, you should have run." Allred said.

The rest of the 9th had come forward, even Helga but they couldn't quite join up with the rest, cut off by the stalking earless savage soldiers. Scroll's wrestled with his bow, transformed int a serpent.

Allred's leg was bleeding. His side was bleeding. His neck was bleeding. He stood beneath the same palm where Lookout sheltered. Helga screamed, incoherent, waving some other sword she'd found. The summer storm was deafening now, the rain loud; it sounded like standing beneath a waterfall. The face of the mountain which hid the Haunt was sliding mud and began to hide the gate behind it.

The sword was heavy in Lookout's hand. He threw it down and took out his own whittling knife. He'd prefer to die holding that. He pointed it towards the two soldiers with the same yellow, sick eyes, of their archmage master.

Cole said nothing. Waited. There was no fear in his eyes but a rage which he had not seen in the man before and it made him take another step back to the cliff.

The enemy mage issued a command. The soldiers rushed all at once, closed in to pin and push the warriors against the drop-off. Rearing up behind the last of the soldiers, the flat crimson face of the terrible mage, so close, he could smell its rank and rancid magic breath.

He challenged the beast with his whittling knife and thought for one sweet moment about seeing his father and mother again soon in Allweln's halls.

Their mage lunged in front of the snake. Allred moved towards him, stepping in front of the serpent. The Optri soldiers pressed. Cole slashed.

The crimson thing swung its head down at Lookout. All he could see was the eternity in its jaws. In a blur of motion, Allred slammed into him from the side, tackling him and making the snake miss its strike.

Unfortunately, also sending him over the cliff's edge.

"Fortune," Allred shouted. And then he was falling fast through the mud and the rain and the tops of trees.

His fingers spread out. He dropped the knife. He grasped at

the limbs of tree trunks as his body struck the steep incline, rolling and bouncing off the face of the cliff into the tops of trees, then down through them, down, down and to down.

Rolling, the weight of his body struck another tree. He grabbed at anything as the sky did flips and flips.

He kept falling and between the trees beating his body, there were instants of freefall. He couldn't find purchase. He heard another body falling above him and another and another.

Or was that the sound of his head in the old helmet as it met rock and tree and limb and the feeling of falling and then?

He never knew falling was this fast. And then he didn't because it wasn't and it was dark.

He woke up to the patter of slow rain dripping into his upturned face from burning palm fronds.

Beside him, lay the earless body of one of the enemy soldiers—mangled from the fall, unmoving.

It didn't move. The earless corpse—he didn't move. Which was it now? An it or a he? Lookout studied the man's frozen face in the falling rain as bruises welled up on his own flesh.

Could he move? He watched the corpse. Dead. Safe. He was dead.

I am not.

He trialed a move, put one arm out beside him. Both his arms were covered in scratches and cuts, most of them looked shallow but his vision kept doubling up.

Lookout looked. Looked again. The soldier, yes, still dead. *Still dead.* An odd phrase, if you thought about it.

Every rain drop sounded too loud, like the note to a song buried in mud. But he was so happy to be alive, to hear it. Lucky.

Was he alone? He wagered another movement—yes, that arm could manage to move and the other, too. Good. So, two arms, many raindrops—all moving.

I'm not quite in my right way of thinking, he thought.

He couldn't bear to look up at how high the fall had been, so he didn't. He listened to the rain.

He started to cry. It turned into a laugh and then a cough;

and who cared since it all would wash away in the rain.

His ribs. He found himself in the position of crawling and wondering, can I stand? Then he did, on his feet for a moment, teetered. On his feet.

He looked up the cliff, listening. He couldn't see much above. Dense jungle along the slope, grew thicker the lower down it climbed. It had slowed his plunge—

Something was walking towards him.

He would have liked to fight just once more in his life. He felt like he could now.

"You're alive," Allred said, crawling through some ferns not far away.

Lookout felt a flood of relief but didn't answer the warrior. His lips moved. No sound came out. He couldn't quite make words. Could make them inside his head, not quite spit them out.

"I'm alive, also." Allred paused to consider something then glanced at the body of the enemy soldier. "He is not." His words sounded far away and dull beneath the patter of the rain. "So, it goes."

Allred cocked his head up towards the cliff and whistled what sounded like a bird call and waited there on his hands and knees.

The warrior tried to stand, then thought better of it. Some vines had wrapped around the man's arms, like coils of rope. He picked at them with empty, muddy fingers. His hands looked lonely without a weapon to hold.

He closed his eyes and leaned against a tree. The bark felt good against his skin through his tunic. It had been a good idea to preserve his new tunic, after all. A smart move. He was smart. The sound of the rain on his father's helmet was loud.

"Come here," Allred said, "You gone dumb from the topple?"

He didn't know but this seemed reasonable. He answered by moving, like he was told. Allred had crawled towards the dead soldier.

"Turn him over. Look for anything worth taking."

Lookout did as he was told. He knew if he so much as

hesitated, he wouldn't be able to touch the dead man, so he didn't pause. He rolled the dead man over. Thought of him as a bag of cownuts or a sack of tubers.

"He's got no ears," Lookout whispered.

"The dark arts of that Optri sect. They think they get more holy by being deaf to the world, to hear their master better, that's what I heard Scrolls say, eh—he won't miss them now."

"There's a knife," Lookout said.

"Take it."

Allred put his hands to cup his mouth and emitted his bird call again. It went unanswered. "Lived through that fall," he laughed, "Something to consider. Fortune. You're sure you didn't turn dumber from striking your head?"

He didn't think so. It was just that everything was beautiful in its way here, breathing, alive, not alone and then he realized words sounded far away because he heard them beneath the patter of the rain on his father's helmet. He took the helmet off and set it on the ground.

"What about them?" he said.

Faintly, another call like the one Allred had made reached them from above. The warrior raised his eyebrows and sighed in relief.

"Down here," Allred shouted. Pain on his face. He looked beaten badly, some of the blood the rain wouldn't wash off and a little of it was his. "We won, but I don't know what it cost us."

"I'll yell," Lookout said and turning towards the slope. "We're alive! Down here! Allred! Me!" Then he just started yelling, "Hey."

"Line coming down," someone answered from above.

It sounded like Cole. He would be alive, of course. He had only known him for a few days, but Cole didn't seem like a man who died. An image came to him of Cole wading through a field of gore and then he carefully put that strange thought away and watched the rain.

"Might make it up," Allred said, stretching and trying to stand. "Give me that knife."

"For what?" he managed to ask.

"To have."

Lookout handed it to him as he limped forward. He took it and sat back down.

Allred sighed, closed his eyes and a smile broke out on his face. It made him nervous. He stood, waiting. He felt mud in the bottom of his shoes, a squishy feeling.

"Is there anything broken on you?" Allred asked enunciating each word, as if talking to a fool.

Lookout shook his head, no, but he wasn't sure. Perhaps I am a fool, he thought. That could be nice, a foolish knight.

"Bite your own tongue?" Allred asked, "Answer."

"No," he managed, "I'm alive. If I'm talking, I'm alive, right? The dead don't speak."

This answer seemed to bother Allred even though he didn't look like a philosopher or wear a pensive look on his face, like Scrolls.

"Completely wrong," Allred finally answered.

Lookout smelled smoke, "There's some trees on fire."

"Yes, not all of them, luckily." He dipped his fingers into one of the pockets on his leather armor, pulled out a crumpled, blood-stained, rolled up redleaf. "Go fetch me one of those burning branches or a leaf on fire."

Lookout did it. Several were drifting down around them. Fire from the fight between the mages had set the grass and ferns aflame and it reached down even here. He grabbed a leaf, half of it still burning, the other half thick and waxy and brought it over to Allred.

"That'll work. May be of use after all," he said, and again, the man tried to smile through pain, but he just wasn't skilled at it. It was odd to see the warrior try to do something which he could not. That pain wasn't new, Lookout saw—whatever made his face twist like that wasn't just from today's battle.

"Something I saw going for that leaf," Lookout pointed.

Allred looked past him then back to where he got the leaf. He made it to his feet, exhaling the smoke as he stood and shuffled over to where one of the giant's shields had fallen down the cliff with them.

Allred bent over it. Then went to one knee, staring at it. Without looking up, he said, "I lost my sword. Go find it."

He made his way carefully around the area. They had fallen down through the jungle to this wide flatter place. Not far away the ground tilted and kept falling down, eventually to the sea, he figured. Here they stood on what looked like another curving trail or old road, running around the mountain. He had never been to this part of the island.

He saw nothing, no gleam of metal beneath the litter of leaves, no jeweled hilt glimmering. He wondered if it were a magical sword the Allred wielded, or a named sword like in the legends, Boph told.

"Boph? Boph?" he shouted up above. A voice answered from above but muffled and faint. It wasn't his retainer.

There behind a big tree in a clump of low grasses, a fair ways up the cliff's slope he saw the metal of Allred's sword. He made his way up the incline, half swinging from trunk to trunk, leaping to the next, pulling himself up. He put his back against one of the big trees for balance and caught his breath, then up farther and he leaned down and picked up the blade. It was heavy than it appeared.

"I found it," Lookout called down.

"Bring it," Allred yelled up.

Putting the sword down, he sat down and slid and shuffled back down through the loose soil, feet first with the sword dragging behind him in one hand. He went to Allred and happy to be useful, pointed it at him.

"Does your sword have a name?"

Allred had pulled the big shield closer to the cliff face.

"Not like that. Don't hand a sword with the point facing someone unless you're going to stab them."

"Why?"

"You don't do it like that."

"Alright, but your sword is magic?"

Allred took the sword from the ground with a sigh, stood up, sheathed it.

"It's just a sword. A sword has one purpose. I guess,

anything with one purpose has magic to it."

"Does it have a name like in the legends? Many great warriors have named blades."

The man studied him for some time as if deciding whether to answer or dismiss him.

"All swords share the same name, and the name is death; from the most cheap-got steel to the ornamental things on the hip of a courtier. If a sword is named some other thing—it's poorly named, or the wielder is hiding something. When you hand the sword to me the proper way, you show you know the sword's true name. So, do it right from now on."

He didn't understand what Allred was talking about, exactly, but kind of got it and knew the only answer which would do was, "I will."

"A sword knows it's purpose. This is what I'm trying to tell you."

When he looked down at the hilt, pain flickered through his face at the movement. It was like Lookout had disappeared and Allred talked only to the sword in a trance. It started to scare him, but he figured he shouldn't be scared anymore after what he'd seen and falling off the cliff and all.

"Quiet but for killing. A sword's birth is loud, all banging hammers, heat and force. No one feels sorry for a sword's birth and then for its whole life, it's mostly quiet. One true name—can you remember that?" The warrior swallowed hard. Took a deep breath of the weird smelling smoke and looked up at him—"Well, if they can't get some ropes down here, then we'll be walking."

He didn't like the sound of that. He turned back to the cliff and shouted. "Boph? Boph?" He heard the donkey braying above.

"You did well to find it."

"Are *you* broken up?"

"A little more so."

"You saw who survived?"

"I fell right after you. Wasn't trying to kill you when I pushed you."

"I know," Lookout answered. He felt a lot better that Allred said it out loud, though. "I don't know where we are. If we need to walk somewhere, I don't know where we'll go, and I don't know how."

"Figure it out as we go if we must, but, Stoneburner always packs rope for us. They'll have enough."

"They're alive up there?"

"Most likely."

Allred looked back to where the giant's shield lay.

"That shield?" Lookout asked.

"We'll return it, no matter how long it takes," Allred's voice was flat.

"I'll help," Lookout said, "You tell me what I must do. I'll do it."

He walked over to the shield. He couldn't budge it at first. The metal felt like it wanted to bury itself into the ground, clinging to it after its fall. He felt the pain in his fingers then and saw that his hands looked puffy. He managed to lift the shield from the ground, "I can drag it."

"Bring it here. Then go walk along the slope. Look for rope, they'll be trying to throw it down."

"What if the snake-mage is still around?"

"Then we'll die. But I don't feel it around, do you?"

"No," Lookout knew what the man meant.

When the soldiers had attacked with their mage, a wild heaviness came down on the mountain—the proximity of fearful magic. He thought he could still feel it buzzing about but for the most part dissipated.

He wanted to ask Allred more. He stood there with his mouth open for a bit. There would be time to learn about these intricacies of war, their war, so instead of talking he did as he asked and started walking along the cliff face.

Above, he could hear cursing and the sound of men working. A dwarf emerged from the dense foliage above, descending the steepest part of the cliff. He wore a harness made of complicated knots and ropes and metal pins and a weary look on his face. It was not the crazed dwarf and not the one who had been hit with the arrow but Staah. He stared at Lookout with beady, eyes that were friendly above his wispy blond beard.

Lookout called out and waved.

The dwarf saw him and waved back and shouted something up the cliff. Soon another harness and rope slid down beside him. It held a pack in the harness.

"Me and Allred are down here. He's hurt. There's a giant's shield, too. Does Boph fare well?" Lookout called up to the small man. There were so many answers he needed and all at once.

The dwarf said something, but he couldn't hear it. The dwarf looked frustrated and did something complicated with the knots and a piece of metal, struggling with the ropes running through the jungle brush.

"Be right back."

He jogged over to Allred and told him what he had seen.

"Drag the shield close to where the dwarf is. What was his name? Can't keep them straight."

"I think it's Staah."

"Seems right. I'll follow," Allred said.

"Heard."

He raised an eyebrow, "You see my crossbow?"

"No," Lookout answered, "You want help walking?"

"No. I'd like my crossbow. Keep your eyes open for it. Came off the strap."

While Lookout went to get the shield, Allred slowly shuffled over to where the dwarf was working his way through the trees, down the cliff face. When he made it back with the shield, the bottom of the dwarf's feet rested on a tree limb just above them and he was guiding the rope that held the pack down to where Allred stood to receive it.

"Cole says bury this bag somewhere down here. More coming, too," the dwarf said. From his belt, a shovel had been strapped. He tossed it down.

"How many have we lost?" Allred asked.

The dwarf looked down, "My brother, Shad walked the bright line. Helga lives. Both your giants ... for now. It's not good. His leg is severed, the one. I can't keep them straight, Hortha or Hartha? Aodlen works to keep them both alive."

"My retainer?" he asked.

"Your what?" the dwarf asked.

"Boph, the One-Bead."

"Alive, with his donkey."

A great energy and joy went through him at the news. He knew Boph would make it. Knew the donkey would survive. (Why hadn't Boph ever told him its name?) He felt a new confidence in his step. He couldn't wait to get back to the top of the cliff and relate all that had happened. To hear, Boph tell of the battle in his own words and ask him about the light he was sure he cast.

He thought of the villagers then. The strange snakes where their eyes were and nearly retched. The thing to do was just not to remember that.

"No. No. It is good in the main," he told himself.

Lookout helped take the pack of treasures out of the harness. When it was freed, the dwarf tugged on the rope suspending the now unburdened harness. Unseen arms pulled the dwarf back up through the jungle.

"What do we do now?"

"Bury this," Allred said, pointing at the bag.

He took up the shovel, "Where?"

Allred cupped his hands over his face, lit another redleaf roll from the ember off the last, "Anywhere."

36

Allred

He smoked one redleaf roll after another, as the dwarf guided several packs down the cliff, maneuvering them through the brush growing from the cliff face. It hadn't been a straight drop down from where they fell. If it had been, they'd be dead. There was enough trees and the ground sloped just enough to allow them to survive the fall.

Fair amount of luck, that he was just a bit crippled up and not dead. Some were not so lucky but he put his mind off that for now.

The boy dug holes. Allred watched him for some time, then tried to help; but there was only one shovel, and he was sick with pain from the battle and the fall and the years of watching men he knew die, so he just let the boy do the work. It kept him quiet.

They hid one pack where the cliff face fell to the ground in a pile of rocks. Another they hid under a rotted log. It wasn't perfect but it would take too long to dig a lot of holes. If they didn't move soon, they'd be stuck marching in dark.

A swarm of red-backed beetles, and translucent worms writhed in the muck beneath the log and the boy yipped. Strange boy. He'd shown some real spine or stupidity or both jumping into the fray.

Everything was wet from the rain. Most of the magefire had dimmed and flickered out, leaving it darker under the jungle canopy in the little sloping game trail etched out on the side of the mountain.

"Rainy season here in the south coming on, isn't it?" he asked as the boy dug.

"Yes. It rains a lot here in the season of the Dragon Wash."

After they buried the treasure bags, he and the dwarf fitted the harness around the boy and they hauled him up first.

"I want to carry the shield," Lookout said, already strapped in.

"It could go up in an empty harness."

"Could I try?"

"If you drop it on me, I'm going to toss you back over the cliff."

"Thank you."

Allred hoisted the heavy shield up and the boy got hold of it. The weight made the whole harness dip and the rope strain. The boy's knuckles turned white clutching it, but he held on.

"Pull!" Allred shouted.

The men above pulled, and the boy did his best to keep his footing and soon he was disappearing through the brush. He held on to the shield. Strange boy but maybe he had some promise after all. Fate would decide that, not him.

He went to the body of the Optri soldier, dragged it to the cliff's edge where the valley tipped farther down and shoved it over. With so many wounded, they wouldn't be able to carry it all, but they could return for it in time.

Then the sound of rope and metal and sliding. The dwarf guided the empty harness down the cliff, hanging halfway up the cliff, obscured by trees and tumbling bits of scree when he shifted. Allred fitted himself into it, clipped the metal pin and shouted,

"Pull!"

The dwarf echoed the command, and he felt the ropes pull taunt against his body. He dug his boots into the cliff as best he could or found purchase on limbs and trees and crevasse and ascended in the jerky motion the length of men's straining arms.

His foot slipped on the cliff face up on the steepest part, bare of trees, wet and slick. He spun on the rope and hit the cliff face hard on his side. Pain flared—a solid, familiar thing passed through him. His sword pommel bit into his side, pressed between his waist and the stone and he cursed. He breathed in, his feet scrambling met only air. The tips of his boots he drove into the cliff, then relaxed and let his weight straighten himself out. He spit on the bare rock of the cliff face and studied it. No blood.

Soon he reached the top. Hands pulled him over the lip of the cliff and onto the old road and the devastation there.

Scrolls bowed as Cole grabbed him and pulled him forward. Both men had pulled the rope which was tied off in a spike buried in the ground.

"I am pleased you're alive," Scrolls said.

"Same," he answered.

Down the road, Aodlen squatted beside one of the giants who lay on a wide camp blanket soaked in blood. His brother propped up on his elbow was beside him, singing to him. A large sewing needle threaded with wire shook in Aodlen's hands and his staccato barking laugh weaved with the implement. Beside them, a bit farther off, the mage slumped under a thin, black cover. The cover trembled and green haze drifted up through it. Next to him, was the decapitated head of the Optri mage, its jaws open. Boph stood above Mage, his lips moving soundlessly as if praying. He thought he saw a faint golden light surrounding the Mage's body but then it was gone. Lookout stood beside his friend, with an embarrassed look on his face as if he didn't know what to say. Stoneburner was packing the donkey.

"You can walk?" Cole asked.

Allred unbuckled the harness, worked the knots of rope loose which held him.

"Yes. Mage took the head of the archmage?"

"Hartha's idea. Wouldn't hear otherwise. Said it was his trophy."

"A solid claim."

Cole nodded, "Marching soon."

He went off a few paces where a pile of limbs was gathered. He began stacking limbs and branches for the funeral pyre. Scrolls went down the road to the doctor. Allred joined Cole. They had brought the dead villagers nearby the pyre, too, turned them face down so their hideous vacant eyes wouldn't worry the living. All along the road, the bodies of the fallen Optri still lay dead-eyed to the sky. Beside the cliff, the chopped up body of the archmage lay, headless.

Beside the pyre, Helga held vigil beside Shad's corpse. She looked up at him, as if waking from a sleep.

"I lost them all but Staah. All my Rats besides him and the two on the ship—gone."

Staah the dwarf who'd been in the harness had gone off alone. He was gathering more wood for the pyre with a small hand axe.

"He was brave."

"Aye, and wise not to descend the Haunt and all his wisdom didn't save him," she said, "He was kind and that didn't save him or deflect the arrow that struck him."

"He fought well."

He didn't know what else to say to her. The Upside Fever had gone from her and now she just looked weary.

They would have to gather a lot of fuel for the pyre. Less so, for just the dwarf. He bent beside the dead Shad, found his plaque to the Lady, took it out and muttered a quick prayer, then stood.

"Thank you, cousin. Your lies are sweet."

He turned to Cole, "Faster if we leave the villagers where they lay."

Hartha's shouts grew louder down the road. Cole kept piling the brush and did not turn to look down the road. Neither did he.

"Shad will have proper rites."

"Yes and the others?"

Cole spat, looked out over the cliff ledge out to the volcano.

He was wet, ragged, cut up and bruised.

"They didn't deserve their fate and there's not much remaining of their bodies. Hortha and Hartha can't march, yet. Hartha won't walk at all, unless Aodlen figures something. We'll be slow in leaving. It costs us nothing to give them rites."

"Could be more Optri coming."

"Let them come."

Allred grunted, went back to piling brush. The giant's voice grew louder. Aodlen was cackling. The fury of a short dispute waged again and again and then Hortha's voice singing a verse in Green Island dialect and quiet. The sound of Aodlen's bone saw followed and a final groan and quiet.

Helga stood, "Neither of you attends to Hartha?"

"Aodlen's task," Cole said.

"Best to be out of the way during such things," he answered.

She watched them both, eye squinted. "I'd come to believe you're a kind of demon, or have had congress with them for so long, the difference wears fine. But, you're men, also—You fight and kill and die but you're both of you too afraid to go comfort your fallen friend. You're just men after all."

He didn't have time or patience for her truth-telling.

"Survive not one Haunt but uncountable fights below, cousin. Year after year. Bury or burn dozens of your friends, the ones you can recover, the pieces you can salvage. What would you become? Would you remain a poet? Or would the masks you wear eventually become confused with your real face? Someday you'll wake up wearing a mask you forgot to take off."

She wouldn't back down, as he expected of a woman from his homeland.

"I'm no better than you for my mourning. You took me wrong. I still can see you're a man, a hopeful thing. I just wonder how much longer you can remain so."

"Enough talk. We'll perform rites but we can't tarry," he answered.

They would burn the dead on the Sem-hel-hen road.

37

Helga

Watching the bodies burn, she tried to recall the proper prayers but couldn't.

Her tongue felt heavy in her mouth. She was thirsty for water, though she had drunk her fill. The flame caught finally in the damp of the brush and smoke rose carrying burning flesh into grey sky. The smell was not masked by the odors of heathflower that her people usually lined their pyres with. It was the richest funeral she had attended, but the heathflower did not grow on Esmer and no amount of gold could make it so, nor bring the dead to life.

Now, I am forever far from home.

Was that her own thoughts? Or something the vision of the child inside the Haunt had spoken? She couldn't tell. Since leaving the Haunt, all her thinking was jarred, disjointed.

Somehow, Allred had lived through the fall over the cliff. He stood near her now. He reminded her of the promise of home. She had known of him since childhood, well before meeting him at Cearhardt Castle but she wasn't certain he recalled her back then. She'd left that unspoken. The tale of his name, the story of his clan was told through the hills. Everyone knew it for many days' ride away. He'd won fame before he ever joined the 9th and he'd won it from a bloody blade.

No, her cousin wasn't the type of man to die falling off a cliff. A strange thing now to hear, under his breath low prayers from his warrior's mouth. In a quiet voice, he recited them— prayers to the Lady.

"Speak a little louder, cousin. I can't recall them, anymore."

Her voice broke on the last words. On the pyre, Shad burned. Hortha's leg smoldered beside it. She turned away from him to hide her crumpling mouth. He lifted his voice louder.

"Earth eternal, man escapes it's bounds."

"Speak louder."

"Waters constant, man swims the flood."

"Speak louder."

"Airs untouched, man marches the storm."

His voice rose over the singing of Staah and Hartha. Cole tended the fire and made his own prayers, silently. She had heard a rumor he had been a priest a long time ago or had considered it as an avocation. No one really knew Cole's history. Her lip's trembled but she remained mute. Today, she would not sing, would not play a part.

"Fire, the gods willed, absolute and brief, like the spirit of man—rise, flicker, to warm, to burn and then retire in ash and born again. The Lady holds the world and spins it with each breath," Allred recited.

Cole stood on the other side of the pyre. Another more hastily built consumed the villagers. Cole went to that pyre and prayed there, too. He stood with them, solemn, alert, watching the road for enemies. She couldn't blame him. Understood him better and better each hour. The mage, exhausted, hiding beneath a long, thin veil to block out the light joined Cole at the pyre for the villagers. She couldn't look at him.

All burned except the Optri mage's snakeform. Scrolls had

dissected the thing and pulled Hartha's devoured arm from its gullet. She thought she saw him pull something else out of the body the size of an apple—reaching deep within the flesh of the beast and hiding it away. She didn't want to know all the dark practices of these men anymore, suspecting many more than she had seen.

Mage teetered on the edge of an abyss of madness. The jewels in his teeth glared and his skin looked tighter, paler than usual. He left the pyre with elaborate gestures and still shimmering in the chaotic wake of his power, leaned against Hortha, who stood with the strange half-false mourning smile plastered on his blocky features. The same smile Staah wore. Emerald Island people thought it a sin to frown at pyres. She knew that. For the Rats, she forced her own smile but failed.

Tym, mad but sleeping, curled like an animal on the tether, oblivious to the pyre's stink. He could not make the prayers, half-beast that he was now, but he watched the fire with a curious look at the end of his makeshift leash.

She almost felt jealous of the madman. Then she wondered how they would manage down the stairs, off the island with the mad dwarf, the crippled giant and all the gold.

Still struck her as odd that Cole had taken the time to make the funeral pyre after the battle. Did he want more enemies to find them here? She didn't understand him yet, fully. Taken a lot of risk needling him and Allred, too. She needed to see what they thought and neither men were prone to give away their thoughts without her digging for answers.

As soon as the battle ended, with the Optri mage's death at Cole's own sword, he had gathered those still standing, saw to the wounded and readied ropes to search for the fallen.

Then Cole started on the pyre as Stoneburner lowered the excess treasure down. He had it done for Shad, just a mercenary dwarf in his eyes, and even for those villagers. She despised herself that she hadn't asked that it be done, that deep down she was scared and wouldn't have protested if he'd ordered them leave as quickly as they could.

A shadow ran across her cheek and she swiped at it. Nothing there. Since she had left the Haunt, she twitched and felt things running across her body which she couldn't grasp. Unannounced rivers of power inside her ran rampant, down her arms, through her hair, over her skin—it felt like bugs crawling on her. Then strange bursts of emptiness made her numb and heavy.

The night before the morning's ambush, deep in the thing they called Upside Fever, she recalled Aodlen assuring her this symptom could subside. *Could* he had said, not *would*.

He told her, between his abrupt laughs—which she suspected to be a kind of verbal twitch and permanent, so not particularly reassuring—that these things usually went away.

He was probably lying. Physicians did that. He gave her some potion that tasted like burned up flowers and salt which she drank.

The rites and prayers concluded, the mountain looked gentle in the afterglow of rain, but the sun still sheltered behind thick clouds. Little swarms of bugs darted along the road mingling with the flies drawn to the dead.

Then Cole was giving orders again, forming them up, and moving them away from the Haunt on the island of Esmer.

She thought she hated Cole, but she also knew she couldn't trust her own thoughts yet.

Because when the attack had come, he had stood at the front with the others, in the teeth of the Optri mage, fighting not beside them but in front of them all.

She didn't hate him for the orders he gave, or the cool calm of his commands, or his stolid, burned face, or for allowing her to come here—that's what she had sought after all; she didn't even hate him for her greatest suspicions, that he was not entirely a man at all; she hated him because he didn't suffer the same way the rest did.

It wasn't truly hate after all. It was wonder and fear and a species of envy. To him, this fight on an unnamed mountain was a small thing, and he meant much more blood in the future. Well, if it *was* hate, she'd live with it because she knew she'd ask to follow him wherever he went.

If there was an inside to Cole there was a lot of space there, like a Haunt of flesh and blood, therein dwelled a greater hatred than what she could fathom. It had made him more than a human—a hero and a subject of song, so why shouldn't she write that song? Through her one good eye she could see it—Cole was a spirit of vengeance more than a man at all.

In the depths of her Upside Fever, she had slept at the pinprick of Aodlen's needle, but she thought she recalled, some time later, Cole leaning over her, watching her, a shadow in the night, a quiet monster, bloodless. It felt like a giant piece of steel hovering over her, suspended by a thin rope. It might have just been a dream and probably was but the figure spoke in his voice.

"I would march every inhabitant, man, woman and child of the Throne City straight into the jaws of a hungry Haunt far worse than this to see my plan through. And if it required my own marching into the damned places below this land—and it will—I would step lively into its slavering jaws. Because I am the death of a dynasty. Helga of the Rats I give leave to follow me. And you will. "

Had he said that?

Of course not. It didn't sound like something he would say. He spoke practical words of practical command when he spoke at all. The truth was every time she'd seen him, here on Esmer and at Cearhardt's Castle, he didn't act like a warlord in his speech or manners.

She found herself on her knees on the old cobbles of the Semhelhen road. Her body was moving strangely. That was sobbing, wasn't it? She felt hands on her, picking her up.

"One foot in front of the other, cousin," Allred said.

Staah looked up at her. He reached out and took the rope to pull Tym along. She looked down at him. There was fear in his eyes, fear that his leader would not march.

She understood Cole then and the hatred left her and her weeping, also. She recalled her vocation. The actor took over and her face regained composure. She wiped the tears away with grime-stained hands.

Maybe Cole was a cold bastard, probably so. Maybe something worse than that. She understood him though, finally. Ahead, she saw him, back turned to her, at the head of the line she was holding up—everyone stood around, most pretending not to see her.

"One foot in front of the other, yes," Helga replied, "It's that simple, cousin."

She opened her mouth to shout ahead. Maybe to curse Cole, maybe to thank him. She wasn't sure. Before she could speak, her cousin left her and joining Cole at the front of the line, signaled the march and the living started the long journey back, not to home but away from Esmer.

38

Allred

Their pace was slow. Both giants were lamed. Leaning on a makeshift crutch, Hartha sang songs until he passed out, guzzling wine until his torc and tunic were soaked in it and refusing to give up his grip on the Optri mage's decapitated skull, saying, "I've plans for it. Aodlen knows!" Finally, almost falling down the mountain, Hortha convinced him to mount the skull atop his pack which despite his lacking a leg, he still carried. His brother held him up when he lost consciousness, and the others took turns hoisting the giant when he grew cross with his brother and his care.

Lookout carried the man's shield for him, and the giant bestowed many good-natured curses directed at him and taunted him at his poor dice play, which the boy didn't understand since he'd never played, but took to be friendly enough.

As they descended, Cole marked a tree here, an upturned rock there, leaving signs and signals only they would be able to see if they returned. He cast other visible marks, sending unwary bands away from the Haunt, through the valley paths towards the barrows they had avoided.

Hartha still sang but quieter now and at some point, Aodlen made him drink some potion and the singing stopped. For his part, he couldn't look at him too long but could only manage a weak smile when he turned his head to watch the giant man limping behind.

When they reached the tower, they didn't pause for long. Lookout ran ahead, rushed up the rickety steps, disappeared for a moment, gathering some belongings and then raced back down with eager eyes, afraid they would leave him behind.

Cole conferred with Stoneburner.

He smoked and checked his weapons and ignored his wounds. The survivors stayed quiet as survivors often do. Nothing more to say. The rain had stopped. The sky sat heavy on his head, grey and laden with humidity. The clouds were thick, and he felt like he could reach up and grab them. The season was turning to rain. He wiped the sweat from his brow and thought of the north and how it would be good to escape the heat.

Aodlen had fixed him up after he finished with Hartha. He gave him some potion dripping from the edge of a hollowed thorn which pierced him and it killed the pain. He couldn't feel his toes much. He wished he had time to take his boots off, wash his feet in that creek nearby but there would be time enough to rest if they made it off Esmer.

Cole split them up. He'd go alone to get the boat. He didn't argue. Would be happy to be on his own. It made sense.

Lookout climbed down the rickety tower, paused and smiled and saluted. It had been the boy's home for a good year. He went over to Cole, tapped him on the leg and said something, pointing back at him.

He checked his pack, tightened the straps that held everything in place, so nothing rattled, no dagger, or blade made noise. He'd lost his crossbow in the fall, but Scrolls would make another. Still, that bothered him. It was a beautiful piece of work.

Making another would pass the time. Stoneburner had handed him a good bow to replace it for now. He longed to be alone for a while.

"I'm ready, sir," the boy said, looking at him, "I'm going with you, Cole says, me and Boph and the donkey and you."

"Fine."

"And I'm sure now. I want to be a knight like you. Aodlen's work, it's good...it's not for me. Neither is the stuff Stoneburner does. My father was a soldier and I want to be a knight which is a type of soldier, too."

"Alright," he replied.

Lookout narrowed his eyes. In his hand, he held one of the small, whittled figures he must have retrieved from his room above.

"You don't believe me."

Cole gave the command to move before he could answer. Helga would go with Cole and the rest down to the village to secure it and to meet up with her surviving Rats on their fishing boat. He'd meet Glume and bring the Black Boat around.

"No talking until I say so. And I'm not going to say so for a long time."

Boph nodded. Lookout opened his mouth to answer then shut it.

The trail turned out uneventful. Despite the medicine Aodlen gave him, he felt the echo of the impact of the fall with every step.

When night came, they camped near the same spot, where the Relic hunters had gathered just a few nights ago. He found the wire they had set, still undisturbed. It meant likely, the Optri had come up some other way.

The boys didn't talk much that night. From their eyes, he could tell it was setting in that they were leaving all they knew behind, and it scared them like it should. A better man would have tried to console them, but he wasn't a better man, so he smoked and sat alone and guided the donkey to some grass and let it eat. He was tired. Better for everyone he didn't waste the air talking. The boys and the donkey all fell asleep soon enough.

"You better get used to wearing your shoes when you sleep," he said, when Lookout took them off. "You never know when you have to move fast."

"The demons could come this far down the mountain?" he asked.

"I think they won't send more."

"You're sure?"

"No, but I'll keep watch."

He didn't sleep. He kept the watch all night, smoking redleaf, watching the approaches to camp. Nothing moved in the shadows but he still jumped and scratched skin that itched for no reason. He tried not to think about the future, about Hartha's burning leg or all the wounds of yesterday and the future and he didn't take his boots off from his aching feet.

The next day they neared the beach. The air was heavy and thick. Low ground. The jungle didn't stop dripping this close to the sea, but the sky stayed clear.

He halted the boys at the end of the trail where it met the beach and estuary. The Black Boat wasn't at anchor but he hadn't figured it would be. There was no sign of the Optri ship, either.

He crouched in the low ferns waiting and watching the beach for a long time. No sound besides gulls. In the distance a hawk circled something in the sea. After a long time, he rose and gestured for the boys and the donkey to stay put.

The beach was empty. The sound of the breakers grew sharper away from the cover of the jungle and the salt air burned his nose and lingered in the back of his throat.

Out on the horizon, he saw it. The hawk was flying above the Black Boat waiting off the coast.

Shuffling through the bright yellow sand, he whistled, and the boys came out onto the beach. They trudged through some dunes, staying close to the tree line. The smell of seaweed drying on the shore mixed with the dank, salt-rot smell of fish beached in the sun.

"There might be villagers soon. They come to harvest the beach of fish when the Dragon's Waves comes in with the rainy season," Lookout said.

He grunted acknowledgment. The sun was bright. Walking in sand annoyed him. It cleaned his boots some though.

They walked in silence, backs bent by the weight of their loot to the roll of the sea and the sound of seabirds fluttering in the palms and nothing more. He found the arrow with the light green tip on the point in the quiver Scrolls had given him.

Voices followed the coastline far down the beach. He covered his eyes to block the sun. Dozens of tan men carrying sacks were making their way towards them.

"Who're they?"

"Villagers scavenging," Lookout said, copying the way he sheltered his eyes from the sun.

Allred said nothing. A cloud passed over the sun, dimming the day. He held the flame of the redleaf he was smoking against the tip of the dart until it began to spark and then pulled back and aimed in a high arc towards the Black Boat and let go. It sailed up into the sky and exploded in a shower of sparks.

"What was that?" Lookout asked, "That'll scare the villagers away, probably."

"Calling Glume and our boat."

Allred slung the bow over his shoulder. His pack was heavy, and he put it down on the beach. He kept eyeing the villagers who had stopped and were arguing with each other. They watched the strangers on the beach, pointed out to sea. He watched them. Soon the boat looked to turn but it was too far away to tell.

"It's enough, I think."

He saw a man pointing. The two larger of the group approached. He didn't want a conversation right now. Might not work out well for anyone but especially the villagers because, no one needed to know who they were or what they were doing. He had a thought.

"Go down there and meet those men and tell them whatever lie you need to tell them, to keep them from bothering me."

"Lie?"

"Handle it how you want. Keep them away. I don't want to

answer questions and I'm not in the mood to lie, myself."

The boy drew himself up to full height. The light of the sun made him look very small for some reason. He was covered in bruises and his helmet scuffed and in poorly condition and something about the boy and his courage made him laugh a little, "I'll tell them something. I'll handle it."

Lookout jogged halfway down the beach, waving at the villagers. He turned his back on them and slipped another arrow from the quiver, then turned back and sat down, hiding the bow behind him.

Boph came over closer, stood above him, watching his friend, "I think he'll be a knight. I know why it's stupid to think it, but I still think he will."

"Well, supposedly you got some mage in you, or you're born to sight or something, so I won't argue it. He's brave enough, that's true. You weren't exactly at the front of the fight up there."

The boy laughed, "I'm not a fool."

For a second, they said nothing, then Allred laughed, too and the One Bead boy took it up again and bent over gasping from it. The donkey nudged him with its nose, and he stood straight and pet it and their laughter resided like a wave.

He could hear the boy talking to the men, pointing backwards, pointing up the mountain and waving at the boat. The villagers nodded and turned around, returning to their group who stood watching warily.

The ship neared the shore. Lookout came back.

"What'd you tell them?" Boph asked.

"I told them the truth. I told them I am the son of my father, who served the Throne and who is buried on Esmer. I told them his name and my own. And I told them that I am the guard of the watchtower on the island of Esmer but that bad things have come to the island, so they are ordered to go home."

Allred nodded, "You might turn out useful, someday."

Lookout stood there on the beach smiling and he finished his redleaf roll as the ship drew closer. He could hear the sails snapping and though he hated ships, he looked forward to boarding it.

They all watched the villagers retreat down the beach, who cast looks out to sea at the large ship making its way toward the little estuary. He walked out into the gentle surf; warm water filled his boots. Glume stood on deck. His men lowered a simple rope ladder from the side, its ends splashing into the sea.

"Going to come in close," Glume called out between cupped hands.

"I can't swim," Lookout said.

Allred called up to the judge, "You spot an Optri ship?"

Glume cupped his hand to his sunburned head and called back some exotic expletive of the sea.

The boat got closer. When near the shore, a big wooden door, near where the hull met the water lowered with a splash.

"I really can't swim at all, Allred," Lookout said, again.

"Don't fall over the side. That's all you need to know about boats. That's all I know about them. You just wade out here a ways. The donkey, too."

They made their way through the crystal clear, blue sea. Once onboard, inside the dim cargo hold, they unpacked the donkey and their own haul. He stretched his shoulders, relieved, unburdened.

Glume stood watching them, directing his sailors. He told one to remember fodder for the animal. Shelves and nets held a hundred things; tools and canvas, rope; the implements of the art of sailing filled up the dim hold. Up ahead, there was a ramp and it led to the deck.

"Can I bring my donkey up there?" Boph asked.
Allred shrugged, "There's some stalls onboard for horses and things. A sailor will show you."

"I'll sleep in the stall then," Boph said.

"Cole says head to the port on the other side," he told the captain.

Glume nodded to another sailor who stood waiting behind him, hands folded behind his back. The man hurried up the ramp and started shouting orders of his own. Soon, he felt the boat shift beneath him.

"Go on both of you," he said.

"Find the boys and the animal quarters," Glume said to the remaining sailor. The two boys and the donkey followed him, Lookout casting unsure glances behind at him.

He sat down on a wooden box, hunched over, hands folded. The captain stared at him in the dimness of the cargo hold. Neither man said anything for a while. He could feel the ship pitch and turn. It was dark down here though it was lit by two lanterns and for a moment, he wavered in a spike of Upside Fever. He closed his eyes. Breathed. Glume stood watching him, saying nothing, a half-deaf, grizzled seabird.

"Dead?"

"None of our lot. Some others showed up, Helga and the Rats. She lost some. Hartha lost a leg and Mage is wrung out but we're alive."

"Dread things that but could be worse, so it's Fortune, I say."

"Optri found us just out of the Haunt. You see them?"

"No. You want to come up to the deck?"

He felt like falling asleep there and then on the wooden floor of the ship. Just slink down off the box, curl up, and sleep the whole voyage through. Instead, he followed Glume up the ramp.

"Didn't see them. Hortha won't walk, you say?"

"Hartha."

"I get'em mixed up."

"Leg got gnawed off by an Optri archmage."

"You killed them all or I need to be watching out?"

"All of them but always keep watching out. Captain—I'm all beaten up and still got Upside Fever on me."

"You've been beat up for a long time and you don't seem to notice. Don't seem to die, either. I suspect if you took too much notice that'd do you no good. The Fever hasn't left any of you for a long time, but I'll look after you well enough onboard the Black Boat, I will."

"Truespoke."

The light above hurt his eyes. He wanted to go back down into the hull. Sleep. Rest. Forget. He hated the trapped feeling he got from the belowdecks though.

400

Glume watched him. A crewmen came down a small ladder from above, looked at them both and then turned around.

"You say this Helga somehow was on the island?"

"Blond woman, named Helga of the Rats, you recall her?"

"At Cearhardts, aye."

"She followed us all the way from Port Shamhalhan."

This vexed Glume because he should have seen that, and he didn't. The man didn't answer with words but a string of exclamations and short outburst of animal grunts, finally clearing his throat and spitting out to sea.

"They used a mask. No sailor has eyes sharp enough to see that."

Again, Glume disputed this with incomprehensible indignation but let it go with a question.

"Those two are spoken for?"

"Spoken for," he agreed.

He realized how much had happened in just the time he had last seen him, and the story felt heavy and too much to tell and the captain could see it on his face.

"Good. Had enough blood for some time. You're tired as Allwein on the tenth day in the cave and I see it. I have a village to find and a ship to pilot. Call out if you need something."

"Aye," Allred said.

"Your quarters are ready."

"I'll stay up here for a bit."

"Aye, like you do."

Glume turned around abruptly and started shouting commands to his crew that he didn't understand—the language of the sea and sailing people. He'd never learned it. Had no plans to.

Alone. He put both hands flat on the deck rail, stretched his fingers and dug his fingernails into the wood just a bit, feeling the pull against them—wanting to feel and hold something besides a weapon. He watched the beach. The villagers Lookout had sent away still stood on the beach and stared at the boat. One of the men waived at him. He returned it.

The Upside Fever was still on him. So, he lowered himself to the deck and closed his eyes and among the racket of the crew, the swell of sea, the sway and creak of hull and the whipslap of sails that beat the wind; he found a little sleep in an uncomfortable place, as a soldier learns to do.

He woke beneath a star-draped canopy of purple. Glume stood on the deck, beside him, saying nothing. The night had come, and the dark wood of the boat was dipped in little golden domes and halos of lantern light which moved at the pulse of the waves.

"We'll find port soon," Glume said.

Allred got to his feet, with a friendly waving-off of the proffered hand of the Captain.

"Are the arbelests mounted?"

"Aye," he pointed down the length of the rail, midship with a rope-hardened, craggy hand. The big bows were covered with sacking, so as not to give other ships warning that they were armed. Below them, bolted to the railing an oversized leather quiver contained at least twenty large bolts.

He sniffed, his head congested from the sleep and smoke and stumbled around stretching and trying to keep his feet on deck. He fished a redleaf from his vest, and lit it from one of the flames of the lantern, holding it over the fire down through the glass, "The rest are well-enough?"

"What?"

"The boys and the donkey haven't given you any trouble."

"Yes, good. They been fed."

"I'm going to stay up here a bit."

"Aye."

The old sailor stared at him for a while, squinting. He looked to say something but didn't and moved off down the deck.

He smoked watching the dark sea below. The coast was near, crawling, heaving, seething just like the water. He kept his eyes on the dark waves. A crewman approached with purposeful, loud footsteps and brought him bread and wine and a cloth full of dried fruit.

"Captain says, you ought to eat," the crewman said.

"Should do," Allred answered and took the things from him, "What is the wine?"

"The kind the captain ordered me to bring, sir."

He eased himself back down on the deck. The man went away.

They rode the sea keeping Esmer in sight.

A sailor stood high up in a crows nest shaped by ropes holding a magemade looking glass and studied the shore.

Below, the sea was deep indigo in the moonlight and here and there, patches of floating phosphorescent green swam and tossed in unseen currents, flickering.

The shivers took him, and he went down closer to the deck on his hands and knees as if praying to the Lady and pressed his forehead to the damp wooden planks. His body started shaking and his teeth chattered. The waves of pure fear lapped against his core, drenched him and he fought to keep quiet, to keep from screaming. Something large splashed in the water and he leaped to his feet and unsheathed his blade.

"What's wrong with hm?"

He looked to land, and he could feel the places below it crawling through his guts. Nothing. The land crawling. His throat was dry.

"Stay clear when you see him like this. It happens—a good half of that man lives in hell."

"He saved my life. Allred is a good man."

Those voices were familiar. Not the enemy. Why were they observing him from the dark? Lookout and Glume watching him from afar.

"You know how he got his name?"

"It's not a common name from his lands?"

"You're on a ship heading to a wider world. You said, you want to be a knight and you read a lot of legends? Come away now. I'm the captain of this ship and when a captain gives an order, you follow it smartly."

He wanted to tell them he could hear them talking about him, but he found he was gripping the handle of his sword and so it was not time to speak to friends. His fingernails were white in the moonlight, the dirt and grime outlining them.

Breathe.

"Thought I saw something out there. It's all clear. Nothing," he shouted down the deck at them.

A faint resigned 'aye' came from the dark and Glume turned the boy around with an arm on his shoulder and wagging his finger, sent him off belowdecks.

The sword he sheathed. Swinging at ghosts. He knew it. They knew it.

He watched the ship cut through the sea and considered— He could slide over, into that water with the glowing things and then let go and sink below and there would be a thrashing and then a deep quiet and the doneness of death.

Can't smoke underneath the sea, he thought.

He laughed and the sound should have frightened him, and he watched it skip across the waves like metal ragged bits in the wind.

He leaned against the wood of the ship, still breathing fast through his nose. The feeling was coming back to this body. The Upside Fever had come out of nowhere, gripping him in the familiar infinite panic of the moment. The men and the boys had been watching him and wondering, the young ones confused and Glume certain; and he kept laughing until there was spit running down his chin thinking about the dead.

There was a shifting and a stir somewhere. The sails ate wind. The moon slid down in front of the volcano as the world spun and it was beautiful to watch the orange fire heave against the white belly of the full moon and he kept laughing until he fell asleep again.

A man in the crow's nest shouted something and Allred woke up. His eyes were bleary, and his face felt cool where some wetness had dried in the air. He should have taken his boots off and let his feet dry out but was half afraid to see the mess of his own feet from the marching.

The Black Boat slowed and glided past a shoal as they came into a cove where a small village huddled beneath the jungle canopy.

There was a small pier and some torches lit near it since it wasn't yet morning. Glume guided the Black Boat in. Stoneburner and Cole were standing ashore just down the little pier, talking to the villagers.

He heard the splash of an anchor on the other side of the boat and the crew ran about, tying this and that and doing the tasks of the sailor near to land. Ten or so villagers milled around the pier, watching as the Black Boat came into Esmer, proper. The first time they would have seen it.

The village itself wasn't much to take in. A brown sand beach under moonlight and a dozen buildings, wet-looking, jumbled up beneath the upward slope of the mountain sheltering it. There wasn't a stone building in sight. The roofs were thatched palms and they waived in the gentle warm wind of the night. A dirt road ran up the mountain into jungle and he could see tracks of men and animals in the sand of the beach, leading in both directions away from the settlement. The waves licked at the prints in the low light of evening.

An old man, overweight, bearded and sunburned was dressed in patched and ragged-looking Throneland garb, ornamented by the shell and pearl jewelry of the locals. He stood conversing, one hand on his big belly, the other gesticulating in the air between himself and Cole.

He made his way down the rope ladder, to the pier.

A few villagers crowded around gabbling in pidgin Imperial and gave him broad berth. The moonlight caught the hilt of his sword. This would be the last dry land he'd feel beneath his feet for some time.

Stoneburner bargained with some merchant men, small-traders, gesturing to food covered by stretched tarps in the tiny trading boats which bobbed against the pier. Buying supplies for the trip back to Port Shamhalhan.

Several boys hauled crates and sacks, waiting for the Black Boat to come in. Stoneburner organized it all and they brought the supplies near the ship but did not board it. Stoneburner broke off his haggling, walked past him to the pier, hailing him quietly and went to talk to Glume who stood, a thin shadow on the deck.

Then, despite his dislike for sailing and the sea, he wished to be back onboard, away from this place and on the way to Port Shamhalhan. He even considered going below deck to his quarters on the ship.

Cole broke away from the crowd and the fat man, "Trouble?"

"No, nothing."

He didn't mention the word Optri here. The villagers might pretend not to hear but he knew better. Even if some didn't speak Thronelander, that word had exceeded the bounds of the language by the power of the fear it inspired.

"That's the Attman, the fat one, half-blind and barely glanced at our papers," Cole said, "He knows Lookout, just like the boy said."

Lookout came running down the pier at that instant straight towards the Attman.

"Attman!"

"There he is!"

The Attman smiled and Lookout went up to him and saluted. The Attman grabbed the boy in a quick embrace and Lookout smiled.

"Our distinguished guests, the Throneland's cartographers have told me of your bravery. I knew I chose wisely when I picked you for the watch tower. Your father would be proud, boy. Completed your imperial service and these men here, they've offered you service and a place onboard their ship."

Lookout's smile didn't break, didn't waver there in the torchlight. Maybe the boy didn't lie but he also was starting to learn when to talk.

It took time to get used to the bitterness of a man telling you lies he didn't know he spoke. He studied Lookout's face. The boy thanked the old man. He didn't say anything about the so-called Imperial cartographers. He even managed a convincing Thronelander's salute.

"Thank you Attman. This man," Lookout pointed at Allred, "He knows much about horses. I know you like them, too. I'm hoping to learn to ride someday."

The Attman looked at him, put on a pleasant grin, saluted and then turned away. He wasn't a complete fool, this Attman.

"That's a fine thing. You'll see many places that way. I miss my own gelding a great deal. Now—" he looked at Cole and drew himself up and Allred admired the man's spirit. "Now, of course, if you don't wish to leave Esmer, your position at the tower will be secure for you. You're a citizen of the throne and you choose where you go. This man, he says, they have bought your position out and that you chose to leave Esmer with them. As the Attman, I must officially ask you if this is so."

"Yes, Attman," Lookout said.

The Attman nodded, smiled.

Cole took Allred aside while the boy gabbled on.

"Stoneburner is supplying the Black Boat, made deals with peasants on the way back down the mountain. We appear to be the only Imperials here, besides the Attman."

"Does he know?" Allred asked, not looking at Cole.

"The Attman survived to retire. He's the kind that knows what is necessary and knows what not to ask. That's how you survive to retire. Me and you, we never learned that lesson."

Cole turned to other business and Allred slowly walked along the pier to the have a look at the other boats.

The traders and the curious were astir at the Relic Hunters arrival and had set some torches to light the night. They were thin and brown, the Bead people of Esmer, tanned by the southern sun and gentle enough, these descendants of an ancient empire. People from no place important. The men wore light undyed shirts above thin trousers or short pants. The women wore their dark hair long above smoky smiles on auburn faces. Their bare arms held the signs of their status by the number of the pearls set beneath the skin. They wore necklaces of shells, and their world would change, once word reached the Thone there was a Haunt here and the 9th had visited it.

Stoneburner was bargaining with an older man whose pretty daughter helped her father trade in Imperial pidgin which he himself pretended not to speak with a vacant grin. She kept touching Stoneburner's hand as he measured out coins.

"We'll have decent stores for the ship," Stoneburner said. "Good."

His word came out so flat and abrupt that the girl's father thought he had taken offense at something and started talking much faster to his daughter. She kept her eye on Allred and Stoneburner made a sign for him to go away and smiled at them and clinked coins.

His eyes kept scanning the dock for the flash of knives or the claw of a demon. The small, tarped fishing ships bobbing in the sea would be perfect for a man to hide in and take aim with a crossbow. He would use that cover.

Who waited in the shadows of the little dirt road to attack? When he stared down that road for an answer, he saw the shadows of Dhlams waiting for him, claws sunk in sand ready to bolt.

The village girl had snakes crawling in her eyes. His hand sought the handle of his sword. The movement made several villagers turn and jump.

"Something wrong?" Stoneburner asked in a way that told him, there was nothing wrong besides him.

"No, just too much sun maybe, tired. Don't like ships."

Then he tried another smile and slowly brought his sword hand to his jaw and pretended to scratch an itch there and searched his vest pocket for another redleaf.

He slowly walked away, lit the redleaf from a torchlight near the pier, the bright fire blinding him momentarily when he turned to the relative dusk of the beach.

He went back to the ship. The few village stevedores avoided him, shuffling to the side of the narrow pier as he passed, the way small fish flee the wake of a shark. He muttered a greeting and they answered in solicitous grunts staring at the sea.

Back on deck, he unslung the bow from his back and leaned it against the side of the ship and watched. The crew took the supplies from the islanders, brought them to deck and hurried them down to stow below. He could feel the ship grow pregnant in the water.

Glume broke away from giving orders and came to him.

"There's no point in bothering yourself about yourself. We

made our choices."

"Yes," he answered, "But, keep an eye on me for a while, captain."

"Aye."

Beside their ship, at anchor was the fishing boat of the Rats.

Helga was talking to her Rats on the deck. She turned to him, watched him and raised a hand. He returned it.

He couldn't make out her words from this distance, but he figured she told them of the dead. As a soldier, he'd told the same stories to survivors of the ones who would not return.

Boph came out to the deck with his donkey.

"You going to say goodbye down there?"

The little island boy turned to him, "No. I've already been paid by the Attman. Nothing here for me."

The boy wasn't dumb.

"Aye."

"Thanks for not killing us when it would have been easier."

"We aren't monsters."

Boph didn't look convinced.

"There's a lot of room on this ship. More than there was when you sailed here. All those men who went into the Haunt didn't come back."

He looked down at him and growled, "Being the smartest man on a small island is a good life. Being the smartest man in the Thronelands is a dangerous life. You should learn that before we shove off."

"I should and I will."

"Then you might make it. Your friend will need your help. You can't afford to be stupid."

The One-Bead boy said nothing in return. He moved a little closer towards Allred though and watched the scurrying and the haggling of the people, and the weirdness of Cole in his armor standing among them.

He nodded to the donkey. He could have sworn it acknowledged with a sudden shaking of its mane. Reaching out, he gave the animal a pat on the head and then leaned his elbows on the rail and watched the peaceful scene.

"You see him alone there?" the boy asked, pointing.

Down the beach, he saw the mage in the shadows pacing in circles of sand. He must have summoned a light feint, and he hadn't noticed him. The dwarf on his rope crawled in the surf beside him, biting and snapping at the water. Hortha leaned over his brother, exhausted, head in his hand while his brother slept. In Hartha's hand, a bone cup for rolling die. His brother watching, dropping the dice one at a time within the cup and pulling them out and then tossing them back again waiting for his brother to wake and play. Mage's feint was not strong, but Cole had clearly told them to stay obscured from the villagers. Allred could see through it, would have noticed it if he wasn't so tired probably, he'd had enough practice, but the boy?

"You do have sight. Figured as much on meeting you," he said. "And, yes, I see him."

Cole gestured and the mage caught the sign and acknowledged it, turned to the water, said something to the moon and then the injured he led, slinking down the beach in the slow gloom of magic and night. Allred could hear their unsteady steps on the pier.

"I don't think you're monsters, especially not Mage, sir. But you're killers, that much is plain and I could see it when you first came upon us. Like I said though, thank you."

He leaned against the rail of the ship, "And if you don't take the chance to step off this boat, what do you think you're bound to be?"

"I'm not smart enough to know, sir."

Allred laughed, "You're learning."

His father used to tell him the stars came out every night to judge the day. That's why cloudy, dark nights tended to crime. Soon business was over and all the rest of the men boarded.

The ship began to float away from Esmer. The Attman stood on the beach, watching for a long time. Helga's fishing boat followed in their wake.

Boph's donkey brayed from somewhere belowdecks. The rest of the 9th had boarded and bedded down in their bunks below.

The ship was much emptier and quieter without the cargo of the Black Boat men. The places where they had slept were now heavy with packs of treasure, the contents which Stoneburner refusing to sleep sorted, rated and discussed with Scrolls in the bowels of the ship.

Lookout joined him on the deck. Neither said anything for a long time. The orange sparks of the drowsy volcano faded in the purple sky as they moved out farther to sea.

He spoke first, a rare thing but he felt the boy would ask him of the fit he had witnessed and didn't want to explain himself.

"I learned to ride young in service to my clan. Then later, in service to the Throne, I rode more. I'm not a knight."

Lookout gave an uncertain smile, "Boph said men who ride horses into battle are called knights in the legends."

"Not always."

The boy fretted with his hands and from where he sat on the deck, he could hear him tapping on the rail.

"It feels strange to leave home. I don't think I'm coming back for a long, long time. But it's also strange because this island isn't really the home of my ancestors. Never thought of it much until now that I'm leaving. What will happen here?"

"You have no family there?"

"No."

"Imperials will come in time. Some will stay. No horses on Esmer?"

Lookout shook his head, no. "Just donkeys for hauling and the plow. I've seen a horse in the village once long ago. The Attman kept it—but I don't know how to put a saddle on them or anything."

Allred leaned forward, stretched. He propped himself up and stood.

"A knight serves a House. I serve no House. First, I served my clan. Then I served the Throne and now I serve Cole and the 9th. You grew up there on Esmer," he gestured out to the darkness in the direction of the receeding island. "I come from a place like this in a way—not in the way of the weather or plants but similar because it's not even on the road to anywhere important. There is a House far away from Darkridge but we barely acknowledge it. We breed the finest horses in the world, and we ride better than anyone under Allwein's sky and my clan are known as great warriors—but I'm not a knight."

"I see," Lookout said.

He had taken something from his belt pouch. As he turned around, Allred couldn't quite see what it was and he palmed it, holding onto it. "Stoneburner gave me these new trousers, days ago. They don't quite fit right."

"They will if you survive long enough."

The boy let out a frustrated sigh, "I want to be useful. I must be because I'm far away from home."

"Yes."

"Can you teach me something then. Anything? Even if it's not knightly things."

"I don't know what Cole has planned for you."

The boy took the thing from his belt pouch and chanced a few nervous steps over to him offering it. Allred put out his hand. It was a little wooden doll the boy had whittled—a carving of a horse and not a bad one at that, similar to the ones in his tower. Rough-hewn but even and graceful in the low light; he could make out the wave of its mane portrayed in tiny scoops and dashes of a knife. The musculature of its legs was wrought in knicks and scratches.

"A gift from me. I made it. From when I saw the Attman's horse that one time."

"You have a knack for that. Especially, if you say you'd only seen a horse once," he said.

He lifted it up into the light more to study it, then placed the figure down gently on the deck of the ship, as if unsure it would stand, like a foal on first legs. It stood tall beside his bow, and he nearly smiled.

"My people, a long time ago, were once part of another. Those sacrificed the best horses every year to Allwein in the festivals of the spring. Our fathers thought this foolish and knew it displeased Allwein. So, one year, the night before the slaughter, we feigned sleep and stayed up all night and took all the horses away into the mountains to tend to them and increase their bloodlines.

Each of those men, honorable thieves, became the leader of a clan. Since we had to spread out and live apart to afford pasture for the horses, we grew foreign to each other in time and fought ourselves, but we never forget our common origin. Allwein thought this good. So, that's how we came to have the best horses but also to live in the hills and mountains."

"That is the story of your ancestors?"

"One of them."

The boy thought on this for some time and nodded his head, finally.

"How can I be useful, if I can't learn anything?"

Allred didn't want a 'charge' or an acolyte—was that the word Scrolls would have used? He had lost many friends. He said nothing for a long time. He lit another redleaf, but the boy would not leave.

"It was foolish to walk into that fight on the mountain."

"I had to do something, didn't I?"

"No. Sometimes you don't do anything. Sometimes, you wait, and you watch, and you wait some more."

He inhaled deep. Well...

"It was a certain type of bravery, though. The type that I've seen get a lot of men killed but bravery, still. If we make it to Port Shamhalhan...if for some reason Cole keeps you in our service...if I have time...if I feel like it—I'll show you how to saddle a horse and ride it. This I can promise you and fulfill, no more."

His face lit up in the dark and Allred's stomach sunk, and he looked away.

"Yes, that would be useful for a knight to know how to do," Lookout said.

"Yes, it would. Now be gone and let me smoke and be alone."

"Heard, sir! I'll go tell Boph."

The boy left him, backing up, watching him as if the promise he made might disappear with the man.

The sea remained the same—inscrutable and determined to make him sick. The wooden figure kept its feet on the deck balancing on four wooden hooves. He plucked it up and studied it again, the knife work was quite fine. He tried to fit the figure inside the pocket of his vest, but it was too big. He set it back on the deck.

The sounds of the ship, the sharper unexpected ones made his stomach clench. His neck was tight. Sweat broke out on his forehead and everything looked a little warped; the colors and smells of the mundane world around him threatened him with an unending emptiness.

Then that passed.

After the fighting, this—the agony of peace and the wicked solace of the usual. The flinching at the light and the restless forever of another day and another night above ground.

He flicked the redleaf roll out into the sea. He watched the coal chart its own blazing course through the warm salt wind then burn the sea and sink. He lifted his bow, and he took the figure in his other hand. In the warm light of a lantern, he stole from a hook, he found his way across the deck and climbed down the short set of stairs to find his berth.

Postscript

Travelogue of Vohn Cearhardt, known as Scrolls—
Awarded-Scholar of the University of Mhars, Outlaw

F ar north of Port Shamhalhan, we rode—Me, Cole, Allred, Aodlen and the boy.

Past the last of the sun-soaked city walls, ripe with little lizards nesting in the sandstone warmth, out through the big villages with peasants dressed in their red-white checkered smocks, where the cobblestones gave way to dirt they stared; past a waystation lounging in the shadow of a cypress tree with two old riders out front whose eyes were wise with the knowing of who it was safe to see; down narrow road where the scent of vineyards lingered above the dust, we travelled. For a long time, rows of cedar, date and fig tree groves, shadowed the path and the dust rose and in time our mounts trod less-travelled ground, so the dust rose and coated their bellies and clung to our saddles. We, the surviving men of the Relic Hunters of the 9th journeyed the peaceful paths spiraling out from the free-city of

Port Shamhalhan.

On a roan gelding with stubby legs, the boy balanced precariously. The warrior riding ahead, sometimes wheeled around, and reining his own mount backwards alongside, shared sharp whispers of instruction and then urged his own mount forward until we could barely make out his figure.

We reached a crossroads and then another and took that one farther north and the dirt paths turned to grass.

Haycarts came and went. Farmers hailed us, in the friendly, lazy manner of greeting peculiar to the people of this rich land. Most of them when catching a closer glimpse of well-dressed northerners, mounted on fine horses with good tack, pretended to look elsewhere. The young ones shaking to the rhythm of the wooden wheels running the rutted road stared, untaught yet to pay no attention to such men as us. To them, the flash and glint of the steel we wore at our sides just looked like bobbles and toys and I wished I could see the world so, again.

After quiet hours of riding under the sun, even the trace of a path disappeared. With night coming on, Allred rode straight into a copse of trees marked by a faint sign. Past these trees we followed to find a trail again winding into a gentle valley. In the distance, a small homestead sat at the bottom of the narrow decline hidden by a cluster of fanning branch and green.

The boy pulled in his reins at the top of the steep slope, hesitating to give the horse its head down the hill.

"Drop the reins and straighten your legs," Allred told him, and he obeyed. The horse quit his shy and followed down the path behind Cole.

In the valley below, a woman stood in front of her house watching the men, hands on hips covered in the same red and white the peasants wear in the country surrounding the city, though she wasn't born from it. She hurried inside and then back out.

We did not dismount.

"Stay here. Listen to the woman," Allred told the boy.

The boy shot a distrustful look back at him, then said,

416

"Heard" and bowed to the woman, who humored him with a tired frown on sun-split lips. He stood there with the reins of his horse in hand, petting its muscled neck, shy around the woman.

I stayed in the saddle with the rest. The woman pointed to a barn and the boy moved off. She went behind the house to a well I know and came back out and brought cool fresh water to us.

Cole said something to her. She shook her head; no. Allred had already led his ride out and away from the place.

We thanked her and rode on up the other side of the valley, deeper into the interior. Our horses were weary with the weight of the riders and the packs Stoneburner had sent us with.

Night was coming on when we arrived at the location for the pre-arranged drop. The land had been quiet for hours, but the grass came alive with a chorus of crickets when the sun set. There were no more farms only forest. Cole took out a small sun and pointed it at an unassuming tree. The light illuminated a small slashing blue mark.

We waited there building no campfire. Cole sent Allred out to the next village to signal to someone to meet us and then took the watch and we slept. The time spent on the ship and the few days of rest in Port Shamhalhan and the not-knowing what Cole would decide had made us all nearly mute—even Aodlen did not speak much but on occasion barked a low laugh, answering his own magic-addled monologue.

In the morning, Cole remained sitting in the same place he had taken up before we slept, like a statue left out in this wilderness by an older civilization whose history I cannot find written in any of the scrolls or libraries of Mhars.

Allred came back and said there was no one from the rebellion waiting. No one had come to meet us. Maybe caught. Maybe dead. Allred thought he smelled corpses. No one would talk about anything in the little village.

Halfway through the next day Aodlen spoke.

"Ha! No one's coming, Cole. No, not at all!"

We had brought two orbs of pure magic, bundled carefully beneath a bag full of potatoes and roots. Some of our relics, I had traded in the markets of Port Shamhalhan for gold and those coins we carried, too. I realized then what the woman at the homestead had likely told Cole, "Haven't seen anyone."

"We'll wait," he said.

We waited. Another day. Another night. Cole allowed a small fire that night and I wrote these words in its light while the rest said little. The only sounds were Aodlen's shuffling cards and the crickets and the crack of twigs in the campfire. Allred knew where a creek ran and led our horses to water there.

I rested my eyes from penning these words, words which if Allwein prevails shall not be consumed by time or war. I followed Allred to the creek and found Cole there, too. The men stood side by side, talking.

"No one. Again," Cole said.

"Maybe delayed," Allred answered. His horse finished drinking. In his hands, he toyed with the reins, separating them, bunching them, passing the leather from hand to fist, to open hand.

The doctor had followed us. For a man, so ill from his own concoctions, he could be stealthy when he wanted.

"Ha!"

Now we four all stood by the creek in the dark, not looking at each other but watching the cool play of water over smooth rock.

"Speak, if you have something to say," Cole said.

Allred let the reins go. The horse grazed around the creek, snatching clumps of creek-wet grass in their teeth. He looked at me and back at the doctor and we waited.

"Mage is damaged, maybe forever. Hartha won't walk again—"

"We'll see about that, ha!" Aodlen said.

"We are rich. Whoever was to meet us here isn't at the village anymore. When do we go back?"

"Soon. Shamhalhan then maybe to Coldewater and then on to Lord Cearhardt's lands."

"Let's figure—at least there's an organized army back there. Out here, most of the agents are dead. Optri nearly killed us, they've probably killed most of the agents of the 9th. Maybe we'll find their bodies in Haunts we haven't reached yet. Maybe Optri buried them instead of the other way around. We remain. You can lead the army that already stands."

"The timing is the thing," Cole said.

We stood there by the creek, and I knew that no one would come to take the treasure we brought.

"We have enough to buy our own army, if there's consequences for leading Cearhardt's men," Allred said.

"There's politics in my father's court," I told them, but Cole knew this.

"We'll return when it's the right time," Cole said.

Neither man spoke and the horses grazed as the moon came up over the forest, fat and full and red.

The next morning, we carried the treasure with us, no one to receive it. We rode back to the homestead—a safe place we had kept for some time outside the city.

I write these words to keep them for the future and to keep my thoughts away from Mage back in Shamhalhan and the drunk giants with their three legs and the sad rattle of the bone cup between them and the woman Helga, and her message from my father, and how my friends will recover from their wounds or won't and if my brother still lives.

We tarried at the homestead for some days before returning to Port Shamhalhan. Allred busied himself with new foals in the stable. He took time to show the boy the brushes and the blankets, the rasps and stirrups.

When I wasn't writing, I watched them both while Aodlen dealt cards to no one. Neither saw me; the warrior describing the many names iron takes when wrought and twisted and the boy looking up with hopeful eyes, striving to remember the names of sharpened metal which might be turned to peace or war.

About the Author

Justin A.W. Blair lives in Florida.

www.justinawblair.com

Acknowledgments

I couldn't have written this without my mother and father. She taught me to read and to love books. He encouraged me to never give up.

A few friends have listened to my ideas and complaints when the editing got hard. Mathew heard out early ideas and bad drafts. Grant read through the first finished text and came through with some helpful edits and kept yelling at me to finish the book.

Kernal is small and helped me keep rockin' even when I found myself at the bottom of the Haunt.

Made in United States
Orlando, FL
23 March 2024